Blood to Blood

Blood to Blood

The Dracula Story Continues

Elaine Bergstrom

ACE BOOKS, NEW YORK

BLOOD TO BLOOD: THE DRACULA STORY CONTINUES

An Ace Book / published by arrangement with
the author.

PRINTING HISTORY
Ace edition / October 2000

Cover art by Jim Griffin.

For information address: The Berkley Publishing Group,
a division of Penguin Putnam Inc.,
375 Hudson Street, New York, New York 10014.

The Penguin Putnam Inc. World Wide Web site address is
http://www.penguinputnam.com

ISBN: 0-7394-1440-2

ACE®
Ace Books are published
by The Berkley Publishing Group,
a division of Penguin Putnam Inc.,
375 Hudson Street, New York, New York 10014.

PRINTED IN THE UNITED STATES OF AMERICA

Though the others do not speak of it, I know there is a moment of choice for our kind. . . . Do we kill? Do we use? Do we feast on ecstasy? I know this now, and that Illona made certain I would be a killer like her.

From the journal of
Countess Karina Aliczni

Prologue

Joanna Tepes lay on the bare earth floor of her chamber, hidden deep within the labyrinth of caverns that cut through the rock beneath Castle Dracula.

There were few mortals who had ever possessed the courage to venture into the vampires' lair, and none who had ever prowled so deep. Nonetheless, the man and woman upstairs were like none she had ever known before, and she trembled and, wary, forced back the daytime sleep.

An impotent rage filled her, one she did not possess the courage to satisfy. Wasn't she also a Tepes? Didn't she deserve revenge? She tried to rationalize her terror. Even her brother knew that when the battle had been lost, it was suicide to face the enemy again so soon.

She forced a breath into lungs that had no need of air and exhaled a high-pitched, hysterical laugh. By the time she found the strength to confront that pair, they would be long gone from this place.

Could she follow them? Did she dare?

After centuries of nights each the same as the last, she realized that, no matter what her decision, everything had changed in the passing of a single night.

The rest were dead, truly dead, and for the first time in centuries she was completely alone.

She shuddered again, turned onto her side and clawed the soft earth beneath her with her delicate, killer's hands. A tear rolled down the side of her face. She brushed it away, then licked the dampness from her hand, tasting the salty warmth of her own blood.

Tepes, she thought. *Tepes. Tepes. Tepes.*

As if she were claiming a legacy that wasn't her own, claiming a name that even when whispered could still cause fear.

one

May 25, 1891
Dearest Jonathan,

By now Van Helsing would have told you everything that happened to us on our second trip to Dracula's castle. You've undoubtedly also read the story the two of us invented to account for Lord Gance's death. The story is not so unlikely in that part of the world and was the sort of blatant lie Gance would have relished, I think. Hopefully, Van Helsing's many titles will allay any suspicions about the actual cause of his death.

Though I wished to do so, I did not accompany the body back to London. I feared that were we to wire Gance's family about his death, the press might have been alerted and been on hand to interview his traveling companions. Had we simply arrived with his coffin, another strange death stemming from a journey east, I might have been forced to identify myself. Though I do not care so much about my own reputation, I am pleased that no scandal has fallen on you or the firm.

This time I know it is over, Jonathan. Dracula is truly dead and his dark bride as well. As to the fair Countess Karina . . . no, I still cannot speak of her. I think it will be years before I can accept what we did to her and to Lucy.

I wish I could say that everything has changed, but in truth, dearest, it hasn't. I am no longer troubled by the dreams that forced me back to his dread castle to face him once again, but I am not free of the passion he forced me to feel. And I know now that it is no sin to give into it with one you love.

So come to me, dearest. I am staying in Paris and have enclosed the address. It is a beautiful house in the heart of a most incredible city. It is a place for lovers and for those who need to rekindle their passion for one another. I almost wrote "love" but in truth I love you still and I know you feel the same for me.

So come and let me hold you and kiss you and touch you and reveal to you all the passion that life has trained you not to feel.

With all my heart, your Mina.

It had not surprised Jonathan that the letter had been waiting for him when he returned from Lord Gance's funeral service. He had not wanted to attend the service of his wife's lover. However, as Gance's solicitor and a known friend of Van Helsing, who had brought Gance's body back, suspicions would have been aroused had he not attended. So he had stood in the back of the ballroom of the Gance estate, listening to Van Helsing explain how after the attack on Gance, he had been called to Gance's side by the Romanian authorities, who needed both translator and physician. Van Helsing added that Gance had undoubtedly saved the lives of the others in his party, then died when the exertion of the battle opened a recent near-fatal wound.

Perfect. Even the examination of the body by the authorities could reveal nothing to contradict Van Helsing's account. And the advanced state of decomposition, brought about by the damp hold of the ship, made it clear that no stakes and holy water were needed to ensure that Gance remained in his grave.

Now Jonathan sat behind the dark wooden desk in his office, holding Mina's letter as gently as he had once held her, looking out the window at the sunlit sky. He thought of Mina, her hair unpinned in an auburn cloud over her shoulders, her chemise fallen from her body into a satin halo around her bare feet.

Yes, he thought. Yes, he would go.

He picked up his pen, found a sheet of paper, and began to write a reply when Tom Pierson, a young man recently hired for Jonathan's old position, knocked on his office door. "Your first appointment is here to see you, sir," he said, passing Jonathan a calling card.

"In a moment," Jonathan replied, lovingly folding Mina's letter and placing it in his desk drawer.

Something in his expression made his clerk pause and ask, "Is everything all right, sir? If you wish to reschedule. Well, with it being so soon after the funeral, I'm sure Mr. Seeley would understand your situation."

Situation, Jonathan thought. The situation was dismal indeed, and he should have his mind on business as least while he was trying to work. Managing Lord Gance's estates had been an almost full-time duty for one of his clerks, not to mention the business that Gance's referrals had brought his way.

If he didn't replace it, who would he let go? Tom, who seemed so like himself not so long ago, and just engaged to be married? Frank Wallace, a bit irresponsible in his personal life but with excellent business sense?

Perhaps he was worrying over nothing. Perhaps Lord Gance's family would follow his lead and stay with the firm.

It was, he decided, a time to look industrious, confident. He conveyed both in his afternoon meetings, as he met with one client after another.

Late that evening before he left the office, he consulted his schedule and saw that it would be at least two weeks before he could get away. He had so many depending on him that he had to think rationally about his future and, he would make clear in a letter to Mina, her own as well.

He would remind her that she was in no danger now, and that if she were, he would not be writing but already on his way to her side. Then he would ask her to come to him instead. She had been practical once, determined to be a supportive wife. With a bit more understanding on his part, she could be again.

With these thoughts tumbling around in his mind, he took the information Mina had collected on Dracula and his wives out of his safe and went to meet Van Helsing and Arthur for a late-night supper.

Van Helsing had arrived at Robert's Pub a half hour before the others in order to claim a secluded table in a windowed alcove, a place where they could talk freely.

He had hoped that all the band could be together but Jack Seward had begged off, noting his duties at the asylum in London made the trip to Exeter impossible. Perhaps it was better that way, Van Helsing thought as he sipped a lager and waited for the others. Three men had loved Lucy Westerna. One was dead; two were still mourning. It might be best to speak to Arthur separately, especially since Seward knew most of the story already.

It never occurred to him to think that there were some things Arthur didn't need to know. Honesty above all had always been his motto, even in a case like this, where the truth seemed to constantly shift.

Poor Mina actually mourned the death of one of them. Incredible!

Jonathan and Arthur arrived at the restaurant at the same time, stopping just inside the door to shake the rain off their hats before joining him. Jonathan had a bit more color in his face than usual. Perhaps he had walked from his office, or perhaps he felt naturally embarrassed at what Van Helsing would likely reveal. Nonetheless, he'd agreed to the meeting, trusting Arthur's discretion as Arthur had trusted his.

Under normal circumstances, Van Helsing would have preferred to dine first and discuss the situation after the table was cleared and they would have no interruptions. But Jonathan seemed to grow more uneasy by the moment, so Van Helsing took pity on him and started in as soon as they'd been served their drinks.

"As I told you in my letter, Madame Mina discovered some additional information about the vampire and his consorts," he began telling Arthur. "It was in the form of a journal she found at Dracula's castle."

He went on, explaining how she had not wanted to worry

them before she knew the contents, and that once she did, she understood why she felt so pulled to return there. "Unfortunately, Jonathan did not believe her, nor did Jack Seward."

"So Gance became her ally," Arthur said. Noticing Jonathan's surprised expression, he added, "I was a friend of his, after all. Probably the only one who understood what he'd discovered. I suspect I know why he went. Such power would be a terrible temptation to someone like him."

"We have the complete translation of the vampire's journal," Jonathan said, laying a hand on the thick envelope he'd brought with him. "We both have read it all, and Jack most of it. We think you should too."

Jonathan slid the envelope toward him, but Arthur pushed it away with such force he nearly overturned a mug. He started to stand, then looked at the pair, at Jonathan's relief and Van Helsing's concern. "What in God's name is in there?" he asked, falling back into his chair.

"Information on the youngest of his consorts, the one Dracula told Mina reminded him of your Lucy."

Arthur picked it up, holding it lightly as if the paper itself might cause him harm, finally setting it beside his hat on the window ledge.

Out of sight, Van Helsing thought, wondering if Arthur would ever open the envelope.

They changed the subject, discussing everything except what mattered most—Gance's funeral, Mina's absence and the envelope Arthur had set aside. As Arthur was getting ready to leave, Jonathan said softly, "When Dracula came to my Mina, he told her that Lucy would have had no choice but to become in time, as he was. Remember that as you read this account."

"Are you saying she wasn't, not . . . then?"

"She was a vampire, yes," Van Helsing said, "but her soul was not yet his to command."

Arthur looked down at the envelope. For a moment it seemed that he would toss it back on the table. Instead, he clutched it more tightly. "Will we ever be free of his curse?" he asked.

"I no longer dream of them," Jonathan said gently. "Mina writes that she does not dream at all. And you?"

"Only of my Lucy," Arthur said and left them without another word.

Jonathan started to stand, but Van Helsing motioned him to remain. "What do you hear from Madame Mina?" he asked.

"She wrote me. She asked me to meet her in Paris. I intend to write and ask her to come home instead."

"Is that what you want to do?" Van Helsing questioned as gently as his nature would allow.

"It's what has to be done if we are to remain as husband and wife. That's the heart of the matter, isn't it?"

"I would consider carefully before you send that letter."

Jonathan frowned, and Van Helsing could already see that Victorian stolidity surfacing. He thought, as he had more than once since Mina had arrived at his house in Bukovina, that if he were younger he would not be offering Jonathan such good advice. Instead he would fight to possess her. "And I would not consider the matter too long," Van Helsing added. "Remember that she also has much to forgive you for."

Jonathan might have taken a cab home. He chose to walk the two miles instead. The May evening was chilly but not overly so. The walking kept him warm, and he felt a need for the solitude he wouldn't have once he arrived at home.

Van Helsing's words had stung because they had been so true. In the months since their band had invaded Dracula's lair to destroy him, Jonathan had ignored Mina, then all but abandoned her when he thought she'd gone mad.

Now she wanted him to come to her, to walk the streets of Paris and in that beautiful city try to rediscover what they had once felt for each other.

And yet, all around him were signs of misery . . . beggars on street corners, urchins darting among the crowds looking for easy pockets, women in dresses mended too many times, heading for uncertain houses where their last farthing might give them a place to spend the night.

He would never fall so low, but he could hardly hold on to what he had without some diligence.

Send the letter or not? He could reach no decision that night, nor the following day. He worked well into the night, at the office, then at home, convinced that so many extra hours would free up enough days for at least a week in Paris.

He wrote her to say he would be coming on the fourteenth and reminded her that the date was special, the anniversary of the day they first met. He put the letter with the others to be posted the following morning and returned to his work.

That evening, as his employees were leaving, a gentleman arrived to see him. His card identified him as Samuel Perry, a solicitor with the prominent Mayfair firm of Quarles and Brady.

"I'd hoped to find you in," the man said as Jonathan locked the outside door and led him into his office. "Actually, I'd hoped to contact you earlier today, but the train from London was delayed. Some problem with the track."

Perry laid his coat over one of the Chesterfield chairs, careful that the damp side not touch the leather, and ran a hand through his graying hair, smoothing it down before taking a seat across the desk from Jonathan. "This is a private matter," he began with some hesitation.

"Well, that's hardly a problem at this hour, since we're alone here. And this concerns . . ." Jonathan let the question trail off.

"Your wife, sir. I need to contact her."

"May I ask the reason?"

"She's come into an inheritance, the details of which should be first discussed with her."

Jonathan eyed the visitor intently, reading in the blush spreading over his already ruddy cheeks exactly who had left her the money. "Is this from Lord Gance?" he asked. "If so, I am . . . or was his solicitor."

"In most matters, yes. But Lord Gance thought that, given your business relationship, it would be best to alter his will in Mrs. Harker's favor through a different firm."

Jonathan nodded and Perry continued, "Since Lord Gance died without leaving a direct heir, the title and country holdings will descend on a distant cousin. But his private fortune was his to dispose of as he wished. Without being specific, I can tell you that Mrs. Harker is not the only person named in the most recent changes to his will."

And may at least some of the other beneficiaries be male,

Jonathan thought as the man passed him a letter. It was written by Robert Quarles himself, alluding to a brief meeting he and Jonathan had the year before. It was enough to convince him that the man in front of him was who he said he was. Jonathan jotted down the address where Mina was staying and slid it across the smooth wood of the desk. The simple act brought back quick flashes of memories . . . of Mina writing in her journal, of how helpless she had looked when he'd left her at Seward's to go in search of the vampire, of the brush of her palms against his when he'd reach for her during the night. The Gypsies said you could read the future in the palm of a hand. What would they have made of hers? Of his?

"Are you all right, sir?" his visitor asked.

"Just . . . curious, that's all. Well, I'll learn everything soon enough, I suppose," he replied.

"As Wilhemina Harker's husband, you are invited to hear it directly from Mr. Quarles at that same meeting."

After the man had left, Jonathan put on his coat and followed. He stopped only long enough to retrieve the letter he had written from the mailbox and put it in his pocket.

She'd be home in a few days. He would speak to her then,

The house in Paris where Mina was staying was built in the Spanish style in a box enclosing an elegant courtyard. There among the spring flowers, the cobblestone patio and walks, the fountain with its water lilies and sculpted swans, Mina would sit in a sunny corner and drink her morning coffee, her afternoon glass of wine. It was far removed from the foggy damp of England or Dracula's crumbling castle to the east.

Her traveling clothes had been soiled and torn, and at her host's suggestion she had visited a seamstress who had made her three new outfits, two of them romantic in their lace trim and airy summer-weight piqué, the last a simple blouse and skirt. It took the remainder of her traveling funds, but she was already earning money, organizing her host's library and papers, trying not to consider that she might be putting Claude's affairs in order for his descendants.

Not that Claude seemed so old, but that he was damnably evasive about his age.

In the fortnight since she had arrived here, Claude had finished her portrait. He declared it a masterpiece he would keep for himself and hung it above the stone mantel in his dining room. When they dined together, she would look up at herself, then quickly away. He was far too flattering, she thought, surprised that none of his frequent guests saw fit to agree with her even in private.

The weeks were pleasant enough that they might have passed quickly. But she'd written Jonathan as soon as she arrived and had still gotten no reply, not even refusal. Each day that passed with such uncertainty seemed longer and sadder than the last.

She was sitting in the morning sun in the garden drinking coffee when her host joined her carrying a large envelope. He laid it on the table in front of her and pointed to the stamp. "England," he said, then seeing her expression brighten, kissed her on the forehead and left her.

This wasn't Jonathan's handwriting, she realized, and opened the package more quickly, half convinced that something terrible had happened to him. Inside were two envelopes. One, on watermarked parchment, was in Gance's hand and had a note that said simply, *Open me first.*

The letter inside was short, and in Gance's fashion, to the point.

> *My dearest Mina. If you read this, I did not survive the journey. A trite opening, far too melodramatic and hardly witty, but apt.*
>
> *You said that Dracula ordered you to follow your heart. I do the same, but realize how difficult such an order is for a woman without the necessary means to do so.*
>
> *Independence is my gift to you.*
>
> *I leave you the house in Exeter where we spent too few precious hours, and the money necessary to maintain it and yourself in comfort. I have taken great pains to assure that this money will be yours alone to keep or give away as you see fit. This may make your future secure or far more complicated than you wish it to be. That may well depend on what sort of Victorian you*

married. But understand that I do this with as close to purity of intent as I can ever hope to achieve. G.

The second, thicker, packet was addressed to Mrs. Jonathan Harker. Inside was a bank draft for a hundred pounds and a letter requesting her presence in London for a private reading of the will. It concluded with, *Should you wish to stay in London, we will of course be able to make arrangements wherever you wish,*

They must have gotten her address from Jonathan, she thought. They must also have told him something about why they needed it. She realized with dismay how complicated Gance had made her life . . . and how free.

two

In the end it was fear that drove Joanna Tepes away from Castle Dracula.

For days after that woman and Van Helsing had gone, carrying the younger man's body wrapped in one of the upper chambers' rotting rugs, Joanna had hidden in the depths of the castle, in one of the maze of rooms where her brother had kept his slaves, his captives, and later his food. She barely slept, and lived as best she could on the rats, sucking their little bodies dry before flinging them away, furious at her own timidity.

Wasn't *she* also a Tepes? Shouldn't *she* be taking whom she wished, striking fear in the hearts of the lesser creatures in the villages nearby? She wanted to—it was her nature to do so, after all—but she had no experience at it. Her brother had hunted for the women, and when he was absent, Illona had done so. She and Karina had been nothing more than pampered pets, kept because they amused the lord and lady of the castle, each in her own way. Karina with her beauty. Herself, because she was so easy to torment.

For Joanna, it was a bitter understanding, made all the worse because for the first time in centuries she was utterly alone.

Weeks passed. One afternoon she heard the distant creak of cart wheels, the muffled sounds of familiar laughter, the tinkling of little bells. The Gypsies had returned.

From the dark chamber in which she slept, she heard the

gates of the castle swing open, the click of hooves on the ancient courtyard stones. She waited joyously for night so that she could go to them and speak to them as she had so many times before.

Instead they ventured into her world. They pried open the castle doors and moved through the great chambers, stripping them of every article that held any value. Some of the older men were familiar with the lower chambers and invaded them as well. She could sense them, pulling the remaining tapestries from the walls, taking even the charred scraps of those nearly destroyed by the fire. The leader, the one who knew the labyrinthine corridores beneath the castle the best, actually opened the door where Joanna retired during the day and shone a torch into its blackness.

Her eyes glowed red in the torchlight, her face a pale white blur, thankfully unrecognizable in the glance he had of it. He gave a small cry of surprise and retreated, barring the door from the outside.

She relished his terror for a moment, then rushed forward, barring the way from the inside as well, surprised that she'd never thought of locking it before.

It would keep them out, but at night, when her powers were strongest, no bars could hold her.

When it was as dark outside the castle as within her chamber, she left its sheltering walls. For the first time in nearly a century, she ventured beyond the familiar haunts of the mountain, traveling almost to the crossroads town of Bukovina. Stopping just outside it, she hid in the shadows beyond the fires of the Gypsy encampment.

She could recall the Gypsy bands of centuries ago, how they would come into her village, bringing songs and music. Like her, they seemed frozen in time—their wagons, their language, their music. She could hear it, carried in a faint breeze that brought with it the scent of life, of blood.

She watched. She waited, hoping someone weak enough to give her courage would venture within reach.

The band had not expected to encounter any enemies that night, or they would have circled the wagons. Instead, they had pulled into a narrow field just off the road and laid them out in a half circle. The men were on one end of the caravan, close to where the horses were tethered around a blazing fire, no doubt intended to keep wolves and other predators at bay. They drank heavily, telling tales of old conquests, sexual and otherwise.

The women were on the other end of the crescent, well away from them, speaking softly of more important things at a smaller fire. Even then, they were busy, stirring a stewpot simmering over the coals. Occasionally one of their children would crawl out of a wagon, carrying a bowl and asking for another helping of dinner.

Children! The women fed what would be her food.

Joanna's hunger was not isolated, as it had been when she was alive and so often hungry. Instead she could feel it as weakness, a craving too strong to resist.

Yet, when a little girl ventured so close that all Joanna had to do was reach out and clamp a hand over her tiny red mouth and drag her off into the shadows, she found she could not do so.

Not so small, she thought, rationalizing the reluctance while her body screamed for blood.

Later, when only one man still sat at the dwindling campfire, no doubt to keep the horses safe from thieves, she moved closer to him, coming up from behind.

The scent of him—old sweat mingled with the garlic and smoked meat of his evening meal—made her wince with disgust. Had her need not been so great, she would have returned to the shadows. Instead she forced herself to move forward, half woman, half wraith, gliding toward him, silent as the night mists.

When she was almost near enough to touch him, a horse whinneyed, the sound sharp and anxious. The man stood and scanned the darkness. By the time he had turned to look behind him, Joanna had vanished.

He started to call out to the others, then took a deep breath and shook his head. "Too close to their lair," he mumbled to himself, looking up the mountain, then quickly away, as if his interest might attract something unholy. Something dangerous.

He feared her. It gave her some satisfaction.

If he only sensed how terrified she was of him. Joanna, incorporeal, laughed at his fear and her own—a titter soft as the skittering of ground squirrels or field mice, barely noticed by the one who should have been her prey.

Later, while he dozed at his post, she fed on one of the horses. She was too frightened to drink her fill and kill the beast. Instead she let it live, then picked one of the others for her own, leading it away from the herd, daring to mount it only when she was well away from the encampment.

When she reached the castle, she led the shivering beast inside the gates, hung a bag of silver pieces on the outside of the doors, then closed and barred them. If the men returned to the castle, they would know the bloodline of the one who had done this. Perhaps they would respect her name and leave her in peace. Perhaps not.

She'd had no definite reason for stealing the horse. But as she stood at the top of the wall, looking down at the valley, it occurred to her that she had too many enemies in this country and that they knew her weaknesses far too well.

It was time to move on. Tomorrow evening she would force herself to think rationally, to plan.

The heavy pull of dawn was already on her when she willed herself outside the walls again, returning with fresh grass for her mount. The well still held brackish water. She left that for the horse as well. The beast looked at her more calmly now, even standing still, letting her stroke its head.

"We'll be all right, you and I. The wolves won't trouble us here." She released another peal of nervous laughter into the lightening sky.

Later, lying on the earth floor of her bare chamber, she found sleep elusive. Instead the ancient stones of the walls and vaulted ceiling reminded her too much of the centuries that had passed, often without a single worthwhile memory to them; and of her youth, still so vivid that it would never die.

Joanna was born eight years after her half brother Vlad, a fact that like so many others, she learned much later in life.

Her mother had been a princess in her own land, given as a hostage of Vlad Dracul in Tirgoviste, to assure that Dracu' sons, Vlad and Radu, would come to no harm in Turkish hands.

From everything Joanna could later learn, it took only a

few months before the lonely child her mother had been fell deeply in love with her captor.

For years Joanna believed that the feeling had been mutual. Perhaps it had been, but fewer than three years after she was born, mother and child were abruptly sent back to Turkey.

Joanna's earliest memories were of that journey. Throughout her life the smell of lathered horses would bring back the memory of the sudden, swift departure, the hard ride, and her mother holding her so tightly that she could scarcely breathe.

"What do you think her father would have done with her when she returned with the child of his enemy?" Vlad asked her years later.

Joanna couldn't answer because she would never know. The first night of the journey, as they were camped in one of the high mountain passes, her mother picked her up and carried her away from the horses and wagons, stopping at the edge of a high cliff.

In the years that followed, Joanna often wished her mother had given in to her first instinct and killed them both. Perhaps she had feared for her soul if she killed her daughter. Perhaps she thought the Fates should decide if Joanna lived or died, and there was a good chance that wolves would find her long before Dracul's soldiers did.

They almost did. She glimpsed the beasts padding silently through the scrubby mountain trees. One came so close to her that she could have reached out and touched it. She started to, but before she did, its attention was drawn to a snarl farther down the slope. It whirled and left her, bounding off as silently as it came.

"It smelled your mother's blood and that drew it away," Vlad told her so many years later. "When the soldiers found her, there was little left but her clothes and some bones they had not broken for the marrow."

He'd spat out the words, as if by wounding her he wounded her mother. Though he had never known the woman, he'd had reason enough to hate her.

When the soldiers found her and her mother's remains, they followed their orders and delivered Joanna into Turkish lands, leaving her at the first village they passed, along with information on her mother's suicide and a letter from Vlad Dracul to Mezid-Bey, her grandfather.

Whatever Dracul had written had not been enough to soothe Mezid-Bey's rage. And he knew all too well whom to vent it on.

Not a tiny girl, too young to understand and who he often said resembled her mother. Much better to turn his attention to his hostages. The pampered life that Vlad and Radu lived in Mezid-Bey's court came to an abrupt and bloody end.

Vlad was brought to Mezid-Bey's chambers. No words were spoken, no explanations given. The sultan stripped off the silk and fine tooled leather clothes he wore, flung him onto the carpet and fell on him, pleased that the child would not relax, that he fought as hard as an eleven-year-old could fight, that he did not cry when he lost, not that night or for the dozens of nights to come.

And that was how Vlad Tepes, one day known as The Impaler, learned hate.

Joanna never admitted to her brother how much her grandfather had doted on her, how often he said he cherished her as he had her mother. No, he would never have killed her mother, though how was she to know that? It was a piece of her past that she thought best not to share with her half brother, a secret she kept through her life and the centuries of life-in-death that followed.

Though they shared the same house, brothers and sister rarely spoke.

Her happiest memories were of the sultan's garden. She dreamed of it now, of the heady scent of the flowers, the lilting trickle of water in the pools, and the brilliant golden sun beating down.

It darkened her skin until she looked pure Turk. Only the reddish cast of her dark hair gave hint of her heritage, that and the brilliant green eyes with the fire in their center. Sometimes, when she would look directly at her grandfather, he would wince and turn away for a moment, then turn back to her, smiling again.

As she grew older she learned to never look at him directly. He did not seem to notice. After all, it was how any well-bred Ottoman woman would have behaved.

• • •

Night came, pulling her from her dreams. She knew she had work to do, but the nature of it eluded her for a moment. She sat in the darkness, listening to the drafts in the ancient hall above her, the scurrying of rats in the crumbling walls, the clop-clop of the horses' hooves on the packed earth and stones of the courtyard.

And remembered.

She rushed to the courtyard, gave the horse water then led it into the high meadow beyond the castle so it could graze.

There were wolves in the area, so she dared not leave the horse alone. Instead, she sat beneath a tree and guarded the beast, her means of escape. Even at a distance, she could feel its heat, its life; smell the blood that moved through its veins.

Something rustled in the leaves close beside her. She reached out, almost absentmindedly, and closed her fingers over the tiny vole. Its tiny heart beat in terror and she ran a finger down the soft fur of its back, calming it slightly before raising it to her lips to drink. It would nourish, as would any warm-blooded creature, but not in the same way as human blood, whose taste reminded her of the life she had lost so long ago.

It was past midnight when, with hunger appeased by a half dozen tiny lives, Joanna returned the horse to the castle. Once the gates were safely closed behind it, she descended into the lower chambers, places dank with moisture, whose walls glowed with a soft phosphorescence only a vampire's eyes could detect.

In the centuries they had lived here, lord and peasant alike had been their prey. Though Vlad had generously rewarded the Gypsies for their loyalty, his frequent gifts to them barely touched the treasure hidden in these walls.

If only she could remember where he'd deposited the rings and gems and gold of their victims. He hadn't hidden the places from her. Oddly, just before he left for England, he'd told them where to look.

It only she'd paid attention to that or any of his advice on traveling over land and sea. Instead, she had let her mind wander in the past, when she had been young and the sun released the scent of flowers.

If only . . .

She wandered the narrow passages, picturing him in her mind, until she could finally recall a place where they had stopped and he had pointed out. . . .

A darker section of wall, filled in with muck from the damp stone floor. She dug her fingers into the seal, not surprised to find it still wet, and crumbling against their pressure.

The cache was a good one, judging by the weight of the leather bag. She held it tightly and moved on, finding three more caches before returning to her chamber.

She'd found a treasure. One of the bags held rubies, emeralds, and stones whose names she did not know. She emptied another onto the floor and watched gold coins roll away from her. Scurrying on hands and knees, she scooped them up as if they were prey and would escape her. The third bag was more interesting, holding exquisite gold settings. Some had been stripped of their jewels, but there were occasional pieces left intact . . . a signet ring, a necklace with diamonds and black onyx, a dragon-shaped brooch with amethyst eyes.

The last she pinned to her tattered black dress and vowed never to part with it. The dragon was on their family crest. Shouldn't she have some reminder of that?

Tepes, she thought again, and laughing finally from nervous joy, she invaded her brother's library and rummaged among the papers. Since she'd never learned to read and had no idea which were valuable, she loaded any that appeared recent into the sack with the jewels, adding his seal and some wax for good measure. Night's work accomplished, she retreated to her chambers, barred her door, and fell into the dawn sleep.

When it was dark again, she rummaged among the boxes of earth and pair of wagons that the Gypsies had left behind. They were not discards, but had been intended for her and the others at some future time.

She took what her brother had said was the best of them—a wooden box so roughly made that no one would have much curiosity about its contents, but which hid much. There were tiny compartments, cleverly concealed, where she deposited jewels and coins. There was another, smaller, where she could hide the key to the rusty lock that would keep the case locked day and night. An old harnass attached her horse to a wagon.

Without looking back, Joanna started down the trecherous winding road that would take her past Bukovina. Her destination was the port city of Varna. She had absolutely no idea how to get there except to travel east to the sea.

three

Mina wired Jonathan that she was leaving for London but had no time to wait for his reply. Since the reading of the will was to be Tuesday morning, she had to arrive in London the night before. Though the money Quarles sent would be more than enough for a room at one of the city's better hotels, she decided to take the time to visit old friends instead and wired Arthur that she was coming.

He met the evening train at the London station. He was easy to spot amid the crowds of passengers and friends. He was taller than most, and his fair hair shone even in the dim station lights. She'd expected Van Helsing to be with him, but Arthur came alone. "Is the professor still staying with you?" she asked.

"More often than not, but he's off to Dublin, of all places. Meeting with a colleague, some writer who claims to be an expert in the arcane. We'll be staying in Kensington tonight. Three of Gance's old friends are using my Mayfair flat. They're here for the will, as you are. I've been asked to come as well, so we can go there together."

"Did he really own so much?" Mina asked.

Arthur laughed. "Not that little. And he has a flair for the dramatic . . . had a flair, I suppose I should say, though it's hard to believe the rake is gone."

The comment seemed to sober him, and he said very little on the ride to Kensington. The butler carried Mina's bag inside and up to the guest room. Dinner was nearly ready, and the two of them dined at a table that could have easily seated ten. They shared a bottle of wine and brief, light conversation. But Mina had a feeling that her host was biding his time, and that as soon as the servants were safely out of listening distance, their conversation would become darker and far more intense.

She wasn't wrong. After they finished their chocolate mousse, he suggested they retreat to the rose garden and catch up on the past. They sat in a gazebo in its center, close enough to each other that he could hold her hand. "You went east with Gance. Please tell me the details," he requested.

She told the story to him, leaving out only the more intimate aspects of her relationship with Gance. An hour passed as she spoke softly and gently of their journey, and what followed. By the time she was through, she felt light-headed and free, as if by finally telling it all to someone, she had broken the hold the events had on her soul.

"Now all that is left is the countess's memoir, written after her death, so to speak. What did you think of it?" she asked.

"I have it, but I haven't read it. I confess that I'm afraid to . . . because if I see even one of them as human, does that mean that she was still human as well?"

"Karina did not choose her life, any more than Lucy did. They were victims. As were we."

There! She said Lucy's name, the name they had tried so hard not to mention in all the hours they'd been together.

"And we're still victims," Arthur added, his voice pitched a bit too high, as if he were on the edge of tears. "Van Helsing asked if I still dream. I said only of Lucy, but I didn't say the rest. Too often I wake hearing her last terrible scream echoing in my mind. Van Helsing said she looked at peace when we were done. I tried to see it that way, but when I think back on it, she merely looked dead."

Mina knew no words to comfort him. In truth, she could not comprehend how she could have killed someone she loved so brutally and remained sane afterward. So she squeezed his hand and said, "I would give you any help I can. As would the others, I am sure. We are bonded by what we alone witnessed."

He moved closer to her. "It's a comfort just having you here," he said.

They sat together without speaking until the silence grew too awkward. Then Arthur took her inside and rang for a servant to show her to her room.

Mina woke early the next morning and dressed in her best summer gown, in that pale shade of green Jonathan always said made her look her best. She and Arthur arrived early. As he went to greet friends, she waited near the door, glancing nervously at it each time it opened.

Even though Arthur had warned that there would be a crowd, she still had not expected so many people, including two of Jonathan's other clients, her close friend Winnie Beason, and Winnie's husband, Emory.

Winnie seemed a bit out of breath from emotion. "The hospital is a beneficiary," she said to Mina, then looked past her to the door. "And look, there's Jonathan."

He looked at her from across the room, and from his expression Mina guessed that he was not certain how she would receive him. He'd suffered enough; they all had, she thought, and held out her hands.

He smiled as he took them, then kissed her cheek and explained about some problem on the rails. She was about to suggest that they step outside for a moment, when Robert Quarles took his place in front of the crowd.

Jonathan sat to the left of Mina on one of the half dozen long wooden benches, his hand resting atop hers. Arthur sat on her right, also holding her hand. She felt restrained by them and the oppressive social convention that made her glance around the room, wondering if anyone was observing Arthur's impropriety.

Arthur noticed her watching the others and pulled his hand away. "It seems to trouble you too much." He spoke softly, then dropped his voice to nearly a whisper to add, "Damn them all, as Gance would say."

"Damn them all," she repeated in the same private tone and grasped his hand once more. Jonathan heard her and looked at both of them, frowning.

She leaned toward her husband, intending to whisper that

she loved him, and always had, when Robert Quarles cleared his throat, took a sip of water, and began to address the now silent room.

An hour passed. Two. Quarles was still listing estates, then factories, then finally . . .

The house in Exeter she had expected. Some funds to cover taxes as well. But an apartment in Bloomsbury and a hundred thousand pounds?

As he had for some of his other beneficiaries, Gance supplied a reason, noting that she was *my most loyal friend, and the only truly honest creature I have ever known.*

Jonathan's hand stopped pressing hers so tighty as if he'd managed, finally, to relax. Gance's reason for the fortune he'd left her seemed almost pure, as if she were his conscience and not his. . . .

Winnie, who was sitting behind her, leaned forward so quickly she nearly lost her black felt hat. "Did you hear that!" she exclaimed. "Fifty thousand for the hospital. I think we will have to name some part of it after him!"

Quarles glared at her, the iciness of his expression quelling even her enthusiasm, and continued on.

Another hour passed. The bequests grew smaller, covering everyone from Arthur Holmwood, who received the bulk of Gance's wine cellar, to Oscar Wilde, who received "not one but three" casks of amontillado (a literary reference hardly lost on the more euphoric members of the crowd), to a favorite music tutor who inherited the Steinway from the ballroom of Gance's Exeter estate. The reading concluded dramatically with a final, huge sum to *to Asha Kumar of Delhi, who may not have possessed my heart but certainly had everything else.*

"And more than once. I'll wager one of my casks on that!" Wilde called from the back of the room. Laughter followed. As the group broke up, most of the conversation concerned the absent Asha and her relationship with Gance. How like him to be discreet, even in death, Mina thought, wondering how many other mistresses in this room had escaped notice because Gance had directed everyone's attention elsewhere.

As soon as the reading was over, Winnie mumbled a quick congratulations to her and headed for the back of the room to speak with one of Quarles's associates. Arthur pulled Mina aside. "Are you still planning on going to Exeter today, or will you be staying at the Bloomsbury place?" he whispered.

"I'll go to Exeter. I don't know if Jonathan is coming, though. He may have more business here." Mina hesitated, then confessed, "We haven't spoken."

"But you have an agreement, don't you?"

"He never wrote either."

Arthur seemed about to say something, then shrugged and looked over her shoulder at Jonathan instead. "I'll be staying in London indefinitely. But if it should happen that you need any assistance whatever, please wire me. The house is livable, I suppose. But if not, I'm sure the Westenras would be delighted to put you up for a time."

"Thank you for your concern, Arthur, but the house is charming. You'll have to come and see it soon," Mina replied, wondering if the little cottage would soon become the heart of her problem. She noted Winnie and Emory standing at the door, and whispered a final thanks to Arthur before joining them. "If you wait a bit while I say a few words to Mr. Quarles, we could travel together," she suggested.

Quarles had papers for her to sign, and keys to the house and flat. He thanked her on her good fortune, without giving the slightest hint that he had any knowledge of why she had received it.

As she turned to leave, she found Jonathan standing close behind her. He took her arm and led her from the room.

She half expected that he would abandon her outside, but instead he traveled with her and the Beasons to the station and sat with them on the train. He seemed oddly silent, but that was hardly surprising with Winnie's chatty enthusiasm for the hospital's newfound fortune and her grand plans on how to spend it.

Sometime during the journey, Jonathan and Emory began discussing business, leaving eventually for the familiar comfort of the smoking car.

As soon as they were alone, Winnie took a small case from her valise, pulled a flask of sherry and a pair of shotglasses out of it and poured them both a drink. She held up her glass.

"To change," she said. They drained them, and Winnie poured another pair.

"So you two haven't spoken?" she asked as she put the cork in the bottle.

Mina shook her head and looked away. It was the first time since this ordeal had begun that she felt like crying.

"And we've intruded. Should I claim Mr. Beason and take him to a different car?"

"No. When we do finally speak of the future, I want to be able to walk away from him if need be."

"Then tell me everything that happened. Every detail."

Mina adjusted her traveling bag on the end of the long seat, leaned against it and put up her feet. "Everything was exactly as I'd suspected, and so sad," she began.

Mina told her story while the train rolled on, carrying her to an uncertain ending. Occasionally she looked out the window at the twilight mists blurring the edges of the landscape. She was finally free of the vampire's blood. How much longer before she could be free of his memory?

The train pulled into Exeter a little before midnight. Without asking what her plans were, Jonathan retrieved Mina's bags. Since they lived close to the Beasons, they shared a cab. Winnie and Emory got out first, Winnie pausing to grip Mina's hands tightly. "If you need anything at all, come to us. I'll be sleeping with one eye open," she whispered, then kissed Mina on the cheek and said good-bye.

In the few minutes it took them to get home, Jonathan said nothing. Instead he held her hand as he had that afternoon, and kept his eyes straight ahead.

She waited until they pulled up in front of the house, the home she considered his, not hers, then asked, "Do you wish me to come back to you?" She hadn't wanted her voice to sound so cold, but he was taking too much for granted.

"If we can reach an agreement, yes."

"That might have been easier to reach somewhere else."

"My aunt is away, I made sure of that. We can speak as openly as we wish."

He carried her bags inside and up the stairs. She stopped in the foyer, inhaling deeply. The room smelled of lemon wax and Jonathan's cigars, of roasted onions and cinnamon. Familiar scents, welcome ones until Jonathan had brought her here and left her like some decorative piece of porcelain while he went on with his work.

Yes, she thought, moving into the parlor and lighting a gaslight. Agreements had to be reached. She went to the sideboard in the dining room and poured them each a brandy, then took a seat at the table and waited for him.

"Wouldn't the parlor be more comfortable?" he asked when he saw her there.

"This is a better place to discuss our future, I think."

He said nothing, only took the brandy she held out to him and sat across from her, solicitor and client, it seemed.

"Did you get my letter?" she asked, as gently as she was able.

"I did. Then I heard about Gance's will. Since you were coming to London, I thought it better to wait."

"I was in Paris for days before I received the solicitor's letter. Why didn't you come earlier, as I asked?"

He looked away for a moment, jaws working. "I suppose I should say I'm sorry, but I can't. I couldn't drop everything . . . again. And yet, I am sorry for everything that happened earlier. I should have believed you. Instead, I . . ." He couldn't go on, but took a drink from the glass instead.

She moved around the table, kneeling at his feet, his hands in hers. "Jonathan, I forgive you that."

He bit his lips, then blurted the words she'd expected to hear. "Was he . . . Gance . . . because of what that blood in you made you feel?"

"In the beginning. At the end it was how I felt," she answered honestly.

"And if Gance hadn't died in Transylvania, would you be here now?"

"I don't know," she answered. She poured another brandy, noting his disapproval—silent and obvious as always. She looked at him and added, "Should I be here at all?"

"I brought you here because it is your home. I'd like us to go back to the way things were when we were first married, before any of . . ."

She had to struggle to keep from shuddering, from revealing

any of the terror she felt at the thought of that life. "Never again, Jonathan," she whispered. "I can't abide being useless, and that is what I have been in this house. What I should like instead is a position. I am skilled enough to be a clerk in your office. We could work together."

"We're not shopkeepers, Mina. It isn't done."

"We'd be the first, then."

"It isn't done. But there are other things. In your free time, you can work with Winnie Beason at the hospital. Take some of that money Gance left you and put it to good use. I can help you with that."

She considered the compromise, then asked, "And what would you expect of me?"

She leaned toward him as she spoke those last words. The sweet taste of brandy was on her lips, the heady warmth of it already running through her, driving out the chill of the journey. All he had to do now was kiss her and everything, everything that had happened would be forgiven.

But he didn't. He actually looked as if he were forming a list in his mind. She picked up the bottle and took a candle from the sideboard. "I'll sleep in the guest room," she said and started up the stairs, moving slowly, begging him to stop her.

He said nothing, just as she knew he would say nothing the following day, and the months and years after.

At least he had made her decision easy.

Concentrating on that small bit of happiness, she went to bed.

She woke late in the morning, not surprised to find that Jonathan had already left for the office. His note mentioned an early appointment that would be impossible to postpone. It asked that she please stop by the office so they could go to lunch.

Not likely today, she thought. There was too much to do.

She stepped outside, inhaling the damp June air, taking in the quiet of the street, the splashes of sunlight in the puddles from last night's rain. A messenger on a bicycle passed by and she hailed him, asking him to find her a cab and send it to the house in an hour. She tipped him well and went inside to pack.

There wasn't much she wanted to claim, and little that she really needed. From her room, she took her clothes, the pictures of her parents, a few keepsakes. From downstairs, her typewriter and her favorite photograph of her and Jonathan, taken soon after they returned from her first journey east. Since they'd recently married, she considered it their wedding picture.

She moved through the rooms, running her hands over furniture willed to them by Mr. Hawkins, realizing that nothing in these walls mattered at all to her.

Except the memories, she thought. And in this house only the earliest ones had been good.

Jonathan's Aunt Millicent would undoubtedly tell him that at least he should be thankful she left so soon.

She heard the driver outside and went to the front door, where she already had her trunk waiting. She reached into her handbag, her fingers closing around the key Mr. Quarles had given her, the freedom Gance had spoken of.

For being an utter libertine, he was remarkably astute.

The trip took them past the children's hospital. Mina aske the driver to stop for a moment. As she expected, Winnie wasn't in so early, so she left a note with her address and an invitation for Winnie to call as soon as possible.

The cab continued on through narrowing streets.

Exeter did not have the slums of London, but like any large town, it had poverty of its own, and the shortest route to her new home took her straight through it. The driver took her past factories and dilapidated rooming houses. Glimpses down the narrow lanes between them revealed small children playing in the gutters, splashing in the water from last night's rain, water mixed no doubt with the droppings from slop buckets. Young beggars stood on the corners, rushing to her cab and asking for pennies every time her driver was forced to slow down.

She wanted to give some of her wealth away, but she knew where the generosity would lead. The poor would flock to the cab like geese at a morning feeding until the boldest of them realized that her voluntary generosity could be easily bypassed.

So she kept her eyes straight ahead and ignored any approaches.

In the narrow passage between two buildings, she saw a woman leaning against a man, her skirts lifted and wrapped around them both. Later she spied another woman leaning on a man's arm, both obviously drunk or drugged. The woman's hand against the man's dark coat revealed two missing fingers. Her skirt was ripped and filthy. Had one of these factories maimed her, then spit her out when she could no longer work? Had pain driven her to drugs or drink?

Mina tried to keep her eyes straight ahead, but she kept glancing at the sadness around her—women leaning against sunlit doorways, women holding children as ragged as they were, women in taverns, on benches in workyards sharing bread.

And last, a copper-haired young woman whose blue dress and bonnet were worn, but clean and mended. She had just left a workhouse, and her expression appeared desperate. But there was still color in her cheeks, and she appeared well fed. Most likely this wasn't the sort of work she was used to, Mina decided. Her driver had only traveled on a few hundred feet before Mina rapped her umbrella on the side of the cab and asked him to stop.

Stepping out of the cab, Mina called to the woman. She wasn't surprised when the woman looked at her as if she might know her. As Mina suspected, she had been someone's servant. "What is your name?" Mina asked as the woman approached her.

"Estelle Toth, mum. Essie." She smoothed back a lock of honey colored hair that had escaped from under her bonnet.

"And are you employed, Essie?"

"No, mum. I was. I was a maid for Judge Charles Proctor and his wife."

Judge Proctor. Mina frowned, trying to recall why the name sounded so distasteful. "And you are no longer there?"

"No, mum. I had a disagreement with Judge Proctor."

Mina suddenly recalled a piece of gossip about the man, told her by one of the children's nurses at the hospital. Given the attractiveness of the girl, Mina could easily guess the reason for the disagreement. "Can you read?" she asked.

"A bit. More than I need to get by."

"Can you provide a reference?"

"Only Mrs. Proctor, mum. But she is an invalid and may not be up to answering your inquiry."

"I'll check with her anyway. Can you come by my home the day after tomorrow?"

Essie sighed and shook her head. "I'm sorry, mum. I need to find something sooner, and if I do, then it wouldn't be right to desert my new employer."

Mina had always prided herself on knowing real character when she saw it, and she was sure she saw it now. "Then you shall start as my maid immediately," she said. "Can you come with me now?"

"I'll need to collect my things, but I can be there by two."

Mina wrote down her name and an address and pressed the paper and a coin into Essie's hand. "Get something to eat and someone to help you bring your bags."

As the cab pulled away, Mina watched Essie stroll down the street toward the rooming houses, walking faster now than before. Mina had given Essie a most unexpected gift, and another to herself as well.

She had a house, and now a servant to help her maintain it. Best of all, she was following her instincts, and they felt so correct.

The day was starting out much better than she'd ever expected.

four

Dr. Felix Chandra Rhys sat at his desk in his Exeter clinic, carefully explaining the needs of his tiny patient to its mother. As he spoke, he dangled his pocket watch before the toddler, noting the boy's lethargic interest in the bauble. He doubted the woman understood half his explanation about nutrition, so he relied, finally, on a simpler set of directions. "Every morning I want you to go to the Loden Brewery and ask for Mike Farrell. Tell him you need a bit of the unfermented malt blend. Have Roddy suck down as much as he'll take for the next few days."

"Beer?" the woman asked, shocked.

"Not beer. Hops and barley and molasses. Just what Roddy needs for the next few days. Can you do that?"

"I've a couple shillings that I was planning to—"

He understood. "No need to pay me now. Just see that Roddy gets what he needs." He showed the woman to the door, hoping that she would follow his orders, but hardly certain. Still, he tried. If the child survived, so be it. If he died, well, Rhys shared his own mother's beliefs in reincarnation and hoped the child would have a better life the next turn of the wheel.

Rhys had a successful practice in another part of Exeter much like the one he'd abandoned in London the year before, but once a week he spent a day in this dingy storefront just a few blocks from Winnie Beason's charity hospital, tending to the needs of Exeter's poorest citizens, just as he had in

London's East End. Over the past year his main surprise was how many poor there were in this small city and how, in spite of the huge numbers who died far too young, their numbers seemed to grow so quickly.

But he did not abandon the charity work he'd begun years before. His charity cases were, after all, in keeping with a promise he'd made a decade ago to his mother. He didn't care that she was long dead when he made it, since he knew her spirit was with him. Now every person he saved was a way of thanking her for ensuring his own survival through infancy. He could scarcely remember her, yet his aunt told him often enough that she had been a remarkably courageous woman.

And he had a gift for dealing with the poor. Hardly surprising since his first few years had been spent among them in London's East End, a place that made this dank section of Exeter seem like Paradise.

He'd hated it there—the poverty that made children into beggars and thieves, the drink that turned men into brutes and women into harlots. And the terrible way that vice spilled from those who inflicted it on themselves to the innocent whose only crime was to trust too well.

Then there were the ones like this mother—well-meaning but destitute. He did not mind his vow so much when he worked to heal ones such as these and the innocents they bore.

As he watched the woman leave with her child, he spied Essie Toth coming down the street. Her bonnet was a bit skewed, her hair windblown, but she had a wide smile on her round face. The factory must have work for her, though he shuddered to think of the sort of labor she would have to do. She wasn't trained for it, but she would learn. They all did.

"They hired you, did they?" he called to her.

She walked toward him, waiting until she was close to answer. "Better! I have a real position. Servant to a Mrs. Wilhemina Harker."

"Even after what—"

"She acted like she'd heard the rumors about Judge Proctor. Perhaps I should have tried some of the other families instead of thinking that no one would have me when he let me go."

He shrugged. Treading in both worlds—and because of his

race, accepted in neither—he knew how shallow the rich could be when it came to scandal.

"So I've come for my things," she went on.

He took a key from his coat pocket and opened the door of a cupboard that took up all of the rear wall of his office. Hers was one of many bags and boxes, treasures he kept safe for those with no rooms of their own in which to store them.

Essie's canvas satchels were two of the newest and cleanest, recently given to her by Mrs. Proctor. He wondered if the poor invalid had guessed that they would be parting gifts. "Shake your things out well before you go inside her house or you might regret it," he suggested as he handed them over. The office was as clean as he could keep it, but that hardly kept bugs and worse from invading in his long absences.

"I'll stop and do it sometime during the walk so Mrs. Harker won't see."

He frowned. The name was familiar. He would have asked Essie about her, but he doubted the girl knew anything worthwhile yet. "Where does she live?" he asked.

"On River Road."

"That's quite a hike from here. If you wait a bit, I can take you there," he suggested.

She looked from him to the door, the pair of women waiting outside, one leaning against the other. "Looks like you have more patients. I wouldn't want to keep you from them."

He glanced at the pair, then remembered that he had promised Winnie Beason that he would definitely come by the hospital today to look in on a couple of her children.

He smiled at Essie as he opened the door for her. She accepted the gesture naturally, as if she were one of the ladies she served. In a way, she was, especially when compared to most of his patients—derelicts and whores, some half insane from poverty and drink and the diseases that stemmed from them.

Essie paused as she passed him. "Thank you for everything," she said.

He watched her go, repeating the name of the woman she would be working for. "Wilhemina Harker."

As soon as he could, he would find out everything he could

about her. Essie was one of his special charges. He vowed to look out for her, and make certain that she came to no harm.

He motioned to the next patient to come inside. Both women did. "She can't walk without help, sir," the healthy one said.

Rhys studied his patient—the sweat on her forehead, the deep, hacking cough. Tuberculosis, most likely, though it was possible that typhus was coming early this year.

Sometimes he wished it would wipe out the lot of them, and leave space in the world for more decent folks.

Essie's bags weren't heavy, and Exeter was hardly a huge city, so she decided to walk to her new home. The route took her north, through the center of town, then up a narrow road that ran along the Exe River. The houses weren't grand, but they were well tended enough that she guessed most of them employed a gardener. It made her feel better about her future, until she spied number 37, her mistress's home.

The stone wall and iron gate in front of it seemed imposing enough, and the entry garden with its stone fountain was untended but still beautiful. Needs a bit of work, not much, she thought as she slipped through the half-open gate. There was no narrow path to a side entrance, so she walked toward the front door instead, listening all the time for some sign that Mrs. Harker was at home.

The door wasn't locked, and no one answered her call, so she stepped inside.

The first thing she noticed was that the air smelled of a man—sweet pipe tobacco and bay rum cologne. And it was a man's house, with its thick oriental carpets and dark leather settees. Essie ran a finger along the sofa table, noting the sharp line she left in the dust. "Mrs. Harker," she called again, and heard a reply, faint with distance, from the rear yard.

She moved quickly through the house, frowning when she saw its small scale, and the disappointingly tiny kitchen, then went through the rear door into another garden, this one sloping gently down to the riverbank.

Mina Harker had changed into a light green dress. She was stooped down, pulling vines away from the rose bushes. "I always wanted to see this garden in its full summer beauty," she said. "I hardly guessed that I would have to restore it first."

"Did you purchase the house recently?" Essie asked.

Mrs. Harker looked up at her for the first time, and Essie saw that her eyes were wet. "I inherited it from a friend. It belonged to Lord Gance," she explained.

Essie turned away to look at the house again and to hide her knowing expression from her employer. Having worked for a wealthy family, she'd overheard enough gossip to know Gance's reputation.

"He was no gentleman as you would think of them," Mrs. Harker said, as if reading her mind. "But he was hardly the sort of ogre your last employer turned out to be."

"You've checked my reference already?" Essie asked, amazed.

Mrs. Harker stood and smiled. "Merely remembered," she replied. "Let's get out of this heat, shall we? I'd forgotten how small this house was. After we have something cool to drink, we'll have to find you a bit of privacy until I can arrange to have some rooms added on."

Essie pumped water from the well, cool and tasting faintly of iron. They cut the taste with wedges of lime. When they'd finished, her employer took her on a tour.

Essie blushed when she saw the upstairs bedroom, something out of one of those dirty magazines, and marveled at the bathrub that drew water from the heater in the kitchen. As Mina opened the doors that led to the narrow second-floor porch, Essie saw a bug scurry toward the fringe on the carpet. She caught it with her boot before it could escape.

"How long has the house been unoccupied?" she asked.

"It was never . . ." Mina began, then concluded, "eight weeks."

"Then it needs a good airing, mum."

"Call me Mina, Essie. Let's just shake out the bedcovers and worry about the rest tomorrow. I'm sure you're as exhausted as I am."

Essie spent the night on the setee in the solarium with the doors that led to the rest of the house shut to give her some privacy. She wasn't used to such huge windows, nor the view of the open spaces beyond, and when she woke in the middle of the night, it took her a moment to get her bearings.

When she did, she stood and with blanket wrapped around her, walked closer to the glass. Outside, the half moon lit the garden and turned the river into a precious glowing ribbon.

Without really thinking, she opened the doors that led to the garden, intending to step outside. Something unseen scurried away from the door, and she heard a beating of wings, the ghostly call of an owl. She shut the door quickly and stood with her back pressed against it, shivering with fright and exhilaration, like a housecat who had just realized the freedom that lay beyond an open door.

"There's nothing there. Nothing to be afraid of. Nothing at all," she whispered, then padded quickly back to her makeshift bed.

five

Joanna Tepes learned to read the night's shadows . . . the blinding ones thrown by the full moon, the dimmer ones of the partial moon, the softest ones unseen by any but night birds and vampires, the shadows of the stars.

And when these shadows began to dull at the edges, she would find shelter. There were always small canyons where the horse could graze, overcroppings of rocks beneath which her box of earth—her haven—could rest. The horse had a Gypsy coin embedded in its bridle. She added to this a coin of her own, a gold one stamped with the likeness of her brother. If a man ventured too close to the animal while she slept, the likeness of the Gypsy coin would keep all but the Gypsies from stealing her mount. As for them, the other gold coin would give them pause.

She doubted that any found the beast, though. She was careful in her resting places, and the land was so empty.

It took her two weeks to reach the settled areas along the coast. As the cities and farms grew more numerous, she was forced to take greater precautions during the day until the night when she woke at dusk she realized she was not alone.

Silent as the mist she became, she spilled out of the hairline crack in the side of her shelter and rolled along the ground until she was some distance from her makeshift camp. There, she took form and studied the intruder.

A slender youth no older than twenty, about the same age she had been when she was taken from her grandfather's palace. Sexless in appearance but the scent was female. Joanna moved closer, trying to decide what to make of the thief.

Not Gypsy. Not Turkish. The hair was too golden, the skin as pale as Karina's had been. Joanna moved closer and let her form become solid. Closer yet, until she was so close she could grab the girl and feed. Then she inhaled and spoke, her voice loud, intending to provoke fear. *"Nu te atinge de acela!"*

The girl only turned and looked at her curiously, saying something in a language Joanna did not recognize.

Had her own speech become so dated, or did the girl perhaps come from somewhere else? "Say something I can understand!" Joanna ordered with the last of the air still in her lungs.

"I thought the horse lost . . . ah . . . *am gîndit cal pierde,*" the girl said slowly in Romanian. Her accent was thick and foreign to Joanna, but the words were understandable.

"Pierde." Joanna tittered and grabbed the girl's arm. She felt the pulse, barely noticeable to another human or the girl herself, rolling through her, rapid with fright.

"Yours?" The girl pointed to the animal. "I am . . . *îmi pare rau.*" She reached into the dirty leather tunic covering her body from shoulders to knees and took out a coin, holding it out to Joanna.

"Not thief. For you," she said. Fear did not motivate this, Joanna thought. It was honor.

Joanna shook her head. There was something else here that she wanted desperately, though she dared not claim it. The hunger in her was immense, overpowering even her hysteria. If she gave in to it, the strength of it would fade, and with it her tenuous hold on sanity.

She shook her head again.

The girl backed away, then turned to face the road. To Joanna, who understood the feeling all too well, she seemed ready to bolt for freedom.

Something Joanna's brother had told her came back to her. She needed to find a creature like this to see her safely to the ship, across the seas to . . . The name of the place where he had gone, and where his enemies lived still eluded her. "Go Varna?" she asked simply, hoping the girl would understand.

The girl turned back to her, frowning. "What did you say?"

she asked in that same language. Joanna realized that she had heard it before, not long ago. English, her brother had called it. The language of her enemies. He spoke it. So did Karina. Joanna had learned a few words of it from the English in the castle; hardly enough to get by.

"Go Varna?" Joanna asked and gestured toward the horse and cart before pointing to herself, something the girl seemed to understand more than the Romanian words. She nodded.

"You. I. Go," Joanna added in English and saw the girl's suspicious expression break into a happy grin.

The girl built a small fire. Joanna brought her meat, the remnants of her own kill, to cook and eat. During the next hour, through a mixture of English and Romanian spoken slowly, Joanna learned something of her new servant. She was Colleen Kelley O'Sh——, some name Joanna could never pronounce. She was from Ireland, and just eighteen. Through some quirk of fate Joanna could not understand, Colleen had stowed away on a ship she thought bound for her homeland, not realizing that it was not going to Ireland, but east. She nearly starved because she was afraid that if she came out of the hold she would be thrown overboard or raped. So she foraged at night, surviving as best she could. When the ship finally landed in Constanta some weeks ago, she had run as far from it as possible.

Since then, she had lived off the land, and begun to realize that this was not at all a haven for her. She had been making for the port at Varna, hoping to find a ship bound for the west, when she'd spied Joanna's horse.

And, though she had picked up a few words of Romanian, she had thankfully learned nothing about vampires.

If she had, Joanna would have been forced to kill her probably a dozen times during the two-day trip to Varna. Instead, the girl seemed to take Joanna's pale skin for granted, and accept her own story that she was an escaped hostage, a noble in her own land. Joanna told her that she had been traveling by night to avoid detection, and that she would continue to do so, hiding in the wooden box during daylight hours when she would be more likely to be seen and perhaps recognized.

She made up an incredible tale about concealed breathing holes, and how she was a queen in her own land but unable to return to it. Colleen believed it all, or seemed to, and the language problem made any questions difficult.

The ruse seemed so easily accepted that Joanna let out one of her anxious giggles when she'd finished. Colleen didn't question that either, but instead looked at her, head cocked as if trying to decipher the joke.

So they went on, reaching the outskirts of Varna three days later.

Colleen did as Joanna had ordered, and stopped some distance from the city. When Joanna joined her for the evening, Colleen had already made a fire and was eating bread and cheese she had purchased from a farmer earlier that day. "Would you like something?" Colleen asked when she saw her, holding out the bread so Joanna would understand her question.

Joanna shook her head.

"There's an inn just down the road, we could go there and have the stable tend to the horse. You could have a real meal."

Colleen was no fool. She knew her employer had odd habits. But what she saw when Joanna deciphered her suggestion was unconcealed terror. Though she pitied the woman, Colleen thought there was some benefit to her timidity. Colleen would have to be the strong one, the clever one, if they were to survive.

"Or we can stay here," she said in a soothing tone. "And where do you want to go tomorrow . . . into Varna? From there you can arrange passage to Russia? Turkey?"

Joanna shook her head, still trying to remember.

"India? Sweden? Egypt?"

Colleen spoke the names slowly, so Joanna would understand. Joanna frowned, struggling with the memory of her brother's destination. "Your language?" she finally asked.

"English?" I don't understand

"English, England . . . London, England. I wish to go there . . . London," Joanna said at last.

"Then I'll go too! I think we can find someone who can help us once we get there—that is, if you have the passage . . . the money."

"Money." Joanna repeated the word, savoring it. Her brother had often spoken of money, and of places where it was kept.

She suspected that she even had papers that would help concealed in her box. "You come. I pay and you come."

"You want to employ me, you mean?"

Joanna understood the words. She pulled in another breath of air and agreed.

"We have to buy tickets. And we ought to dress up like ladies, British ladies. There are enough foreigners in Britain that you will fit in. No one will be looking for a lady and her maid," she went on, watching Joanna to see if her words were understood.

"Yes. We do that," Joanna said. It pleased her that Colleen seemed to understand her words, seemed to actually relax now that she had some idea of their relationship to each other.

Joanna stared into the fire, remembering how she had treated her servants so many years before when she was young.

There had been so many that she could not remember even one name. But there had been one among them, a girl her own age who had become more than a servant, more even than a friend.

No! She would not think of that. Illona gave her good advice when she said it was not wise to dwell too often on the past.

And yet? She watched Colleen build up the fire that would keep predators away. She watched her comb the tangles from her light brown hair and twist it up under a loose-fitting cap to hide the weakness of her gender. She kept on sitting there, watching in silence, until Colleen wrapped herself in a blanket, lay between the blaze and the fire and went to sleep. Then Joanna rose, thinned to a mist and flowed down the road into Varna.

The city's life teemed around her, more life than she had experienced in centuries. Had she possessed substance, she might have lost her mind in its presence, but incorporeal, her emotions were as soft as her form. She moved through the most crowded streets, controlling her fear and that ever-present hysteria, searching for the fortitude to replace it with hunger and desire.

On the edge of town the buildings grew grander and farther apart, separated by expanses of lawns and gardens. She moved closer to one of the largest, certain from the number of people inside that she had discovered an inn.

She waited in the shadows until the lights inside were extinguished, then moved closer to the building. The night was oppressive, stuffy and hot, and a pair of European women slept on their third-floor balcony, thinking themselves safe from harm because they were so far above the ground.

Their open door and the public nature of the shelter were invitations enough for Joanna's kind, but she hesitated anyway. Half formed, she ran her hand over the younger woman's chestnut hair, thinking of the one who had killed Karina and her brother. The woman stirred in her sleep, rolled onto her back, the half smile of a pleasant dream playing on her lips.

Dare she take? If she pressed her lips against that pale neck, if she drank, if she killed, what rumors would circulate among the rabble of Varna? Suddenly fearful, she fought the urge to kill and instead moved quickly into the room, digging among the clothes scattered on the bed, taking only a pair of dresses and some shoes, dropping a coin to pay for them. She left the way she came, drifting over the balcony to the ground, fleeing in the shadows with the dresses fluttering behind her like kites tossed in the wind.

SIX

Colleen woke after midnight. Weeks as a fugitive, first in France, then on the ship, then in this strange land, made her instincts sharp, and so she lay still a moment, listening.

The horse stomped and snorted. A man whispered something. Beneath her blanket, Colleen's hand moved slowly up her side toward the knife she kept hidden in her belt. Before she could reach it, something came down hard on the side of her head. Dazed, she felt hands moving over her body, taking her knife, then realizing her sex, fumbing with her shirt.

She tried to roll out from under him but he was too quick for her, his body too heavy.

He reeked of old sweat, rotten teeth and brandy, and she turned her head sideways in disgust as he tried to kiss her. As least there seemed to be only one. Perhaps if she lay still and just let . . .

No! She'd had enough of that before she boarded the ship. She was through being passive. She jerked a knee up between his legs, hitting him hard but not hard enough. He grunted and hit her, not a slap this time but a punch that stole all thought of fight from her.

She wished he'd hit her harder; she didn't want to be awake for what would follow.

Half dazed, she felt his fumbles at her clothes and his own until she heard him grunt again, the weight of him jerked off her.

She forced her eyes to open, tried to focus on the sight of

him struggling with nothing, or so it seemed. She did not understand the words he spoke, but heard the terror in his tone and in the final words he called: *"Strigoaica! Strigoaica!"*

A cloth fell over her face, whispy soft and scented with sweet perfume. Colleen pushed the fabric away and looked with terror at her enemy.

He was a huge man, larger even than she'd thought when his weight rested on her, yet something unseen had lifted him off of her, and now held him doubled over at the waist, his feet off the ground, kicking the air. Breathing hard, Colleen slipped backward on hands and feet, away from the firelight and into the comfort of the shadows. There she watched with growing horror as her attacker's head was jerked backward and his throat ripped through, cutting off the name he called again.

"Stri—"

His blood flowed for only a moment. Then a shadow covered and seemed to close the wound, a shadow that slowly solidified into dark hair and pale face, the long, thin arm that held him, the long, thin hand that grasped his grimy hair, holding his head up and back.

Colleen choked back a scream, turned and lurched down the road, then up a hill and into a stand of trees. There she crouched, trying to keep her knees from shaking, her breath slow and silent.

Joanna found her anyway. The woman's face and hands were smeared with blood, and there was a dark, shiny stain of it on her tattered black dress. "Come," she ordered and held out her hand. Colleen cringed at the sight of it but stood and, resigned, followed her mistress down the hill and into the firelight.

The body lay where Joanna had dropped it. The throat was ripped open, the head at an odd angle to the rest of the corpse. He had died horribly, yet Colleen was hardly sad that he was dead. She looked from the corpse to her mistress, noting the flush of pink in Joanna's cheeks, the fiery flash of life in the centers of her emerald eyes.

"What are you?" she whispered.

Joanna repeated the dying man's word, adding another.

"Strigoaica mort." The words were said with no emotion, as if she were beyond caring what Colleen thought of her.

Colleen wanted to step back, to run. Reason might have told her it was futile, but something else intervened before it could.

She looked from the corpse, bloodless and still, to the one who had killed him. And for the first time in all the fear-filled weeks of stealth and hiding, she relaxed. Convinced that loyalty was the only thing that could save her now, and that loyalty would somehow keep her safe, she bowed to the woman who stood before her and humbly took her outstretched hands.

For the first time since they'd met, she saw Joanna smile. Her canines were far too long, too sharp. Her look too triumphant.

Colleen stifled a shudder, pulled away slowly and crouched beside the body. She pulled the knife from her belt, only half aware of how Joanna crouched beside her, how she nodded as Colleen whispered, "Damn you!" She lifted the blade and brought it down hard into the man's belly, once then again and again, repeating the curse all the while until, finally, the tears began to flow. She fell against her pale mistress, lay her cheek against the lifeless breasts, cold, sticky with blood.

She cried, hardly aware of the one who held her, moving her wrist to Colleen's mouth. Blood pooled along a wound the man had made in his struggles. Without thinking, Colleen sucked it as she had her little brother's frequent scratches, pulling out the dirt so the wound could heal cleanly.

But this was not a protective gesture. There was too much purpose in how Joanna had held up her wrist, too much strength in how Joanna gripped it, holding the wound open so it would bleed freely.

And too much emotion in how she trembled as Colleen took in that small bit of herself. Tangy. Smoky as a long-aged red wine. Colleen swallowed and felt a fire not unlike that of strong drink fill her. As she moved her lips to the wound again, Joanna pulled away.

"Enough," she whispered. Her form thinned to a mist and vanished.

Colleen built up the fire, and sat with her back to the corpse, staring into the comforting light. She thought not of the attack but of the creature who had saved her. Oddly, she felt no fear until she sensed rather than heard Joanna return.

She'd found some river or pond and washed the blood from her clothes. Now they clung to her body, weighted down by the water, showing how thin she was, how seemingly frail.

Joanna grabbed the body by one foot and dragged it effortlessly into the trees. "Wait!" Colleen called. "He may have some money. We ought to take it."

A tinkle of laughter said Joanna had heard. Moments later she returned, carrying a muddy sack and a handful of coins that she dropped into Colleen's lap. Though Joanna seemed to have no interest in the rest of what was inside the tattered scrap of cloth, Colleen did. She pulled out a filthy shirt wrapped around a bottle. She yanked out its cork, sniffed the bottle's contents, then took a taste. Spicy-sweet and heavily alcoholic. She swallowed; swallowed again.

The drink gave her strength. She looked from the fire to Joanna sitting beside her, rested her hand on her mistress's, feeling a hint of warmth in it. She touched Joanna's chin, turning her head so they faced each other.

It was time to learn what she was traveling with.

By the following afternoon, when Colleen hitched the horse to the wagon and to begin the final journey into Varna, she understood many things.

She understood that her mistress was not alive, and had not been alive for nearly six centuries.

She understood that, as a result of this condition, Joanna was forced to spend the daylight hours in the box she carried with her, and that to expose her body to the sun would most likely end her existence.

She understood that the blood she had drunk, such a tiny amount, had bound her to her mistress in a way that no human loyalty could have accomplished.

She understood that if she continued to drink it, she herself would begin to slowly change.

Last, she understood that she did not care.

Colleen had put on the simpler of the pair of stolen dresses and taken them those last few miles while Joanna hid from the relentless sun. In town, people stared at the strange combination of an Englishwoman on a Gypsy cart, but used to the eccentric ways of foreigners, did not try to question her.

She moved through the center of town, to the wilder streets north of the wharf, where the shipping firms were located. She stopped occasionally to ask directions until she located the shipping firm of Steranko and Summers.

She pulled her wagon in front of the door and went inside. A tiny office opened onto a large warehouse filled with containers of all kinds. She saw mesh bags of cured hams, crates of wine and, oddly, what looked like bottled water, stacks of cured hides and sheepskin. So much wealth behind an unlocked door, as if the owners feared nothing. "Is anyone here?" she called.

In response, someone laid a hand on her shoulder. She cried out, whirled and retreated, her hand instinctively falling to the place at her waist where she'd kept her knife hidden. "I am Mr. Summers. Can I help you?" an old man asked in cultured English, blinking at her from behind a pair of glasses thick as bottle bottoms.

"Yes . . . that is . . ." She took a deep breath and went on. "I'm here on behalf of my mistress, who wishes to obtain passage to London for her and myself."

"And why does she send you instead of coming herself?"

"Her knowledge of English is not good," Colleen replied, hoping the answer would be enough.

"Then she could speak to my partner, Mr. Steranko."

"That would hardly be—"

"Of course it would be," he said, cutting her off. "We need to know whom we are to arrange passage for."

This wasn't going as Colleen had hoped. She guessed it was her accent—that strange blend of cockney and Irish—that gave her away. Though she'd worked hard to learn to hide it, and to get an education of sorts, she'd never been able to leave the slums of London and Dublin behind. There seemed to be only one option. "She'll be along soon. If Mr. Steranko can wait, he can speak to her."

"Mr. Steranko just stepped out for a little while. I'm sure he'll return soon enough."

He took her back into the office and brewed them both a

cup of strong black tea. By the time they sat down to drink it, the sun had already fallen behind the distant western slopes. Colleen could feel her mistress wake, feel their minds brush. The intimacy gave her comfort.

She turned toward the door, but the form she saw there was not Joanna's but that of a large man, well dressed but with long, unruly dark hair. "Mr. Steranko?" she asked.

He nodded and stepped forward. Some years younger than his partner, he nonetheless seemed to be the one in charge. He took her hand and kissed the back of it. "Please," she said, pulling it away from his grasp.

"Her mistress will be coming soon to arrange passage west," Summers explained.

"Ah, yes. I saw the wagon outside and the emblem on the bridle. I was wondering when the others in the family would decide to follow the count. Which one is leaving next?"

Before Colleen could decide how to answer, she saw Joanna take form in the doorway. She looked far more beautiful in the pale blue gown than in the tattered clothes she'd been wearing, and the flush of the life she had taken was still on her cheeks; but her pallor, the silence when she moved revealed everything to a knowing eye.

Steranko walked quickly to Joanna, taking both her hands, bowing so that his forehead nearly touched them. "Enter freely and be welcome, Countess," he said, revealing just how much he understood.

Colleen watched how Joanna took a seat in one of the office chairs. Her bearing was stiff and regal, and yet Colleen could sense in how her hands gripped the chair arms, her fingers playing with the turnings in the wood, how her unruly hair seemed to shiver in some unfelt breeze, that she was on the edge of another bout of hysteria.

What did she dream about in her long days in dark confinement? Colleen wondered. Did she dream at all?

Joanna had never looked into the eyes of a man who understood what she was, and yet was unafraid. She had to fight the urge to bare her fangs and arouse that fear, had to remind herself that he was undoubtedly someone who was used to her kind and whose help she needed. She wisely managed to keep it at bay, even while she grew more and more flustered as he spoke words she could scarcely understand, pointed to documents she could not read.

She had revealed that fact to Colleen last night. They had sat by the fire, sifting through the stack of papers she had taken from her brother's ruined castle. There were crumbling edicts written centuries ago, letters written in a language strange to both of them from someone in Szged, notes to a banker in Bucharest, and the most recent from some gentleman in England concerning the shipment of her brother's belongings to his new home.

Those last had provided the name of the shipping house he'd used, and brought them here. Now Steranko sat with the documents spread over his huge desk, explaining to her what each of them meant. She didn't understand half of what he was telling her, but there was no need, especially when he assured her that there would be solicitors in London more than willing to handle all her affairs.

He then took a map and showed the route their ship would take, and last explained the papers they would both need to travel openly.

"Don't worry, Countess. Everything can be handled through us," Steranko explained. "We are quite used to handling the affairs of nobility like yourself, as well as those with other unique needs."

Beside her, Colleen whispered in a voice so low only a vampire's ears could detect any sound at all. "Unique needs. Banshees. Dearg-dul. Rakashas."

"And you can handle this all?" Joanna asked.

"All of it. We can even keep you safe until the ship departs tomorrow evening."

So easy! So very easy! Joanna pulled in a quick breath, then realized how insane her laugh would seem, how out of place. She pressed her lips together tightly, feeling ready to explode.

"It will cost, of course," Steranko went on.

How dare he try to cheat her! Her eyes flashed with anger and he quickly added, "But no more than any set of forged papers, I assure you."

Forged? "I go under my own name," she insisted.

Steranko considered this. "I think you must once you reach your destination, Countess. If you do not, you will have no part of your brother's wealth once you've arrived in London. According to these documents, he has sizable holdings there."

"And why not now?" she asked.

"It would not be be completely wise, Countess. You see, your brother's name is too well known in this country, and the fate of the sailors on the *Demeter* only added to his reputation. You might end up on a ship where some part of the crew knew the *Demeter*'s story and would wish you harm. And by day . . ." He left the thought unfinished, a polite gesture.

Joanna shut her eyes, struggled to remember the distant past. "There is another name that is also rightly mine," she said at last. "Princess Joanna Mezid-Bey."

Steranko bowed again, lower this time. "I thought I detected some eastern blood in you. I'm sure it will do for your travel papers, Princess. I will also prepare a second set for London."

Joanna glanced in Colleen's direction, but the girl seemed to understand the language as poorly as she understood the meaning of the words. Frowning, Joanna faced the man again, adding another request in quick, dated Romanian.

It was his turn to be confused, and she repeated herself more slowly. "I wish a private cabin for myself and my servant. She will watch over me to be certain there are no mishaps."

"It shall be done, Princess," Steranko said when she had finished. "And may I remind you that this will be a long voyage with few stops. I suggest that tonight, you head north from the wharfs. The area is poor and wild. You will dine easily there, and the one you choose will not be missed."

Joanna did giggle then, out of joy, not confusion. With that quick statement she felt more at home than she had in the long, confusing days that preceded it.

On the other hand, Colleen felt suddenly ill. She didn't understand every word the man said, but it seemed that he spoke of murder as casually as he might the food at a well-respected inn. When Joanna gripped her arm, Colleen had to fight the urge to pull away, to dig in her heels as Joanna led her into the darkness outside.

"Will you . . . kill?" she asked Joanna when they were some distance away from the building.

Joanna shrugged. Her grip on Colleen's wrist had grown painfully tight as she led Colleen in the direction Steranko had suggested.

The streets grew narrower and muddier, though there had been no recent rain. A stench filled the air, one far too familiar to a girl who had spent too many months in the London slums. Under normal circumstances, she would be keeping to the shadows, moving in quick, silent bursts, hoping to escape notice. Now she walked with her mistress, and though she was still frightened, it was not for herself.

A man reeled out of an open door, falling against her. She pushed him away with all the force she could muster. He looked at her, eyes glazed, mind clouded with drugs or drink, illness or exhaustion. "Go!" she ordered in a harsh whisper.

Close to her, so close that Colleen could feel the chill of her flesh beneath the layers of cloth, Joanna tittered.

"Please," Colleen begged softly. "Please."

Joanna's hand covered Colleen's eyes, her free arm circled Colleen's waist, pulling her closer. Colleen felt her feet leave the ground, her body propelled upward. Lips were pressed to her neck, drawing blood with deceptive delicacy. When she opened her eyes, she saw the stars whirling above her, then slower, and slower, until they vanished, leaving only darkness. . . .

When she came to her senses, she was stretched out in the cart, in the narrow space between its sides and her mistress's shelter. Steranko was standing at the back of it, holding a plate of spicy stew and a mug of beer. "I suggest you keep your strength at its peak," he said. "It's going to a long journey for both of you."

He left the plate and mug on the edge of the cart and turned his back to her, walking away as if she were one already dead.

seven

When he left the restaurant after meeting with Jonathan and Van Helsing, Arthur Holmwood had vowed not to read the translation they had given him.

He managed to ignore it until a week after the reading of Gance's will. That afternoon, still exhausted from a long, sleepless night brought on by too much wine at an impromptu wake for Gance that Wilde had tossed with his legacy, he found himself too weary to run away from his curiosity any longer.

He made a grand gesture of uncorking a bottle of Gance's well-aged Merlot and pouring a glass before opening the transcribed journal of Countess Karina Aliczni. When he came to the reference that implied that perhaps vampires did not need to kill, a shudder rolled through him, then another as he realized that he was thinking not of Lucy but of Mina and what they might have done to her had their mission failed.

Though he had loved Lucy, he understood her shortcomings. She had been loyal but flighty, a bit eccentric but lovely, flirtatious, but in time she would have made a marvelous mother for his children. All in all, the perfect wife as long as she did not face undue adversity.

Then she would have wilted and given in.

And yet?

He recalled Jonathan's words to Mina—that if she were to change, he would change with her so she would not go alone into that dark and terrible half life. It had seemed a grand gesture at the time, but not now.

Suppose that when Lucy had tried to give him that dark, eternal kiss, he had pushed back the others with their crosses and their stakes and their hosts and holy water. Suppose that he had let her change him as Dracula had changed her. Would he have possessed enough self-control for both of them?

He didn't know. He had never looked closely at his own defects. But he was certain of one thing: The faith that might have sustained a better man had long ago left him. It would not have been God that kept him from breaking that most basic of all commandments—it would have been the memory of what human contact had once meant to him.

No. In the end it would not have been enough.

Mina, on the other hand, would only grow stronger in adversity. She had already proven that far more than once.

He thought of her, of Lucy, and last of himself. Then he cried, until there were no tears left in him—one final grand gesture of grief for her memory.

In the morning, he took stock of his pounding head, his eyes red-rimmed as some widowed woman's, and vowed to take Gance's advice from months before and put the matter behind him.

It was not so easily done. Arthur had lost his own parents when he was thirteen—a father to a riding accident, a mother to grief. He had been raised by a bachelor uncle who had more money than common sense. Some ten years after his parents' death, he lost his uncle when the ship taking the man to India sank off the Cape of Good Hope.

With a title and the money to accompany it, Arthur drifted for a few years until he met Lucy. No sooner had he started courting her than her family adopted him as their own.

He'd reveled in their exuberant attention. But they were just as exuberant in their grief. The family still draped their doors in black ribbons and their bodies in black wool, and most still had to reach for kerchiefs when her name was mentioned, as if she had been laid to rest last week instead of nearly a year before.

He has lost a fiancée. Would he lose her family too?

Yet he knew that the best way to begin his own healing was to stop his constant visits to her family and instead mourn with the stronger ones who also had loved her.

And so his thoughts turned to Mina. He intended to send her a letter telling her that he was coming to Exeter and wanted to call. Before he could do so, he received a telegram from her, inviting him to come and visit and see her new home.

He'd heard about the house; all Gance's close friends knew of it. But it had been Gance's private retreat. Few even knew the address, and of those who did, none had ever been invited inside.

Seeing Mina had been a pleasant idea. Now curiosity made the journey downright irresistible.

He sent a quick wire to her asking that she meet him at the station. The following morning he packed a traveling bag and caught the first train west.

When Mina received the telegram, she immediately realized the turn their conversation would take. In a house the size of hers, privacy was nearly impossible. Working side by side with Essie on setting up the house, Mina realized how rare their camaraderie was. And though Essie would undoubtedly learn part of the vampires' story someday, she hardly needed to hear it all so soon, and thinking her employer mad, or worse, resign. So Mina suggested that the woman take a few days off to visit a cousin in Plymouth whom she had not seen for the year she had nursed Mrs. Proctor.

Mina walked into town with Essie, seeing her off on the northbound coach as if they were friends, not mistress and servant. She had just enough time for a quick cup of tea at a little café near the station before Arthur's train pulled in.

He was easy to spot, with his fair hair seeming to glow in the precious rays of midmorning sun breaking through the interminable British mists. When he reached her, he dropped his small satchel and gave her a long hug, smiling while she rearranged the jade green bonnet that had gone askew from his exuberant greeting.

"I only saw you for a few hours while you were in London and have been missing your company ever since. Has it only been two weeks?" he asked as he linked her arm in his and patted her hand. "It's an unnaturally lovely day. Is your house too far away to walk?"

"A bit of a hike. Nothing I don't do often."

"Then let's walk. Are there places you need to stop along the way?"

"A number of them. I'm glad you asked, since I could use your advice. If you had come just a week later, you would not have seen the house as it was when Gance was alive."

"You're changing it?" he asked, his shock half serious, as if the museum to licentiousness must remain completely intact.

"Expanding it is a better term. It's more of a cottage than a house. And scarcely big enough for one, let alone my servant and occasional guests."

"If space is a problem, I could stay with the Westernas."

"There's absolutely no need. Essie and I have been making do. I've given her a couple of days off so we can catch up on things."

She took him to the job site of a carpenter she was thinking of hiring, to a woodworker's shop, a seamstress to get fabric swatches for draperies for the new rooms. He offered advice when asked, seeming just as content to watch her excitement as she planned her addition.

When they were close to her home, he suggested that they stop for an early dinner.

They chose a place he knew well, one that served excellent Cornish hens and brewed its own ale. They were midway through dinner before she realized that his gaity was strained, and probably had been since his arrival.

She reached across the table and rested her hand on his, a gesture that she hoped would reveal what she felt in her heart but did not have the words to say.

"There's not an hour that passes . . ." he said and looked away. When he turned back to her, his expression seemed almost merry again, as if he had shrugged off Lucy's memory one more time. He ordered them each a snifter of brandy, drank his fast and ordered another.

It was early evening when they reached the cottage, all the magnificent shades of the late summer walkway muted by the dusk. She led him up the walk and inside without speaking, as if it were a museum, then took him through the back doors and into the garden.

"Gance said this was his favorite place," Mina told him after he'd taken it all in.

"No wonder. All the flowers, and the huge bare windows that expose your life to the world, even if the world is filled only with roses and delphiniums. Not at all like the shutters and draperies of polite society. I've grown to hate those velvet cages."

"So have I," she said. Then added, "Damn them all."

She poured them both a drink—sherry for her, scotch and water for him—and they settled into the slatted wooden chairs in the garden. "How is your friend Rose Lewis?" Mina asked, recalling the showgirl Arthur had been seeing.

"Off touring the Continent, this time with the London Opera. The last note I received from her was condolences when she heard of Gance's death. She asked me to come to see her perform in Berlin, but I have no interest. I'm afraid I've become a bit of a recluse as of late."

"I'm sorry to hear it. Are you still in mourning?"

"If you mean are my doors draped in black, not anymore. Now I merely want to tell everyone I care about exactly what happened to all of us. I suppose it's no secret anymore, but I doubt anyone would believe it. Most would think me mad. So it's better to avoid polite company altogether."

"I've told some people. They believed me."

"But you're so sensible, how could they not?" He smiled as he said the last, sheepishly, as if realizing that some women might take his words as an insult. "I did take your advice, though, and finally read the journal." He paused for another large gulp of his drink before going on. "Then I read it all twice, then some sections again. I admit that I did not like it at all.

"I can see no point in asking Van Helsing his opinion on the story since he's convinced of the justice of what we have done. As for Seward, he's far too rigid to think beyond black and white. And Jonathan's response would be colored by what happened to you.

"That leaves only you, and your opinion is the one I value above all others. Tell me, did we do the right thing in killing Lucy?"

She had to force herself to look at him while she considered how to say the truth as gently as possible. "I can only say what I believe, and that is that given everything we knew and everything that happened, we did what we thought best."

He stood and came to her, towering over her. "You didn't answer me," he said.

"It was all we could do," she went on.

"I could have followed my instincts. I could have loved her, as she asked. Then she would have come to me—"

"And killed you in the end, or changed you into what she had become. Could you have resisted that constant desire to do the same to strangers, especially if you hunted with the one you loved beside you?"

She diffused his anger with that, but with it gone, there was little else. He sat beside her and, as he had at the reading of Gance's will, took her hand. "I know it's insane, but I would give my fortune to spend an hour or two with one of those creatures and see for myself what they are like."

Evil, she thought, but knew it wasn't true—not of Karina, probably not Joanna, either, though from everything she knew about that one no one could be sure.

He looked down the hill at the river, now a dark ribbon in the dim light of the stars. "My friend Beardsley says that Death is an entity, hovering close and watching us all. That's how I feel about Lucy sometimes, like she is on the edge of sight, watching and reproaching me for what I thought I must do."

Dracula had been an entity at the end, Mina thought. Incorporeal. Waiting. And Lucy? No, she decided, Lucy could never have done the same. She never had the power. And Gance?

The shadows suddenly seemed too close, too alive. "It's getting chilly out here. We should go inside," she suggested.

He sat in one of the wicker chairs in the solarium, watching her intently as she moved through the room, lighting lamps and candles, filling the space with soft, dancing light. She was a beautiful woman, with that mane of bright chestnut hair and those arresting dark eyes. Was she the real reason he came here?

"I don't want to pry, but I am curious. What's happened with you and Jonathan?" he asked.

The candle she was holding to light another lamp flickered for a moment as her hand trembled. "He won't find the time to discuss anything. I think that even the thought that there might be a scandal unnerves him."

"Brave women invite scandal."

Mina turned to look at him, a smile dancing on the edge of her lips. "Did Rose tell you that?"

"Actually, my mother. She was giving advice on the sort of woman I should not marry. I've always found the other sort boring, though." He hesitated, then made a quick decision and blurted, "Jonathan's a fool."

"Arthur!"

"Don't pretend to be shocked. He is. And I feel . . . I feel as if we are all related now through what we have been through. And if Jonathan wishes a separation or divorce, then may I be considered as an alternate?"

"We scarcely knew each other before this all began."

"And no one else will ever know us as well as we know each other because they can never understand what we have been through."

"That bond won't be enough."

"Won't it?" He pushed himself and took an unsteady step toward her. She would know he had far too much to drink, so he did his best to keep his speech clear as he added, "When you were Jonathan's wife, how could I have ever looked at you with anything more than affection?

"I'm still Jonathan's wife," she reminded him.

And even drunk, he was too much of a gentleman to disagree. "It's gotten late," he said, turning toward the open doorway, wondering if he had the ability to leave. It would be a long hike to the cab on the main road, but it would sober him up, at least.

"So it has." She looked at him, undoubtedly realizing that he was somewhat unsteady on his feet. "I think you'd best leave in the morning. The sink and closet are at the top of the stairs if you want to get ready for bed. While you're up there, I'll fix us both some chamomile tea."

She turned toward the kitchen while he pushed himself to his feet, uncertain whether to follow her suggestion or slump back in his chair. He did neither. Instead, he looked at the room around him. "Do you think his ghost is here?"

She looked back at him, frowning. "Gance's? I haven't felt it."

"I hope it is. I hope he possesses me and shows me what he did to possess you."

"He convinced me that the act would be inconsequential. It was a lie I chose to believe."

"Mina!"

Later he was convinced that it was the anguish in his tone that made her stand where she was as he went to her, wrapped his arms around her and kissed her. But though his passion was genuine, she did not respond.

Instead, she stood passive in his arms, whispering gently, "And it *was* inconsequential in one respect. In the beginning, I didn't care a thing about what happened to either of us. I care far more about you, Arthur. And Jonathan."

He backed away, certain the flush on his cheeks would be noticeable even in the dim light. "I've made a fool of myself. I'm sorry."

"It's not foolish to say what you feel," she responded and went into the kitchen.

He stayed where he was for a time, then joined her just as she was putting the kettle on the stove. "Is there any reason to hope?" he asked.

"If Jonathan and I cannot come to an agreement, there would be reason enough," she said without a trace of the coy tone Lucy might have used.

Would he be condemned to think of Lucy at the most inopportune moments? Perhaps he deserved it.

He pushed aside the memory and grinned at his hostess. "Then something came out of my declaration. I can wait." He grabbed his bag from beside the rear door and started for the stairs.

"You'd best take a light," she called after him.

Gripping the banister, he carried a candle in front of him up the narrow flight of stairs to the second floor. Its dark woodwork seemed to absorb the rays as the thick carpet absorbed his footsteps. Even his breath seemed muted. The scent of the space was familiar, as if the smoke from Gance's pipe had merged so completely with the plaster that they could never be parted. Had he seen his friend standing in front of him, he would have been only mildly surprised.

Mina had not invited him to explore the second floor, but once he was there, curiosity got the better of him. He lit the lamp in the hallway, a second beside the bathroom sink. Together the lamps threw enough light into the bedroom that he could see an oversized and exquisitely carved canopy bed cloaked in blood-red lace and strewn with wine-colored cushions so dark they seemed almost black against the white crocheted duvet.

The lace, he decided, had come from Mina. The rest was clearly Gance.

He sat on the edge of the bed, noticing his reflection in the mirror beside it. He looked gaunt and pale in the dim light, more like Gance than himself. He lay back and thought of how many women Gance had brought to this bed to use as he wished. Women often told Arthur that he had wit and looks to turn their heads, but he never possessed his friend's predatory nature. Gance could have whomever he wished, while Arthur had to be content with harmless flirting or a night with women purchased for pleasure.

The well-respected Victorian to his friend's classic libertine.

He shut his eyes and prayed to whatever power might watch over a house like this. He asked for a greater Gance inheritance than mere wine—some small piece of Gance's soul.

With that thought fixed in his mind, he drifted off to the soothing scents of lavender and musk.

Mina waited in the solarium until the tea grew cold, then climbed the stairs to the second floor. As she'd expected, Arthur had fallen asleep on the bed. She looked down at him for a time, at the boyish peacefulness of his face as he slept. Would Gance have called her a fool for refusing him? She would never know, but it made no difference. She found her nightclothes and changed quickly in the bathroom. Returning to the bed, she slipped a pillow from beneath the coverlet, blew out the lamp and left him.

She'd slept on the seetee before and, like Arthur, her thoughts were of Gance as she drifted off.

Later, she woke suddenly, straining to hear what had roused her. But there was only the rustling of breeze through the bushes beyond the open door, the faint sigh of the house as the current of air shifted. A distant strobe of lightning gave her a logical reason for the sounds. A storm was coming. A large one, judging by the tingling of her skin.

She'd left their glasses and the decanters on a small table in the garden. A good gust would send them crashing on the cobblestones. As she went out to retrieve them, she paused and relished the wind in her hair, the kiss of the satin nightdress against her bare skin, even the cool, tumbled stones beneath her feet.

Without thinking, she untied the ribbon holding her gown shut and let the rising wind blow against her skin. The pleasure it gave seemed perverse yet harmless, the sort of thing no good woman would ever confess to doing.

She fell into one of the chairs and pulled her gown completely open, spread her legs wide apart, feet flat against the ground.

She had never felt the wind brush against her there, never knew this pleasure. Barely thinking about what she was doing, she slid her hands up her thighs, pressed her thumbs against the folds of her sex, as he had done. She threw back her head, inhaling the damp night air as her fingers began to move.

Gance, she thought, as she felt the first waves of pleasure roll through her.

In answer, she felt a drop of rain on her face, as if he were here with her, mourning the body he had lost.

She glanced up at the bedroom windows, and in a stroke of lightning noticed the curtain move. Was there someone standing at the window, or just an illusion caused by the sudden burst of light? She clutched her gown around her and rushed inside.

With the raindrops cool on her face, she held her breath and listened. No boards creaked on the floor above her. No sound at all except for her heartbeat and the rain beating on the stones outside.

What a strange, mad creature I've become, she thought and

let out her breath with a soft ripple of anxious laughter. It's the house, she thought. That and the constant reminder of what she had done here that made her so reckless.

On the long trip back to London, Arthur sat in his private compartment, drinking Yankee bourbon from a jacket flask, mind rolling like the wheels against the track.

She had refused him. Not Gance, but him!

Not unthinkable. She'd even done it with a certain flair, managed to give him some hope, but not much. It was clear as well that nothing he had told her would be repeated. She had always been one to keep a confidence, especially when she privately agreed with it.

And that was good. So good. He'd gotten a bit too drunk and hinted at a marvelous fantasy. At least he thought he'd hinted. Perhaps later he'd revealed too much. But if he had, she gave no indication that she was at all horrified by it.

He opened a copy of the morning *Post* and began to read, looking for all the world like the proper British gentleman that he usually was.

But that would change—his life, his fortune, all of it.

By the time he reached London, he had put away the flask and drunk enough tea to be waterlogged and sober. Nonetheless, he hailed a cab and called out a destination. Not the best part of town, even so early in the evening, but he had need for companionship. Besides, the hunt for it gave its own pleasure, as if he were already a predator and the girl he purchased to do with as he would no better than prey.

He decided on the Bostonian Gentlemen's Club because he had heard it was clean and none of his circle ever went there. Skipping the drinks, he chose a woman from the night's line whose chestnut hair and proud bearing reminded him of Mina.

The room she took him to was opulent, plush and dark—like the bedroom Mina had inherited from her lover.

Once the door was shut and locked and the red glass lamp turned down, she started to speak. He pressed his fingers against her lips, silencing her. "You do as I say, replying only to my questions. No false displays of passion, no coy, seductive maneuvers. Understand?"

"Yes, my lord."

That may have been a false display, he thought. She had no way of knowing his title. He let the answer pass. Tonight he was her lord. "Good. Take off your clothes," he ordered.

She did as he asked, exactly as he asked, then stood in the center of the room, hands at her side, waiting for his next order.

"Now, what may I do with you?"

"Whatever you wish, my lord. You have me for the night."

"I understand. Now, if I were to hurt you just a little . . ." He deliberately left the sentence unfinished, watching a quick shudder pass through her. The moment of pleasure he felt at this was beneath him, but he accepted it. If he were going to have a vampire's mind-set, he should expect such disquieting feelings.

"A little only, please," she whispered.

"I was only asking. Now I would like to ask something more. Do women ever come here?"

"Two of us, you mean?"

"No, no. As customers."

"Not here, my lord. But there are other places."

"Name them."

She listed three. Of them, only Impostors—such a marvelous name!—was known to him. He recalled it as being particularly discreet, so much so that he had no inkling that women were ever admitted. Ladies, duchesses, contessas. He wondered which of his friends' wives frequented such a place. "Do they offer men or women?" he asked.

"Both, my lord."

"Or both at once?"

"Yes. I have been told that women who come alone are not welcome, unless they are already known to the staff."

Intriguing, even more than the girl before him. But she was his for the night, and it had been a long time.

"Come here," he said and placed her hands on the buttons of his coat.

Later, in a moment of supreme passion, he asked her to hurt him just a little. Anxious to please, she bit harder than he expected, but he only learned that later when, just before leaving, he examined the marks she'd left.

He turned back to her, still lying on the bed, still naked as if he might change his mind and return to it. "Do men often request you to do that?" he asked as he brushed his finger over the wound she'd left.

"Sometimes. Not often in so public a place."

"Well, it will be ascots for a while," he replied mostly to himself, and handed her half a crown as a tip. He could afford it, and she had been more than generous with her favors.

As he left the establishment, he considered that London would be a perfect place for a vampire—but only if it were male and rich.

eight

As he had promised, Steranko handled every detail. Joanna and Colleen had an inside cabin with not even a porthole to let in the cursed light. And when they boarded the ship together, shaking hands with the captain, who greeted everyone as they stepped onto the deck, they were wearing Western clothing. These things seemed finer to Colleen than anything she had worn in her life, and she tried not to think where Steranko had found them so quickly.

And because he had explained to the captain that the noblewoman who had booked passage suffered from extreme seasicknesses and fear of water, the captain made a point of whispering reassurances to her, then commented that she could get below because she seemed so terribly cold. Joanna understood enough of what he said to take a breath and laugh. The sound, so close to hysteric, had an unexpected effect. Throughout the voyage, the crew never questioned Joanna's being constantly in her room. Everyone was certain they understood.

As for Colleen, she dined with the servants of some of the other passengers, but said as little as possible about her mistress. They would all be lies, of course, and the less told, the less likely she was to be caught in one. But they were curious.

"I hear that you travel with a princess," a woman commented one morning over breakfast.

Colleen swallowed down a mouthful of dry biscuit with a

bit of warm tea. "And a poor traveler," she said, hoping to change the subject.

"Russian?" a man asked. "It seems that every one of them has some title."

"Turkish," Colleen answered.

"And she's going west, alone?" The woman's voice was incredulous. "I've never heard of such a thing."

"Turkish women are no more than slaves to their husbands," one of the men said. "Perhaps she's run away."

Someone from the end of the table called out, "What does she keep in that trunk the porters carried on board? It looks big enough for the body of her husband."

More laughter. They must have thought it a joke, but the curiosity behind it alarmed her. "Her clothes and some books and keepsakes."

"Well, they must mean plenty to her, considering the lock on the thing. And why is she going west?"

"I don't know very much about her reasons," Colleen replied, then lied as instructed, "but I've been in her service a few months and she's always treated me well."

That had the desired effect. Someone asked what she'd been doing in that part of the world. Now she could answer honestly, as she had when Joanna had questioned her. Indeed, after the experience, she had promised herself that she would explain it to everyone and perhaps help some poor, unfortunate girl from making the same naive mistake. "I'd been living in London for three years working as a cook's helper. The family I served was transferred to India. I didn't want to go, so they made arrangements for me to be employed by a cousin of theirs. After they left, the position fell through. Months passed. My savings ran out.

"I was trying to get some job in a textile mill when I met a woman who told me that there were good jobs for ladies' maids in France."

"There was a job, but it was hardly what I'd expected. As soon as I realized what my intended duties would be, I ran."

"One heck of a distance," one of the cooks said. The girl beside her began to giggle, reminding Colleen of Joanna.

The woman beside her pulled her gray shawl higher on her shoulders, patted Colleen's hand and said with sympathy,

"You were taken in, dearie. It happens, especially when you're hungry."

"Someone told me the ship leaving Calais that night was bound for Ireland. Since I had enough of France, and nothing for passage, I stowed away. Only it sailed to Varna instead. Then I met my mistress."

"She could well be an impostor, dearie," the woman continued.

"I could hardly know one way or the other, but she's been good to me," Colleen answered. "Does anyone know what I might do to make her more comfortable? She hasn't a hint of sea legs."

"Peppermint and chamomile tea and honey," the woman said. "No spicy foods or things with too much fat. Which, of course, means she'll be eating biscuits and tea all the way to London."

"When she's up to it, add soup with plenty of salt and crackers," the man across from her suggested.

"Brandy . . . lots of it. Put it in the tea," the ship's cook called from the stove.

"It works for him, dearie," the woman beside her whispered. "But look at the slop we eat because of it."

Colleen finished her meager meal, then claimed a plate for her mistress from the cook. While the servants were given biscuits and tea and a bit of cheese for lunch, the better passengers got pieces of orange or apricots in syrup, and often boiled eggs.

Once in the room she shared with Joanna, Colleen would sit on the floor with her back pressed against the door and eat the best of the small fare. Of the rest, some of the meat and cheese were used as bait to lure rats into the room for Joanna's meals. The remainder was returned to the kitchen or tossed overboard under cover of night.

And the rats did come sometimes, stealing softly into the room. Joannan would wait until they took the bait before pouncing quick as a cat, then turning her back so Colleen would not have to watch what she did with them.

But the rats did not come enough. And on those nights when her hunger grew too strong, Joanna would open her arms, and Colleen would move into them and shut her eyes.

Were the lips of these creatures always so soft, so pleasant against the skin? Were their teeth so sharp that the piercing seemed almost pleasant, and the slow drawing out of life so pleasurable that her body would shake with delight?

And did their hair always smell of the sun they had lost, of wildflowers blooming in summer meadows? Colleen would lay in those arms, her eyes shut, dreaming of her youth, her first carefree lover, those days under the Irish sun.

And when Joanna had taken her fill, she would lift the girl gently in her arms and carry her to the bed they were expected to share during this journey. She would lie beside her, feeding her wine and bits of food, and sometimes, when she thought her servant had grown too weak, a bit of her own blood.

Her brother would have said you must take care of the servants who earn your trust. Joanna understood that, but this was more, far more.

Affection had been there even before the blood had formed a bond between them. With it came deeper understanding of the girl's feelings, her culture, even the ability to speak her language. It was as if in taking life from her, she stole knowledge too.

As she kissed the girl's lips and stroked the side of her face, she understood that without this brave creature to face the world with her she would be utterly lost.

So they traveled south through the Black Sea then west across the Mediterranean. On some days Colleen felt as healthy as ever; on others, overcome with fatigue. But she tried to go about her business as always, certain that any marked change in her schedule would cause ill luck for the pair of them.

Late one stormy afternoon, as she sat with others in the kitchen, she heard Joanna calling her name, the mental summons so unexpected and so sharp with fright that she winced from the pain.

"Something wrong, child?" the cook asked.

"A headache, that's all. I should go below."

"In that downpour? Come closer to the stove and dry off while I fix you some tea."

The ship lurched from a sudden gust of wind. Colleen

gripped the table for support, nearly upsetting it. No wonder Joanna, trapped and helpless, was alarmed.

She started for the stove when she felt the cry again, this time so piercing that she put her hand against her forehead, as if by placing her hand on her head she could muffle the thoughts thrust into her mind. Why hadn't Joanna warned her of this power? In the wrong moment, she might have given everything away.

"I'll come back for it soon," she said, and hurried below.

When she got there, she discovered that the box, which had taken up most of the center of the little room, was missing.

She rushed to the narrow hall, but there was no one in sight. The doors on either side of her were locked, but the second one she tried opened a moment later, and a man, clutching a towel and looking miserable and sick, peered out at her. "Someone knocked. Is the ship all right?" he asked.

Colleen looked past him but saw no sign of the box. "The ship is fine," she said. "But I seem to have lost my mistress, and it appears that our cabin has been robbed."

"A woman missing! Go into your cabin and lock the door. I'll go topside and find the captain." He grabbed a coat and rushed down the hallway, nearly falling when the ship took another unexpected lurch.

As she watched him go, Colleen heard her mistress call to her again, this time softer, as if she knew Colleen had already answered.

Colleen stared at the hallway floor, trying to devise some story to explain what Joanna was doing inside the box. An idea had just begun to form when the man returned, along with the captain and two of the crew.

"You say your mistress is missing?" he called from the end of the hall.

"And our large steamer trunk too."

"Not an easy piece to carry," the captain said. He turned up the flame on his lantern and crouched, studying the floor. "The thief came my way. I can see the marks from the trunk." He turned and followed the trail down the hall until it ended at the door to a storage compartment at the bow of the ship.

As expected, the door was bolted. While the captain

searched the ring he carried for the right key, Colleen heard a sound in the unused cabin to her right, the hissed intake of a breath of air, a grunt, a stifled cry—things that the others did not seem to notice.

They did hear the scream, though, and the struggle that followed. This time the captain didn't bother to look for the key but instead slammed his own shoulder against the door. His two crewman joined him on a second attempt and the door fell open, held upright but askew by just the lower hinge.

To the others the dark room must have seemed empty, though Colleen could see the deep red glow of Joanna's eyes before she turned away from the lamplight. It must have smelled of mildew rather than the overpowering scent of blood. I am becoming like her, Colleen thought.

Then her mistress, the one no one on the ship ever called by name because the name was too foreign to them, stepped into the light.

Her pale face was streaked with blood, her hair dripping with it. The bodice of her dress was ripped, one shoulder and most of a breast exposed. But it was her terrified expression, her trembling lips and the quick gulps of air she took in, that made the captain raise the lantern higher and move past her. He looked down into the open box, then at the papers and clothes that had been inside and were now scattered through the room, then to the place where the thief lay, his own knife buried in his neck.

Joanna whispered something in Turkish and fell against Colleen, shivering as Colleen patted her back, whispering sympathetic, soothing words.

The captain stepped forward. "Princess," he began. "Princess, can you tell us what happened here?"

"The box!" Joanna whispered. "He opened it and . . ."

She stopped before she said too much, and she buried her wet face against Colleen's neck. "It's clear that he was going to kill her and put her body in it. He had a knife," Colleen said, lying for her. "She got it away from him . . . and thankfully, or she would have suffocated long before we found her."

Joanna stopped trembling and lifted her head. Though Colleen could not see her face, she knew Joanna was looking at the captain, doing what she could to control his mind. After a moment of silence, he lowered his lantern and called out, "Will someone bring a blanket for the poor woman?"

Their neighbors rushed to help, and moments later Colleen was assisting her trembling mistress down the hall to their room, while the crewmen dragged her trunk behind them.

Not one of them, even the Romanians, ever whispered the dread words Colleen had first heard only weeks before. "*Strigoaica* . . . vampire."

But they were much on Colleen's mind as she sat with Joanna in the cabin. The cook had sent them a bucket of cold, soapy water. As Joanna stripped off her clothing, she paused to suck the still-wet sections of blood from the cloth before handing it over to Colleen for cleaning. The vigor with which she did this convinced Colleen that she had not taken much from her attacker before being discovered and that she would need more soon.

Strigoaica mort.

And herself? She ran a finger over a still-bloody section of cloth and held it close to her lips. The smell tantalized, but the thought of tasting it sickened her.

That would change, and soon, she thought, and looked at Joanna with something akin to love.

nine

Mina had left him without so much as a note of explanation—as if one were needed after the shoddy way he'd behaved, Jonathan admitted to himself. In the week since then, Jonathan had gone about his daily routine with wooden precision. He thought that work could keep his mind off her, and how she had looked at him over their glasses of brandy.

I should have had more. Maybe then . . . ?

Now his work held no joy for him because it had no purpose. Instead he looked forward to the smaller pleasures. The walk to and from the office seemed to energize him—the stop at the bakery in the morning, the stop at the pub on the way home, often late at night.

His aunt had written from Reading, asking if Mina had come home. He understood what she really wanted, but he couldn't face her and tell her that they had reached no decision about their future; worse, had barely even talked. He sent a vague reply that he hoped would keep her away longer.

A week of emptiness passed. Another. Then something happened, something terrifying and strangely exhilarating: He began to dream again.

It wasn't of Mina or of the dark vampire bride who had seduced him so easily in those cold and empty halls. Instead he dreamed of the strange vampire woman, the shy one who had always stood close to the door, as if ready to flee if he took a step toward her. She had always waited while the dark one had stolen his will to fight with her strange hypnotic stare, the licentiousness of her body and her cold and hungry lips. Then the shy one had come forward to join the other two. She had always seemed the plainest of the three, except for those eyes, cat's green with fire in their depths.

In these dreams, she wasn't shy any longer. Instead, like a wolf, she attacked, ripping at his clothes, his skin, the flesh beneath. Nothing pleasureable in this touch; only pain, searing and horrible, until her lips pressed against the wounds, drawing away his blood, his life, his—

He would wake with a start, heart pounding, bathed in sweat with the sheets tangled around him.

He began using brandy to help him sleep. From the state of his bed in the morning, it seemed to make the dreams no less vivid, but at least he could not recall them when he woke.

But as the dreams grew stronger, the remedy lost its effectiveness. He thought of consulting Jack Seward, asking for some drug to help him rest, but wisely knew where that could lead. Instead, he began working longer hours, though lack of sleep made concentration difficult. One afternoon, when one of his employees reluctantly suggested that he take some time off and get some rest, he admitted defeat and left.

He walked through the streets of Exeter, aimlessly it seemed until, well after dark, he found himself on the river road and guessed his destination.

He had not visited Mina's house before, though the infamous address was already fixed in his memory. Fortunately, the sky was clear, the half moon bright, and the polished brass numbers on the gate stood out like a beacon, calling him home.

The gate was half open, and he slipped through it. From the outside, the house seemed less the den of sin it had been rumored to be when Gance owned it than a charming cottage. He walked to the door but decided not to knock, not yet. Trying not to tread on the violets and lupine that marked the narrow path, he went around the house to the back and into a rose garden.

Moonlight glittered off the water in the fountain and the little white stones that marked the path to the water's edge. The space smelled lovely in the still damp of this warm summer night—of wild roses and wysteria and other, less familiar blooms. In a place like this, he half expected to see the woman in his dreams, waiting with pale arms outstretched.

Shaking off the thought, he approached the little house. Work was under way on one side, the wooden shell of an addition already in place. He avoided it and moved toward the vast expanse of glass that made up almost all of one corner, where he tried to peer inside.

Until an hour before Jonathan's stealthy arrival, Mina had been lying awake in bed, reading the morning paper she had not had a chance to look at earlier. It had been a hectic day, one of many in the past week.

Two days after Arthur's visit, carpenters had come and begun the addition, a larger one than she'd planned on, since she realized that she might want an occasional guest to stay over and would need at least one extra room besides Essie's. She and Essie had been trying to keep the dust at an acceptable level and the knicknacks from being destroyed by the pounding. At the same time, they were attempting to set up the house for full-time use rather than an occasional quick visit. Mina sent Essie shopping for pots and pans while she handled the more delicate task of picking out china and silver, and a dining table and chairs small enough to use in the solarium.

Like Jonathan, she was trying to find consolation in her work, and at last she was succeeding.

She had just drifted off when she heard Essie's frantic whisper coming from the hall outside her door. "Wake up, mum—Mina! There's someone prowling outside!" By the time Mina opened her eyes, Essie was already in the room, shaking her.

Mina put on a robe, handing a second to Essie, who came upstairs wearing only a thin slip. Mina felt oddly calm as she pulled the revolver from the bed-table drawer. With Essie close behind her—"I couldn't bear to be left alone now, mum!"—they went downstairs.

There was a man standing outside the doors, his face hidden by the dark, his form outlined by the moonlit landscape behind him. As Mina walked through the dark room, with the gun aimed at his chest, she recognized the form. Confident that she was right, she lit a candle and threw open the doors.

"Please, mum!" Essie begged.

"It's all right, Essie," Mina said as she lowered the weapon. "It's just my husband." She pulled open the door and drew him inside.

"Go sleep in my bed, Essie," she added. "I think I should talk to him here."

Essie looked at her a moment, frowning, then obeyed.

Once they were alone, Mina lit a lamp, then studied her husband more carefully. He was blushing, justifiably so, and looked ready to bolt from the room if she said a word of reproach. She noticed that his hair looked uncombed, his suit a bit rumpled, and his face lined from care or exhaustion. It was so unlike meticulous Jonathan that she wanted to laugh, but she knew it would be cruel to do so when he seemed so obviously miserable.

She went to the settee where Essie had been sleeping, folded the girl's blanket and sheet and laid them on top of her pillow. She sat on the edge of the settee and motioned Jonathan into one of the wicker chairs.

"If you're going to pay a surprise visit so late, don't you think you ought to use the door?" she asked.

"I didn't intend. It just . . . happened."

"Happened? You mean you were sleepwalking?" she asked, more concerned now.

"I was afraid to sleep. I have dreams again, and these are more vivid than anything before."

She moved to his side, took his hands. "Jonathan, are you certain that when you were their prisoner you never drank a drop of their blood?"

"Never that I can remember, but there were many nights there that I can't remember at all. Perhaps I was wrong about that. Perhaps I am—"

She cut him off. "Which of them do you dream about?"

"The green-eyed one, who always seemed a bit mad."

"She was mad, and she's the one still alive, if you can call that sort of existence living." For a long time they didn't speak; then Mina offered an opinion. "I believe the dreams mean that she's coming, Jonathan. It may take her months or even years to get here, but she'll come. You have to be ready when she does."

"Not 'we'?" he asked.

"I'm hardly certain of our future yet and neither are you," she replied.

She hadn't intended her voice to sound sharp, but perhaps he caught some of her anger through her tone. He moved closer to her and kissed her cheek. "I do love you," he said.

His touch brought back so many memories. She wanted to kiss him, to love him. But Essie was sleeping in her bed, and she doubted that Jonathan would ever consent to any intimacy here, when Essie might walk in at any moment.

Hardly a night for romance, so she suggested instead, "Sleep here tonight. In the morning, we should wire Arthur to see if Van Helsing is still staying with him. I think you need to ask his advice about this."

"He hardly helped you before," Jonathan reminded her.

"But he may know something of her history. It may tell us what sort of a threat she'll be."

"I'll have to leave here early tomorrow . . . work, and all that. I could wire him from town."

"I'll do it. I was intending to write Arthur anyway. He came and saw the house a week ago, and soon after he left, he wrote me and said that he'd read Karina's journal. It was not a pleasant note, and I need to keep in touch. Perhaps he and Van Helsing would like to come here. The two of them can stay with the Westenras. There's scarcely room for me and Essie here, especially with the carpentry work going on."

"And I'm imposing. I should go home."

"You'll do nothing of the sort." She pointed to the dark windows. "It's misted over. You'll have no moon to light the way to the main road. Now lay down here and I'll sleep with Essie upstairs. We'll have plenty of room." She handed him the blanket and sheet. "Perhaps I'll see you in the morning."

She climbed the stairs slowly, half expecting him to call her back. Or follow. Or say good-bye and leave. He did none of that. She heard him moving in the solarium, the swish of the sheet on the damask upholstery.

She found Essie stretched out on the carpet beside her bed, wrapped in a spare blanket. Given how difficult it had been to convince the girl to sleep on the settee, she should have expected this. She decided not to wake her. Instead, she slipped off her shoes, stepped over Essie, and lay down.

Downstairs, Jonathan lay awake in the darkness. He felt foolish for startling that poor servant and for disturbing Mina at such a late hour. Worse, he was afraid to sleep. He'd been alone in his house for weeks, and if his dreams made him cry out, there was no one to hear him. But here . . .

Mina had dreamed like that once, and he had not been nearly as understanding as she was now. If he had the means to make amends, he would. Now that they were allies again, perhaps she would repeat the offer she'd made that night in their home.

He vowed that next time he would not refuse her.

He thought of this as he stared out at the lawn, struggling to stay awake for just a few moments longer, until he was certain the rest of the house was deep in sleep.

And then, just as he was about to give way to his exhaustion, the moon broke through the fog, painting the garden in silver and gray. He stood and walked toward the windows. As he did, he saw something move near the edge of the lawn. Some animal perhaps, or another intruder with less benign intent than his.

He pulled the doors open, stepped into the yard and started down the path.

The earth was soft beneath his feet, the night air chilly against the bare skin on his exposed arms and chest. He was close to the river when he saw the figure move again, this time downstream, near the thick hedge fence of a neighbor's property. He followed, wondering if he should call out or if he might only startle someone else with his foolishness.

As he watched the distant indistinct form, it seemed to wink out like a snuffled candle. Frightened now, he turned to rush back to the house and found himself face to face with his nightmare.

But she did not look so terrible now with those red lips and eyes so green that even the moonlight could not steal their color.

"Come," she whispered, and he followed her back to the

water. They stopped on the edge, and she faced him and reached out her hand.

He did not know how it happened, but a touch of her hand removed the last pieces of clothing he wore. A quick, disdainful toss sent them into the river, where they floated into the current at its heart and flowed slowly downstream.

He paid them no mind. His eyes were trapped on hers, his body on the feather touch of hands—enticing, almost real.

Was this a dream?

These creatures were from the realm of dreams. How was he to know?

Then she kissed him, her lips soft but cold. Her body pressed against his, colder still, so cold it made him ache at his core. He felt no fear, only pity for this creature, and he would give whatever he could to help her.

Her hands continued the soft brushes against his skin. Each touch made him shiver, stole a bit more of his will. When they finally reached his crotch, it only took a quick brush against the tip of his penis to make him hard and ready.

She stepped back to undo the laces on the bodice of her gown, leaving him with a sense of loss that he was out of her arms.

Was this how Mina had felt when the other . . . ?

He looked past the vampire woman toward the house, and saw the huge black form of a wolf slink through the doors he had left open.

"Mina!" he screamed and tried to run past the woman.

She grabbed his arm but he continued an ineffective struggle, crying out her name again and again, "Mina! Mina!"

"Shhh, Jonathan. Hush. It's all right. I'm here."

The vampire woman released her hold as Mina tightened hers. He felt his wife's hair, soft against his face, scented with lavender water. "I'm such a bother," he whispered.

"I'm glad you were here so that I could help you," she whispered, her breath warm against his icy skin.

He expected her to push away from him, but she seemed as reluctant to leave as he was to let her go. Instead, she stretched out beside him, pulling a quilt around both of them and pressing close. "You're so cold," she said.

"It was the woman. That creature." He felt her shiver and

tried to reassure her. "It was only a dream, but so vivid. When she touched me, she seemed to steal all the warmth from me. She was—"

Mina touched her finger to his lips, silencing him. "It's all right," she said.

Caught up in the dream and the passion it had aroused, he kissed her once, then again. She responded with a fervor he had rarely felt in her before, one she had probably learned from the master of this house. Did he care? Should he? She was here because he had been dreaming of another—fantastic, yes, but the creature's effect was no less real.

He moved back to give Mina room. As he did, he saw a flicker of light from the front hallway, the serving woman's white face. She retreated without a word.

She reminded him of where he was, and the uncertain future he and his wife faced. Passion somewhat quelled, he nonetheless held Mina close, relishing the lavender scent and the familiar shape of her against him.

Mina seemed content to lie beside him, silent but close as he drifted off to sleep.

When he woke in the morning, she was gone. He could hear her and her servant—Essie, was it?—talking softly in the kitchen, trying not to wake him.

Now that it was daylight and he was alone, he studied the opulence of his surroundings—the thick, crimson oriental rugs that softened the slate floor. The glass and iron table perfectly sized for an intimate meal. The tapestry-covered divan on which he'd spent the night was wide enough to sleep two. The—

"Stop it!" he whispered and moved to the doorway.

It would be polite to greet his wife, to say hello to her servant. But he was not thinking of politeness anymore. Rather, he wanted to find a bathroom and do what needed to be done to get him out of this place before he saw anything more. With that in mind, he started up the stairs.

It was the scent that made his mind return to thoughts best ignored—the mélange of old tobacco and ladies' perfume. Scents of ballrooms and the hotel restaurants where his mother would take him for a plate lunch when she "felt flush" and wanted to "explore how the better class dines."

Aunt Millicent had called their lunches a foolish waste of time and money, but Mother had been the one to teach him how to sit properly at a table, how to use a fork and knife and napkin like a gentleman. He suspected that the training had impressed Mr. Hawkins as much as his conscientiousness, and both had led to his good fortune.

Mina had found a swifter way to an even richer end.

Not that she had intended it, of course. He had to remember to tell her this as soon as he could. Perhaps he could get her to give up the house, rent it out or better yet sell it and transfer the money to Winnie's charity or some other good cause. He'd have to suggest this gently, move slowly. But if she would agree to the sale, then they could be recon——

The happy idea fled when he reached the top of the stairs and saw the bedroom—its excesses in color and decadence the antithesis of everything a proper gentleman would provide for his wife.

He walked through it, touching the wine-red curtains, feeling the carpet soft and thick even through the hard soles of his shoes. He noted the rich wood of the fireplace, the carvings on the mantel, the red flocked paper on the walls, the tall mahogany posts of the huge bed, the brocade quilt beneath the lace coverlet folded back to reveal its black satin lining.

He looked up at the bed's canopy, at the mirror beneath it, then at the cheval mirror near the far wall, angled to reflect the firelight on whomever slept in that bed.

He laughed without mirth. Sleeping was hardly the idea.

How could she have gone with such a man? He was outraged at the thought, wounded and yet—he could feel himself responding to a vision of her here. He felt a fluttering in his stomach, the sudden pressure against the seam of his pants.

A glance in the bathroom mirror was enough to make him realize that he needed to go home before he went to the office. His beard had smudged his face. His shirt was wrinkled, and he needed a bath. He turned on the faucet, splashed water on his face.

As he dried off he noticed the tub, big enough for two, the little table beside it filled with dainty soaps and bottles of oil.

Not Mina's, or if they were, he had never noticed them before.

"There's a razor in the cupboard," someone—Mina—said.

Startled, he jumped at the sound of her voice and turned to face his wife. He could feel the heat of his flushed face, as if he had been caught going through her things.

"I haven't gotten around to sorting through what was left here," she explained. "If you draw a bath, Essie can press the shirt for you, or I could find you a clean one."

He wanted to say that he would leave. It was the polite thing to do. But his office was a long walk from here, their home a far longer one. She was only being practical.

"See what you can do with this one." He took it off and handed it to her and began to run the water.

He was surprised to feel how warm it was—spring-fed, given the clarity and pressure. He undressed quickly. Once in the tub, he lay back and shut his eyes. Half dreaming, he seemed to look out the door at the dimly lit bedroom beyond it and thought he saw not Mina or Gance, but the vampire women from the castle. Seductive memories, made even more seductive by the horror of them and their sudden resurrection at the most inopportune times.

Today, at least, they kept their distance, and he drifted slowly into a deeper sleep until Mina's arrival jarred him awake.

She carried a tray of biscuits and jam, a pot of tea and a pair of cups. "I'd like to sit with you awhile if you don't mind," she said. "I thought that we could compose the telegram to Van Helsing together."

He wanted to tell her that her presence was unseemly, but of coursc it wasn't. She was his wife, he reminded himself, more his wife now than she had been in weeks. They were allies again, and it pleased him.

She brought her little writing box from the bedroom, pulled out pen and ink and was soon hard at work setting down Jonathan's jumbled thoughts.

ten

After Jonathan had gone, Mina sat for some time and considered how to deal with Essie. It seemed to her that she had acted rashly when she'd hired a servant. At the time she had been so pleased with her choice that it never occurred to her that she might be putting the girl into some danger. At the very least, she had to warn Essie about what she might face.

She tried to begin a few times that morning, but was always interrupted before she began—first by delivery of her china and linens, second by a cartload of supplies for the addition, then by the carpenters themselves. So she waited until late afternoon, when the workers had gone and they were alone, then asked Essie to join her for tea in the garden.

Essie put down the polishing cloth she'd been using on the new dinnerware and followed Mina outside. "Is something wrong?" she asked.

"Not exactly, but there are some things we need to discuss. It concerns my husband's visit last night."

Essie blushed. "It's hardly my place—" she began.

"In this case, it is." Mina motioned for her to sit down and poured them both a cup of tea. Essie's innate discretion made it difficult to begin the conversation, so Mina decided to simply tell it all.

"A little over year ago, Jonathan was sent to Romania on behalf of his employer," she began.

She continued, leaving out only the most lurid details. She didn't want to frighten her servant, though it had been her observation that servants often had far hardier spirits than those they served.

"What an adventure! Just like old Varney!" Essie exclaimed when she was done.

"You've read those stories?" Mina asked.

Essie frowned. "I *can* read," she said. "I wasn't always in London. My village had a school. I went six years before my family gave up the land and moved to Manchester."

"I didn't mean I was suprised at that . . . only that the story was published long before you were born."

"It was my grandfather who kept the old books. He taught himself to read using the penny weeklies. He said that was easier than the Bible because it was how people spoke. When I was younger, he would read the stories to me. I loved to hear him, all dramatic and frightening. So that's what the count was—a vampire?"

"Yes. Do you believe me?"

Essie hestitated, then answered diplomatically, "You don't seem like the sort to make things up."

"I'm not. And I wouldn't have ever told you any of this, but my husband is dreaming about the one creature who is still alive. I don't know if that means that she is coming here, but I need you alert and prepared. And I wouldn't be surprised if you wanted to leave my employ, given the circumstances. You've been a treasure to have with me, and I'll certainly help you get another position."

Essie frowned, considered, then shook her head. "I may someday think myself a fool for this, but I'll stay. Now what do I need to know?"

Mina described Joanna as best she could, then added, "Since she may have means of disguising herself, you should never give a strange woman permission to enter the house, especially after dark. Don't even open the door. If I am not here, be sure to tell anyone you don't know to wait outside for me or to return later."

"Can they wait in the garden?" Essie asked.

Mina smiled. "I think the garden would be fine."

They finished their tea in silence. Then Mina poured more and asked, "Your family farmed. Where?"

"In Surrey. They'd worked land there for as long as anyone could remember. I was small when the first drought hit. We had three more in five years. No one can survive that. We left there in '81 and moved to Manchester. A horrible place. When my father died, my mother thought we should try London."

"Did you find it better?"

"Even dirtier than Manchester. But my mother had steady work in a bakery, so we always ate. Not like some. We shared what we had, though. My mother said charity would bring us luck, if only in the hereafter. It did, at least for as long as she was alive."

"Are you also religious?" Mina asked.

"I am. But I haven't been able to go to church recently. After her last attack, I always had to stay with Mrs. Proctor."

"Well, you have Sundays to yourself to go or not as you please."

"Good. And I think a few prayers might be in order . . . and perhaps a bit of holy water?"

Mina nodded. A little extra protection might prove to be best. She watched thoughtfully as Essie gathered the glasses and went inside. When the woman returned some minutes later, a small metal cross dangled from a chain around her neck.

"Should I get back to the kitchen?" she asked.

"I'll come and help you. While we work, I want you to tell me everything you can about the poorer parts of Exeter."

By the time the kitchen had been set up for daily use, Mina had learned a great deal about sections of Exeter she'd rarely visited. There were at least a dozen women Essie knew who had fallen on bad times due to the deaths of their husbands, or being let go from some position. She learned that the Beasons were held up to near sainthood by the poor who sent their children to the charity hospital, and that Dr. Rhys was someone the older folks could rely on.

Essie explained about the charity clinic Dr. Rhys had opened a year earlier. Though he had a thriving practice among the gentry, he opened a free office two days a week to tend to the needs of adults and children alike, usually without cost. "I stored my things in his office. If I hadn't, I would have owned only the clothes on my back the first time I fell asleep."

"Terrible people."

"Not terrible, Madame Mina. Poor. The luckiest work. The rest beg, and when they can't, they do what they must. I don't judge them. I can't anymore."

"Are there many like you . . . that is, fallen from better circumstances."

"Too many. These are hard times. I'd always hoped for a husband and children someday. Now I am glad I never had that responsibility when I see how the poorest ones live."

Mina considered her words through the morning. Later she asked Essie to go into town with her the next time the clinic was open and introduce her to Dr. Rhys. She had no certain plan in mind, not yet, but she was beginning to see what she wanted to do with some part of her sudden and awkward fortune.

Dr. Rhys was just seeing the last of his morning patients when Essie arrived with her mistress. He noted that Essie seemed excited and her mistress quietly anxious. Though he was curious, he asked them to sit in the outer office while he gave some final advice to a patient.

As he turned his attention back to the young woman who had consulted him, he frowned. In truth, he had nothing he wished to tell her. She was in the final stages of syphilis. Had she showed some sign of honor, he might have given her some funds to keep her from plying the trade that had infected her in the first place. But he knew she would only spend the money on drink and be on the street the next night, willing to infect some other unsuspecting john.

Not unsuspecting now, he thought. The exact nature of her disease might not be clear to a casual observer, but the fact that she was ill certainly would be.

Let the bastards draw their own conclusions.

At times like this, it was best not to think of his mother, but he could not keep the thought at bay. When he told the woman she had at most a few weeks to live and all but ordered her out of his office, his voice had a hard edge—deserved, but not in keeping with the oath of his profession.

Better to save his judgment for the nights when he was not

Dr. Rhys, but just a man, and a good glass of rye or bourbon would make the anger dull.

As he went out to meet his guests, he recalled what little gossip he had heard about Mina Harker. Though he found it intriguing, he thought her actions less than honorable. He was even prepared to dislike her until he mentioned her name to Winnie Beason and learned that Mrs. Harker, though new to Exeter, had become one of the most reliable volunteers for the Children's Hospital. It had been his experience that libertines did not engage in direct charity work, but if she was a virtuous woman, why had she taken off to the Continent with the likes of Lord Gance?

A mystery he hoped would not intrigue him overly much. As always, he had more important things to think of.

Essie stayed only long enough to make an introduction, then declined the cup of tea he offered and went off to visit a friend in the neighborhood while the two talked. As he expected, Mina Harker asked about his work.

He explained that he had left London a year earlier following a lengthy illness brought on by his charity practice there. He had come to Exeter because in a city far smaller than London his charity work might make a difference and not prove too taxing to his health. He was a physician to the wealthy and poor alike, letting one set of fees cover the expenses for those he treated for nothing.

"I still go to London occasionally to consult with colleagues and see some of my patients. When I visit the worst of that town, I try not to look too closely at its misery or I would be drawn back into a battle for its innocents that I think not even an army of saints could win."

"Essie tells me that you have been a godsend to her. I wanted to thank you, and volunteer to provide some support for your work. However, I would like to ask a favor in exchange."

"A favor?" He looked at her with open curiosity as he added, "Ask, and I'll do my best to grant it."

"Essie said that there are many women like herself—good women who have fallen on hard times. I should like to help them if I can, the way you helped Essie."

"And why would you do this?"

"Why?" she looked at him, confused. "What an odd thing for you to say."

"Not so odd, to inquire about motive."

"I came into an inheritance, and I wish to share it."

She said this without the slightest trace of self-satisfaction. The tone convinced him that whatever gossip there might be about her, it could hardly be true. "All our lives are uncertain," he said. "We brush against one another's souls and alter both—in this life, in the past ones and in the ones to come."

"Reincarnation, you mean?"

"Exactly. I believe in it because there is a justice at the core of it that all other religions lack." He explained the philosophy, pleased to see that her interest in it had not the slightest hint of condescension. Yes, Essie was right about her. She had a remarkably open mind.

"Then if we are all to be reborn, why do anything for anyone that will extend a miserable life? Why this clinic and the work you do?" Mina asked when he'd finished.

"We do acts of charity because it makes us feel more human. And the gods do notice. They reward us for them in the next life."

"An odd way to put it," she said thoughtfully.

"Not so odd, especially since charity suits some of us so well."

She smiled then, beautifully. On impulse, he took her hand and impetuously raised the back of it to his lips, a courtly gesture.

"And your favor?" he asked.

"I am looking for assistance in finding a small building that could be converted into a home for widowed and abandoned women, one that will allow space for their children as well. Then, if I haven't taxed your patience too much, I would like referrals of women you think would benefit from such an arrangement."

He smiled. "You mean women who would not bring scandal on the house or the other tenants in it, don't you?"

As he expected, his directness caught her off guard. She hesitated, then answered, "I suppose that is what I mean. Though I care not a bit about scandal and am hardly prudish, I would not want those I mean to help subjected to abuse or drunkeness from others in the house—not the women, and especially not their children."

Her aims were higher than he'd expected, but hardly unreasonable. A practical woman, he decided. "I'd be pleased to help," he replied. "I have no patients to see tomorrow. Shall we start searching for your house then?"

"Please! The sooner we begin, the better." She glanced into the outer office and saw it was empty. "When Essie arrives, tell her I've gone over to the hospital to see Mrs. Beason. Tell her that I'll meet her there at three."

Mina had been gone nearly an hour when Essie returned. "Sarah's husband's had a bit of luck," she said happily. "Steady work on the docks, at least for the summer. The boys look better. She sends her thanks."

Rhys shrugged. "Mrs. Harker asks you to meet her at the children's hospital at three."

"Then I suppose I should be starting."

"Not just yet. Tell me about her. Are you as pleased now as when you began working for her?"

"I am. She's a marvel. Mrs. Proctor was a good mistress, bless the poor thing, but not like Mrs. Harker."

"Does she live alone?"

Essie looked at him, the hint of a smile on her lips as if she guessed why he asked. "She does, but she is married. I met her husband. Unexpectedly. He came by late one night." She described how she'd seen him in the garden and the scare he'd given her.

"You say he walked all that way? At that hour."

"He'd had a bad dream. And another later that night. Mrs. Harker is most concerned about them."

"Do you know what sort of nightmares they are?"

He'd asked too many questions, saw her retreat from the easy conversation into the natural discretion a servant should have for her mistress. "The reason's not important, really," she replied.

"It could be. I might be able to perhaps suggest something to help him sleep if I better understood the sort of nightmares he has."

That relaxed her, but only a bit. "She would be so thankful. Promise you won't tell her or anyone what I say?"

He nodded. "They'll be like patients to me."

"It's like old Varney."

"Varney?"

She explained, and as she did, he found himself remembering the tales he'd heard long ago of the rakshasas who stole the life from the living. "He dreamed of women like them," she concluded.

"Of demons? How strange."

She shook her head. "Not strange at all." He thought to question her further but decided against it. Besides, she'd told him more than enough already.

The woman was married but living apart from her husband, a man who just might be unbalanced.

Perhaps it was for the best. If he ever became involved with a woman, he would want one of his own race, someone who would understand him.

Reason wouldn't make the attraction for Mina Harker go away. But at the least he would never let on how he felt. And there was some logical rationale for courtly love. He might never declare himself, but being close would have its own pleasures.

When Mina took the doctor's hand and said good-bye, she'd felt a chill at her core. It wasn't really him who made her anxious, she decided after thinking it over. Rather, it was the magnitude of the task she was about to take on. That night she prayed that she would be capable of it.

Nonetheless, she could not help but feel wary of the doctor—his exotic looks, his long face and wide-set eyes more striking than handsome, smooth voice and the odd way he looked at her when she said she wanted to help.

It must be his race, she decided. There would be so many who would judge him inferior because of the color of his skin. Of course, that would make her offer of charity suspect.

A rational enough explanation, but the wariness stayed with her on her visit with Winnie, and bothered her through the night. It even extended into her meeting with him the following day.

She met him at his office. He had shed the white collarless shirt he'd been wearing in favor of a cream-colored coat and brown vest. The suit made his complexion look lighter, and he seemed more a businessman than the doctor of the day before.

And though she wondered at his intentions, he was every bit a gentleman as they took off in a cab. Yet she would sometimes glance in his direction and find him turning his head away too quickly. He was watching her and did not want her to know it.

Perhaps he wasn't so proper, or perhaps he'd heard rumors about her and Gance and wondered if they were true.

When they returned to his office, he asked her to wait a moment, then brought her a package wrapped in brown paper. "This is for you," he said, handing it over, then continuing to talk as she opened it, his voice gaining intensity with each unfolding of the wrapper. "It's something I found in a local bookstore I visited yesterday afternoon. As soon as I saw it, I immediately thought of you. Consider it a . . . my first assistance for your new endeavor."

Inside was a book covered in tooled leather. She opened it and saw that the pages were blank.

"It is to record your life, to try to find the balance in it, especially now, when your life has taken a new turn that will affect so many others."

That evening she sat in her garden and fingered the soft leather binding, the smooth vellum pages.

Such an appropriate gift, she wrote. *Had Winnie mentioned to Dr. Rhys that I kept journals? Or did I merely look like a woman who would scribble down the intimate details of her life, including the most fantastic adventure a woman—or a man—could ever have?*

There is even a balance scale tooled into the cover. I commented that it was the sign of Libra and most fitting, since I was born in September. Dr. Rhys said he hadn't thought of astrology at all. "One finds balance in the collection of thoughts, the sorting that comes before setting them down," he told me. "I kept a journal through my school years. I still consult it from time to time, to compare my ideas then with the ones I hold now. People's minds, like our species, evolve."

The doctor might say it was kismet that put this book in my hands at this time. I think it more his own inspiration. Now, as I sit with my pen and ink, I realize how much I've missed writing in my journals.

I think, too, on how helpful he was today and I believe I've misjudged him.

We visited with two local ministers, both of whom have a number of clients to refer to me. We spoke, too, with a pair of women Rhys knew. One was a native of Exeter who had lost her husband the year before and had a four-year-old boy. The second, in far more desperate straits, had recently arrived from London with two small children, fleeing an abusive husband who had sworn to lock her away as a lunatic if she tried to leave him.

She even confessed to me in a clandestine sort of whisper that she believed her daughter had stolen the money she'd used to ferret them out of London, since the story the child told about where it had come from was so implausible. I looked at her little girl, scarcely six and thin and ragged, and told the woman that no court that believed in justice would pass judgment on any of them.

Winnie would say we are no better than horses or land to some men, but it isn't true. Often we are less valued. I said as much to the woman, coaxing a quick, anxious smile.

This meeting reinforced something I have believed for some time. I am fortunate to have found a man like Jonathan to be my husband.

eleven

In the last days on their journey to England, Joanna began to dream of the past. It had been so long since she had recalled her youth. Perhaps it was the swaying of the boat in the choppy Mediterranean waters, the dry air blowing from the south, or the Arab passengers they took on during a stop in Tripoli and lodged in the cabin next to hers. In her long days half sleep and confinement, she would hear their whispers through the walls of her room and her box, soft syllables in a language similar to the one spoken in her grandfather's house. And so she dreamed.

Not unpleasantly. She cherished the memories, kept them with her during her waking hours. As they crossed into the Atlantic swells, she and Colleen often sat on the deck at night, and she would look up at the stars, remembering.

"What is it?" Colleen asked after she noticed a faraway look in Joanna's expression.

Joanna drew in a breath, and continued to stare out at the sea as she exhaled the words, "I was on a ship like this once before—a long time ago." She shut her eyes and fought down the urge to howl at the memory of all she had lost.

Colleen moved beside her and took her hand. The touch, willingly given, always excited Joanna. It had been centuries since any living person had ever known what she was and touched her without fear.

All the memories surfaced, glorious, bringing with them a bittersweet feeling akin to love. With Colleen's warm flesh pressed against hers, she fell into the happiest years of her past, relating part of the memories in quick, hushed breaths.

When Mezid-Bey received the news that his daughter had borne a child of his enemy then killed herself rather than face him, he guessed the truth. She had not been raped, or even seduced. She had loved the infidel and knew she could not keep this from him.

Her death had saved him the trouble of killing her himself.

He told that to Joanna years later, when she was old enough to understand. He said he might have killed her too, but when she was brought to him, he had looked past the tangled hair and ragged clothing and seen not his daughter but her mother—the wife Mezid-Bey had loved above all the others and who had died only months before Joanna had been brought to him.

"She would not have approved my killing a child as innocent as you were then," he explained to her.

So he had let her live with his own children in their private quarters in his home. There were no walls here; Mezid-Bey was no barbaric warlord in a dangerous country, nor did he have enemies among his own people. Instead there were gardens and fountains, tapestries lovingly created by his wives and favorite slaves.

They taught her deportment, how to act like a princess. Though she could never aspire to a noble marriage, her grandfather thought that perhaps he could find her a good match in spite of her tainted Western blood. "Perhaps it might even be an advantage," he told her one afternoon as they sat together.

"Advantage?" she asked, speaking with her eyelids half closed, looking at the flowers at her feet. The slaves had never taught her this, but she knew that the color of her eyes troubled him.

"The wars continue west of here. Some might think that a woman with the enemy's blood would perhaps have some insight into their thinking."

"Will the fighting come here?" she asked, glancing at him for some reassurance.

He pulled her close. She inhaled the scent of his perfume as he held her and whispered, "Of course not, child. We live far away from it all. But perhaps if you were to listen to the slaves from the West, you might learn something of value."

And with that briefest suggestion, she became a spy for her family. She was nine years old.

Slaves from the Western wars who proved to be trustworthy were allowed to tend their captors. Among them were a handful from her father's house. She could still recall the few words of the language she'd acquired. They taught her more, and through them she learned something of her father as well.

She feared him. To the child, it seemed that by sending her mother away, he had killed her as surely as if he had plunged a knife into her heart. Years later, when she thought of it, she realized that, in truth, he had.

But though her father frightened her, her brothers did not. Radu she despised, because everyone who knew him seemed to. He was overly fastidious, fawning over his captors and making it clear to anyone who would listen that had no desire to ever return to the barbarity of his father's house. In a land where blood ties were so important, his opinions were seen not as a triumph for his captors but as a flaw, strong enough that he was not trusted.

Vlad was a different story. Joanna would sometimes see him walking through the palace, always guarded, as if his captors were afraid to leave him alone. She was too young to guess that they feared him. She only saw the worn clothes, the oily hair, the frequently bruised face of a slave.

They might never have met had it not been for a night when she attended a state banquet. She sat near the back of the hall with the other children, aunts and uncles who were often far younger than she. At the start of the meal, Vlad and his brother were brought in and introduced to visitors from the West. Vlad was dressed well for the occasion, but had men surrounding him. She recognized them as palace guards, though they tried to look inconspicuous as they led him to the visitors.

She watched a quick exchange between the guests and her half brother, then listened in amazement as Mezid-Bey asked the boy to share his table. Vlad looked as starved as the lowest beggar, but declined. She watched as he left the hall so quickly that the guards who tried not to look like guards had to struggle to keep up with him.

Curious, she slipped away from her family and followed the group, keeping to the shadows along the walls, darting out the door as quickly as a mouse. Once in the hall, she stood behind a post and listened to the exchange—her eavesdropping made all the more difficult by the sudden shift between Turkish and Romanian.

"Did he really think I would share food with him?" Vlad responded to the youngest guard's whispered comment.

"Keep your voice down, fool!" the head guard said, grabbing his arm as Vlad tried to walk away.

Vlad wrenched it free. "I've half a mind to go back inside and—"

She would have heard more, but his angry words were cut short by the sight of the head guard's sword. "I would not think that wise for yourself or our guests, young prince," he said, his voice low and lethal.

As they walked down the hall, she noticed the youngest of the guards pull one of the small meat pies served at the banquet out of his pocket and slip it into Vlad's hand. As it disappeared into his robe, Vlad responded to the kindness with a quick nod.

Joanna began to understand why he looked so lean, so tattered. Did her grandfather know that they starved him? Would she dare to ask about it and discover that he had ordered it as punishment?

She followed the group, keeping well behind them and in the shadows, where the flickering lamplight did not touch. Under normal circumstances, she would not have tried to meet him, but tonight it seemed that she could at least find out where they kept him, then return to her group without ever being missed.

So she went on, down turns in the hall and up a twisting, narrow flight of stairs to a plainer section of the castle, one where the most trusted guards of the family were lodged in comfort but not extravagance.

She peeked around the final turn in the hall and saw the far room open and her brother step inside.

She prayed that luck would stay with her, and it did. The

chief guard and two of his men continued down the hall, leaving the kind guard and another behind.

She had not intended to do anything more than what she had already done, but this seemed too fortunate an opportunity. Taking a deep breath, she stepped into their sight and walked confidently toward the pair.

"And what brings you here on such a night, young princess?" the kind one asked.

"I should like to see Vlad Tepes, please," she replied.

He knew why she had come alone. Would he dare to help? She waited while the men looked at each other, saying nothing. "Do you order this, young princess?" he finally asked.

She had never ordered anything and did not know if he were joking. "I understand that he is my brother. I would only like to meet him."

The look that passed between them was longer this time. "Do you suppose he'll strangle her?" the second guard said.

"He has not survived so long in this place by being a fool." The younger guard slipped the bolt, glanced into the room, then let her pass.

A single candle lit the space, and there was a stench to the room that told her it was rarely cleaned or aired. He sat at a bare table, lit by a single candle. As soon as he saw her, he relaxed and casually finished the small meal he had been given.

"Welcome, Princess Joanna," he finally said, his eyes glittering in the light, intense with interest. "Come closer so I can see you better."

She did as he ordered. Thinking of the guard's comment, she stood out of reach. He opened a drawer in the table and pulled out a scrap of parchment. It flared as he held it over the candle flame, then closer to her face, letting it fall to the floor when it burned too close to his fingers. She stepped back quickly to keep from being burned, watching as the ashes died on the bare wood.

"I'd heard that we looked much alike. Close up, it's more obvious," he said, commenting no further.

She stared at him, trying to see what he saw. The long silence grew oppressive, and when he took a sudden step toward her, she cried out and jumped back.

"Features mean nothing," he said and laughed. "You may look like me, but you've no more strength than Radu."

"I'm so much smaller than you are," she retorted, her chin starting to quiver.

"I understand that your mother was eaten by wolves. Do you dream of them?" he asked.

"Sometimes," she admitted. "But they don't frighten me."

"They should. They're the strongest army of my land, protecting what is theirs. Perhaps they let you live because you are one of us."

She looked at the bare stone walls, the tiny window near the ceiling, the small hinged door within the door. This was not his chamber, but his cell.

"I came to see if I could help you," she said.

"Help?" He laughed. "I've been beyond help since I set foot in this cursed place." He paused, then added, "But if you do wish to do me a favor, I can think of one. I'd like a knife."

"To escape?"

"Escape! Now, where could I go?" He'd moved closer to her again, so close she could feel his breath on her cheek as he whispered, "No, small sister, I want to kill a man—two, if I can manage."

"The punishment for murder is—"

He cut her off with a quick laugh. "If Mezid-Bey intended to kill me, he would have done so long ago. He can't because he needs me. There's no one else to take the Wallacian throne but a Hunyadi, and he's wise to fear them."

She understood only half of what he said. "Why do you want to kill someone?" she asked.

"For justice."

"Justice." She frowned, considered, answered finally, "For that there is my grandfather's court."

"Yes, he would have some interest." He smiled, his lips pressed together, his eyes oddly out of focus as if he were watching the deed. "But it's not the same as holding the knife my . . . self."

She knew that other boys his age did not speak of such things. And though she wanted to understand, she still had a hundred questions, all unformed. She was about to speak when they were interrupted by a quick knock, the door flung open. "Child, someone's coming!"

Vlad jumped backward, away from her, lost his footing and caught himself against the stone wall. "Crimes," he mumbled and shut his eyes.

The guard who had helped her pulled her into the hall and thrust her into an open doorway across from her brother's room. "Stay there until I come for you," he said, closing the door to hide her.

She put her ear to the wood and listened to someone walking down the hall, a new set of voices. She recognized the head guard's, then another, even more familiar one.

She was certain she heard her uncle, her mother's brother.

He had no position in the castle save that of a lesser relation, and certainly no reason to be visiting her half brother. Now more curious than frightened, she lay down on the floor and placed her ear close to the crack at the bottom of the door. Though she struggled to hear, the voices were too soft, stopping altogether as the door to her brother's room opened and shut behind them.

When she'd listened awhile longer and heard nothing, she risked opening the door. The hallway was empty. Certain she would be missed by her family, if she had not been already, she decided to leave while the hall was clear. But before she could bolt to the stairs and safety, the door to her brother's room opened.

She fled into the room where she'd been hiding and flattened herself against the wall behind the door.

"I want to know who is responsible for the drug!" her uncle bellowed. His voice seemed strange to her, menacing. She had never heard him speak in such a tone before.

"He may have bribed someone. We couldn't be with him every moment while we were in the hall," the guard commented.

"Just see that it doesn't happen again," her uncle warned. She heard his footsteps grow softer as he walked down the hall. Before the guard could come for her, she left the room herself, and curious about her uncle's words, peered into her brother's room.

He lay on the floor, one cheek scraped as if from the fall,

a long cut on his back. The clothing he had been wearing had been ripped from his body. His expression was dreamy, as if he did not care what had been done to him. But as he focused with difficulty on her face, she saw that his eyes were still alive and so filled with rage that they seemed to glow.

She tried to comprehend what she saw, but before any meaning came to mind, the guard noticed her standing there. Before he could say a word, she turned and fled down the long marble hall.

Her fears had been groundless. She had not been missed. This was due in no small part to her cousin, the son of the man who had visited her brother. "Did you hear what Kemal did?" her younger cousin asked.

Joanna nodded. "I think so," she said. "What could you expect from him?"

"And poor Osman, laughing so hard he began to hiccup. Little Grandma had to take them both to their rooms. Kemal will get it this time."

Joanna hoped not, since he'd saved her from a scolding or worse.

But though her journey escaped notice, the consequences of it did not. That night, for the first time in years, she had another nightmare. In it, she was again stealing down the halls and stairs that led to her brother's chamber. His door was open now, the guards away from their post. She moved closer, heart pounding, and peeked inside. There she saw her brother, starved now to nothing more than skin-covered bones, lying naked, face down on the table. Around him were a pack of wolves, front paws on the table, their nuzzles pressed against him, pulling the meat from his bones.

She cried out, covered her mouth with her hand to stifle the sound and backed away. But it was too late. The beasts had seen her. As they turned their attention from Vlad to her, she saw that her brother was not yet dead. He raised his head and stared at her, green eyes glowing in the skin-covered skull, his form slowly shifting from human to wolf.

She turned and tried to run, but the wolves were faster. One knocked her down. Another pulled at her shoulder, turning her onto her back. They tore at her clothes until finally one stood over her, his paws heavy on her chest, his green eyes glowing. He ripped through her gown until he reached the skin of her belly, and bit hard and deep.

She felt something wet against her legs. Her blood!

She woke screaming, her thighs and back wet. When Little Grandma came running at the sound of her cries and pulled the cover back, Joanna jumped from the bed and looked down with horror at the sight of urine mingled with drops of blood.

"Shhh. It's all right, child," Little Grandma said, stroking her tangled hair. "This happens to girls. It means you've become a woman."

Of course she knew that, but pretended not to; better that than to try to explain the dream and its origin. She buried her face in the folds of the old woman's skirt and relaxed as the woman's hand stroked her long, dark hair.

That evening they held a ceremony for her, a small gathering of her older cousins. As they sat drinking apricot juice and eating sugared almonds, Little Grandma and a younger servant packed her clothes and the gifts her grandfather had given her and carried them down the castle halls to the wing where the older, unmarried girls were lodged.

Though the space was larger and far more beautiful, there was no one to share it, no one to listen to her cries in the night, to wake her from the nightmares of wolves, of battlefields overrun with wolves. She had not one friend with whom she could share her fears.

For a time she thought about her brother often, then less, until weeks passed without her worrying about him at all. She ceased to feel any guilt for not trying to help him. Instead, with no real vanity, she thought only of herself.

Her mother had been insane when she jumped to her death. Young though she was, Joanna was certain the same sad end waited for her.

She was drawn out of her reverie by the sudden shaking of Colleen's hand, the cry of a sailor in the crow's nest far above them.

"Look, Princess!" Colleen exclaimed. "We're pulling into a harbor. Oporto, Portugal."

"Portugal?" Joanna walked to the rail and looked out at the town. Inhaling, she smelled sweet flowers, spices, and the sweat of the men unloading cargo from their ship—bundles of hides and bottles of water from the warehouse where they'd made their arrangements for this voyage.

Joanna leaned over the rail, her attention fixed on a tall young man on the edge of the dock, directing the crew in stacking the bottles on the back of a half-dozen wagons parked there.

Sensing he was being watched, the man turned and stared up at her. Joanna felt suddenly human. Her knees shook, and she gripped the rail to keep from falling. As she did, the man flashed a smile and made a slow, almost courtly bow.

Joanna was scarcely aware of Colleen at her side, gripping her arm to hold her steady until the girl spoke. "He acts as if he knows you," she said.

Joanna stared at the man a moment longer, then turned to the girl. "You are standing beside a legend," she whispered. "There are others, far more than you will ever know."

They stood on deck until the wagons pulled away with their load. Then Joanna let Colleen draw her out of the darkness and into the dim lantern light in the hall below.

That night she lay on the bed with Colleen, holding her close, so close that Colleen shivered from the chill of her flesh.

"There are so many wonders in this world," Joanna whispered. "There are the *strigoi,* mere children compared to the old ones in their mountain keep. There are the werebeasts, their strangeness unknown except in the rays of the full moon. There are the ghosts of my own . . . and so few of them now, all dwindling quickly in your crowded world."

"And the banshees, the elves, the dearg-dul?"

"I don't know them. But perhaps . . ." Joanna's voice trailed off, her thoughts lost in the past.

They had hours until dawn, hours until she would sleep. Hours to purge the memory from her thoughts and, hopefully, her dreams.

twelve

Colleen moved away from her, turned up the lantern as high as Joanna's sensitive eyes would allow and took up the mending she'd started earlier. They had so few articles of clothing between them that they had to preserve every one until more could be bought.

"Are you really a princess?" she asked after a while without looking up from her work. "That man on shore bowed to you as if you were."

"I was, but that was a long time ago." Joanna settled onto the bed they often shared on stormy evenings. Perhaps it was better to tell it all to someone. There was a legend among her father's people that to speak of a tragedy would lessen its effect. There was wisdom in that, and so she began. "Mezid-Bey was a prince of his empire, and my paternal grandfather, Vlad Dracul, had the title in his for a time, as did my brother before his death. And there was my husband, also titled, though there again I was not directly royal. I was his third wife."

Colleen looked at her, startled though she said nothing.

"What is it?" Joanna asked.

"We don't do that in England. One husband. One wife. Your way seems . . . wrong to me."

Joanna laughed. The feeling seemed so odd in her throat. When had she last done so? "The wrong husband with the wrong wife would be barbaric too. But yes, it was barbaric in much the same way that watching larger animals prey on smaller ones is barbaric. And I was the smallest of them all . . . at least in the beginning.

"You see, the oldest wanted to be the only wife but bore no sons. The second wife bore a son and a daughter and so was hated by the first. I might have been her ally, but she was my husband's favorite. And they both knew that I was chosen as third partly to court Mezid-Bey's favor but also because of the blood tie between my brother and I."

"He wasn't a prisoner anymore?" Colleen asked, thinking of the bits of his story that she had already learned.

"Vlad? No. Though the empire . . . through my family, starved and abused him, they never broke him. They taught him to hate and gave him a hunger for revenge. And later they uncaged the wolf with nothing more than a quick agreement between them. Vlad did what hungry wolves often do and gave back to them far more injury than they had ever dared inflict on him."

Joanna paused and trembled, thinking of the whispers of his atrocities that invaded even the scented gardens and opulent rooms of her grandfather's palace, that place so distant from the bloody wars. She pushed the stories from her mind and took another deep breath. She was getting so good at breathing like they did, of learning their language, of speaking like they did, even of making sounds when she walked so as not to startle the crew. She felt as if every mile she put between her and those lands was a lifetime of separation from that horrible past. Certain she could purge it all in the telling, she went on.

"Kemal was my husband's name. His lands were near Burgas, close to Varna, an area often threatened by my brother. I knew the language and customs of the Romanians, so he married me and took me west to lands that bordered my brother's unstable holdings."

"Did you care for him?" Colleen asked.

In the beginning, Joanna thought she had. That all changed so quickly when on their wedding night, the first night of the journey west, she had joined him in his bed only to be kicked onto the dirt floor because the scent she wore did not please him.

She wanted to be like her brother then, strong and silent,

but her tears would not hide, nor would the sobs that followed. He sent her off to sleep with the servants. "I hated him from the start," she lied. "Our marriage was never consummated. For that, I am still thankful."

Again, she lied, though she doubted the act would have altered the tragedies that followed.

"I was sent to live with the servants, some of them slaves from my brother's land. Since I was dressed in castoffs from the two privileged wives, and rarely given a moment of time by my husband, they looked on me with pity.

"One of them had known my father and commented on my resemblance to him. I had been coached to tell the truth about who I was, and so I did.

"They trusted me then, telling me what they knew of my brother and his battles. By now, filled with hate for the one who brought me here, I told my slaves much and my husband many stories that were mostly false. And as I told them, I thought of my brother and cherished the rumors of his every triumph.

"Then Fate smiled on me one last time. My husband's cherished second wife died, leaving not two but three children, one young enough to need her mother's breast. It was not a time to trust servants, so they trusted me instead.

"They were not at all the sort of little tyrants I had expected. Instead, as they warmed to me they showed me love—infinite and beautiful."

Colleen smiled from her own memories. "My brothers were that way. So much younger that I felt like their mother."

"So I was mother in truth to those children, especially the infant, Sophia, who shared my bed as if I had given birth to her. No one else cared for my husband's children as I did, certainly not my husband's first wife, who hated them. Whatever pettiness I harbored retreated. I grew calmer, almost serene, and certainly content as I had not been since my first years in my uncle's gardens."

Her tone must have shifted, because Colleen set aside her work and moved to the bed, sitting close to her mistress and taking her hand. "You don't have to go on," she whispered.

"I must." Joanna shuddered once, but when she spoke, her voice remained steady, strong. "Their lives and my happiness,

I had already doomed. I had told too many lies to my husband and too many truths to his slaves. A surprise attack in early morning of our holy week ended as I had once hoped it would.

"I saw my husband's head on a pike, his first wife stripped of her finery and given over to my brother's guards for their pleasure. I would have followed, but one of the Romanian slaves spoke up for me, explaining to the soldiers who I was. Their attitude changed in a moment. Once I might have felt triumph. Now I had the children to consider.

"I could not protect the oldest boy. He died like his father, but at least was too young to know fear before the pain. I begged one of the Romanian women to claim the other two as her own. She did as I asked, and so we were taken north and west."

"I was well treated on the journey. While the others walked until they were too tired to walk any longer before being allowed to share the soldiers' mounts, I had my own horse from the beginning, as did my servants and the children they claimed as their own.

"We rode for four days before we entered Romanian land, five more before we reached the Arges River and the castle Vlad had built there."

She recalled her first sight of it too vividly. How vicious it had seemed, with its sharp stone walls jutting into the sky, how cold, how gray. The inside had even less life.

"The captain of our troop spoke to my brother first. Then I was brought to him and we were left alone. He pulled away the veil I wore, then forced me to look at him. 'I remember the eyes,' he said. 'What else was there?'

"I told him what I remembered of our first meeting and how I had seen my younger uncle in his chambers. He looked ready to strike me for that, then smiled instead. 'He taught me to be strong,' he said. 'I've always felt gratitude for that."

" 'You were always strong,' I responded, thinking of those whispers about him even when he was so young.

" 'And growing stronger,' he said. Someone entered the chambers where we sat. I heard a woman's laughter, turned and saw her—my brother's wife.

"She was Illona Ilsabeta, a woman of odd, sharp beauty. I

seemed exotic to those in my mother's country because of the color of my eyes and the red cast in my hair. With her, it was nothing so obvious. The eyes seemed too wide-set, the nose too straight, the skin a bit too pale. Her hands and feet were large. Later I discovered that her legs were long and muscular. The men in my mother's country would have found her unattractive. In Wallacia, men could not keep their eyes off her.

"'There are two small children downstairs who are in need of their mother,' she said as she came forward. 'Some say they're yours. Is it true?'

"I was afraid to tell the truth, almost as afraid to lie."

Joanna stammered something about love making them hers as Illona walked forward. She had a knife in her hand, one she held so tightly that Joanna was certain the woman meant to use it on her. Instead, she ripped through the thin linen of Joanna's skirt and the layers beneath it. One hand held her by the neck, the other moved over her belly. Illona's fingers moved between her trembling legs, pulling apart the folds of skin, pressing hard.

"She pressed her hand against my sex," Joanna said. "I cried out in surprise and pain. She laughed again. 'They can't be yours,' she said.

"They brought the children to the hall. They rushed to me, the little girl leaping into my arms like the monkey she seemed . . . all legs and arms at that age. What followed . . ." She shivered. Colleen held her close.

"You don't have to speak of it," she said. "Put it behind you, it was long ago."

Joanna shook her head, gulped another breath of air. "Someone—probably Illona—pressed a knife into my hand.

"I wanted to do the deed. I thought I would be merciful and do it quickly, and in doing it a part of me knew I would gain favor with the woman who was undoubtedly mistress of this cold place in the months when her husband was gone. But I could not. Instead, I dropped the weapon and ran, Illona's dark laughter following me down the bare stone hall.

"I spent the night locked with the children in a tower room, listening to them cry with hunger and fear. I tried to calm myself enough to calm them, but each time I touched them to soothe their misery, my own only made theirs worse. Children are too perceptive in those things. In the morning, their heads were raised on pikes beside those of the fallen Turkish officers."

She began to tremble again. Colleen held her close, murmuring words too soft for Joanna's overwrought mind to translate. She was lost in the past, in the days of delirium that followed the execution of the only children she would ever know. She took another gulp of air, but Colleen pressed tightly against her as if to force the means of speech from her lungs.

"You needn't talk about the past. You mustn't."

Joanna pushed her away and continued, her voice shaking, "The war went on and on. My brother won some battles, lost others but led a lucky life for a number of years. Hardly a scratch, though he was often in the thick of the fighting.

"Though I hated Illona, I never doubted that she loved him. When he was gone, she would spend each night in prayer. Her servants were ordered to pray with her, though they had their work in the morning. I was excused. 'God would not heed a heathen's prayers,' she often told me.

"Nor did He heed hers, at least not forever. The battles turned in the Turks' favor. Vlad was wounded, more than once. Frantic, Illona turned to soothsayers and shamans and witches, followers of old religions. They promised protection; then, when she paid them a pauper's fortune, they promised even more.

"She listened. She learned. That last time, when he was carried home, he was not expected to live the night.

"He did, for he was marvelously strong. But the fever was taking hold of him . . . and of her as well. She abandoned his side, spent the night in the chapel now profaned with symbols of old dark creeds.

"That night, I stayed at his side and held his hand. He was so delirious, he looked at me and whispered her name. I confess that I kissed him more than once, thinking it a small lie when it gave him so much comfort.

"It was nearly dawn when she came to us. I could sense the change in her—the triumph in her expression, the deadly passion glowing in her eyes, the same passion that glows in mine when I am hungry or enraged. 'Leave us,' she ordered and told me to close and lock the shutters and admit no one to the chamber until nightfall. 'Keep watch outside if you must, but follow this command,' she said.

"I would not dare disobey her. So I sat and waited, dozing occasionally since I had not slept for so long.

"It was the last day I would ever be completely awake and free. And I spent it in a dark stone hallway.

"At dusk, she opened the door. I had never seen her look so triumphant. 'Come in, sister,' she said.

"I was instantly wary. She never called me that unless she had something unpleasant planned for me.

"I peered past her and saw my brother sitting up in bed. Though his face seemed pale, his hair damp from sweat, there was no sign of fever. She had found a cure for him, I thought. I smiled at her, real joy in my face, for I thought that as long as he lived, my life would be far less miserable. He would protect me from her.

" 'Go to him,' she said and pushed me forward.

"I dared not disobey. In truth I had never embraced him in all the months I had lived under his roof. I hardly expected him to embrace me, but he held out his arms. Just before I fell into them, I sensed that something was wrong. But it was too late. He had me and I could not move, not even when I felt his teeth rip the flesh of my neck.

"Some say a *strigoi*'s kiss is sweet. They lie." She paused, considering the hour she spent locked in his arms.

"And then," Colleen asked when the silence had grown too huge.

"As I faded, I thought of the time we first met, when I was so young and he hardly more than a youth himself.

"Memories share through blood. I think the reminder of our kinship was too sharp. As soon as his hunger was appeased, he pushed me away. 'Turn her as you did me,' he ordered his wife.

"She tried to protest, but he would not listen. 'I will not have my sister's life on my hands. Do it!' She obeyed him then. I had no idea what they had done, but I feared them both. Had I any strength left, I might have struggled. Instead I let her guide my lips to her breast, suckling blood as a child might his mother's milk.

"I slept. The following evening she called my name, and I awakened to a different sort of life. Sadder than my mortal one. Far lonelier than even I could have imagined."

"What was it like, that awakening?"

"Different for everyone, I believe. For some, especially those who fear death, it must be a liberating experience. At first, I did not even notice the change except for that odd silence."

"Silence?"

"Shut your eyes and listen to the beating of your heart. Now listen to your breath moving in and out. Those were the soft sounds I missed. And when at last I realized what had happened, I tried to cry out and gagged from the attempt. I had to force a breath before I spoke. When I did, I turned on her. 'What have you done to me?' I demanded.

"She forced in a breath, but only so she could laugh.

"And sadly, the power that filled me brought no relief from my hysteria, or my dreams. They made things worse, it seemed, because I had a feeling that a different sort of life was within my grasp if I only had the courage to reach for it.

"I never dared, not with Illona present. She made sure of it that first night. When I awoke, confused and frightened, she laid an infant in my arms—one stolen from a nearby village. Knowing how much I missed the children they had killed, she brought it to me to taunt me. It was my first meal.

"I ignored the child as long as I could while it lay on the stone floor screaming with fear and cold and hunger, as the children I had thought of as my own had screamed. Finally, unable to bear the sound of it any longer, I did the merciful thing and killed it.

"After that, I never dared raise my voice to her. If I did, she would hunt up infants to bring to the castle to be my food. As the years went on, I avoided her as best I could. Her death freed me of that fear. And you . . ." She paused to press her lips to Colleen's cheek. "You have shown me love. The man who attacked you showed me my power. And now, a new land."

She lay back, drawing Colleen close to her again. Her fingers circled Colleen's wrist as she marveled at the constant beauty of the woman's pulse. "Tell me about London."

"It is like a forest of stone, teeming with life. Not all of it is pleasant." Her voice grew softer at the end.

"What are you thinking of?" Joanna asked.

"The man you killed for me. And the sailor . . . I think you will like London, and I am afraid."

"Afraid?"

"The English hunted your brother. They killed his wife as well. I don't like to think of them hunting you."

"Ah!" Joanna tittered, an honest display of humor. "It is hard to kill something already dead."

She felt Colleen shudder and try to pull away. She held her servant tightly and moments later drifted off with the dawn, her lips pressed against the fresh wound she had made on her servant's shoulder. As her arms relaxed, she felt Colleen leave her, then the quick draft of air as the cabin door opened and shut.

Joanna was awakened just before dusk by the clanging of the ship's bell, running feet and a sudden rush of air into the room. "The sun is nearly set. You should come topside," Colleen said.

"Topside?"

"We've reached England."

Joanna rose, stretched as if by such close association with a human she had begun to think like them with their constant aches in aging bodies. She drew a cloak tightly around herself and followed her servant up the narrow ladder to the deck.

The land was on both sides of the boat, which pitched uneasily in the shifting currents. She drew in a breath. She could smell the land, its farms, its people. "London?" she asked, pointing to a stand of buildings to the north.

"Just a village. Romford, I think. The captain says we will be putting in at Gravesend. We'll take a barge the rest of the way."

Joanna didn't answer. She had moved to the rail, gripping it, watching the buildings grow denser as they moved inland. The flatter landscape seemed so alien to her, and the land so populated. Did her brother really mean to settle them here?

"How soon will we be leaving the ship?" she asked.

Colleen went in search of an answer, coming back a short

time later with the captain. "I understand you are still feeling ill," he said. "We'll be going into port on the next tide. That will be around midnight. We'll unload through to morning. You may leave whenever you wish."

Joanna nodded and took his hand. "You're so cold. You should go below," he said, then turned his attention to his crew.

"The city is too big," Joanna whispered. "We'll be lost in it."

Colleen wrapped the shawl around her mistress and led her away. "It's time for you to rest. While you do, I'll see to everything," she whispered. "I promise that everything will be all right."

thirteen

Since they had landed in London, Colleen had taken charge of her mistress's affairs. It was not that she wished to, but Joanna's moods seemed to swing between reckless elation and long periods of utter silence. While she brooded, Colleen did what she could to assure their survival.

She found them a hotel room, later a place in a rooming house—two adjoining rooms on a lower level, one windowless with a stout door with a lock, the other with a private entrance to the street. This seemed to cheer Joanna, and she took to disappearing late at night when most decent folks were sleeping, coming back just before dawn with her hair in tangles, her dress soiled. But she had not eaten. That much was clear in how avidly she reached for Colleen in those moments before sleep claimed her.

In a few weeks' time, their rent and Colleen's necessary supply of food had exhausted most of their funds. With no other resources left them, Colleen asked if she could pawn one of Joanna's gems.

Since they'd been laughing just moments before, she thought she'd caught her mistress at a good time. But the suggestion was met with such a long, sullen and unblinking stare that Colleen wished she'd taken to begging in the streets instead of being practical. Finally, at just the moment Colleen was thinking of breaking into tears and asking forgiveness, Joanna pulled out of her quiet fury long enough to rummage among her papers and hand Colleen the written advice Steranko had given her in Varna. He'd composed the note in English as well as Romanian, as if he guessed that Colleen would be the one reading it.

Steranko directed them to find the solicitor who was listed on a number of the papers in Joanna's collection. The man replied the same day to Colleen's message, writing that he would be happy to meet them that evening.

Harold Siekert's office was near Hyde Park, on a street that seemed mostly residential. Colleen could only remember being in such a grand place once, and she'd been too young to recall much of what she'd seen. She sat stiffly on one of Mr. Siekert's office chairs, holding tightly to its wooden arms while the solicitor sorted the papers, arranging them into a number of different stacks on his desk. He tried to explain her mistress's holdings. Colleen seemed to be suffering from the same lack of luck as Joanna, but perhaps they misunderstood different parts, and when they were alone together they could sort it all out.

"Your brother's solicitor was a Mr. Hawkins of Exeter. I hear that he has passed on, as has the Mr. Renfield whose name is on so many of these deeds as a witness."

"And that is problem?" Joanna asked, speaking slowly so he would understand her in spite of her thick accent.

"Problem, you say? Not exactly. I was contacted by Mr. Hawkins because of my knowledge of London properties. I arranged some of the deeds for him before he sent one of his employees east to visit your brother. I must advise you that the man who would know the most about your holdings is Jonathan Harker, whose name is on many of these papers and who inherited Mr. Hawkins's firm in Exeter."

Joanna paused. To Colleen she seemed about to laugh again, but instead replied carefully, "I have come long way. I do not want to travel more."

"You do not have to, but you should at the least write him and tell him you are here. He may have other news for you."

"News?"

"Information," Colleen volunteered, wondering why her mistress's speech always seemed to deteriorate when she addressed someone else.

"Ah! I do not write English well . . . the letters are unfamiliar. And I have no need, I think."

"As you wish." He shuffled through the papers for some time, then showed them a map, pointing as he summarized. "Your family has a number of holdings in London here and here, as well as Purfleet, Whitby and Exeter, but many seem to have been acquired as investment only. I cannot imagine anyone living in them.

"But there are two that would serve you. One is a small apartment under lease near Oxford Circle in Mayfair. Another is a cottage on the edge of Chelsea Gardens. There is one in Exeter as well. If you would like to visit the pair in London tomorrow and decide—"

"Gardens," Joanna replied.

"Well, if you don't like it later, you can always move or lease something of your own."

The rest of the meeting settled some financial matters. At Joanna's request, he even suggested a jeweler he thought would give Joanna a fair price for some of her gems, and said he would open an account for her at a local bank, using her brother's funds.

As they were preparing to leave, he made one final comment: "I have not seen your brother since he came to me some months ago to sign the leases. Do you have an address for him?"

She frowned, then shook her head.

"I could contact Mr. Harker. Perhaps he knows it."

Joanna looked at him, her expression blank as she deciphered the meaning of his words. When she did, she drew in a deep breath and laughed. The sound, so unnatural, caused the solicitor to step back. His hands shivered, then fell straight at his side, as if he longed to cover his ears and did not dare to give insult. "I do not think so. But perhaps I visit Mr. Harker later, after I have gotten to know your country better. Then I ask him for you," she finally said.

She stood up, prepared to leave. Siekert stood just as quickly. "Would you like me to hail you a cab? There might be one out, though it is quite late."

She didn't answer, only pushed past him to the door. Colleen moved quickly, to stay close behind.

Once in the street, Joanna let out the emotions she had suppressed in another, longer, peal of laughter. She spun on one heel so swiftly that for a moment her features blurred. Stopping too quickly, she lost her footing and fell against an old man with a cane who hobbled slowly down the street.

Then, for the first time in all the weeks they were together, Joanna pulled Colleen close and kissed her. Not out of gratitude for what Colleen gave so freely. No, it was exhilaration, perhaps, or some sense of daring others to notice them. Colleen had no way of knowing. She only knew the coldness of Joanna's lips, the dryness beyond them, like the dust she should long ago have become.

"Come," Joanna said and gripped her arm, pulling her east toward the wilder parts of town, the places Colleen did not wish to visit ever again. "Come, you are safe with me."

Safe? She might be safe, but what of the others, the people who might cross their paths, who might out of drink or desperation make some foolish move Joanna would choose to interpret as an attack?

It was what Joanna wanted—that excuse, that permission to let loose her rage and kill.

Colleen wanted to scream, to fight, to run. She did not dare.

Instead, she dug in her heels. "Not that way," she said.

But her voice seemed too small, lost among the cacophony of carriages and newsboys, street vendors and beggars.

"Please," she whispered, drawing close to her mistress. "Please. I would like to go back to our rooms. I doubt I am needed any more tonight."

"Then go. Collect what little we brought. Tomorrow we'll move into the space my brother prepared for me."

Joanna walked on. Colleen watched her go, her form becoming thinner and fainter in the dim gaslights until it vanished completely long before it should have been out of sight.

Joanna went on, moving silently above the dark, narrow streets near the river, sensing the life beneath her. Hers for the picking if only she dared. She stopped outside taverns, brothels, hovels where decent people tried to sleep in spite of hunger and vermin.

The life still walking the streets seemed aimless, except for a man too well dressed for his surroundings, who walked stiffly down the dark and narrow wharf. A long tweed coat made his age difficult to fathom, and the carved wood cane he used was too familiar a weapon against her kind. There would be easier prey later in the evening, drunks who would not wake when she touched them, and through slumber survive her need.

She was about to move away when she noticed a woman step out of the deeper shadows between two rotting buildings and walk toward the man. Joanna noted the exaggerated swing of her hips, the thin fabric of her gown and her seductive smile. A ripple of pleasure went through her as she watched their brief greeting, how the woman dropped the fringed shawl she had draped across her shoulders to reveal a blouse so low-cut that only a shrug was needed to bare her breasts.

There had been women like this in the villages near her brother's keep, and even in her grandfather's castle. "Little harlots," her grandfather had called them, a term as affectionate as it was quietly disapproving. The old man had never gone to one, but many of his relations had. From what little she had seen of polite British women, she was amazed there weren't thousands more of them in London.

The couple moved into shadows so deep that only a vampire could detect them. She watched the woman raise her skirt and slide a bare leg down the man's side, lower her hands to his belt and the buttons on his pants. He reached for her, moving her closer to the crumbling stone wall of the nearest building, no doubt to use it to steady her as he . . .

A sudden hard thrust of the man's arms pushed the woman backward against the stones. As the recoil sent her falling forward against him, Joanna saw a quick flash of moonlight on metal, a spurt of blood, the man jumping sideways to avoid staining his coat.

What had the poor creature done to deserve an act like this? As enraged as she had been the night Colleen was attacked, Joanna fell into human shape on the stones behind him.

She must have made some sound because he turned, catlike, and glared at her.

Flee. Attack. Join him. All the emotions of her conflicting

natures held her motionless and trembling, a stance he must have mistaken for fear. He took a quick step forward, stabbing with the knife he had used on the girl. The blade cut too quickly, and her reaction was hardly what he'd expected. But the blade's thin wooden handle made her gasp and double over, one palm flat on the ground.

She looked up at him, her eyes blazing. He made a small, strangled sound and backed away from her, then whirled and ran down the wharf and disappeared around a corner.

Joanna started to follow when the woman's moans and the scent of blood drew her back.

Joanna moved to the woman's side and rolled her over. As she'd expected, the wound was mortal. Blood flowed from the break in her skull and poured from the deep cut in her sternum, presenting an opportunity that hunger made it difficult to ignore.

Murmuring something soothing, she lowered her face to the bleeding wound and began to drink from the river of life flowing away from the poor creature. She felt the heartbeat quicken, then slow, the final intake of breath. Only then did she look down at the victim—ragged and dirty, obviously young but with a face already scarred and lined from dissipation.

Illona had told her that to kill brought power, then had denied her that. In the castle Joanna had always been the last to take, sucking the last bits of nourishment from Illona's corpses. The thug she had killed on the road to Varna gave her nothing but satisfaction and confidence, this one nothing at all but a vague feeling of uneasy grief.

Though Joanna left no marks on the body, she carried it the few steps to the river and let it slide, with only a tiny splash, into the murky water of the Thames. Returning to the site of the murder, she picked up the girl's shawl, dipped it into the water, and used it to wash away the stains on her dress, the puddle of blood on the wharf.

And though it might have been some trick of her blood-clouded senses, she felt the murderer still nearby, watching her; wondering, no doubt, what she might be. But when she scanned the dark wharf she saw nothing, heard nothing.

What sort of monsters were there in this city—this sorry,

dangerous city? The thought stayed with her as she made her way back to the rooms she shared with Colleen.

Colleen frowned when she saw the rips in the dress, the wet patches near the hem. She seemed about to complain about them, but the intensity in Joanna's expression silenced her. Usually Joanna would try to soothe her. Usually she would stay awake until dawn and tell her what she'd seen. Tonight she said nothing as she stripped off the soiled dress and went into the back room. Shutting the door, she lay in her box and pulled shut the lid. Drawing in a breath, she smelled the musty, comforting fragrance of earth, of home.

fourteen

In the two months he'd been in England, Van Helsing had grown thoroughly sick of Arthur Holmwood's—Lord Godalming's!—hospitality.

Not that Arthur wasn't a gracious host . . . indeed, Van Helsing's problem was that Arthur seemed *too* gracious. Whenever Van Helsing visited London, Arthur insisted he stay with him at the modest—at least by British standards—estate in West Kensington that he'd inherited from his uncle. Ian, the aging butler—or gentleman's gentleman or whatever someone like him was called—who stayed wherever Arthur was staying, had been instructed to see to his every need. Van Helsing, unused to servants, had no idea how to tell the man he merely wished to be alone.

In the evenings, Arthur constantly dragged Van Helsing away from the library he'd given him leave to use, and the contemplation and meditation that kept the doctor's cerebral life at its best. As a result, Van Helsing had seen more of London than he had ever hoped to see, and met a number of its more eccentric characters in the process. Though he found it interesting to eavesdrop on the cutting wit of Oscar Wilde and or share the odd adventures of Arthur's theater crowd, he longed for the silence of a good library or bookstore. There was plenty of both in London and he stole away from Arthur's presence as often as he could, until Arthur suggested that he might be more comfortable in Mayfair, at a small flat Arthur kept for theater friends and those nights when he didn't feel like riding home.

For solace, Van Helsing often found himself seeking out the droll company of Arthur's artist friend Beardsley. Barely twenty, the young man always looked as if he would be dead within a fortnight.

"Aubrey's been that way for as long as I've known him," Arthur explained soon after he introduced the pair. "I hear that he's known he is dying since he was seven."

As have we all, Van Helsing thought, though he admitted that for most, death had far less of a presence.

Though most of Beardsley's work was far too risqué for Van Helsing, he could not help but admire the young man's talent, his drive and his deep philosophical acceptance of his dwindling future. He soon found himself scouring texts and writing fellow physicians in Germany, hoping to find some new treatment for consumption that would prolong the young man's life or at least diminish his pain. He did discover one odd prescription, which included an elixir made from moldy bread, unfermented beer and lemon juice. Though Van Helsing was doubtful about the efficacy of such a foul-tasting drink, the physician who recommended it swore by it, as did Aubrey after only a few days of treatment. Soon the old man and a companion a third his age were strolling the streets of Mayfair on sunny afternoons, often stopping for lunch in their favorite outdoor café near the Arcade. Van Helsing wasn't certain which of them was slowing his pace for the other's sake, but it made no difference.

They were dining when Arthur found them. He joined them at the table, laying his hat and walking stick on an empty chair.

"I've received a note from Mrs. Harker," he said, sliding the unopened telegram across the table.

As Arthur ordered a glass of wine, he watched Van Helsing open and read the telegram, trying to judge the tone of it from the older man's expression. He needn't have bothered. As soon as Van Helsing was finished, he handed the note to Arthur. "She's asking me to come for a visit," he explained, "and hopes that you will be able to come as well."

Arthur read the telegram, nothing more than the doctor had

already conveyed, disappointed that Mina did not say more. But telegrams were hardly private, and she promised that a letter would follow and that they would receive it soon. Hopefully more would be explained then.

Arthur leaned back in his chair and stretched his long legs out alongside the table. This was a charming spot to dine and he knew why Aubrey and Van Helsing chose it so often. The tall buildings on either side of it kept the cold sea wind away, and in early afternoon, with the sun beating down from above, the place seemed almost tropical—good for old bones and for weak lungs as well.

Last fall he had sat at this same table, feigning disapproval while Oscar and Gance planned a bachelor party for him that would have done the old Hellfire Clubs proud. But the wedding had ended in death and mutilation, and with Lucy and Gance rotting in their Exeter crypts. In spite of his vow to discard the past, it was no surprise that Aubrey was the one he turned to for solice, even though he could hardly explain the real reason why. Even after so many months, he still felt most comfortable among the near-dead.

Before his thoughts grew too dark, he ordered a glass of wine, then forced himself to concentrate on the story Aubrey was relating to him and Van Helsing. It concerned a woman he'd encountered the night before.

"I tell you both, I have never seen a creature of such incredible beauty . . . well, not beauty, not exactly. "Presence" might be a better word. Even with all the smudges on her face, I could not take my eyes off her."

Dirt?" Arthur leaned forward, his fingers playing with the stem of his wineglass. "Where did you see this ragged creature?"

So Aubrey finally had Arthur's interest. And his concern. Aubrey easily guessed why and tried to brush the matter off. "I never said she was ragged, just dirty. I saw her on the embankment on Cheyne Walk near Battersea Bridge. I'd just left King's Head when I glimpsed some motion, a darkness against darkness in the shadows along the river close by the bridge."

"Darkness! Good lord, Aubrey! You should have been at home!"

Van Helsing moved his foot under the table and kicked

Arthur's shin as Aubrey's frown twisted into a bitter smile. "My days are numbered, damn it! Must my nights be too?"

Arthur laughed. *"Touché,"* he said. "Go on."

"I called out to her and she looked up at me. Her face, filthy but exquisite. Her eyes, especially. They were . . ." His voice trailed off, surprisingly. Arthur had rarely seen him at such a loss for words. "They were strange—that is, when they focused on mine I felt myself the complete center of her attention."

"You should have been a poet instead of an artist, Aubrey."

"Do you think so?"

"And of course you were the center of her attention, if she meant to rob you or worse."

"I could have knocked her flat, she was that thin."

"And you followed her?" Arthur asked, more concerned.

"It was early evening. There were still plenty of people about. Yes, I followed her. But when I reached the bridge, she seemed to have vanished."

"She probably crossed it and you couldn't see her."

"I thought of that, but it was a clear night. I should have seen her cross. Then I thought she might have jumped, her expression was that frantic. So I looked over the side. There was hardly a ripple on the water."

"Did you go on?" Van Helsing asked.

"There was already mist rising from the water. It did not seem wise to be outside much longer. I may never see her again, but at least she gave me an idea for a drawing for Le Morte D'Arthur. She'll be The Lady of the Lake, I think."

"I'd like to see it when you're done," Van Helsing commented.

"The final will be finished within a few days, but I have the rough with me." He opened the sketchbook he carried everywhere and handed it to the professor.

Van Helsing studied the drawing for a moment, then handed it over to Arthur. "Beautifully done," he said.

Something in his tone made Aubrey look at him curiously. "It's just a rough," he said. "More her than the finished piece will be." He retrieved his sketchbook from Arthur before his friend started turning pages and reached for the check.

Arthur moved faster. Aubrey smiled and protested as he always did, then as always gave in. His friends supported him, and he was thankful, since he never had more than a pound to spend on himself in any month.

Arthur saw to that money, too. He owned a dozen original Beardsley drawings, purchased anonymously through the man's publisher and hidden away where no one would see them. He never let on that he owned them, lest Aubrey think his motive pure charity.

It wasn't. Someday they'd be worth a fortune, whether or not Aubrey survived to enjoy the fame.

"He's looking better, isn't he?" Arthur commented after the artist had gone.

"And eating better, as well. Even steamed pudding for dessert." Van Helsing lit a cigar, something he refused to do in Aubrey's presence lest the smoke start another bout of coughing. "Did you notice the face on the woman?"

"Much like Aubrey's other caricatures," Arthur said.

"The straight brows and nose, the deep-set eyes. They are much like his and his sister's."

"I'm sure there are many who look much like him." They never spoke the count's name in public, rarely when alone.

"It's more than that. Did you see the morning *Times*?"

"I suppose you're referring to the murders," Arthur said stiffly. "Nothing out of the ordinary for summer in London."

"A woman killed. Her body tossed in the river."

"My point exactly," Arthur countered.

"That river can hide so much."

"And has for centuries. Besides, it could be the Ripper again."

"The Ripper always mutilated his victims, then left them for the police to find, no?"

"Madmen evolve," Arthur countered, not liking the turn this conversation had taken. He had no desire to ever go near stakes and mallets again. He suspected that a game of croquet might make him queasy. Van Helsing ignored the last remark. "Three ships arrived from the Black Sea in the past two months. There were two women passengers on the most recent one—one of them from Turkey and the other a servant who had been in her employ for some months, or so the captain told me. But there was only one death—an act of self-defense on the part of the Turkish passenger. The captain did not think it unusual, given the reputation of the sailor who was killed. Even so, it would be best if we did meet with the Harkers, and soon."

"Should they come here?"

"No. No, it would be too dangerous for them if she watches us. Better we go to them, I think."

Arthur looked at the professor and saw the determination in his expression. No use arguing, he thought. "I'll send them each a telegram," he said.

"That is good. We will go on Saturday so we may meet when Jonathan is not occupied."

His tone, Arthur thought, held a hint of distaste.

Arthur sat a while after Van Helsing had gone, composing the telegram on a piece of paper he begged from the waiter. After dropping by the telegraph office, he flagged a cab and headed for the docks to do some investigating of his own.

The ship had long since left on its return voyage, but after buying two rounds in a rowdy dockside pub, Arthur found a sailor who'd served on the crew. He ordered the man a meal, watching as he devoured the sausage rolls, licking the grease from his fingers, washing it all down with another pint.

"She kept to herself. Her servant was a lively one, though. I learned a lot more about her than the other."

"Did you ever see the woman?"

"See? I suppose. Never spoke to her, though. She only came on deck at night."

"Strange, isn't it?"

"Not so. Passengers who are seasick often come up for air when it's dark. Easier on the stomach when you can't see the horizon bobbing up and down."

"What did she look like?"

The sailor looked up from the last of his dinner, frowning. "Why do you want to know?"

The man's sudden shift in tone made Arthur thankful that he had paid the hansom driver to stay outside and act as a bodyguard were he needed. "Curious, that's all," he said and grinned.

"Curious. Her servant says there's plenty that's curious."

He paused, his thin mustache a dark, stubborn line above his tightly closed lips. "I'm an Englishman. I would not mean the woman any harm, I swear on my father's grave."

Arthur wasn't sure if his tone or the potential for more coin broke the silence, but one of them did. "Okay to talk now, I suppose," the sailor said. "Never saw her anyway . . . well, not so's I'd know her face. She was a bit bloody after the attack. She stabbed Gorty with his own knife. An expected end for a bastard like him. He was even lifting from his mates at the end, so why shouldn't he stoop to robbery and possible murder? One of us would of thrown him over if she hadn't finished him first."

He went on, describing the sort of man Gordy had been and how he'd tried to lock the woman in her own steamer trunk.

"He undoubtedly deserved what he got," Arthur said when he'd finished the story.

"She must of been terrified. She looked it, with her dark hair all soaked in his blood."

There was one thing he might have noticed, one important thing. "Half a pound if you answer two questions for me: How much baggage did she carry, and what color were her eyes?"

The man seemed to stop even his breathing. He looked across the table at Arthur and waited. Arthur didn't want to reach for his billfold here, but he had no choice. Holding it close to him beneath the tabletop, he pulled out the money and slid it across the table.

The man smiled. "Such an easy thing to answer," he said. "Just that one trunk. And her eyes were green," he said. "The deepest green I've ever seen on anyone. She might of even been pretty if she weren't so thin. I suppose she didn't get much to eat, given how she was running away."

"Running?"

"Turkish women aren't exactly allowed to come and go as they please. She never said, but we all knew that someone was looking for her. But she's safe now, she is."

"Do you know where?"

"I wouldn't say even if I did. I figure now that she's here, someone might be trying to take her back. What do you think?"

Arthur shook his head and downed the rest of the only pint he'd ordered. "I'd say she's as safe as anyone can be in London," he agreed.

He started to leave, but the man stopped him. "I think you ought to buy another round for the place. Stay in their good graces when you leave, if you catch my drift."

Arthur glanced around him. The men at the bar and the tables around him did seem overly interested in his departure. It occurred to him that he might have dressed a bit more poorly for a visit to this side of town. He laid a half pound on the bar, enough for three rounds for a crowd this size, he reckoned, and left just as the first was being poured.

Clever, he thought, and stored the experience for future use as he got into the cab. "Mayfair," he ordered the driver, then hesitated and called out again. "Better yet, Chelsea. Cheyne Walk near the bridge."

He knew the city was huge, so much so that he'd never see all of it. Yet the eyes on the woman Aubrey had seen had been the same color. He'd go hunting tonight.

His heart pounded on the rest of the ride—a combination of anticipation and dread he'd experienced only a few times in his life, all in the past few months. The uncertainty of what he would do—and what *she* would do—when they stood at last face-to-face, added its own measure of excitement. By the time he handed the driver his fee and tip, he felt as aroused as an adolescent on his first assignation.

He walked across the road to the park that had been created out of muck and weeds recently enough for him to recall the transformation. The young trees were thick in their late-summer foliage, their lower branches just brushing the top of his head as he made his way to a bench where he could sit and watch both the bridge and the land around him.

As he sat and waited, the air cooled and a thin mist rose from the water, sending its tendrils across the land.

This was the sort on evening on which Aubrey had spied the woman. Arthur hoped he would be as fortunate. Though he had never seen Joanna, if she resembled her brother at all, he would know her. If not, he decided that a vampire would have difficulty hiding its nature from one who understood it.

So he waited.

On the bank behind him, he heard music coming from one of the cafés, laughter from the open door of a gallery, horse hooves on the stones of Beaufort Street. He inhaled, stifled a cough brought on by the damp in the air, and thought suddenly of Aubrey. What sort of art might a genius create given centuries in which to perfect the craft? If he were one of those creatures, he would go to Aubrey and offer him that gift.

And so he waited, watched.

It was well after dark. The fog pressed close, muting sounds along with sight. The streets behind him had quieted, and only an occasional whisper of a passerby made him recall that he was among people. Once, well after dark, he felt something colder than the mist brush against his temple but decided it was only his own excitement playing tricks on him.

fifteen

Joanna watched him go, one more dandy in a city filled with them. He was a handsome man, lanky and vibrant. The pale, almost white hair curled over the collar of his cream-colored jacket and bright blue scarf. She'd noted a rose pinned to his lapel. She wondered who he'd been waiting for, surprised that he hadn't whispered the name of the lover who had stood him up. And it was a lover—that much seemed clear enough when she noticed how quickly his heart beat, and how anxiously his head turned in response to every small sound.

No matter. The time to dream about that sort had passed centuries before. He might be beautiful in the masculine way, but he was obviously wealthy, the sort who could be a threat if alive, more of a threat if found dead. Better the East End, the docks, and the waterfront.

When he was well out of sight, she returned to human form and stood on the bridge. It was so beautiful in the moonlight, the filthy water below it iridescent, the gaslights from Cheyne Walk flickering like St. Vincent's Fire across its rippled surface.

She stood a moment, gazing into the water like a Gypsy into her crystal. Memories and possibilities rushed through her mind, bringing the familiar hunger. Shrugging, she walked to the embankment, then east, toward the wilder parts of town.

Joanna floated, incorporeal as the mists from the Thames, through streets that grew dirty and crowded. At times like this she was thankful that she did not have to travel in her human form, for to do so would be to smell the stench of the open sewers, the alcohol reek of the taverns, the sweat of those who crowded close in the narrowing lanes that made up the poorest section of London's East End.

She had made Colleen guide her here—was it only a week ago?—to show her the worst that London had to offer. She had seen for herself what Colleen had tried to escape on her dangerous journey east. She would do so herself, if she still had life to cherish. Now she could only pray that she could find life to claim.

There were so many, so many who would not be missed. And almost as many whose death would cause rejoicing. She stopped, close to a group of men, drunk and loud. As she hoped, one noticed her, but something in her eyes—the need or the wildness of them—made him halt in his approach, return to his friends and whisper something to them. They moved away with never a glance in her direction.

She went on, stopping finally, with her back to the mouth of a dark alley. She could sense someone in there, could smell fear, need. "Come," she whispered. "Take me from behind. Take me."

Nothing moved. She turned and peered into the darkness. Only a rat digging through a pile of refuse.

She frowned. She had not sensed an animal; something else hid beyond it. Moving out of the shadows, she traveled deeper into the narrow space, her feet above the ground so as not to dirty her shoes.

It was the sound of the hunter perhaps, her little hiss that dissipated nervousness, that brought a response. She heard a quick intake of breath, a startled cry.

Crouching down, she peered into a rotting wooden crate tipped on its side. She saw a child huddled against the back of it, knees drawn tight against its chest, eyes wide and white-rimmed with fear. Though Joanna was certain the child could not see her in the darkness, some change in the current of the air alerted it. "Shoo, snake!" it whispered. Then in a louder, little-girl voice, "Shoo!"

In one swift movement, Joanna pulled the child from her hiding place.

"No!" the girl screamed, kicked her leg and beat at her, but so ineffectively that she posed no real threat. Joanna held her, waiting for the hunger to overpower her, to let her kill. It came, but a glance at the frightened child's face brought something else as well—the memory of another child, dead so long ago.

She had never understood why she let the Gypsy child live while she starved. Having recently relived her past life, she finally saw the truth.

Whatever she was, there was still some ghost of a soul in her, some shred of conscience.

No children. Not ever again. She had put that horror behind her when Illona died.

"It's all right," she whispered to the girl, and tried to smooth back her dirty, tangled hair. "I will not hurt you. Are you hungry?"

The girl looked up at her, trying to see her face. She nodded.

"Then go back to sleep and wait," she said.

She watched until the girl scrambled inside, then shifted again to a mist and rode the almost imperceptible currents of air back to the narrow street and down it to a more prosperous area filled with shops. Though thought was difficult in this form, she focused only on her goal. . . .

Something good. Something sweet. The smell of yeast and honey. Yes. Yes. Here.

. . . And willed herself into the half-open door of a bakery. Though it was still more than an hour until dawn, the owner was already flouring his boards, getting ready to beat down a second batch of dough and start it rising for the ovens.

She took form in the shadows behind his counter and reached for a loaf.

"Who's there? The baker rushed from the back, his face red and wet with sweat from the heat of the ovens. "I told you damn beggars to stay away! This is for decent folk."

He had a long, flat-edged knife in one hand. Joanna stood, human formed, making no move to leave or advance on him. His choice, she thought, make it his.

Her calm made him hesitate. "Get out!" he screamed, then

looked to the door and saw that it was still held shut by its chain.

Too foolish to be frightened, he advanced on her. "How did you get in?" he asked.

She pulled in a breath. "Door," she whispered.

"The hell you did. Now get out the way you got in."

He was close enough to touch now, but she wouldn't move. She could sense the doubt in him, and for a moment wondered if he would back away. But he was too foolish for that. Instead, he grabbed her and began dragging her toward the door.

She pulled away and he slashed with the knife, cutting deep into her arm, again into her shoulder.

It should have been a deep cut. On a mortal, it certainly would have bled or perhaps been fatal. But even before he could attack again or apologize, it began to close.

Illusion, he must have thought, and dismissed what he saw. But the nagging uncertainty led to a rush of fear that only fueled his anger. Though unsteady and slow on his feet due to his girth, he followed her as she scurried back to the narrow space behind the counter where he had first spied her. She retreated until her back was pressed against the wall. He followed, then saw in the dim light from the kitchen the expression on her face—triumphant rather than fearful, as if somehow she had him trapped.

He stepped back. "Get out!" he bellowed.

She did not move.

They stood their ground for a moment—victim and thief, prey and predator—until his patience vanished. He rushed forward, knife in one hand, the other stretched out to grab her. She fought silently, letting the blade cut her more than once, letting the feel of it—that half-remembered mortal pain—give her strength.

Still, the battle between her vampiric nature and her timid human past was stronger than the other, more obvious one. Then the baker slipped on the floor and fell against her, the weight of him dragging her down. The knife he had intended to use more to frighten her than to do actual damage sank deep into her stomach.

She should have died or at least gone slack above him. Instead, she looked down at him as if merely winded. But he saw that she was not even that, because . . . because . . . because there was no breath.

"What are you?" he asked, scrambling away from her. Without warning, he began to scream and stab at her harder and faster, as if by energy expended he could kill.

The choice of life or death was no longer hers—he had made it for her. She pulled back her lips and bit hard into the fatty rolls of his neck, taking out the windpipe as she dug for the main artery. His breath bubbled against her chin. By the time he would have needed another, he was dead, and she sated by the rush of blood and the scent of fresh bread that clung to his hair.

Her brother. Illona. Little Karina. Would the English hunt her now, as they had the others? Uncertain, and wanting to guard her secret, she took the baker's knife and cut through his wrist, stabbed into his chest far more than once, then his neck as well, mutilating the corpse and praying that the cause of death would seem a "typical" human killing.

With that done, she went to the cooling rack and grabbed one of his flour sacks. She filled it with fresh-baked rolls and pastries, then put in the coins he had intended to use as change for the morning rush. She carried all of this through the streets to the narrow alley where the girl waited and laid it all at the mouth of her makeshift shelter. She saw the girl's eyes grow wide when she opened the sack and, in the dim light of a breaking dawn, found the bread and coins.

The girl sped out of the alley and down the narrow street. Keeping to the shadows, she moved quick as a feral cat down a second dirty alley. Joanna followed, watching as she slipped through a window. She heard a cry, a delighted giggle, murmured thanks as the child shared her wealth.

Joanna, unnoticed as the morning mists, watched it all. The feeling that she had somehow atoned for a cowardly act committed centuries before warmed her even more than the baker's blood.

She'd made another important discovery. She could feed in more ways than one.

Embracing the damp air of early morning, she floated back to the shop. There was something more she needed to do.

• • •

When Joanna left the bakery, she'd left the door unlocked, releasing the smell of fresh-baked bread into the misty air. A beggar passing by stopped, mesmerized by the scent. Seeing no one inside, he stole in for a quick theft of a single loaf from a cooling rack near the door. A more timid unfortunate, seeing that no one gave chase after the first thief, did the same. Another followed, then another, scurrying like vermin in the front of the store. Only after the sales racks were completely bare did a woman venture toward the ovens in the rear kitchen and discover the mutilated body behind the sales counter. She screamed, but only once, and she did her best to stifle the sound. Rather than run for the police, she took a pair of hot loaves from the oven, wrapped them in her overskirt and fled.

Above her, unnoticed, a bodiless thing hovered. Watching. Absorbing what was happening below. This latest thief had no knowledge of that presence, but she sensed that others were watching the shop, perhaps the man who had done the deed among them. The woman hurried off as silently as she was able, toward the narrow streets and familiar crimes of her own neighborhood.

At least she would eat well this morning.

The first paying customer in the bakery that morning found the man's body. By then the store was empty, stripped of bread, even the burned ones from the oven and the rising, unbaked loaves beside it.

Later that morning, when Joanna lay on the edge of sleep, she considered the sight of the poor stripping the loaves from the bakery.

When she learned to trust her strength, she would prey upon those poor, the desperate, the ones who would risk anything to better themselves . . . and who had reputations that would ensure they would never be missed, let alone mourned.

Yet there was something wrong with her pleasure, the memory of life gnawing at what remained of her soul.

sixteen

The afternoon following his vigil, Arthur headed down Cheyne Walk, listening to the gossip of the gallery and café owners, straining to pick up any odd piece of news that might be associated with the vampire woman. Nothing, except for the account of a baker's murder that had taken place on the opposite bank, south of Battersea Park.

He'd stopped in a pub for something to eat and was about to finish his brandy when he heard three patrons at a table near his speaking of the crime.

"I hear that the bakery had been picked clean after the owner died. Well, murder's to be expected when there are so many filthy beggars on the streets these days."

Arthur, who had never known a day of hunger in his life, let alone real starvation, nonetheless silently agreed.

"The baker was stabbed, I hear," a patron at a nearby table added.

"Least twenty times. Body looked like mincemeat."

"Jack's back!"

"And moved from whores to bakers?"

"So he finally realized that food is what really matters," a portly man commented, patting his belly.

The men laughed, but nervously. Better to blame the Ripper than some hungry man with no conscience.

After Arthur left the tavern, he stopped at Whistler's to ask if the artist had been sketching the night before but found him absent. Just as well, he thought. His quest was futile, and there was no need to have a gossip like Whistler whispering to others about him. Perhaps Aubrey's consumption had even caused some hallucination. Besides, weren't artists prone to hallucinations anyway?

Nonetheless, he continued the search, walking over the bridge each evening just after dusk. But he saw nothing, and after that first night, felt nothing but the peace of knowing that he had not given up.

In a few days the new habit became a ritual, one he could not abandon, not even for a trip to Exeter.

The night before they were to leave, Arthur pleaded business concerns to Van Helsing, then noted that he had no real need to visit the Harkers. After all, Van Helsing was the expert. His own presence was hardly necessary.

He must have been persuasive, because Van Helsing did not argue. Arthur saw the doctor off at the station that Saturday morning with relief. Now that the old man was gone, Arthur could begin his search. Having thought of one creative way to start, he headed not for Chelsea but for Mayfair and an early luncheon he'd arranged with his family's solicitor.

George Hunt Brooks was not the kind of man Arthur preferred to confide in. He was too old, for one thing, and too strait laced. But he had served Arthur's father and grandfather with the same impeccable attention to details he used in his dress, and he could be counted on to keep a confidence.

He was waiting for Arthur at a quiet table near the back of the restaurant. "It seemed to me on previous occasions that you were often distracted by acquaintances. I thought this would be more conducive to a business discussion," Brooks said when Arthur joined him.

"Quite correct," Arthur said, choosing to ignore the polite criticism. He hadn't told Brooks this was a business discussion, but then what else would he have in common with the stodgy old man? He signaled a waiter to bring him a cup of tea, ordered, and after a few more polite near-pleasantries, got to the point.

"I have a friend to whom I made the mistake of loaning a sum of money. He was about to pay me back when he fell upon some hard times of his own. It seems that he made some investments with an individual from the East who has disappeared with most of his money and, indirectly, a good part of mine."

"That is hardly your concern," Brooks said. "I would stay out of it."

"The man is a friend I value, and he's in a state that makes a legal suit far too expensive unless he is sure of a good outcome. I said I would assist him in getting his funds back. The foreigner we believe stole his investments owns property in England. If it's worth the expense, my friend would like to put a lien on it and make some recovery of the stolen funds."

Brooks actually smiled, convincing Arthur that he believed only the more likely scenario—that Arthur himself had fallen into a bad financial state. Natural, since it would hardly be the first time.

"It would help to know the name of the firm who assisted in the purchase of them," Brooks suggested.

"I know that, but it might not be wise to contact them, considering their duty would be to warn their client."

"I never said you should contact them," Brooks corrected. "But if the purchase was recent, they needed to record it. You can then consult with Frederick Spoerl, who has his offices on Chesterfield. The Germans have a talent for making sense out of our tangled public records."

A second party! And Arthur had been trying to think of how to get Harker to part with the information without putting him on the woman's trail. Brooks had only stated the obvious. "I should have thought of that myself," he grumbled.

"Then I should not be eating this excellent shepherd's pie at your expense," Brooks countered and smiled at his joke.

It was the first time Arthur had ever seen Brooks's teeth beneath that huge mustache he'd cultivated. "Then we should finish with lemon tarts, don't you think?"

"And a brandy. Then, if you've the time, we could walk over to Chesterfield. Spoerl is an acquaintance. If he keeps hours today, I'll make the introduction."

Arthur made the final order immediately, then sat back

and considered his good fortune. If the woman who had come here was indeed Joanna Tepes, she would need her brother's funds and his lands, and the other gifts Dracula would have left for her.

He wanted to find them first.

seventeen

Some two hours before Van Helsing was to arrive on the afternoon train, Mina stopped at Jonathan's office. She paused outside to shake the rain off her umbrella, then waited in the outer room. No stranger to his staff, she chatted with Tom Pierson about his wedding plans until Jonathan's last appointment left, then joined her husband in his office.

Though he had been expecting her, Jonathan felt confused by her presence and the formal note she had written asking if she could stop by early. He wasn't sure if he should kiss her, or pull out a pen and paper and begin discussing the division of their goods. So he merely held her close a moment before returning to his desk chair, frowning, the expression all the more pronounced because of the dark circles under his eyes. "You of all people don't need to make an appointment," he said.

She sat across the desk from him; stiff-backed, awkward, her hands folded in her lap. "In this case, I felt that I should, because it is business advice I need.

"I'm here because I can think of no one I would trust as much as I would you to help me now," she continued, her eyes fixed deliberately on his face.

"I don't quite understand. Are you speaking of a financial matter? Or is it something more?" he asked.

"A charitable matter. The money Gance left me is far more than I will ever need in a lifetime, so I would like to do some good with a part of it, as Winnie and Emory have with theirs."

"You could donate some to their hospital," Jonathan suggested.

"I could, but they already have enough funds to cover their expenses and there are other needs just as pressing. I have already begun searching for a building near the factories, something large with perhaps a bit of land around it. I've spoken with the Reverend Barnett, who runs a charity at St. Jude's in London, about my arrangements—"

"You visited there?"

"I'm not a fool. I wrote him, Jonathan. We met here when he came to address a woman's group about his charity.

"I've also spoken with Dr. Rhys, who operates a free clinic for the poor in our town, and with Winnie. They both suggested a building close to the tanneries. I've looked it over, and consulted with a number of masons and carpenters. It's the right place to lease, or better yet, buy outright."

The tanneries gave off a noxious smell, one that had been thought to cause no end of illness in its workers. And that neighborhood, filled with poor and desperate creatures, was hardly one he would travel through, let alone allow his wife to go there. The thought of her anywhere near that dreadful area filled him with concern, but he kept silent as she continued.

"I would like to create a cooperative rooming house for women with small children. A place where they can leave their children during the day when they go to work and be assured they will be well cared for. I want the children taught the things that will give them a better chance in life than their mothers ever had."

"So you're going to become one of *those* landladies?" he asked.

She scowled at him. "Hardly! I don't intend to profit off misery, as so many do, nor will I have unrealistic expectations regarding women's morality. I merely want to provide them with a safe place in which to live. But, yes, I do intend to charge a modest fee for the service. Perhaps in time the home might even pay for itself and I could use the profits to open another."

"A noble idea . . ." he began cautiously.

"But you have a concern."

"It's the area, Mina. So much thievery. What if someone tries to steal from you and things get out of hand? Or if—"

She cut him off. "I don't intend to run the place myself. I'll have a supervisor and staff for the house, and have the women themselves see to most of its upkeep. Does that satisfy you?"

"I'll be concerned every time you have to go there."

"I'll go in daylight, Jonathan. One thing the past has taught me is that I can face anything in daylight."

He reached across the desk and took her hand, squeezing it lightly.

She pulled out the papers she'd collected on the building as well as estimates from the carpenters and masons who would be needed to make it inhabitable. Jonathan recognized the name of the agent handling the building but none of the rest. "How did you find these people?" he asked.

"Through Winnie and Dr. Rhys. Many of them live in that area. It seemed wisest to use local craftsmen and add to the wealth there. But I have no idea how to determine if they're reputable."

"I have a client who owns a number of properties throughout the city. He might know of them."

"You will help, then?"

"Mina! As long as you are careful, I think the plan is admirable. Just don't name the damn place after him."

The moment he said the words, he regretted them. They reminded him and Mina both of the wall surrounding her, making them both prisoners of her wealth.

She apparently did not share his thoughts, because she placed her gloved hand over his and said sweetly, "Dr. Van Helsing's train is due at the station in less than an hour. The sun has come out again, and the air will do us both good. Shall we walk?"

They did. And during the length of the half-mile stroll, he held her arm. He patted her hand often, and when they stopped near the cathedral, kissed her on the forehead. "Whatever happens, know that I care for you," he whispered.

She looked at his face. In daylight, the circles beneath his eyes seemed deeper, his pallor too light, as if he were being possessed by the memories of those creatures and the dreams he had. "I can come home for a time, Jonathan. I would like to do that and to care for you."

"Then she would possess us both. I know it."

"Perhaps it isn't her doing the possessing," she said and kissed him again, on the lips and with such ardor that he found himself responding with open eyes, trying to see who might be staring at them.

She moved away, and they went on slowly, arm in arm, until hearing the distant train whistle, they moved more quickly toward the station.

Van Helsing was in a gruff state of mind. He'd been trying to read while on the train, but the uneven tracks made it impossible. He'd tried to meditate, but a gaggle of unruly children kept breaking through the moments of calm. Worse, he could blame no one but himself for the past two hours, since he had opted to save some money and travel by coach.

However, the sight of Mina standing beside her husband at the station cheered him. She hadn't spoken of any reconciliation in her letter, but it seemed from their expressions that things were going well.

He soon learned that their happiness had been directed less at each other than at seeing him. It troubled him that they weren't together, for after what they had been through and the love they so obviously possessed for each other, they deserved a happy ending.

He was hardly well versed in matters of the heart, but perhaps on this visit he could think of something to bring them together. He considered this on the long, silent ride to their home.

The brick house seemed charming on the outside, yet once through the doorway he was astonished at how stuffy the place seemed. His study had the same feel, but he was an old man and used to claustrophobic surroundings. Had Mina done nothing during the time she lived here?

It occurred to him that this had not been so long ago and that the couple had just been married when Dracula arrived in London. Had it only been a half year since their trials began? It seemed that they had all aged a lifetime during them.

• • •

The three settled into Jonathan's study; Van Helsing with his pipe, Jonathan with a cigar. Mina seemed the most ill at ease, moving between kitchen and parlor, bringing them tea and a light meal of sliced beef and cheese and fresh bread they had bought at a shop near the station. When Jonathan began to describe his dreams in detail, she left the room altogether to spare him the embarrassment of having to relate such erotic details in her presence.

She sat at the dining room table, sipping a second cup of tea while watching a bronze sliver of the setting sun that had forced itself under the storm clouds and through a thin crack in the heavy draperies. It crept slowly across the carpeted floor until it reached the far wall and ascended. She should leave for home now, if she were going. But now that at least a part of their little band was reunited, she was loath to abandon them and thankful that she had told Essie that she might not return until tomorrow.

As she paged through a day-old issue of the *Times,* she could hear Jonathan's voice, almost a whisper; Van Helsing's occasional, louder, reply. The words were indistinct, and she did not try to make them out.

An hour passed. The sun set, the stillness of evening marred with the distant sound of another approaching squall.

She'd just begun a second magazine when Van Helsing called her into the room. "You should both hear what little bit I know about the creature," he said.

Mina sat beside Jonathan on the sofa, the pair of them facing the doctor like two schoolchildren in the presence of a revered tutor. She wanted to correct the old man, to tell him that this was not a "creature" at all but a woman. But pupils did not correct their teachers.

"Joanna is Dracula's sister, that much is certain from the records I have studied," Van Helsing said. She was apparently of mixed Arab and European blood. Most likely her mother was a slave or servant in Vlad Dracul's castle. She was sent east with her mother when she was just a child, perhaps because the man truly cared for them both and thought they would be happier among their own.

"The mother's fate is lost in time, but Joanna apparently lived as some sort of prisoner in the East. During one of Dracula's raids, he rescued her from her captors. They have been together some little time." He smiled at this. "I would think she must miss him, and if her blood runs true with his, she will come."

"Would that Karina had written more about her," Mina commented. "But I wonder if she possesses the will to move from that crumbling ruin. She seemed quite mad when I last saw her."

"She may not have that strength," Van Helsing said. "But the so-terrible force that animates her body is tenacious. I believe she will be forced to leave that place and follow her master's plan. Jonathan's dreams are those of a victim sensing an imminent attack. Yes, she will come."

"Then why don't I dream of her? Or you? Or the others?"

"She did not feed on any of us. It is his blood in her that binds them. We can only hope that she does not feel the same terrible pull. But if she does, we must be prepared."

As soon as Van Helsing spoke the words, Mina looked at Jonathan. He tried to hide his alarm, but she knew him too well for him to succeed. As for her, she felt unusually calm. It was if the faith in Fate that Dr. Rhys had spoken of had altered her perception of life, much as the experience she had been through had altered her belief in the hereafter. Once she had been an agnostic. Now the phrase "all things on heaven and earth" came often to her mind.

She explained that she had already warned her servant. They discussed whether Jonathan should do the same with his clerks. "Not if I wish to remain in my profession," he grumbled.

"Tell them that you have been threatened by a madwoman. Make up some story to go with it so they will tell you if they see her," Mina suggested.

"Better to send them home each night well before dark and keep my reputation completely unsullied."

"And if you will die at her hands, it will be as a proper gentleman," Mina commented, her tone sounding almost innocent.

"What do you want me to do?" Jonathan shouted, then looked at her, stunned by his outburst.

"What you are doing," Van Helsing answered. "But she is

right: Be aware of the greater risk you take with this discretion."

The conversation soon shifted to more mundane subjects. Van Helsing spoke of his research and his travels through England. Jonathan discussed the firm, but briefly, noting that recent events had not hurt his practice. "If anything, it seems stronger than ever," he said.

All of Mina's spare time for the past few weeks had been spent on the house she'd inherited. She could hardly speak of that. But when Van Helsing asked about her activities, she answered immediately, discussing how she met Essie and the charitable endeavor that meeting had led to.

"You must promise to make certain that you will not let the less fortunate take advantage of your woman's heart," Van Helsing warned. "The poor are more subject to temptation than those who can afford to avoid it."

"Mina has assured me that it won't be charity," Jonathan said.

With growing enthusiasm, Mina explained the rest of her plan.

"And where will you find these women who need a safe shelter?"

"I will take referrals from two people I trust: my friend Winnie Beason, whom you've met, and Dr. Felix Chandra Rhys, who recently opened a charity practice here."

"Dr. Rhys. I know of him. I've had a professional acquaintance speak highly of his skill even though he is Hindu. I should like an introduction if possible," Van Helsing said.

"Hardly difficult. I'm meeting him tomorrow afternoon. You may join us if you wish."

"Good. Now, you will excuse an old man who needs his sleep. Jonathan, I need to know my room."

The question should have been a simple one, yet Jonathan hesitated and glanced at Mina before replying, "The guest room. I'll show you the way." He left with the professor's bag while Van Helsing stopped for a moment to kiss Mina on the cheek and wish her a good night.

Once she was alone, she poured herself a sherry and a second glass for Jonathan. When he returned, she was sitting near the window, both hands cupping her glass and staring out at the stormy night. He glanced at her, then took the second glass from the butler's table and sat in the place where Van Helsing had been.

"There are things we need to discuss," she said.

"It doesn't need to be now," he replied.

"One thing must be settled. Jonathan, do you wish to be married to me?"

"I don't know. Sometimes I think it would be best to part. But then . . . I, I only wish I weren't so certain that when you are with me you aren't thinking of me."

A memory from the recent past surfaced in her. Without a word, she went to Jonathan's desk and opened a drawer. As she expected, his sketchpad was still in its usual place. When she laid it on edge on the desktop, it fell open to the drawing he had made of a naked Illona Tepes, the one she had caught him studying some months before. His face was red with embarrassment even before she held it up for him to see.

"Fantasies aren't sins, Jonathan. We all have them. But what's past is in the past. I think of him more often than I might have if I weren't living in his house, but I do not dwell on his memory any more than you do on the memory of this creature."

He took in her words, considered. "I want you to give it up," he finally said. "The house. The funds. All of it. I want you to come home and be my wife and live with me as we had planned."

Planned, she thought. When had they ever had time to plan? He proposed. She accepted. Then he was gone, off to a strange, foreign land to meet with creatures no one could have imagined existed.

And even when they returned as husband and wife, they'd planned nothing. They were to live instead as society demanded. Yes, it would have been a safe life, secure and empty until the children came to occupy her time. Emptier still when they abandoned her, as children must.

Once she had begged Jonathan to let her work at his firm. But he had placed others' notions of respectability above her wishes. Would he have done so if the vampire had not intruded on their lives? Would he have listened if he had not thought her tainted?

No matter. What was past, was past. Gance had given her freedom.

"I can't," she said. "I won't."

He gripped his glass so hard, she was certain it would break. "Nothing's changed then. Perhaps we both need time."

She finished her brandy in one quick gulp. "Where would you like me to sleep?"

"In *our* room," he said. "I'll take Aunt Millicent's in the attic. She would prefer me there, I think."

Millicent. One more reminder of why Mina could not stay. As she left the room, she saw him walk toward the sideboard where the decanter of brandy was kept.

Since she hadn't brought a change of clothes, she put on one of Jonathan's nightshirts, slipped into the familiar softness of their bed, and blew out the candle. The window had been shuttered through the day and could not be opened now because of the rain. The room's damp, warm air felt stifling. She lay beneath a thin sheet, but every time she began to drift off to sleep, a flash of lighting or roll of thunder would startle her awake. She waited until the rain beating on the roof subsided to a soft whisper, then slipped out of bed and opened the window that looked out on the walled rear garden. The cooler night air fell against her. A distant flash of lightning silhouetted the nearby houses. She thought of how Dracula had first come to her on a night such as this, and how Jonathan had once spoken of the vampire women and how storms made them restless.

No wonder. Even the most protected chamber could be invaded by a downward stroke of lightning, flooded by the rains, ripped apart by the winds. God's judgment, she'd heard a minister call it. She'd been a little girl then, experiencing her first twinges of conscience, and every small misdeed had convinced her that she was deserving of that judgment. She had been terrified of storms for years. She'd eventually outgrown the terror, come to love the wild nights.

As to God's judgment, He had reserved it until much later. He took her father to Him when she was only twelve, her mother some years later. The only things they had left her was the house she'd been raised in and a small sum of money, enough to see her through school and into marriage.

And it could have been such a good one if God's judgment, or Rhys' notion of Fate, or her own too-strong will had not intervened.

The thunder cracked, closer now, as if the heavens were in agreement.

"Are you thinking of him now?" Jonathan asked.

She whirled and saw him standing in the doorway, his hair all rumpled, his nightshirt damp against his skin. "I thought I'd come and open your window, but you got there first," he said.

He'd come to this room for other reasons, though he might not know them. And if she had been sleeping, would he have stood in the darkness, watching her? Watching but afraid to touch?

She bit back the words that came unbidden to her mind, saying instead, "I couldn't sleep. It seemed so strange being here alone."

She lit the candle and looked at him with concern. "Are you ill?" she asked. "Or did you have another dream?"

"It's just the heat. It's even worse in the attic rooms."

"Come here, then. There's a cool breeze coming through the window."

He moved beside her and, more by instinct than plan, she took his hand.

A draft of air slipped under her nightshirt, sending a shiver down her spine. She felt her nipples harden beneath the thin white cotton. Another flash of lightning made his face seem stark and white. He looked at her then, as if possessed, and kissed her for the first time since she'd left him.

She responded, and as they embraced, by some wordless agreement, they moved toward the bed. As they fell on it, she felt a cold moment of calm and sanity. Tonight would complicate things between them. He would expect concessions, agreements she could not make.

But she had agreed to nothing, she reminded herself. And this was too right to resist.

Take the moment and be thankful for it, she thought, then realized it was the sort of advice Gance would have given.

Her hands undid the buttons of his nightshirt as he raised hers up to her breasts, his hands moving over them, his lips following. She responded, being careful to do only the things that would seem natural to him, things they had done together before.

Later, Jonathan lay beside her, sleeping so deeply that she knew he must have been exhausting himself for days. Were the dreams so terrible? More likely troublesome, she thought.

As for herself, sleep came harder. She watched the window, the glass flashing white in the occasional burst of lightning. When it began to rain again, she got up to close it. As she moved toward it, another flash left a shadowy, almost human image on the wall above their bed. Was it a trick of light and rain on the glass? A dream? An illusion created by her mind? If the last, was it Gance or Joanna? She waited, peering in that direction, but in the next flash the image was gone.

"Mina," Jonathan called softly from the bed.

"I'm here. I closed the window." She walked back to the bed and lay behind him, pressed close, and wrapped an arm around his chest.

Outside, the rain came down hard.

She did not envy anyone without shelter tonight.

eighteen

While the Harkers were meeting the train, Arthur Holmwood took possession of the addresses of Dracula's holdings in the London area. He studied the list, crossing off those he and the others had already invaded and made useless for the vampire's rest. After mapping a course that would allow him to see as many of the sites as possible in the daylight, he put the list away and spent of the rest of the evening reading. His choice was deliberate— "A Scandal in Bohemia" by Doyle, which had just been published in *The Strand.*

The next morning, he rose far earlier than his usual custom. He dug in the back of his closet and found a dated black chesterfield and derby he hadn't worn since his uncle's funeral some three years earlier. He put it on, stood in front of a full-length mirror and studied the effect. Yes, he decided, he did look much like a businessman; prosperous, but hardly likely to attract attention in even the worst of the areas he intended to visit.

He rummaged through his desk and pulled out a number of cards that belonged to Derrick Smythe, a young and not particularly ethical accountant he'd had the misfortune of meeting once too often. Their brief association had cost him dearly, but at least all the damn cards Smythe had stuffed in his pocket would serve a purpose. He placed them in his inside breast pocket—ready to be handed out should someone inquire who he was.

As to what he was doing in a place that did not belong to

him, if he were asked, he would say he was inspecting the property for the owner, whom he represented.

And if he were questioned too harshly, he would simply leave his card and ask the questioning party to contact his employer. Smythe, who looked a bit like him, might have an alibi or might not. Arthur really didn't care.

He wondered if there were others who read Doyle's work for education rather than entertainment. If so, the world was bound to become a far more deceitful place soon enough.

He thought of riding but decided a horse would attract too much attention. So he hailed a hansom instead.

His search began in the East End—not in the roughest part, but farther out. The count had, as in many cases, leased two properties close together. The creature was clever, Arthur gave him credit for that. If the vampire were tracked to one and daylight was upon him, he could easily reach another and take shelter. Both of them were single-story places with cellars. Heartened, he asked the hansom to wait and boldly went up to the door of one of them and pounded on it. When no one answered, he made a show of putting a key in the lock and jiggling it for a time. When it would not open, he signaled the driver to wait and moved to the back. There, out of sight of the driver, he broke in.

The interior of the building was musty, the floor covered with dust, the windows with cobwebs and the yellow patina of age. There was no sign that anyone had lived there in the past few months, which surprised him. Given the poverty he saw in the streets, Arthur had fully expected to have to evict a squatter from every property.

Though he already knew Dracula had never been here, he checked the cellar. It was empty except for a rotting board that had fallen in from the outer trapdoor, small bones of birds and rodents scattered around and the reek of a cat.

The second house, some three blocks away, was empty even of feline squatters. Arthur moved on.

By midafternoon he'd seen eight properties in varying states of repair, but only two squatters, a young sister and brother who were using one of the smaller places as a shelter.

The boy, no more than ten or so, tried to duck under his arm and out the door. Arthur grabbed him by the collar and jerked him back, ordering the older girl to remain where she was as well.

The boy rubbed his neck as he stammered some boldface lie about his parents having leased the place. Arthur admired his cheek and handed him ten bob and one of Smythe's cards. "Since you're here and you've done no damage, feel free to stay. Watch the place for me and the other one as well." He provided a description of Dracula's other holding in the area. "I'll check on you from time to time. If you notice anything out of the ordinary here or there, I'll pay for the information. But just you and your sister stay here, understand?"

The boy broke into a grin and nodded. Arthur studied the pair. Beneath the grime, they had good color and healthy teeth. Through theft or begging, they were at least eating well.

When he left, it occurred to him that if Joanna came to this place, they would be in some danger. "Not half of what they'd have on an average street in that part of town," he decided. Besides, they'd be his eyes and ears—his own Baker Street Irregulars, wasn't that what Holmes called them?

It was nearly dusk when he found what he'd been seeking—in a house on a quiet street near St. Giles Church. The moment the hansom pulled up in front of it, he sensed it. The house was in good repair, as were most of the homes around it, so it was unlikely to attract intruders. It also had long, narrow windows of thick leaded glass, far more difficult to break and enter. Most interesting were the basement windows, boarded up from the inside.

As he'd done before, he asked the driver to wait. This time he didn't even bother to try the front door. Instead, he went around back and knocked as always. To his surprise, the door was opened by a young woman. Clean and well dressed, she could hardly be a squatter. But she was nervous, terribly so. When he looked past her, he saw only a table and two chairs in the kitchen, and an empty pantry beyond. Since she looked ready to slam the door on him, he decided to put her at ease as best he could. "I am Mr. Smythe," he said. "I represent the gentleman who leased this house. He's out of the country for some weeks and asked me to check up on his properties."

She stepped away from the door, and the frantic look on

her face made him add, "Not that there have been any complaints, of course. But I do wonder who you might be."

"Stella Cunningham. My father owned this house until he died two years ago. My husband and I had a . . . disagreement. I had heard the place was empty and tried my key. I don't think he will look for me here."

She hid her emotions well, but Arthur sensed that she was desperate. He could well guess what sort of disagreement could send a woman into hiding. "Did you plan to remain here long?" he asked.

"I've sent word to my sister in Leeds. As soon as I receive her reply, I'll be leaving."

He already knew what he would do, but for effect considered the matter. "I suppose that since you've done no damage, it would be all right if you stayed for a few more days. He'll never even know you were here. I do need to inspect the house, however . . . check for water leaks, that sort of thing." He walked past her, his black hat in his hand. The pantry was empty, the rooms beyond it as well. In what would be the bedroom, he found a pile of blankets serving as a bed, and a bag full of clothing, apparently quickly packed.

Returning to the kitchen, he opened the cellar door and saw dust on the damp and narrow steps leading to the basement. Could his instincts be so wrong?

"There's an outside door on the north side that might be easier than this," the woman told him.

And he'd walked right past it! Buried in the bushes, no doubt. "I prefer to try the stairs," he said. He pulled a candle and light from his pocket. A draft from below blew out the light before he reached the third step down.

"Wait! I have a lamp," Stella suggested, and brought it from the bedroom.

He went down, gripping the rickety railing. Below it was a small room, separated from the main room beyond. In it, he found the box.

It was much like the ones that he and the others had blessed in the area around Purfleet—long and narrow and plain enough to escape any attention. The hinges looked sturdy, the lock less so. He pulled out a screwdriver and broke the hasp easily.

With his heart pounding from too many memories, he lifted the lid. But this box was empty, blessedly so, for he had no desire to come upon his quarry too early in the hunt. But it did have earth beneath the false floor. He suspected that it would bc heavy, but not impossible, for two people to carry. He checked the outside door. As he'd expected, it was barred on the inside. Vampires had no need for doors, no concern for locks, but they did know the value of keeping the curious well away from their lairs.

The woman was waiting for him at the top of the stairs. "Will you be here another day or so, Mrs. Cunningham?"

"I believe so."

"Good. My employer has a trunk in the basement that he wishes moved. I'll be coming by tomorrow with some movers. I wanted to tell you so that you wouldn't be alarmed when we arrived."

She smiled, and nervously brushed a stray lock of hair off her forehead. "Thank you for being so understanding," she said.

"No thanks are needed. I wish you the best," he said and left, feeling more than a little pleased with himself. Not only had the search been a success, but also he'd done a pair of good deeds. And tomorrow when he came, he'd do a third and bring a bit of food for the woman just in case she was too frightened or too poor to shop for herself.

"You were gone so long, I thought you'd left," the hansom driver grumbled when he saw Arthur. "Then I remembered that you hadn't paid me fare."

"I'll pay more than that if you can get a cart and a couple of strong fellows for tomorrow morning. I need a trunk moved."

"That's all. You and me could handle it, if you don't mind getting your suit a bit dirty."

"It can wait until tomorrow."

"Well, it won't be hard to get fellows to help on the Sabbath these days," the driver commented. "Too many hungry to observe the Lord's demands. Where to now?"

Arthur glanced at his pocket watch. "Take me to Cheyne Walk."

"Another stop?" the driver asked. "Me horse has to eat sometime."

"This time I'll be getting out. But you can meet me tomorrow at ten at Grosvenor Square."

He sat back and shut his eyes. In spite of the lurch of the hansom, he dozed off until the driver called that they'd reached his stop. He left the man with a generous payment for the day's work and reminded him of tomorrow's meeting.

He had accomplished the first of his goals, and was convinced that the second would soon follow. He should have been excited, even elated. But as he started across the bridge, a terrible sense of doom pressed down on him. The course he would follow went against every piece of advice he'd been given. But he had no choice. He needed answers, and the only one who could provide them was the vampire.

He sat on the same bench in the center of the park and waited as the mists closed in. As always, he saw nothing, and sensed nothing but the feeling that someone was watching him with great and terrible interest.

"Soon enough," he whispered, and with a resigned shrug, headed back across the bridge toward Hyde Park and home.

The following morning, the hansom driver met him as arranged. He'd brought an open cart and a pair of young Irishmen to help them. More coins than words were exchanged before Arthur took a seat in the back, as far away from his companions as possible. Did the poor of London ever bathe? he wondered while the cart alternately lurched forward, then stopped with little warning, throwing him against one of the dirty creatures as the driver tried to avoid hitting anyone in the early-morning throng.

Arthur had brought a round of cheese and some biscuits for the woman, but when they arrived, they found her gone. So his reassurance had no effect on her. In her position, he wouldn't have trusted a stranger either. But she had done him one good turn. She'd left the back door open, saving him an explanation of why he was breaking into the place.

The box was heaver than he'd expected—"lead bricks," one of the men called it—while another was sure he'd committed murder and they were carrying out the body.

"No body weighs this much unless it's made of stone," the driver said. The others laughed, but the mirth was short-lived. With much swearing, the four of them maneuvered it out of the cellar and onto the cart. Arthur and the driver got in the front, the Irishmen in the back to watch the box so it wouldn't break loose of the rope holding it.

"Where we be taking it?" the driver asked once they were settled in.

Arthur gave his Kensington address.

"That's a damn fine distance in this traffic," the driver grumbled.

"And well worth your while," Arthur reminded him.

The Kensington estate had come to Arthur through his uncle. In the past, Arthur had used it rarely, much preferring the trio of rooms he kept in Mayfair for his forays into London society. Since his tastes lay with the theater crowd and their late-night hours, so long a drive would have run counter to common sense as well as inclination. He left the estate in the hands of its gardener, who regarded the acre around it as his personal Eden, and his wife, who acted as maid and cook.

But then he became engaged to a woman who could not have fit her closet into all his bachelor quarters. So he added a maid and stableboy to the Kensington staff and sent his butler, Ian, on ahead to see to organizing the staff and getting the house ready for his bride.

After she died, he could only walk into the house he'd come to regard as hers with the greatest of difficulty. But he could hardly let the staff go, not when the place was finally coming into its own. Though he could hardly sell it in these troubled times, he thought to keep it up and dispose of it as soon as he could.

Then he decided to woo a vampire, and again the Mayfair flat was hardly the place. Even without the presence of one old and inconvenient houseguest, it was too busy, with too many friends coming and going at all hours. He did not know Joanna except through Mina and the journal translation, but he knew enough to understand her need for solitude. And she had been royalty. The Kensington estate might suit her.

So, reluctantly, he returned to it and began to ready it for another, far more exotic, conquest.

He'd planned his arrival well. Once they passed through the iron gates of his acre estate, he had the driver go round to the servants' entrance at the back and carry the box through the kitchen, up the rear stairs and into the large windowless storage room at the end of the guest wing. It was Sunday, so everyone was at church. They would not be disturbed, no questions would be asked.

After the men left—each pleasantly surprised by how much Arthur had paid them—Arthur opened the box again. He pulled up a corner of its lining and rested his hand on the cold earth.

"How could they live like . . ." he began to say aloud, then broke into laughter. They didn't live like this. They were already dead.

The room was about six meters square and only half full. He cleared away the crates and odd pieces of furniture from the dimly lit rear of it and slid the box into the farthest corner. He covered it with some of the boxes that had originally been stacked there, then placed others around it.

An hour later, he stood in the doorway and surveyed the result. He could see that things had been moved, but he couldn't see the box itself. A needless precaution. Judging from the dust on the clutter in it, the room had not been opened in years.

With this part of his work finished, it was time to begin the quest.

He'd already compared the addresses he'd been given with the place where Aubrey had seen Joanna and had a good idea where he would find her.

nineteen

When Mina opened her eyes on Sunday morning, she saw Jonathan lying above her, his head propped up on one arm. She stretched, reached up and brushed her hand over his hair. "Do you always watch me so?" she asked.

"Only when it's been too long since I've awakened to find you here. The same side as always, the same pillow."

His tone was not needy, nor demanding, but the words implied both. She smiled, kissed him on the cheek and slipped out of bed. Stretching, she inhaled and detected the faint scent of Van Helsing's tobacco. "Your guest is awake. Perhaps we should go down and prepare some breakfast."

"He got up a little while ago and settled in the study. I don't think we need hurry."

He looked so rumpled, so happy, so unlike the neat Jonathan of the carefully pressed suit and polished boots and starched collar. She wanted to return to him and yet . . . what had happened last night had been a beginning to reconciliation, no more. It would be too easy to fall into that old stifling pattern.

"We should go down," she repeated, softening the words with another touch, her hand brushing the top of his, her lips on his forehead. "The professor may wish to go to church. And I am meeting Dr. Rhys at two." She took off his nightshirt as if there were nothing unusual in her being here, and began to dress.

Three hours later, after a pleasant breakfast and a quick

service at a nearby church, Mina and Van Helsing left Jonathan and walked to the doctor's lodgings.

It was hardly in the best part of town, something in keeping with the doctor's inclination to live among those he served. But Mina had expected a more prosperous-looking building than the two-story brick structure with its dirty windows.

The doctor had a lower apartment, and so his own doorway. He answered the door wearing loose-fitting pants and a long tunic, both in white cotton. The room was dark and smelled strongly of incense.

"I hope you don't mind, I've brought a friend to meet you," she said. "This is Dr. Van Helsing, also a physician."

As they were introduced, Van Helsing shook the younger doctor's hand, holding it a moment while he noted its strength and steadiness. "Have you done surgeries?" he asked.

Rhys shook his head. "Cuts and such, yes. Even amputations. But the rest . . ." His voice trailed off. He paused, then added, "I have no constitution for that, and without it I am more than useless."

"Not useless, for Mrs. Harker speaks too highly of you."

"I do what I can to treat illness, but we have so much to learn about the soul as well as the body."

"Yes, yes. The soul," Van Helsing said, then asked the doctor, "Are you familiar with young Freud's work?"

"Enough to agree with most of it." He added something in German.

Van Helsing replied in the same language. The conversation between them continued. Mina, who did not understand, found herself studying the sparse office until she heard her name mentioned. "Yes?" she asked.

"Ah, Madame Mina! I am sorry. I sometimes forget that not everyone—"

"It's fine, Professor. I'm glad to see you so animated."

"And will be for a time. Dr. Rhys has a most interesting philosophy. He has invited us out for an early dinner. Shall we accept?"

"You accept, Professor. I'd promised Winnie that I would stop by tonight. Emory is off to London on some business trip, and I said I'd keep her company if I were free. Will you be going back to Jonathan's?"

"No. I wish to go with you, Madame Mina. I should like to see your home."

Direct. But then, he was always direct. She often thought that the professor's ability to see through fashion and manners to the core of things was his most charming virtue.

They arranged to meet at five. As she left the dark apartment office, she turned back to see the two men, so different in looks and age and background, conversing with quick, excited gestures.

After a long visit with Winnie Beason, Mina walked the few blocks to the house she still thought of as home to retrieve the professor's bag. Rather than disturb Jonathan, she used her key. As she'd expected, he was in his study, going over his schedules for the following week at work.

"I'll see you home," he said and began putting things away.

"The professor can see me home. It will be late by the time we get there, and I would worry about you."

He walked around the desk to where she was standing. "You will come again, though?"

"Do you wish me to?"

He walked around the desk to where she stood. She expected an answer, not the kiss he gave her, one that left her a bit breathless from its unexpectedness and intensity.

She leaned against him for a time, reveling in the feel of his arms, the warmth of his body. "We still haven't settled anything," she reminded him after a time.

"This was how you wanted us to settle it in Paris. I think you were right."

She found herself amused by the need to mentally consult her own schedule, then out of conscience compare it to his. "Tuesday," she said, knowing Wednesday was usually his least busy day. "I'll meet you at the office if you wish."

"Here, please," he suggested. "I want to come home and find you here."

She had been a fool to agree. A fool!

She met Van Helsing just as he was saying good-bye to Dr. Rhys. As they drove along, Van Helsing told her a bit about his evening and plans he and Rhys had made to meet in London later that month. She tried to listen, but her thoughts were on Jonathan until they reached the house.

• • •

Essie had been busy in her absence. The added rooms were a long way from finished, but the windows and doors were all in place, and Essie had swept the smaller room and moved her things in there. "I expected you would have company," she said.

And there was a hot stove to start some tea. Essie served it, then retreated to continue setting up her room. Mina and the professor sat at the little table in the solarium with their cups and sugar. It was twilight, but Mina did not light a lamp, and the professor did not ask her to. Finally he said, "This seems more your place, dear Mina."

"It feels so. Then I go home and I wonder."

"I wanted you to come back to him immediately. I see you now, so sure of yourself and what you want to do. Then I worry. I think you will not be there for him in his time of need, or that he may not want you. Thankfully, I misjudged the affection beneath the love."

"There will be enough of both, on both our parts."

He sat without responding, tamping his pipe, waiting for her to go on. When she didn't, he commented, "Your Dr. Rhys speaks well of the work you plan."

"You've seen so much more of the world than I. What did you think of him?"

"I thought him less as an Indian than an Englishman with a curious philosophy."

"How so?"

"He is so rigidly English in his beliefs. Something is right, or something is wrong. There are no in-betweens, yet he says he believes in reincarnation and Fate. The philosophies are hardly compatible. So fascinating, though. I enjoyed our discussion, as did he. We have already agreed to meet again in London next time he visits there."

"Should I rely on him so much?"

"I believe you should. That hardness at his core will make him a better judge of those you can help than your too-soft heart would ever be."

"And I can help so few."

He pointed at the river, glowing in the twilight. "When you

throw a stone in the water you start a ripple. The few you help will help others. And you are not done."

Arthur would seduce me. Jonathan would contain me, and Dr. Rhys and the professor would likely canonize me. All of it seems too silly, she wrote in her journal just before bed. She summarized the events of the past few weeks, ending with an account of the night before and Jonathan, then added a final introspection:

> *I left him, head reeling with the possible consequences of what I had agreed to. Am I capitulating too fast, victim of a woman's heart? I do not know the outcome, but I had already examined my feelings, enough to know that I still love him. He is the man I fell in love with, the man I married. But at my core, I am not the woman I was. He needs to see me for what I am now, then judge.*
>
> *But to put myself apart from him will deny him that chance. And so I will go to him, as I vowed so recently that I would not, and I will try to see him as a mistress sees a lover—one night at a time.*

twenty

This July, London was warmer and sunnier than during any other summer Colleen could remember. Or perhaps it only seemed that way to her. But though it would have been natural for her to adopt her mistress's habit and rest by day, Colleen fought the desire. There were things that had to be done in daylight—and so she would put on her largest bonnet, a black cloak that made her look like some impoverished governess, and go about the mundane business of life. She shopped for food, enough nearly for the both of them, though only she ate. She had curtains made for all the windows—heavy velvet that would keep out nearly all the light so that should Joanna rise early, she would not be burned. She visited seamstresses, ordering gowns for her mistress from the measurements she herself had taken and the ideas Joanna had conveyed to her during their rare hours together.

The house in Chelsea was so tiny it seemed to be a cottage lifted from some tenant farmer and plucked down in the center of the city. It had a small front parlor, a smaller kitchen and two sleeping rooms. The larger of the two had a pair of north-facing windows that, like those in the parlor, looked onto the street. The second, tinier, room had no windows at all and a stout door with a recently added lock. Joanna told her that her brother would have found the place perfect because of the room and door and lock but that the rest would have no meaning for him at all.

Perhaps a male, and a barbarian, would not have found the little place charming, but Joanna did.

"The first home that is mine," Joanna called it as she handed Colleen money to furnish the place. "Fill it with colors," she ordered.

Thrifty by nature, Colleen found a bed for her room, a pair of wicker rockers, and a table and a lamp for the parlor. Not colorful, but she added bright cushions to the chairs, a red glass shade for the lamp, then spent almost as much as all that cost together on a tapestry-patterned rug for the floor.

Joanna approved of each addition, but especially the rockers. In early evenings when the sun hid its burning face behind the thick British clouds, she would rise and open the window and sit beside Colleen. As they talked, she would look out at the people rushing by. She confessed that she felt as if she were one of them, separated by language and culture, not by centuries.

But after a few weeks in the house, Joanna began to explore the city. Soon it seemed to Colleen that she lived alone.

Joanna would rise at dusk or a bit earlier if the day were cloudy. She would say a few words to Colleen, then be off, leaving Colleen to worry until she returned sometime well before sunrise. Often the new gowns were ripped or stained.

"What do you do out there for all those hours?" Colleen demanded one evening as she sat close to the lamp, mending yet another tear. She knew the words and tone made her sound so much like a jealous lover, but she felt helpless to stop them from coming.

"I watch. I learn," Joanna replied.

The last was true. The vampire's English had improved so markedly that most would assume she had lived in London for years.

"But you don't hunt," Colleen went on, examining one of the stains on the hem to see if it might be blood.

"Just that once," Joanna said, and moved close to her, running her fingers lightly down the side of Colleen's face, her neck. She pressed her lips against Colleen's, then the side of her neck, her ear. She whispered, "Would you like me to do it now, *draga*? To make you my companion forever?"

Colleen fought the urge to pull away or to scream. "No," she said softly, "you need someone for the daylight."

"I can find someone else to take care of us, someone for the daylight."

But though Colleen accepted, and sometimes thought she would welcome that change, there were parts of that future that frightened her. She had always hated closed spaces, and so the thought of that necessary daytime box and the smell of cold earth beneath her made her uneasy. Then there was the unsettling thought that for those hours when she slept, she would be at the mercy of anyone who found the box and opened it, even if their intent was merely idle curiosity. Most of all, her mind dwelled too often on a comment Joanna had made when she first explained the change—that silence that death would bring. "Let me be your daytime eyes a while longer," she begged.

"For a time," Joanna agreed, long fingers undoing the laces on the top of Colleen's workdress and the chemise beneath, green eyes watching the folds of fabric fall off her servant's shoulders, revealing the marks of Joanna's feedings on her breasts—two older wounds nearly healed, the most recent so deep that it never quite closed. Colleen took to pressing scraps of cloth against it before she laced up her thin corset.

Occasionally even that wasn't enough. The blood would seep through, something she did not notice until she saw people staring. Once someone in the market commented to her that she was bleeding. Flustered, she'd stammered something about a scrape and rushed home to soak the stain out of the white cotton.

Her mistress's touch sent a shiver of pleasure through Colleen, reminding her of a question she'd not asked. "Can you take a lover after the change?"

Joanna smiled, revealing the sharp front teeth; the longer, sharper canines. "Haven't I?" she asked.

Her hands, demanding, pushed the cloth down over Colleen's hips, to fall in a heap on the floor. The corset. Her arms circled Colleen's waist. Colleen gave into the pressure, falling backward, knowing her mistress could easily support her. As she did, the wound stretched open, waiting for those lips.

Tonight Joanna took far more blood than usual, and as Colleen weakened in her arms, her legs gave way. Joanna caught her, and lifting her, carried her to the bed, arranging her on top of the covers. Kisses light as mist brushed against the girl's body, hands fluttered on breasts and thighs. Only half awake, with neither the strength nor the inclination to resist, Colleen let her legs be pushed apart, let the cold, delicate hands rub against those private parts until she responded finally with the shudders and small moans of pleasure Joanna remembered from so long ago.

She stretched out beside her lover then, and with one hand still pleasuring, brought the girl's face to her breast to nurse.

The blood brought its own pleasure, and soon Colleen was fully awake and hungry for her. Their passion peaked, then waned. Joanna pushed the girl away, and they lay side by side. While Colleen slept, Joanna remembered another girl and then another from those days before Illona replaced her life with another, darker one.

The first had been an older cousin in her grandfather's house. They had shared a sleeping room, often a bed. A normal thing except that her hands were too active, her endearments too mature, and Joanna too young to completely understand. When she did, finally, they swore to a secret, lasting love—one that ended far too quickly when the girl matured and was taken to sleep alone and dream of some nameless husband who would be chosen for her.

Joanna saw her only at family functions, and once, when they were alone, she had stammered some quick endearment, then asked, pathetically, it seemed now, "Do you think of me?"

The girl's cheeks had reddened. She'd looked away, giving the answer Joanna had dreaded but almost expected.

The second had been a slave in her brother's keep, but she had died years ago. Joanna could not even remember her name, though the face framed with the pale copper curls of the Circassian race still came unbidden to her most pleasant dreams.

She held Colleen close, murmured some endearment in a language the girl barely understood. This one had discovered what she was, yet still loved her. This one Joanna loved most of all.

The sun was rising. She moved away from the bed to the

place where she must hide. The lid came down, bringing the welcome darkness. She slept. Her dreams should have been pleasant but instead were restless, unformed, and at dusk too easily forgotten.

When she woke, she found Colleen in a chair, facing the front door, clearly agitated. "I am going out. I must," she said, thinking Colleen's emotion was concern or jealousy.

"I was going to go to the baker's this morning when I passed a blond man waiting outside. He followed me," Colleen blurted.

"To steal?"

"No. I didn't even think anything of it at first. But then everywhere I went I would see him nearby. Watching. All he did was watch."

"An admirer?"

"No! Not that. I was afraid for you so I rushed back, but he was always close behind. Then, just as I was about to unlock the door, he tried to talk to me. I began to push past him, but he gripped my arm and gave me a box he said I must give to my mistress."

She gave Joanna a small box no bigger than her hand.

Instinct made her thrust it back at Colleen. "You open," she demanded.

Colleen did. Under the plain paper wrapping was a second layer of paper, gaily colored with tiny flowers and hummingbirds. Beneath that was a jewel box covered in black velvet. Colleen held her breath and lifted the lid. Inside was a gold ring with a blue stone in the center, diamonds on either side of it. "Look!" she said, holding it up so Joanna could see. "How beautiful."

Joanna took it from her, holding it lightly in two fingers. In her experience, gifts often brought harm, and one from a stranger was doubly suspect. When she felt no burning of her flesh, no weakness in her body, she examined it more closely, fighting down the urge to laugh at the strangeness of it. It had been days since she'd felt that hysteria, and would not give in to it. "Who sent it?" she asked.

"There's a card under the lid. She stared at it. "Flowery script. You found a dandy to admire you." She spoke with a hint of irritation that Joanna understood. They were outcases, the pair of them, and her servant wanted no one to come between them.

Joanna looked at it, uncomprehending. Her English might be nearly flawless, but she could still read little in her own language, none of Colleen's. "What does he write?" she asked.

Colleen's skill also was limited, but she managed to make out enough. "He writes that the real gift is beneath the wrapping. How odd!"

She turned the box over, and as she did, a small tissue-wrapped package fell to the floor.

Joanna picked it up. "No!" Colleen warned. "It may be a trap. Let me—"

But Joanna already knew what it was. She opened the tissue slowly and carefully and let the spoonful of earth fall into her palm.

Once it touched her, she could no longer deny what it was. Her hand began to shake, and the grains scattered on the floor.

Colleen, misinterpreting her reaction, moved close, taking her hand and examining it, trying to find some injury. "What was it? What did it do to you?"

"It's soil from one of my brother's boxes. Someone found it. Someone knew." The thought made her frantic. Frantic! If he knew, then . . . then . . . then . . .

"But why would someone threaten you with a gift, and one so obviously expensive?" Colleen asked.

Colleen was so sensible. And so right. The ring brought some comfort, enough that she could think clearly. "If you see him again, ask him why he did this. Tell him that I need to know his intentions."

"I won't see him, at least not in daylight. I won't leave you alone. I promise."

Now it was her turn to be logical, to calm the fear. "*Draga,* if he meant to do harm, he could have done so today while you were gone."

That quieted her, and they sat together for a time. But as always, Joanna grew restless, pacing catlike and staring often at the door. As she started for it, Colleen said with a trace of annoyance, "I won't sleep at all tonight until you're back."

Joanna didn't bother to answer that, merely walked to the

closed door. Colleen, always disturbed by what would happen next, looked away. When she looked back, Joanna had thinned to mist, and in a moment even that was gone.

One with the air and fog, Joanna watched from outside as Colleen unlatched the door and cracked it open. She noted that the girl was staring across the street with an expression both curious and frightened. Turning her attention in the same direction, Joanna saw a man standing there, his hair white in the gaslight.

He looked toward the door and the space around it. With a strange, sad smile, he turned and headed south and west toward the embankment and the bridge.

This was the night Arthur had been anticipating—the night when he would learn if he would live or die. Somehow it made no difference to him, for if there was one thing that Mina's experience with Dracula had taught him, it was that there was indeed a soul that lived on.

And so he walked down the embankment to one of the rare stands of trees still left from his youth, aware all the time that she was watching him go, following at a distance. He turned around often, trying to get a glimpse of her in some form. But there were no women, no wolves, no bats, only tendrils of mist all around him, and if she were a part of them, he would never know.

Close to the water, he stopped, and with back to the land whispered, "I am waiting, Joanna Tepes. I mean you no harm."

He heard a rustle of fabric on flesh, the snapping of a twig. Turning, he saw her there, her thin body lit from behind by the distant gaslights. Sensing that a move toward her or away would invite attack, he stayed where he was and bowed as a commoner might to a princess.

She inhaled, then exhaled words. "Why such a gift?" she asked.

"The obvious. I know what you are, and I mean no harm."

"Harm is not always intended."

He was astonished at how well she spoke, at how much a woman she seemed. Dracula had seemed larger than a living man, a being too powerful to face. But this one with her thin body and nervous, green eyes seemed more likely to bolt from him than attack.

But wild things, even those in human guise, could not be trusted.

"I discovered the ship you came on," he explained. "I spoke to a crewman. He said you had brought only one box. Your brother had at least a dozen. I've found just one that is usable. I've taken it for safekeeping."

"Taken it where?" she asked.

Should he lie? The idea crossed his mind, but a lack of trust would only cause problems later. "I took it to my home. I will give it to you, or give you safety there, if you will do one little thing for me in exchange."

"And that is?"

"That you will come with me to my home. That you will stay with me for a time or visit often so that we may talk."

"Talk?" The word seemed spoken with her last bit of breath, the "k" barely pronounced.

"I have reasons. I will explain them all."

"And your home?"

He handed her a card, spoke some directions to get her there. "Will you come with me now . . . Countess?"

"I need consider. Maybe tomorrow," she replied.

Far better than he'd expected. "I will be waiting there for you," he said and began walking away from her, a casual stroll that he hoped hid his fear.

Two more steps and she appeared in front of him, her thin cotton gown moving slowly in the breeze. "You were one of them?"

Not quite a question. She might have seen him. Again, he decided on honesty. "I was."

"Then why come to me alone, without the others?"

"I want to know if I was right to be one of them."

She frowned, most likely trying to decide if he spoke the truth. She seemed remarkably logical for one Mina had thought mad. Perhaps that crumbling castle had only made her appear so. "Until tonight?" he asked.

She stepped aside and let him pass.

He walked away, his boots leaving dark tracks in the dew-covered grass.

twenty-one

There were flowers on the street where Joanna dwelled—daisies and verbena and snapdragons in bright window boxes, occasional clumps of tall hollyhocks in the narrow sideyards. Though the colors in her night-keen vision were raucous and beautiful, few of the blooms had any scent at all, and none so sweet as those in the gardens of her human youth. But as she followed the fair young man through the cluttered streets of Chelsea to the walled and iron-gated estates in Kensington, the gardens grew larger, the plantings more intricate. Some were given over entirely to roses, others to arbors of hanging purple and yellow-flowered vines. There were huge beds of orange and yellow with a spicy scent, so strong she could taste it as she moved over them, light as mist.

The gates of the young man's estate had already been opened to her by his invitation. She stayed close until the house was in sight, then hung back in the trees, falling into human shape. Watching. Watching.

The house was not as sprawling or ornate as her grandfather's, but it had a similar detailed charm in the delicately curved black iron of its porches and balconies, the design repeated in the benches on the forest path. Drawn by the fragrance of roses, she moved down one of these paths, stepping through wrought-iron gates in a low brick wall, her bare feet making no sound on the smooth cobblestones of the path.

On either side of her, beds of lavender and mint gave off a calming scent, lilies a spicier aroma, summer phlox their marvelous sweetness. Behind them were hydrangeas and taller lilies. Hedges walled off this charming space, and as she moved through a gap in them, she found herself in a larger space.

She had never seen anything like this—hedges cut into strange balls and triangles, beastly shapes and stars as if they were pieces of marble, the gardener their artist. An artist of scent as well as form, it would seem, since caught in the center of the lower, sculpted shapes were mounds of sweet alyssum punctuated with occasional sprigs of verbena.

Another hedge gave way to a vast expanse of lawn surrounded by a different set of flowering bushes hedged with violets and woodruff. She walked on grass now, keeping close to the shadows on the edge of the lawn until she came upon a gazebo nestled in a clearing in the bushes. It was a charming platform, three steps above the lawn and scarcely big enough for the bench and two chairs on it. She sat and took a deep, human breath, drawing in the mélange of scent and the memories of the garden of her youth.

She had come across half a world on an uncertain voyage, and if she had known that this, only this, was at the end of it, the garden alone would have made the journey worthwhile.

She sat and dreamed of the garden of her youth for a time, then got up and walked on. What if she were mortal, the lady of this house, the princess of this castle? A pleasant dream as long as it lasted, a dream shattered when, lost in reveries, she did not notice a servant, a thin, small man, coming toward her until they nearly collided.

He dropped one of the pieces of wood he carried but ignored it. "Who are—" he began to ask.

She placed one finger over his lips, silencing him for a moment.

"So cold," he whispered. "Come inside. The cook is heating water for tea. Perhaps she'll give you something to eat before you have to go."

She shook her head and stared at him, trying for the same expression Illona had so often used with her. He backed away a few steps, then turned and ran, silent until he reached the kitchen. Then she could hear him babbling on about some intruder in the garden. She watched the staff from above as, holding lamps high, they traveled down paths seeking her.

"She was here, I tell you," the man insisted when, grumbling, they gave up the search and started for the house.

"Sure she was, Petey. And the sight of you in all your strength frightened her off, did it?" the cook taunted.

"More likely my promise of a meal from you," the man retorted, then added mostly to himself, "She was here. I saw her. It makes no difference if anyone believes me."

"He's been in the brandy again, that's what," the cook went on.

"Was not," he said and headed toward the rear grounds. "Well, not much, anyway," he added when he was out of earshot.

In time, even he gave up the search and went inside.

She waited as one by one the lights were extinguished and the house went dark.

Around her there was silence broken only by the howl of a stable hound, the rustling of some small creature in the leaves close to her feet.

Dare she go inside?

She did not have a beating heart to beat faster, no quickening breath to gauge her fear. But every nerve in her body vibrated a warning. She trembled, retreated almost to the edge of the lawn, then stopped and drew on the courage that had brought her across a continent and an ocean.

If he had meant to harm her, why this strange ruse? Why lure her here when he had already discovered her lair? When he knew that her servant was out?

Take him at his word, she thought, and forced herself forward and inside.

Two servants slept in the little room she'd entered; one a scullery maid, judging from the smell of lye soap that clung to her skin. The other had to be the cook, and as Joanna hovered close to her bed, she smelled wine and spices, onions and dill. And she slept so soundly. It would be such an easy matter to pull back the coverlet, undo the top laces of her nightshirt and take what she wished. She was so close to acting in her hunger, almost too close, when the thought of what might happen if she did and the woman woke made her pull back.

Hardly a fitting beginning to any sort of relationship with

the man who owned this house. With one reluctant look back, she moved through the open door and down the empty hallway to the spotless kitchen. Through the pantry lay the formal dining room, the gilt-edged china on display in a glass-doored cabinet, a cut crystal vase of roses on the lace-covered table.

Beyond it, behind a pair of pocket doors, was the music room, with its benches and coffee tables, and a huge piano in the center. She pressed lightly on a bass key, and a low moan seemed to echo off the walls, as if the room itself were the sounding board. Startled and afraid that someone might hear and come to investigate, she moved quickly to the opposite side of the house.

Possessions were more numerous here—collections of paperweights and china flowers, tapestry pillows and lace doilies. Strange for a man to treasure such things. Perhaps they had been collected by his mother or grandmother and he could not part with them.

Was that how mortals held on to life after death? How they remembered their past?

So sad. So futile.

And so beautiful. She ran her thin fingers over the smooth curves of delicate glass flowers and intricate wood carvings polished to a rich patina. She sniffed empty cloisonné spice jars still holding the scents of India and China. Places he had visited, his family had known.

She sensed him in the room above her, and with concentration heard the steady in and out of sleep breath even through the thick walls.

She had intended merely to explore, but the temptation to observe him when he was helpless—to do what he could have so easily done to her—was too strong. In human form, every sense alert to danger, she climbed the stairs, moved down the hall. She might have been floating, so soft was the carpet, so light her step.

She entered the room as she had the garden, in human form, using the stealth she had perfected in her youth. The room was huge, the tall windows flung open as if he, having given an invitation, welcomed her to come. He lay on his stomach in the center of the huge four-poster, a thin coverlet over him. A half-finished glass of brandy lay within reach on the bedside table, not the first he'd drunk, given the sheen of sweat on his body in spite of the cool night.

What had made him so foolish as to seek her, challenge her? He had issued a challenge but had been uncertain of the outcome. That much had been clear in the quick beating of his heart, the smell of fear that hung about him as he'd left her standing in the park. She thought that if she stood here long enough, she would see through flesh and bone to the core of him and understand the puzzle he presented.

One she needed to solve; but carefully.

Afraid to wake him, startle him, perhaps force his hand and hers too soon, she moved away from the bed and studied the room. She saw nothing out of order here but a half-empty brandy bottle under the nightstand. Beside it was the photograph of a woman with fair hair and a heart-shaped face and an expression that, in spite of the formal pose, hinted of innocent wickedness.

She had left him? She had died? No matter, he mourned her and slept alone.

She wanted to touch him, wake him, speak to him as he had asked her to. But not yet, not until she was ready.

Though he did not wake, he seemed to sense her. He cried out in his sleep and rolled onto his side, one arm rising to brush against his face, the side of his neck.

Startled and nearly certain he was about to wake, she faded into mist and floated above him. When his eyes remained closed and his breathing slowed once more, she descended slowly. The mist enveloped him, air against flesh, cold against warmth. She fought the urge to take human form, coalescing finally into a ghostlike human shape. She lay with head against his shoulder, hand on his waist, thighs against his thighs, the mound that once would have taken him inside and given out life, pressed against his groin.

His breath was warm as it passed through her, and where he touched her she could feel the steady beating of his heart, the river of life it pushed through him.

She wanted the fantasy to continue, to be mortal for just this night. Instead, she'd become painfully aware of their difference, then of the passing hours, and the need that was growing inside her that must be met.

Enough! she thought, and retreated to the doors, the garden, the path, the wall, the poorer parts of the city—her city, now that she had learned the layout of its streets and rivers and claimed it for her own.

Tonight was different from the ones before. Tonight she could not be an observer of the life around her. Her hunger was too sharp to carry home.

Besides, she needed to be strong to solve this puzzle, not half-starved from a trusted servant's blood. And Colleen needed to be strong as well in case the man surprised her and turned out to be a danger.

She found a drunk sleeping in a narrow passage between two rotting houses. He didn't stir when she undid the putrid kerchief around his neck and bit, deep enough to take what she needed, shallow enough that he would live. The drink that warmed his blood assured that, if he was ever conscious enough to notice her, he would assume she was some phantasm in his sodden mind.

Sated, she returned to the house in Chelsea where Colleen waited, lying in bed in the dark but still awake.

As always Colleen tried to hide how frantic she had become. She lit a candle and glanced at her mistress. "You saw him?" she asked.

"More than saw. I spoke to him. He gave me his card." She handed it over to Colleen.

Colleen sat up and lit the lamp, then looked at the name. "Arthur Holmwood. Lord Go . . . Godalming," she read, frowning. "A lord. Does the name mean anything to you?"

"He tells me that he was one of the men who came to the castle. He knows so much." She got up and began to unhook her dress.

"Is that mud on your sleeve? No, blood! I can smell it. What did he do to you?" Colleen demanded.

"Nothing. I was hungry, so I took from someone else, that's all. You should be thankful when I do."

Colleen blew out the light and rolled onto her side, facing the wall.

Joanna stared at her back a moment, then stripped off the dirty clothes and lay down beside her.

Colleen's body was tense, but once she shuddered. She seemed to be holding back sobs. "I'll clean the dress in the morning," she said.

Not so long ago, surrounded only by her kind, Joanna would have given no thought to the girl's sorrow, or the hunger of that child she'd fed or the callousness of the baker she'd killed. But now, surrounded by the teeming human life of this city, she could feel a part of herself remembering back centuries to when she had been human, and all the emotions that a human soul possessed. She kissed the nape of Colleen's neck and stroked her hair, quieting the misery with her touch. "I saw the most marvelous garden tonight," she whispered with only the faintest breath. "Someday I will show it to you."

Colleen rolled over, pressed against her, nuzzled the wound Joanna had opened on her breast. She began gently, then became voracious, biting hard when the blood refused to flow. Joanna winced but held her tight and let her nurse.

Grow strong, child of my love, she thought. Grow strong.

twenty-two

When Arthur woke the following morning, he immediately felt the side of his neck. It was not some instinct of Joanna's visit the night before, but a reflex he had possessed since he'd first heard that the vampire might be in London.

Ian Woods, his butler, had already laid out his clothes, and he could smell the faint scent of fresh biscuits rising from the kitchen. These had been made by Wendy Leyton, who had a master chef's touch. Besides the two, he also employed a maid and a gardener. Not the grand staff that had been here in his uncle's day, but more than adequate for his needs. The fact that their presence was more for security during his frequent absences than to actually serve him, also pleased him. He gave them a home they might not have had otherwise.

He considered sleeping in, but a glance at the windows made him decide against it. They had been nearly closed last night but were fully open now. It might have been a breeze, but it could have been she. If she had come, one of the four might have seen her. There would be no need to directly question anyone; all he had to do was open the topic.

He went downstairs and took his place at the table where a copy of the *Times* was waiting for him. Mrs. Woods brought him tea and wished him a good morning.

"And the same to you," he replied. "Did you sleep well? You look a bit tired this morning."

As he expected, this was all he needed to say. The woman was always ready to talk about some worry or another. "I suppose I am. Patch thought he saw a beggar walking in the garden. He and Ian searched the place, but she was gone."

"She?"

"Plenty of she-beggars out there. More than the other kind, since they aren't likely to turn to crime to eat."

"No use losing sleep over her, then," he said, unfolding the paper and pretending to scan he headlines.

"Beggars come in packs like wolves, sir. Some of them might be dangerous."

"Well, if this one comes back, give her something to eat and a few pennies. No use being stingy, no matter what the law."

When he was alone, Arthur poured himself another cup of tea and smiled to himself. So she liked his garden, did she? What else might she like?

He rang for Ian. "I should like your key to the storage room, since I seem to have lost mine," he said to the butler.

"If there is something you need from there, I would be happy to get it now."

"No, just some old papers of my uncle's that I need to sort through."

Now that he had both keys, he could set about redoing the room, making it more appealing to the woman, more what a princess would covet. And he considered what trinkets to leave to convince her that he meant no harm.

Over the next few nights, Joanna found gifts waiting for her, arranged on a table at the end of Arthur's bed. There was a scarf of supple black silk trimmed in jet beads, a ruby ring only a bit too large for her thin fingers, a hair clip holding a spray of peacock feathers that fell in long strands that brushed against the side of her neck light as kisses.

Each was accompanied by the same note, the one Colleen had to read to her the first time: *When you are ready, wake me.*

Joanna had no idea what he wanted of her, but the gifts were beautiful. She would return to the house in Chelsea and lay the new one next to the one that came before.

She expected Colleen to be as enchanted as she was becoming, but the girl grew more agitated with every new trinket. "If I see him on the street again, I'll scream for the police. I won't be able to help myself," Colleen said.

"You won't see him," Joanna replied. Since he'd finally lured her to his house, he hadn't been seen in the area day or night.

"If you don't make a move soon, he will," Colleen said, repeating what she'd been saying since Colleen's first visit.

Joanna didn't bother to answer. They'd had the discussion too many times before. "Come and lay beside me," she asked instead, knowing that a touch would sooth in a way her words never could.

Colleen did as she asked, trembling in her arms. "What will happen to me if you leave me now?" she whispered.

"I will always come back for you," Joanna said, brushing a hand over the girl's soft hair.

Colleen's concern made her cautious, so Joanna did not return to the estate the next night, nor the night after. Finally curiosity got the better of her, but instead of gifts at the end of the bed, she found a key and another note. Different words this time, and she could not decipher them.

The key was similar to the one in his bedroom door, so it likely belonged to some room in the house.

She moved down the hall, noting that the room keys were all in their locks, and unlike the man's, all on the hall side. She tried the first few doors and found they were not locked. She moved quickly to the opposite wing, finally discovering a locked door that had no key.

She did not need to open the door to go inside, but she wanted to make certain this was the room the man had intended her to find.

It unlocked easily. As the door swung open, she could see light coming from somewhere inside. Likely a candle, certainly dim for human eyes. For hers, huge in the darkness, it blinded, and she looked away until her eyes became accustomed to it.

Colleen might accuse her of being a fool, but though Joanna was cautious, she was also curious. She paused at the threshold for a moment, all senses acute. Certain it was devoid of life, she stepped inside.

The fragrances of beeswax and oil were similar to those in her cottage when Colleen had been cleaning, but beneath them was a mustiness that told her the room had no window to let in fresh air—a stale, earthy scent, reminding her of her long years in the bowels of her brother's keep.

She moved deeper into the room. Stepping around a pile of crates and boxes and a folding oriental screen, she found the source of the scent, the box her brother had brought to England.

It had been placed in the center of a cleared space, the rough-hewn top polished until it shone in the light of the single red-cased votive candle placed on a table beside it.

There were three other tables around the box, and each of them held a dozen or more small candles—tapers, votives, poured pieces in shapes of griffins and cats and multicolored flowers. There were real flowers as well—cream-colored lilies in crystal vases. Most marvelous of all, from the ceiling hung clear glass prisms so delicately made that they caught even the dim light and sent it scattering as colors through the room.

Enchanted, and fearing that enchantment, she lit another pair of candles. As the flames flickered to life, she walked to the box and opened it.

Inside, she saw the thin piece of ancient fabric, brittle to her quick, cautious touch. Nothing burned her, nothing warned her that the earth below had been tainted. She pulled back the cloth and fingered the soil—cold to her touch. The earth that would have made her grave.

But the man had added two things to the box: a sheet of soft brushed silk and a silk pillow filled with mint, chamomile and lavender—a mélange of pleasant dreams.

Had he known the herbs' significance? She guessed that he had, just as he knew so much else about her kind.

What did he want of her? The question had been uppermost in her mind for days. Now, knowing the answer had become irresistible.

Probably the same thing the other one had wanted. He had a fortune to dispose of; all he needed was time.

Arthur, Arthur Holmwood, Lord Godalming. She thought the name, then whispered it, letting out the rest of the air she'd taken in with a thin, nervous giggle that seemed to hang in the air long after she had vanished.

He had raised too many questions. Too many! Before her courage failed her, she would wake him.

She wondered if he would find the experience pleasant.

twenty-three

From the journal of Mina Harker, August 17, 1891:

Everything is happening so quickly now, as if God or Fate or merely luck is on my side.

It took only two weeks for me to obtain a long-term lease on the property I intend to use for the shelter. I owe Jonathan for that. He has persevered with tremendous determination through the maze of owners and lessees and managers and tenants who allowed the structure to fall into such terrible disrepair.

Each of our meetings to discuss the matter quickly turned from business to personal ones. I spent two nights at our home. Then, one morning when Essie was away visiting her sister, he came to mine.

He approved of the changes I'd made in the house, saying that the guest rooms and larger kitchen had feminized the space. I made other changes too—subtle ones. I changed the dark downstairs walls to a pale shade of green that reflects rather than absorbs the natural light. As we sat and ate a quick meal, I watched him studying the surroundings, wondering, no doubt, which possessions were mine and which had belonged to him.

He often became silent at odd moments in our conversation, and I guessed the questions he longed to ask. I found myself thinking of the truthful answers—how Gance had taken me here and here. How he had filled the solarium with roses to brighten a gloomy day. How he . . .

And so my mind went round and round, but always back to Jonathan, who had never eyed me with such intensity before, save when he thought I was about to turn into some monster before his eyes.

I was about to ask what was wrong when he stood and walked behind me. "I like what you've done here," he said. "You've made the place your own, somehow. It reminds me of you," he said and began, with no warning, to unhook my blouse, his kisses following his hands as they moved down my back. I wanted to ask what he was doing with so many hours of work ahead of him, but of course I knew, and knew as well that any question, any words at all, would ruin the time to follow.

So I let him continue with the skirt, the chemise, the loose corset I wore out of convention rather than because it served any need. I reached for him, then, and as I began to open the buttons of his shirt, I heard him moan. His eyes were closed. He might have been thinking of Gance or of the woman. I would have none of it, just as he would have none of my fantasies at a moment like this.

"Jonathan," I whispered. "Jonathan, look at me."

And so I called him back to me. There he stayed while I stripped off all those stifling layers of cloth that civilized people are forced to wear even in the heat of summer, and I took him to the settee.

Odd how I, who had relished setting down every small detail of my meetings with Gance, cannot do the same with my husband. It might be considered some sort of prudery, but I have found in the past that I have so little of that dreadful virtue. Instead, it is because I sense a permanence in our relationship and see no need to note details.

I need only say that we wound up in the tub, relishing the cool water against our skin. It was almost noon when he left, only after getting a promise from me that we would meet again tomorrow evening.

How many times will we meet this way before we decide what our futures will hold?

Mina put away the journal, pinned up her hair and changed into a different, simpler dress, one better suited to a day in the garden. She was in the front, cutting the spent blooms off the flowers, when a hansom drove up. Winnie waved and paid the driver.

She'd been expected, but Mina had forgotten all about the meeting. Hardly an unwelcome surprise, Mina thought, thankful her friend had not arrived early.

As she made them tea, she considered how everything was falling into place so quickly—due in no small part to Winnie and the doctor. Even before she had legal possession of the property, Winnie was taking the carpenters and plumbers who had helped construct her children's hospital on a tour of the building, negotiating the best price for the work that needed to be done.

Meanwhile, Mina found a mill that would donate fabric for sheets and table linens and a firm that would give the house a pair of sewing machines so the women could make their own clothing, draperies and linens, and perhaps take in mending and sewing work later. Dr. Rhys contacted a patient of his, a cabinetmaker who was willing to do some of the finishing work at half his normal fee.

The less skilled labor came from the neighborhood around the building. Mina had suggested this as a way of making the funds help more than her clients. Winnie was in favor of it, Rhys was not. "People so shoddy about themselves will not do the work well," he explained, his voice stiff with disdain for all of them.

"But it gives them a sense that this is theirs, not charity," Winnie added.

And so the women won, as did a half dozen men from that sorry neighborhood. Some drank in the mornings before they came to work, but those were soon let go. The others worked as the women had hoped. Soon the walls were going up, dividing the space into small rooms for single women, adjoining ones for those with children. The first rooms finished were already occupied with three single women and a male caretaker—a bear of a man and a bit simpleminded, but honest. He'd been doing the same sort of work for the hospital, and Mina had hired him at Winnie's suggestion to keep vandals and thieves away from the site and to protect the women after the house was finished.

Mina had intended to start the house with ten women, but soon found she'd underestimated the amount of space she'd acquired. The place could easily hold sixteen.

Mina showed Winnie her own nearly finished addition before they set to the afternoon's work, going through the long list of applicants she'd had to turn away.

They had planned to do their work in the garden, but a gusty afternoon storm make that impossible. So they worked at the dining table in the solarium with the outside doors cracked to let in the soothing sounds of wind and rain.

They paged through applications, many of which had been filled out in Essie's precise script on behalf of those who could not write. Mina stopped at an application for a woman with five children whose husband had drowned the year before. "If it were just her and a single child, or even two, I would have room. But five? Winnie, where can she go?"

"There's the church, or she could place them all in a charity home until she has the means to care for them. The option is hardly pleasant, but at least they'll have a warm place to sleep and three meals a day. If they stay together they may live on the street, but there's the Temperance League Soup Kitchen, not the tastiest fare, but nourishing."

Horrible options, all of them. "Perhaps I should have started my work on a less grand scale," Mina suggested.

"Settled, you mean?"

"Settled?"

"You're creating a model for the future, just as Mr. Beason and I did with the hospital. Yes, I could have done some work on sanitation, or arranged to open a clinic as Dr. Rhys has, but I wanted more. Recently two charity groups from the North visited my hospital. They plan to start hospitals much like mine. If I had settled for less in order to help more, I would have set no example for anyone to follow. Dr. Rhys did the same in London, and now we've inspired you."

She raised a subject Mina had longed to discuss, and with Essie gone, it seemed an ideal time. "Dr. Rhys approaches this work so strangely," she said.

Winnie grinned. "Of course he does. He's a man."

"Be serious. He doesn't have the same feeling about his work as you and I do. Sometimes I can't imagine why he does it, and at others it seems so . . . natural."

"He intrigues you?"

Mina knew exactly what her friend meant, and laughed. "Yes, but not like that. It's his beliefs that intrigue me. He says he runs the clinic not out of any concern for the poor but because of a promise he made to his mother long after she was dead."

"I know a little about that. Actually, I was going to give you some good bits about the doctor but then you and Jonathan seem to have reconciled or—"

"We are reconciled when we see each other, which isn't often enough. But at least we both have things to talk about when we do."

"That isn't what I mean, and you know it."

"There's been a bit of that, too." Mina looked away and laughed, silencing her. "That doesn't mean I wouldn't like to hear some bits about our Dr. Rhys."

"First you must promise never to repeat it, or Mr. Beason will be furious, since I learned most of it from him."

"Maybe it would be better if you didn't—"

"No, it wouldn't. I may not be playing matchmaker, but you work with him, after all, and in a few minutes you'll understand a great deal about his behavior. His mother was Indian—from Delhi, I believe. His father was a member of the House of Lords, though hardly noble, given his conduct. His mother was the man's mistress. When his business in India ended, he brought her to London, where she lived in nearly total isolation. She gave birth to Dr. Rhys there."

"Though the man supported the woman and her son, he did not much care about either of them. They never lived together, and he never acknowledged the boy as his. She apparently was a simple creature who thought of them as married and was subservient to his every demand. Eventually he contracted some disease from the other women he frequented and passed it on to her. I understand that he died when Dr. Rhys was a small child, the mother soon after."

"How terrible! How did Rhys survive without them?" Mina asked.

"The father was no cad, at least not completely. But he waited until he was on his deathbed to spring his bastard son and dying mistress on his family. He'd also made provisions for the boy and arrangements to send him to a private school. During the holidays, his father's sister took him in, just as she cared for his mother during her last days. She was a rigidly religious woman with a low opinion of her brother's vice, and apparently sex in general, since she never married. She is responsible for the doctor's rigid view on vice and virtue, I think."

"Yet the doctor is no Christian."

"Nor was his aunt, and I think Christ would be the first to agree with me."

"Winnie!" Mina exclaimed. "You may be right, but the words seem blasphemous."

"You're right. I shouldn't speak the obvious so openly. It has a nasty way of leaking out in more inopportune moments."

"Is the aunt still alive?"

"No. And though, out of deference to her church, Dr. Rhys was never publicly acknowledged as her nephew, she gave him her name and a healthy allowance then left her estate to him."

"So he's a wealthy man?"

"Not as wealthy as Gance was, or Arthur, but since he has rental income from a number of properties, he has no need of a paying medical practice. He does the paying work to keep busy, I think, and the charity clinic he's already explained."

"And he never married?"

"I suspect he's never been attracted to a woman before. But lately I've noticed that he seems to be flirting with you."

Those long, questioning looks, the occasional times when his hand had held hers longer than necessary to help her out of a cab. The solicitous way he saw to her needs when they were together. Until now, Mina had dismissed his close attention as some sort of Eastern custom. "He makes me uneasy," Mina confided. "I prefer direct men. In his case, I have no idea what he wants from me."

"You could ask him."

"I'd rather not acknowledge the behavior. It's better if I just ignore it and keep my distance. Perhaps he'll lose interest."

So they went on with their work, picking out four more women who had children, two younger ones who did not.

Afterward they walked to the main road and hailed a cab to take them to the bank, then the shelter site. There they stopped in the yard, got the invoice from the roofer and paid the man for his work. "One more thing finished," Mina said as they went through the wide doors into the shared rooms of the lower level.

The building had three floors. The first floor had a large kitchen and dining room on one side; there was a second, larger room on the other, where Mina hoped the youngest children could take lessons by day and the women could socialize at night. The last time she had visited, the rooms had been empty. Now there were cupboards in both of them, a huge wood stove in the kitchen and a large potbellied stove in the living room. Hardly complete, but close enough that a number of the more desperate residents would be moving in within the week.

The second stove had been placed near the stairs so that the stove's heat could rise to the upper floors and take away the damp on winter nights. It was hardly the sort of arrangement that would lead to a comfortable warmth in the sleeping rooms, but extra stoves on the upper floors would increase the risk of fire.

The railing had already been put in on the main staircase, one of the few things left in place from the building's previous days. Work also had begun on a second staircase, added as another precaution against fire.

Mina climbed the main stairs to the second floor, where a set of rooms for a woman with children were taking shape. Scarcely three meters square, the rooms seemed small to her, even without the cupboard and bed that would take up most of the floor space. But they, like most of the rooms, had small windows that could be opened for air and every other a rope attached to the sill, another escape route should they need it.

"All these precautions seem so extreme," Mina said. "I'm concerned that we might be challenging disaster."

"With so many living in such a small space, the risks increase. You've seen how many children the hospital has treated for burns," Winnie reminded her.

There was a third floor, reserved for women without children, but the stairs were only roughed in. A dangerous climb for women in long skirts and they didn't attempt it, returning to the ground floor instead.

There Mina paused and looked at the additions one more time, wondering if Gance would approve of how she'd spent so much of his gift to her, then followed Winnie outside. Winnie checked her watch. "We should find a cab," she said. "Margaret is cooking dinner by herself tonight, and I wouldn't want to be late and risk having her burn it."

They'd asked their cab to wait, and as they walked toward it, they saw Dr. Rhys coming up the road. Though he was dressed in a suit and vest, he carried his medical bag.

"Visiting a patient?" Winnie asked when he'd joined them at the side of the road.

"Actually, I'm leaving for London on the last train tonight. I thought I'd catch you here to see if Mrs. Harker and you were interested in having supper with me before I go."

He'd spoken to Winnie, but looked at Mina as he did. "Actually, I have plans already—" Mina began.

"She and Mr. Beason and I are dining together. You're welcome to join us if you wish, though I really hadn't planned on—"

"If you mean that you're likely having a brisket or such, yes, I do eat meat. But I would not wish to impose, and I'll need to dine closer to the station if I am to leave tonight."

Again, he watched Mina as he said this, waiting no doubt for her to second the invitation. "Then since we're going near the station, you should share our cab. They can be hard to come by at this time of day," Mina said instead.

They dropped him close to town. As he left, he took her hand as always. This time he kissed the back of it. "Those you help would never dare to do this. They should," he said and left without looking at her again. His hand had been damp and had left patches of dampness on her own that cooled and dried in the breeze coming through the open doorway. Mina watched him walking away as the cab started on.

"If you had said one word," Winnie commented.

"Which is why I did not."

"For the best, anyway. You know, I have heard that he doesn't have any patients in London at all. That he goes to carouse in the worst sort of places."

"Then why does he take the bag?" Mina asked, smiling.

"It's filled with sheaths."

They giggled, but though Winnie might not realize it, there was a grain of truth in the jest. The doctor's actions reminded Mina of Jonathan's when they had first met—those reluctant, almost chaste touches, the glances that quickly ended when he saw she was watching. With the doctor, unable to speak to her of how he felt, they seemed to grow in intensity. Then he would go to London for a night or two and return far more relaxed. Well, there was a large Indian settlement in the city. Perhaps he had a sweetheart there.

Mina hoped he did, someone to lighten the quiet intensity of the man.

twenty-four

It was fewer than three weeks since she'd first spoken to Arthur Holmwood, but Joanna began to wonder if the feeling, the strange, flustered feeling that she'd never experienced before, was something akin to love.

No, not love. Love was too enduring an emotion to feel for a creature whose life was so fleeting. Infatuation, perhaps? Not just with the man, though he was handsome and attentive enough; no, there were his possessions as well.

After she found the box of earth and the place he had arranged, obviously for her, she had gone to his room confused and angry from that confusion. She had lain behind him, wrapped her arms around his chest, holding him tightly.

"Arthur Holmwood. You wish to speak to me. Wake up," she'd called.

And he had. For a moment, he struggled; then, realizing who held him, he stopped testing her and relaxed in her arms. "Did you like the gift?" he whispered.

"This is a terrible game you play," she said, gripping more tightly so he had to fight to catch a breath.

"I've been nothing but honest. And I have no intention to harm you. Do what you wish with me."

The anguish in his tone was obvious. It recalled a similar surrender in herself, memories centuries old but too intense to forget. How many times had she said words so similar? How many more times had she thought them?

She let him go, and moved away with scarcely a rustle on his bedcovers.

He wrapped the sheet around himself and sat on the edge of his bed. "I stayed awake so many nights waiting for you. Finally, I was so exhausted, you caught me asleep. I'm sorry."

"Sorry?" She hissed the beginning of the word, then held the remaining breath for her next response.

"One should remain awake for a guest."

"I was late." She began to giggle, fought it and won, standing still and silent, as Illona might have.

They looked at each other in silence until she asked, "Why did you do all this to bring me here? What do you want of me?"

"To know you." She frowned and he went on, "Not what you are. I know that already. I want to know what you feel, how you exist, your dreams . . . all of it."

What could she answer? She had no idea how to start except, perhaps, with the story she had recently told Colleen. But it was already late. She didn't need a clock to tell her that she had at most two hours to dawn and a long way to travel.

"Tomorrow night," she whispered and vanished.

Used to being awake when her mistress returned from her travels, Colleen was up well before dawn. The mantel clock said it was after four, far later than Joanna usually roamed. Though she knew it was silly to worry, Colleen could not help herself. She paced the little house, moving from room to room as if convinced that Joanna would try to avoid her altogether.

Joanna had no reason to do so. Indeed, she wanted a human perspective on what had happened that night. But seeing Colleen so angry, she said nothing to the girl. She even took refuge behind the locked door of her own chamber when Colleen, completely forgetting the deference a servant owed to her mistress, demanded the information. Joanna might have reminded Colleen of her place but the girl meant so much more.

And so, minutes before dawn, she returned to the room where Colleen pretended to sleep and kissed her lightly on the cheek. "I will never leave you," she said, repeating a promise she had made more than once, then retreated before the hungry light of the rising sun.

Even in sleep, she could feel Colleen's misery—sharpened by the blood bond between them. Illona and her brother had used the bond to make slaves of their human servants. Joanna looked at it first as a tool for learning, later as a gift. The bond between them allowed her to share the girl's humanity. For that alone she would love her.

At dusk, Joanna dressed in a russet-colored gown, the newest in her growing collection, and joined her now placid servant in the parlor.

"I'm sorry," Colleen said, looking at her with eyes red from crying.

Joanna said nothing, only sat beside her and reached for her hand. Even on this cool evening, it felt warm against her own. She sat there, relishing the peace of the house until the mantel clock struck midnight. "Go to sleep. I'll wake you later," she said to Colleen.

Before the girl could reply, she was gone.

She found Arthur waiting for her in his garden, drenched with moonlight, as if he had guessed that she had spent the happiest years of her life in gardens. But though her grandfather's had been beautiful, they could not compare in scope or arrangement to this one.

Not only one, Arthur had explained on that second night she came to him. There was a cutting garden, a rose garden, vegetable and herb gardens for the kitchen and sachets. There were hedge mazes and topiaries and arbors.

That evening she walked with him through all of them while she answered his vague questions as best she could.

What was her life like?

Endless. Lonely. Filled with darkness.

He seemed so sad at hearing this that she tried to convey the glory of night. But the words seemed hollow, even to her. After centuries, she still dreamed of the sun. "Why do you question me like this?" she asked him in turn.

They were in a hedge maze then, walking aimlessly near the center. A bench had been provided for those hopelessly lost. He sat on it and did not look at her as he confessed his part in the killing of her brother, and why he had done it.

"I saw Lucy die twice. I wanted vengeance that no human laws could give me. I won't apologize for what I did to him. But I mourn for my Lucy and despise my weakness in killing her. That's why I sought you out. I . . . I thought that if I were to find you and speak with you and know you, then I would at least be spared all the doubt. Guilt at least offers the promise of eventual peace, but doubt only seems to grow stronger with age."

How could she answer except with the truth? She gulped in air, convinced that if she had tears to shed she would be crying, as he was. "For as long as my brother walked the earth, your lover would have been his slave," she said. "When you killed him, you would have ended that."

"Then afterward she could have been mine?"

She had no words to answer him. Instead she pulled him to his feet and pressed her body against his. Chest to chest. Lips to lips. He shuddered, tried to pull away, but she held him until he was frantic, then released him. He fell backward onto the bench, and she suspected that only supreme self-control kept him from running as far as he could, trying to get away from the horror he felt.

"There would have been no"—she tried to find the right word and used her own instead—"*relatie sexuala*. No children. No life as other couples have."

"I could have let her live."

"With him she would have been a slave. Without him, helpless as a child."

She considered the weeks after the change, how the new and desperate hunger would not be controlled. Illona had brought her youths and infants, mocking that soft spot in her silent heart. And though it had sickened her to destroy those innocents, she had feasted on them. "Children are all alike," she finally said. "They are brutal in taking what they need."

"But if—"

Incredible! He would continue to protest, continue to find some reason to think he should be damned. She was too weary to argue further. She took a backward step away from him, another, then turned and fled on human feet into the maze.

"What have I done?" he called as he tried to follow, went the wrong way at the second turn, turned back and came face to face with her.

By then she was calmer, "Enough," she ordered.

"I'm sorry," he whispered and offered her his arm.

They went on through the maze and out the far side, down a straight path lined with poplars and flower-filled urns to an iron bench where they sat some distance apart, silent and awkward.

"And your thoughts on London?" he finally asked.

"Too confining. Too dangerous."

"Dangerous? For you?" he actually laughed as he said this, as if she were powerful, not in hiding and constantly afraid.

"For your own." She told him about the starving child.

"There are too many poor to help. And too few people try."

"In my land, parents give their last bits of food to their children. What other future is there?"

"It's different here."

She told him about the murder she'd witnessed.

He wasn't laughing then. "There have been four murders just this summer. You actually saw the man?"

"Just his back, not his face. I've glimpsed him before, I think. And now he has seen me."

"Does he know what you are?"

"He knows I am different."

"Don't go back to those streets."

"You sound like my servant. Always worrying about me. But how should I live, Lord Arthur? Should I feed on the wealthy until someone spies me and hunts me down?"

"Men like that are deadly. . . ." Wanting to warn her, he reached for her hand as if she were fragile, human. His hand passed through her, her form ghostly in the dim lamplight, her nervous laughter vibrating in the air. "Deadly." She repeated his last word.

The air cooled around him and she was gone—up and toward the crowded parts of the city.

The hunger she felt that night was not for blood. Instead she walked the gayer streets of Chelsea and St. James, stopping finally beneath the marble columns of the St. James Theater. The lights were up in the lobby, revealing women with long skirts and elaborate hats, men in starched collars and ascots. She heard their laughter, watched gloved hands with feathered fans flutter seductively.

The lights dimmed slowly. A cue, no doubt, because the lobby emptied quickly, leaving only a pair of bored ushers.

No threat to her. Formless, she moved inside and up to a dark corner of the balcony. There she took form again and stayed, a woman unnoticed in the dark. She watched the audience as they did the stage—never a part of it, intrigued nonetheless. She could hear every breath, every soft whisper to a partner or friend, every rustle of a taffeta petticoat.

The noises around her faded. She stood lost in thought until the heroine on the stage stepped forward and began to sing.

She had an incredible voice, one well suited to her love song. Joanna listened to the deep breaths that gave life to the long, drawn-out notes, the lilting tremolos.

Once, she would have found the creature attractive only for the blood she could give. Not anymore. For centuries she had killed and killed, and convinced herself that that was how she needed to live. The lust for killing had become like the lust for opium or strong drink—a vice impossible to control while caught up in it. Once the others were gone and she was on her own, her fear had made that killing impossible. It was her weakness, not her strength, that broke the hold that horrible lust had on her soul.

And she had longed to be as strong as her Tepes blood. A horrible fate!

Her weakness seemed a blessing now. She took a seat in the empty back row and listened with rapture to that voice rising and falling and rising again to incredible heights. If she had money with her, she would have sent flowers after the performance, or some other gift to show her gratitude for the revelation that voice had given.

So how would she answer Arthur's anguished questions when she saw him next? A lie would be so much kinder than the truth, but she had time to consider that. More pressing was what she should tell Colleen now that her perspective on her servant had shifted.

For that the truth would be kindest, she decided, then sat and thought of nothing but music until the curtain fell.

As the lights went up, she vanished and moved out the second-floor doors to the balcony, the night. She waited until nearly dawn before returning to her home and the safety of her box, her earth.

twenty-five

Joanna never explained where she went on her long night journeys. Colleen didn't ask—first because it wasn't her place to ask, later—after Joanna stopped coming home hungry—because she didn't want to know, later yet because she didn't want to sound possessive or, worse, jealous. Better ignorance than that.

Then the inevitable happened. Though Colleen woke at the time Joanna usually returned, Joanna did not come. Colleen paced the rooms as always, then found her eyelids too heavy. With little warning of her exhaustion, she fell asleep.

It was well after dawn when she opened her eyes again. When Colleen went into the dark room that held Joanna's box of earth, she found no soiled dress on the carpet, nor any other sign that her mistress slept at home. It would not pain Joanna to have the lid opened if the door were shut, but though they were closer than some lovers, Colleen would not violate her privacy. Instead, she went about her usual work until sundown. When Joanna did not join her, she went into the dark room and put her hand on the lid. Before she could lift it, it opened from the inside.

Colleen jumped backward. She would have retreated, but the ruse would only have made her look more foolish. Joanna would have known she was there the moment she entered the room.

Joanna offered no explanation as to where she'd been. Instead she slipped a sapphire ring onto Colleen's finger, gave her a dry, quick kiss and drew her to the bed.

Joanna fed voraciously, then gave even more in return—more kisses, more caresses, more blood—leaving Colleen dizzy, cold and breathless. Her heart pounded. More than once she'd cried out in pain. And yet she clung tightly to Joanna, mixing kisses with tears.

"What is it, *draga*?" Joanna whispered.

"You're forcing my change because you're going away," Colleen said with a sob.

With hunger and need satisfied, all that remained in Joanna was something akin to love. She stroked Colleen's hair, kissed her again, held her close. "Colleen, I promise you that I will not force a change, though I think it became inevitable as soon as you tasted my blood. I regret that sharing. I shared a curse, out of fear and ignorance. I thought I needed that to bind you to me. I was wrong. But at least you will live a full life before you wake to mine."

"A full life . . ." Colleen choked back another sob. "You're leaving, aren't you?"

"Not permanently. I promise that. But I may be gone for a little while."

"No! You mustn't! Who will care for you as I do?"

Colleen would have jumped to her feet, but Joanna held her tightly. "I will not leave forever," she repeated.

"It's that man and his wealth," Colleen insisted.

"I have wealth enough of my own. Enough for you to live well in this house, to marry if you wish, to have children. Our time will come later."

Colleen ceased to struggle, pressed closer to Joanna, close enough to whisper, "Change me now. Let me be with you."

"You don't understand what you're asking. Do you want to die?"

Colleen rubbed the wound on the side of her neck, the second on her chest until the blood flowed freely again. "I'll do what I must to stay with you. Whatever you ask," she whispered.

Joanna looked at the blood. She could not help herself. She was greedy, too much so. Her nature demanded, love demanded and she had so little self-control. She rolled up on one elbow and looked down at Colleen nestled against her. Had she shared too much for Colleen to survive? Too little? No one ever told her these things. No one wanted her to know.

"I'll do whatever you ask," Colleen repeated.

"Then listen to me well. I give you the house and everything in it. And I promise I will not abandon you."

The hands that had been clutching flesh and fabric held only air and memory. Colleen pressed her head into the pillow and, cursing her unfamiliar weakness, cried.

One night's absence followed. Two. Three. When Joanna did not return home for a week, Colleen began to wonder if Joanna were truly dead or merely meant to drive her insane.

Long and lonely nights filled with uncertainty. Bad enough, but on top of that, Colleen felt a thirst in her that a pint or two from the women's room of a nearby tavern did not quench.

But though the alcohol could not kill the need, it could kill the inclination to satisfy it. She slept much of her days, visited the pub at night then returned to the house to roam its rooms, working through the dark hours to keep it spotless, ready when its mistress finally returned.

And if she never did, what then?

Unthinkable! Just as it was unthinkable to believe Joanna might be truly dead. They were bonded by blood, Joanna had told her one would know if the other were in danger. But what if the man had lured her to his estate and trapped her? She might be in pain, or starving—a condition whose torments Colleen had glimpsed.

She made inquiries, discovered Arthur Holmwood's many addresses. She put on her best clothes and took a cab to the estate in Kensington. She had intended to bluff her way inside, but her accent—the blend of Irish and cockney—would not allow her to pass as a lady. As she stood outside the iron gates, a groundskeeper passed by and asked if she were all right.

"I seem to have misplaced my mistress. Is there a woman staying here with Mr. Holmwood?"

"Mister?" He smiled.

"Holmwood," she repeated. "The woman has dark hair and

green eyes and is very thin. She's sick, actually. I'm worried about her."

"I'm sorry," the man said. He seemed about to say something more, then thought better of it and moved on, swinging a sickle to level the grass where the lawn met the wall.

She returned to Chelsea, miserable and hungry, with a sharp headache from the afternoon sun.

That night she tried his house in Mayfair, even going so far as to knock on the door. An old gentleman answered and looked at her kindly. "Is there something you need?" he asked, his English thickly accented; German or Austrian, she guessed.

She shook her head and said nothing as she backed away from the door. To say anything of her prepared speech would reveal too much to the man she guessed was Van Helsing—and the enemy.

"It's all right," he said, voice soothing. "I can help, perhaps?"

"I'm at the wrong address," she replied and whirled.

He followed, calling after her. His voice sounded concerned, fatherly, but she knew how voices could deceive. She ran down the quiet street to a noisier one and into an arcade of shops, lit within and without by gaslights. Blinded, frightened, she rushed on until a top-hatted beadle grabbed her from behind.

"Halt!" the guard ordered. "You have to walk in here, or I will ask you to leave."

She didn't look at him, didn't acknowledge his words.

"Is something wrong?" he asked.

She shook her head. When he let her go, she went on at as quick a pace as she dared. Once outside, she broke into a run, stopping only when she needed to catch her breath.

Once home, she barred the door, wolfed down a quick meal, then retreated to Joanna's little room and shut the door. She moved by memory to the box and lifted the lid. The scent that once had seemed so dank and desolate soothed her. She lay inside, comforted by the darkness of the room, wishing that she did not need air and could close the lid.

This might be as near as she ever got to her mistress again, she thought. The sadness would have made her frantic, but she had traveled so far today and the earth was so soft.

She closed her eyes. Though she did not know it, the dawn was breaking as she finally, peacefully, slept.

For Abraham Van Helsing, sleep came just as hard. Try as he liked to think the woman's troubles were none of his concern, he could not help but consider the frantic expression on her face, the way she had run from him as if she had seen the devil himself.

He thought of the vampire woman briefly, but dismissed the idea as nothing more than monomania on his part. It had been nearly a month since the last ship had arrived from the East, and there had been no sign of the creature. True, two more murders had taken place, but the victims had died from stabbing.

Police held to the theory that the killer wasn't the Ripper but someone imitating his style. And there had been one witness, a woman who had seen a man disappear into the darkness just before she found the body.

As for Jonathan, he had written that though he still had the dreams, they were becomming less intense. Van Helsing attributed that to Madame Mina's comforting presence in his life once more. It was likely that was all the dreams had ever signified.

Perhaps the vampire woman would never come at all.

As for the one he had seen earlier in the evening, she had been well dressed but without the bearing of a lady. A mistress whom Arthur had abandoned? Another actress, perhaps? He did not like to think Arthur could be so callous, but he had been most secretive since Van Helsing had returned from Exeter. Perhaps he had arranged a few trysts, then abandoned the poor child.

He decided it was time to speak to Arthur.

In the morning, he sent a note to the Kensington estate asking Arthur to meet him for lunch. Arthur agreed and suggested a place for the following afternoon.

Arthur's suggestion was a place well away from his usual haunts, on Georges Street in Marlyebone. The distance Van Helsing had to travel for the meeting was nearly as long as the distance Arthur had come. For that the old establishment should have been outstanding, but it was hardly different from a dozen outside dining spots in Chelsea or Belgravia. That alone would have been enough to suggest to Van Helsing that something was wrong; Arthur's behavior made it certain.

Van Helsing arrived first and chose a shaded table near the back, well suited for talking. The moment Arthur joined him, the old doctor noticed a change in him. Not that Arthur wasn't happy; he was. But there was something else, a guardedness Van Helsing had never seen in him before.

When Van Helsing asked where he'd been the past weeks, Arthur explained that he was getting the grounds of his estate in Kensington ready for a fall social, "a small party to welcome my return to society."

"Good. Good. You've put the past to rest, then," Van Helsing replied, the words as much a question as a comment.

"In a way. Gance's death made me think of my own mortality. I don't want to leave a fortune to strangers. I want family. Heirs."

Though he would not usually have pried, Van Helsing asked, "Have you considered someone?"

"Considered? Not really. What made you ask?"

"A woman came by asking about you. Well dressed but . . . well, I am no judge of English accents, but I would guess hers to be Irish."

"Irish! What did she look like?"

"Light-haired. Tall. Thin, like a boy. Twenty, I would say. When I answered the door she became quite agitated, as if she knew who I was and feared me. At first I thought she might be a servant of that creature—" He saw Arthur stiffen and misunderstood. "Do you have news about that?"

"Nothing. I even went down to the wharf and spoke to sailors from the last Eastern ship and discovered nothing new. But I think I need to adopt Wilde's philosophy and demand that something so unpleasant never be discussed in my presence again."

"You did not let me finish. Yes, I thought of that creature. Then I thought of your Rose and considered you might be seeing the girl, but if so, why did she seem so frightened of me?"

"You are too naive, doctor. There are many desperate people in London. She may have expected to find the rooms empty. They often are."

Arthur seemed less concerned than relieved. Thieves would be better actors, Van Helsing thought. "I never considered that," he said. "You may be right. If so, it is good I was there when she knocked, or we both might be missing some part of our lives."

"Well, you were there, thankfully. I should send a locksmith around this week, just to be certain the place is secure. Actually, I should come around myself. I haven't seen Beardsley lately. How is he?"

Having learned all he guessed he would, Van Helsing let the subject shift. "He looks better. He says he feels better. But I think his idea of better is not nearly good enough. He needs to be out of the country this next winter or it may be his last."

"Other physicians have said that for years, and he's still here. Aubrey has strength the rest of us can only wish we possessed."

"I pray that's so. Perhaps when you're ready we can pay a call on you in Kensington. A walk through the garden and an afternoon in the sun would be so helpful."

"Anytime he's able. Just try to give me a bit of notice and I'll be there."

And that might have been the strangest thing Arthur had said all afternoon, Van Helsing thought. In the weeks they'd shared the rooms in Mayfair, Arthur had been home scarcely one day out of four.

They'd met at two. At four-thirty Arthur checked his pocket watch and said he had to go.

Van Helsing watched him head down the street. He considered following Arthur and decided against it. Only instinct made him concerned about the young man's actions, and there were better ways to discover what those might be.

Instead, he headed in the opposite direction, toward his Mayfair rooms. On the way, he stopped at a florist's shop. Though the woman had no garden plants, she did suggest a gardener who kept greenhouses in Camden.

It took the better part of a day to reach the man, but the results were what he had hoped for. He purchased three laburnum vines, a plant the gardener assured him was both exotic and somewhat rare in London. Early the following morning, he took these to Arthur's estate in Kensington.

As he'd hoped, Arthur was not awake yet. He insisted that Ian not wake his master. "It's not important, but I thought of the work he was doing here and wanted to bring a gift." He held out a wooden crate holding the vines.

"Work?" For a moment Ian appeared confused. "Ah, you mean for the garden. Yes, we add to it all the time. Lord Holmwood's family has always had great pride in the Kettering Gardens."

"May I see them?"

"It is more an experience than a seeing, sir. Perhaps I should wake—"

"No. I do not wish to disturb his rest. Walk with me. We older men understand how the young ones need their rest. And the sun will do us both good."

Resigned, Ian lead the way through the house to the wide rear doors that opened onto the terrace, down the steps into the parterre garden with its velvet lawn edged with low hedges and flower beds.

As they walked, Van Helsing learned that Ian had been in Arthur's service since he was born, and in his family's service before that. It seemed a good time to ask if he'd heard the rumor that Arthur intended to marry.

"I would hope he would, and produce an heir in time," Ian replied, adding that it was not his place to pay attention to rumors about any possible fiancées.

Van Helsing tried a number of approaches, then gave up. Ian would have shown him to the gate, but Van Helsing said he preferred to take the winding garden paths around to it and enjoy the plantings on the way. As he ambled toward the gate, he spotted a young man on hands and knees pulling creepers out of the edge of the lawn. Van Helsing waved to him. "Are you the groundskeeper?" he called.

"His help," the man replied.

"I brought three laburnums as a gift for the house. I left them with Ian."

"Ah!" The man wiped his palms on his pants and walked over. "He'll want some new cuttings. Last winter was hard on the vines."

Van Helsing thought he detected the scent of brandy on the man's breath. A house servant would never get away with such behavior, but one who worked outside easily could. He hoped the drink would make the man careless. "I hear Lord Arthur is most interested in his gardens," he said.

"Certainly now."

"Of course," Van Helsing agreed. Though he had no idea what he was agreeing to, he guessed the best way to obtain information was to act as if he knew everything already.

"The lady does love the gardens at night."

"The lady? You've seen her?"

"Once. No one believed me the first time. She gave me a scare, she did, walking alone and so lightly. I see her sometimes now. Walking the paths at night."

"Are you the only one who sees her?"

"No one believed me. But Lord Arthur knows her. They walk together."

"Always outside."

"Once I think they were in the music room. I heard him playing something soft and pretty for her."

Van Helsing's mouth felt dry. "Do you know her name?" he asked.

The man grinned as if he knew he shouldn't answer and didn't care. "I don't, but I call her Cat. She has cat's eyes, you know."

"Green."

"As the grass beneath our feet." He looked down, spotted a beetle in the lawn, and squashed it with the heel of his boot.

Van Helsing could say nothing more. His thoughts reeled. Good God! Could Arthur really have found her? Would he really have been so foolish as to let her inside?

Were it Jonathan or Seward acting so recklessly, Van Helsing would think nothing of marching inside and demanding that he take charge of the affair, just as he had with Lucy. But he had already seen Arthur's obstinate streak and knew he would only be turned away—by force, if needed.

And so he retreated to Mayfair, where he locked the door to the house and sat in the sunniest room, weighing what to do. He decided, finally, that much though he wanted to handle this matter himself, he would not be able to.

With no other choice left him, he wrote a quick, desperate letter to Mina. Wanting her to reach it as quickly as possible, he made two more copies—sending one to Mina's house, a second to her in care of Jonathan's work, and a third to her at the Children's Hospital.

Work done, he spent the remainder of the day trying to work and achieving nothing, trying to rest—for he knew he would not sleep that night—and failing miserably.

She would come, he knew it now. If he had the means to do so, he would take a room somewhere else in the city. It occurred for him, and hardly for the first time, that his obsession with hunting the creatures who had done so much damage to his family and friends would likely lead him to poverty or worse.

But vows had been made, and it was not his nature to break them. It occurred to him that this was what guided Arthur as well.

God help them both.

twenty-six

Mina's days had become long and far more hectic than than they would have been if Jonathan had agreed to give her a position in his firm. She relished her independence in setting up the shelter. And now that she had so many lives depending on her, she could better understand Jonathan's view toward his own work and sympathize with it. He had her and his employees; she, her women and children. When they met, they had much to speak of, and nights to follow. They were, for the moment, content.

There were now six women and four children moved into the first floor of the building while the upper floors were taking shape. Four of the women worked at paying jobs; the others shared kitchen work and tending to the children. Since they were the ones most suited to watching children, Mina thought her experiment was starting well.

One of the children, a little girl not more than six, had taken to her. Every time Mina visited the shelter the child would follow her from room to room or sit in a chair in the room where she went over the ledgers, silent and watching.

Gradually Mina began to understand that the girl was less curious than smitten, "You are from London, I understand. How do you like it here?" Mina asked her

"My mama is happy," the girl replied, speaking as if her own happiness were not important.

"And you?"

The child grinned, showing a chipped front tooth, and nodded. Then, having revealed something of herself, she jumped off the stool and ran from the room. Mina heard a squeal from a younger boy, the girl's mischievous laughter.

Mina smiled. Things were going even better than her most optimistic projections.

She had budgeted twenty thousand pounds for the building. Thanks to all the donations, she would spend barely half that in half the time she'd planned for the work.

She'd nearly finished when Winnie stopped by unexpectedly. "I have a letter for you," she said. "You get so little mail I thought it might be important, so I brought it straightaway."

As soon as she looked at it, Mina recognized the writing. "It's from Dr. Van Helsing," she said and ripped it open, scanning quickly, then deciding to read it aloud. Winnie had been involved in her last terrible adventure. Better to let her know up front what was happening now, since she'd only relay the contents of the letter later.

My dear Madame Mina,

I have unfortunate news that concerns all of us.

Just before I left to meet you and Jonathan in Exeter, I asked Arthur to see what he could discover about passengers on the ships arriving from the East. He did as I asked and told me that he'd discovered nothing.

But after my visit to you, I began to notice how reclusive he had become, even going so far as to leave his Mayfair rooms to stay at his estate in Kensington. I thought perhaps that he wanted to put the past behind him, as he had recently confessed he wished to do. Then I was visited by a young woman looking for him. She was most upset not to find him but would not speak to me. Indeed, she seemed frightened of me, as if she knew me.

Curious, I traveled out to Kensington and arranged a ruse that allowed me to speak to the servants. What I learned is most distressing. He apparently discovered that the vampire woman is in London but did not inform me of this. Instead he took it upon himself to find and meet her. Even then he said nothing.

After all the horrors our little band had seen, he would risk his life and his soul this way. Worse, I have been told that he has even invited her into his house—leaving him open and vulnerable to her attack.

I cannot imagine why he would do such a foolish thing.

Mina paused a moment, thinking that Arthur was less foolish than driven. But then grief and curiosity combined into a terrible drug.

"And you tell me how brilliant the doctor is," Winnie commented when Mina fell silent.

"He hates them, all of them. He cannot imagine how I could mourn for Karina, who was as much a victim as Lucy." She returned to her reading:

I could not confront him, for I could guess the outcome if I did. He may have already realized how much I know. If so, I may never be allowed in his presence again to look with my own eyes for some lightening of his complexion, some sensitivity of his eyes to sunlight, and all the other subtle changes that might come if he does what I fear he may. Indeed, I fear that the next time I see the young man, he will be beyond caring.

So come, dear Mina, for his sake. I think of all of us, he trusts you the most, and in his affection for you he will not allow you to come to harm.

I have sent a copy of this letter to Jonathan. Come alone or, better still, bring him. But come soon. AVH

"What would you like me to do?" Winnie asked as Mina put down the letter.

"I'm expecting two deliveries this afternoon. Could you wait here for them?"

"You're going to London now?"

"I don't know. But I need to speak to Jonathan first." She put away her pen and ink and reached for her bonnet. She'd barely tied the bow when a messenger boy on a bicycle arrived with a note from Jonathan asking her to meet him at his office as soon as possible. The writing was scrawled across the page, as if he wrote quickly and frantically.

She took a cab, promising the driver extra if he got her there as quickly as his horse could safely travel. The driver apparently relished the challenge, for he made it across town at an incredible rate. All Mina could do was dig her fingers into the worn leather upholstery, brace her feet against the front of the cab and try to stay upright in her seat.

"Good ride, miss?" the driver called as she got out, bonnet slightly askew from the last quick turn.

"I suppose I invited that," she replied, glancing at the horse. The beast looked as if he had enjoyed the run as much as his driver, so true to her word, she gave the man half his fare as a tip.

By then it was nearly six. She found Jonathan alone, sitting at his desk, a stack of papers in front of him. He got up when he saw her, all but running to her, his embrace quick and hard. "So much to do, but I want you to stay with me tonight."

His voice had never sounded so taut before, nor had his expression ever seemed so flat. It seemed that he had filed away all emotion for some future consideration.

"You're so busy. While you're finishing up, I'll go to see Essie and pack a bag," she said.

"No!" The word too loud. He looked more surprised than she, and went on more carefully. "That is, please don't. It will be dark before you return. Send a note to Essie. Tell her to bring the bag to the station in the morning."

"And I should leave her alone tonight?" Mina asked gently.

"It isn't she the creature would want to harm."

He's fighting hysteria, she thought, and went to him, holding him close. "It may not be me, either. Or you, for that matter. The woman has been in London for some time. Why do you think she would come now?"

"Because Arthur drew her attention back to us. And now Van Helsing wants you to go to London and face another of these creatures. Damn Arthur! How could he be such a fool?"

She rested a steady hand on the side of his face. "If it had been me who had died and awakened one of them. If it had been you who held the stake that ended my life in death, wouldn't you want to know that you had done the right thing?"

He frowned, then considered as his anger dissipated. "I cannot imagine how I would feel."

She went on, the soothing tone taking the edge off her words. "A year ago, you said that if I went into that terrible life in death you would not let me go alone. You hardly spoke of stakes and holy water then."

"I meant it. I would not have let them kill you, not until I was sure you were beyond redemption."

"But with Lucy, Van Helsing handled everything. How could Arthur have stood up to him? Could you have done so?"

"I . . . I would have tried, because you would have tried for me. You were stronger than the rest of us. You deserved that chance."

She looked at him a long time, trying to think of a way to explain her feeling, her decision. She could find none. "Jonathan, will you trust me?" she asked.

"Not if it means you wish to go to London alone."

"Not that." She smiled, thinking the decision she had reached while being thrown about in the hack was the right one. "I don't want to go at all, at least not yet," she said.

He gaped at her, surprise making the relief he felt too evident. "But Van Helsing's letter, the woman?"

"I've been thinking of the woman, and I do not believe she means us any harm. Have you dreamed of her lately?"

"Shadowy dreams. Nothing vivid. Not for weeks."

"Because she no longer considers you. No, don't look so hopeful. It's what I feel, not what I know."

"And Arthur? We can't just abandon him."

"I will write him. I will tell him everything we suspect and ask if it is true. Then, one curious creature to another, I will ask him to please tell me what he has learned. I think he will reply."

"We should see him, make certain he is all right."

"I've been to Kettering. The house is huge, and there's a wall around the grounds. If he wants to keep us out, there's no way we can get in. If we try to force his hand, he could even have us arrested."

"But until this is over—"

"It won't be such a chore, living with you. But tonight I want you to come home with me. I need to speak to Essie in person, not in a note. I need to explain what I intend to do."

It wasn't his choice. His expression made that clear enough, even as he agreed.

And for the next hour, as Jonathan finished his work, Mina sat at Tom Pierson's desk, writing to Arthur, her words straight from her heart.

Finishing those, the penned a quicker note to Van Helsing.

My dear doctor,

I can understand your concern, but I disagree with your course of action. I, too, have read the papers with care, and there have been no murders in the manner we had feared. Jonathan's dreams are indeed quieter now, though your letter may be the factor that changes all that.

But until I know that the creature means us harm, means ANYone harm, I will not come to London. I am writing Arthur, however, and asking about Joanna. I think this quiet approach is best.

As for you, with what you have seen and suffered, I understand your fear of them. I am making arrangements for you to stay at the flat Gance willed to me in Mayfair. You should receive a key from Mr. Quarles in a day or two. With love, Mina.

The letter was firm, she thought, but not heartless. She took it in to Jonathan to read and saw the relief on his face as he did so.

twenty-seven

Another week passed without even the whisper of Joanna's presence, but Colleen kept up her frantic schedule of cleaning and mending—a schedule broken only by nightly visits to a nearby pub.

But hard work and strong drink could not disguise the truth—no matter what Joanna had wished for her, she had been too late. Colleen was changing, slowly and inexorably. And she faced the change alone.

The infrequent London sunlight still warmed her when it touched, and like most of the sooty city, she relished the infrequent glimpses of a clear sky. But within an hour her skin would redden and blister and she would retreat to the cottage with a pounding headache that no drink could kill.

Her cravings were for stronger stuff.

When she made her way through the London crowds, canvas satchel looped over her arm, a wide-brimmed hat pulled down on her head, she would notice the men, weigh them like no other single women would weigh a prospect. The London dandy was too pale, possibly ill. The merchant was too old. No need to kill when the taste of a younger one would do no harm.

After a week of toying with what seemed a fantasy, she noticed a man eyeing pipes on display in a tobacco shop window. Hardly thirty, so young enough. Tweed coat, badly mended, which meant he likely lived alone. A bit of meat to his bones, as her mother would say, and healthy. A red face that spoke of blood flowing hot and quick. And he looked a bit dim-witted. She might be able to trick him into going with her to the cottage. She would strip off the sage green dress she had borrowed from Joanna's things, remove the tight starched collar of his shirt, flirt with him, kiss him, draw him to the bed. There she would touch him as Joanna had touched her, lovingly, gently, drawing out his passion. And in the moment when he gave it all to her, she would taste him, drink from him.

As Joanna had from her.

What would he make of that? she wondered. Caught up in that moment of perfect pleasure, would he feel it at all?

He noticed her frank stare, walked to her, asked, "Are you all right? You seem a bit ill."

She tried to smile, played with an elusive strand of her hair. "A bit tired is all."

He touched his hat. "My name is Ronald Pepper, and since there is no one to introduce us properly, I must introduce myself. And you are . . . ?"

"Colleen O'Shaunnasy."

"Irish, you are."

"From Limerick. But that was a long time ago."

"Well, Miss Colleen . . . It is 'miss,' isn't it?" She nodded and he went on, "I am recently down from Hull and was just looking for a bit of lunch. Would you like to join me?"

"I would." She linked her arm with his. As they touched, a wave of dizziness rolled over her and she fell against him.

"You're not all right." He led her into the dim interior of the nearest café and to an open, shaded window. "Wait here," he said and wove through the empty tables to the back of the establishment, returning some moments later with a glass of cool water.

"If this weren't London, I'd swear you had sunstroke," he said.

"Perhaps I'm just hungry," she replied, wondering if it were true. She could not recall the last time she'd eaten.

He took it as a suggestion and left again, returning with two sausage rolls and two pints of dark ale. "I thought I'd take a chance that you would want something to wash down the meal. Beer is healthy, you know."

She bit into one end. As she did, grease leaked out the other onto her fingers. The meat was too spicy, the biscuit around it undercooked. She washed it down like some oversized pill with a large swallow of the ale.

"That's the girl," her would-be savior said, beaming as she ate.

"And how would you know about sunstroke?" she asked.

"A dozen years in India. One of Her Majesty's lesser civil servants." He went on, explaining how a brief stint in the merchant marine led to a petty position in vessel inspection. "Then I had a bout of malaria, nothing serious, but enough that it was advised that I come back to the cooler latitudes."

"And now?"

He was happy to supply details of a minor customs job, more details than she was interested in knowing. But as he continued, she began to know him and to like what she saw, enough that she was beginning to feel guilty. He had been so concerned, so kind. How could she use him so callously?

"Would you like something else to eat—kidney pie, bangers and mash, cheese and rolls, barley soup?" he asked, reading the chalkboard over the bar.

"The soup, I think," she replied, and again, he went off and ordered it.

Could she do this? The idea was growing increasingly repulsive, but it seemed she had no choice. The soup was delicious, some part of her was still aware of that; but it tasted stale, corrupted. She'd been raised on a farm, and a sudden flash of memory came back to her, how her grandfather had eaten the raw liver from the sheep he'd slaughtered, saying there was nothing more healthy for a man than fresh blood and flesh and how she must never do such a thing in the city because nothing was fresh there, everything was suspect. The first time she'd seen this, she'd gone behind the barn and vomited, and eaten no meat for days while her brothers and parents laughed at her. Now she wished she were back there with the same opportunity.

From his place across the table, Ronald smiled at her, encouraging her to eat. She forced the rest of it down, swallowed hard to keep it there and said she felt much better.

They ordered another round. She sipped hers while he

gulped, ordered another. She began to wonder if the malaria story was made up, for he did seem to have a problem with drink. Good. She relished the flaw, especially when it made him weaker.

Three hours later, long after the cursed sun had crossed the horizon, they left the pub together. Ronald had far too much to drink but was nonetheless an honorable man. He wanted her address. She warned him that to try for home in his condition would likely lead to robbery or worse, and suggested he come with her instead.

He did not protest her idea overly much.

It was a mere half-hour walk to the cottage, and by the time they got there, Ronald had sobered up a bit. "It's all right, I live alone," she assured him and squeezed his hand before unlocking the door.

Once inside, she shut the door to Joanna's room and offered him a seat. She had no experience with flirting, but that hardly made a difference. He guessed what she had in mind, pulled her close and kissed her.

He was hesitant at first, but when she did not protest, he kissed her again, more insistently. She felt his tongue move between her lips and opened her mouth, inviting it in.

When the time came to move from sofa to bed, she went to lock the door. "You're not one of . . ." he began, voice trailing off, since he had no way of asking without giving insult.

"Just lonely," she replied and joined him.

He was clumsy, standing beside the bed and fumbling with his clothes and hers. She noticed but didn't care, far more concerned about how she would manage to cut him. Her teeth weren't sharp enough and, drunk though he might be, a knife in her hand would hardly be the start of the romantic interlude her act needed for success.

Ronald kissed her again, then lost his balance, sending her tumbling backward. She landed on the bed. He followed her but fell sideways, upsetting the narrow bedside table, landing hard on its edge and breaking the glass that she'd left on it the night before.

He rolled onto his back and swore, then apologized for the mild profanity. She might be acting the whore, but he persisted in treating her like a lady.

"You've cut yourself," she said, crouching over him and tilting his head sideways and down, finger exploring the skin.

"I don't feel . . . ooch!"

She held out a piece of glass. "I just pulled it out of your shoulder."

"A scratch," he said as she helped him to his feet. She sensed he was going to ask about a clean kerchief, and before he did she kissed him again with more urgency and pulled him down on her.

His hands were on her breasts, kneading them mechanically, as if he had been told that was what a woman liked but had no direct experience with it.

Perhaps he hadn't. Country boy, civil service. Perhaps he'd had some Indian woman who never spoke a word to educate him. Certainly he needed an education.

"Slow down," she whispered and rolled above him, one hand behind her playing with his cock and balls. He thrust upward, trying to push her back and up.

"Not yet," she whispered.

"Shouldn't I be using—"

She put her fingers over his lips. She might have no reason to believe it, but she knew it was true. Whatever change Joanna had caused in her had stolen that thing most natural to a woman. "It's all right," she murmured. "I cannot have children, nor will I pass any curse of disease on to you."

With that, she lowered her lips to his, then kissed the side of his neck, the place where she had so cleverly made the wound, licking off the skin that had formed on it.

Barely a trickle, but the taste was enough. Suddenly greedy to possess all of him, she let him enter her, pressed lips tight against the wound, and sucked.

He never noticed, and once when he started to move his head sideways to kiss her again, she began to pound above him, distracting.

He screamed, and in the sudden rush of passion and pulse, the blood flowed quicker, filling her mouth, her body. She screamed with him, head back, one arm wiping her lips dry to hide that unnatural lust, then fell beside him.

Their bodies were covered with a sheen of sweat. His quick breaths sounded almost like sobs. As for her, she could feel him on her lips, her throat, already pulsing through her . . . all the sweet sweet passion of him shared and diffused in a pleasant, rosy haze.

From beside her, he whispered, "Thank you."

She turned to look at him, in wonder. For a moment she had almost forgotten that he was present anywhere but inside her.

"Thank you," she murmured. And as his fingers brushed the taut nipples of her breasts, she shivered with delight.

Afterward there was the awkward fumbling with their clothes, the more awkward silence. Now, sobered through passion, he waited for an invitation to stay the night. Colleen couldn't offer it. This was Joanna's house, not hers, and she could return at any time. It was hardly late, and she hoped he didn't have far to go.

"Is there anything you need?" he suggested, wondering no doubt if her comment about loneliness was a ruse for more concrete needs. She shook her head.

"May I call on you tomorrow?" he asked.

What a dear man! She should send him away, far away, but there was no telling the effect the slight would have on him, or when that terrible need would strike again.

"Not tomorrow. Come the day after if you can."

"And we'll go to lunch, or would you prefer dinner?"

"Dinner." She kissed him good-bye.

Soon after he left, there was a knock on the door, a street vendor carrying a bouquet of yellow snapdragons. She came outside and looked around for Ronald, but he had gone.

The taste of him! The taste of *it*! The day after, she lived in a cloud of rosy haze. She had done it without any help, she was learning to survive! By the following morning, though, she became restless. The feeling grew through the day until, by the time Ronald arrived, she wanted nothing more than to repeat every detail of their last meeting.

He arrived a bit after four, this time in a carriage. She had no idea what a lesser civil servant might get paid, but it wasn't enough for this sort of luxury.

Unless he was courting her.

She was glad she'd worn the blue dress, the one Joanna

had given her because the color was too pale against Joanna's white skin. It had suited Colleen then. Now the color still went well with her blond hair, but she had to pinch her cheeks to get a healthy look of color in them.

As they rode through Chelsea, Ronald told her that he thought she looked much better. "And no more dizziness, I hope," he added.

She shook her head. "And your cut?"

"Healing, I think, It chafes against my collar sometimes, but only a little. I can't really see it, though."

"Let me look." She did, noting sadly that the wound was indeed smaller. "I'll put a bit of alcohol on it later. Just to be safe."

He took her to dinner in a spot close to the natural history museum. She ate what he suggested, barely tasting the food, her mind whirling, trying to find some way to explain her needs, or if not, to repeat the marvelous accident of two nights before.

Hardly possible when tonight Ronald drank little or nothing. At dinner, he did not want to order brandy for himself, and she could hardly put herself at a disadvantage when she was the one with a secret to hide.

By the time they started back to the cottage, she'd become frantic. She needed blood, and nothing but blood would do. Not exactly something to confess to a lover she hardly knew, but something she would do if there were no better choice.

He noticed her preoccupation, apparently noticed too how her attention focused on him every time he touched her. So he touched her often, helping her off with her shawl and resting a hand on her bare shoulder, holding hands with her over dinner, taking her arm when they decided to walk home. And every time their bodies touched, a shiver ran through her and she marveled at the heat of him.

Misinterpreting her reaction as passion, he did not ask permission to come inside. And as soon as they were alone, he was kissing her, his hands quickly undoing the hooks on the back of her dress.

Managing to untangle herself from his embrace, she offered him brandy, which he declined with a sly grin. "I think

I was a bit drunk last time. I'd like to be aware of your needs tonight, my marvelous Colleen."

"Stay the night," she murmured, praying that he was a sound sleeper.

"I should love to see you beside me in the morning," he replied, then kissed her again, the passion of it leaving her breathless.

Once in bed, his kisses covered her breasts and belly and thighs, his hands demanding. And yes, she wanted him more even than before, but her mind was fixed on the thing that was lacking, the blood she could not ask him for.

Then at the moment his passion reached its climax, she demanded hers, pulling him down on her and wrapping her legs around his waist, and she found the spot on his neck and bit.

A taste. She'd only wanted a taste, but her body demanded more, so she bit down hard. He cried out, tried to pull away, but her legs were wrapped around him, holding him tight, her own climax coming hard, her contractions demanding his response.

Moments later, when she lay spent, exhausted, half drunk with what he had given, he pulled away and in the dim light saw his blood on her lips.

"Colleen, what did you do?" he cried, backing away from her.

Later, she knew she should have cried, should have tearfully tried to explain her needs. Instead, sated and joyful, she'd smiled. "I took what I needed," she said, inexplicably astonished when he grabbed his clothes from the floor and darted into the parlor.

She followed soon after, still naked, with drops of his blood on her chin. He was already half dressed, his fingers examining the wound she'd made. "At least get me a clean cloth, damn you!" he ordered.

She did, standing before him, waiting for his anger to dissipate. It didn't. He turned to leave. She grabbed his arm, but he pushed it away. "At least let me try to explain," she said.

"Explain? What's there to explain?" He pulled the cloth away from the wound and tossed it at her.

It landed at her feet. She looked down at the stain on it,

then stepped over it and toward him. "I have to tell you . . . I can't just let you think that—"

"No!" he shouted and with shirt half buttoned, he grabbed his coat and left, slamming her door behind him.

She fell back into a chair. An explanation would hardly have helped, she decided. Most likely she would have had to kill him. That sudden, odd thought made her giggle with delight. Drunk on life, she would worry about the next tryst tomorrow. For now, it was better to enjoy.

She hoped that Joanna, wherever she was, was having as pleasant a time.

twenty-eight

Though it had been lifetimes ago, Joanna could still remember the day she first noticed a rainbow. She'd been scarcely four, the youngest child playing in the gardens outside her grandfather's palace. A quick squall had sent them all scurrying for the shelter of a covered porch. Joanna, smaller than the rest, had lagged behind, then fallen and bruised her knee on the stones.

She'd sat up and took a deep breath, intending to call for help, when the sun found a hole in the clouds and transformed the thin shower into an arch of colors above her.

She'd stared up at it, all thoughts of her pain—slight at its worst—vanishing as the arch grew more intense. The others saw it too, running into the open, pointing at the sky.

Years later, she learned how rainbows were created from sunlight on water. The knowledge didn't ruin the mystery of the sight—why it had appeared to her and stolen her pain.

When she saw rainbows, she always thought of her mother.

"I put the prisms above your box because I wanted you to see a sight born from sunlight," Arthur explained when she finally asked him about the pieces of glass.

How had he thought of a gift such as that? Of all the things he bought for her, the rainbows were the most precious.

Every night, she would wake in an empty room and rise to the sight of lamps burning on the tables, prisms floating above them, rainbows dancing across the ceiling.

Often there would be another gift—a new gown, a coat of

forest-green velvet, evening gloves, a gold ring. She would try the clothes on, and with no way to see the result in a mirror, go to him for advice.

He would tell her she looked beautiful. If she began to pace, or fell into silence, he would plead a need to work or sleep and leave her alone so she could hunt. On nights when she was appeased, they would walk in the garden or go to the music room. He would play while she listened, so avidly that he had to ask, "Do you sing?"

A pause. An answer. "I did. I had a beautiful voice. I can hear it still in your music."

"Sing for me."

Her throat so dry, her voice so little used that even now it seemed most human when she kept it at a whisper. "Music is for the living," she said. "It makes me remember those times."

"Then music it is—the symphony or opera?"

"Opera, please."

He had tickets the following night. Box seats, he assured her. Perfectly private.

Nonetheless, she wore a deep green satin and velvet cape over her green lace ballgown, both intended to help her fade into the shadows at the first sign that anyone looked at her with suspicion. Unused to being out, she sat in the covered carriage, gripping Arthur's hand so tightly that, later in the evening when she looked at it, she saw a bruise in the soft spot near his thumb. She continued to hold it until the lights went down, and in the comfort of darkness she could listen unafraid.

Between acts, she raised the hood of her cape, hiding her face. When friends stopped by the box, she turned her head away so quickly that Arthur led them into the hallway, saying that his friend from the Continent was unwell.

"What are you so afraid of?" Arthur asked when he returned.

"My face. My eyes. My skin. They'll know," she whispered in quick, small bursts of breath. It took all her control to keep from laughing at the absurdity of her in this place.

"Your eyes are magnificent. As for your face and skin, yes, they are too pale, but no worse than my friend Beardsley's.

As to the other, less obvious differences, this is London, not Varna. It's a rare bird who would guess your secret."

"Someone did."

"Ah, but Jack Seward had to import the codger from the Continent. Besides, it's your hiding that makes them wonder all the more what it is you don't want them to see."

He was right, but it didn't help. She sat in silence until the lights dimmed and the singers began. When it was over and the applause began, he felt her pull her hand away. When he turned to her, she was gone.

He found her near the carriage, hood pulled close over her head, body trembling. "I'll join you later. I need . . ." The last word was left unsaid.

"Let me come with you." When she shook her head, he added, "Or let me show you another way."

She thought she understood, and waited for him to repeat the question she vowed would send her away from him forever. He didn't. Instead he asked, "Joanna, will you trust me for a little while?"

Breath in. Out. But no words came to her.

"A little while," he repeated and took her arm so she could enter the carriage like any lady out on an evening with her escort.

He gave the driver an address and climbed in beside her. They moved through the London streets in awkward silence. As their carriage slowed, Arthur put on his hat, brim low over his forehead.

He helped her out, and she followed him on foot down a narrow street in a part of town far better than her usual hunting grounds. Though the rest of the area was well lit, this block was not. Yes, there were gaslights, but they had not been turned on, or else had been extinguished as soon as the lamplighter had gone on his way. In the comfort of darkness, she managed to relax.

Arthur stopped in front of a green-painted door. No sign advertised either the name or the address, but after two quick knocks, a viewing door opened. Arthur handed in a card, and they were let inside.

Joanna shrank back from the collective sounds of passion—whispering to her from the dark corners, through the shut doors on the upper floors, even, it seemed, from the ghosts of those who had visited here before. She noticed others in the room and the larger one beyond it. But like Arthur, the men wore their hats low on their foreheads. The women were even more discreet, keeping their hoods up, their heads bowed, shading their faces from the few dim lamps that shed a weak light through the intimate, dark-colored room.

"Would you prefer a man or a woman?" he asked.

For sex? For feed? She hardly understood. "Woman," she replied. Women always seemed easier.

As if summoned, a portly woman came down the stairs, her tight black dress cut low, revealing the tops of ample breasts behind her fluttering peacock fans.

"Not that one," Joanna whispered, wondering why Arthur smiled at the comment.

"Is Antoinette free?" he asked.

"Usual room," the woman replied, motioning them past her.

Joanna moved quickly, holding her cape close to her body so she would not have to touch even the woman's clothes. Arthur followed close behind, as if he were afraid she would bolt without his constant presence.

He guided her to the end of a long, narrow hall, another closed door. Opening it, he motioned her to step inside, then shut it behind them both.

Her senses drank it in. A mélange of perfumes new and ancient. Scents of sex of countless partners. Dim golden light thrown by a single glass-cased candle mounted to a mirror on the far wall. The girl—Antoinette, was it?—was already on the bed. Her black gown barely covered her pubis. Of more lace than satin, it seemed less for modesty than for erotic effect.

Joanna's gaze moved from body to face—fair she was, skin and hair, blue eyes. Joanna felt a stab of longing, not for this well-fleshed creature but for the one she had abandoned.

And she had promised never to leave Colleen.

"She knows your needs," Arthur whispered, and for a moment Joanna wondered which woman he spoke of.

"All of them?" she asked, wondering what sort of a fool he was to think he knew, and to trust her so innocently. His name was known here; hers was not. If she killed and left, it would be up to him to explain the woman's corpse.

If it would need explanation. She wondered how much he had spent already. How much would he have to spend for a life?

Inviting death, the girl held out her arms.

"May I stay?" Arthur asked.

He'd given a gift. He deserved that much. She nodded without looking at him, took off her cape and covered the girl with it. Perhaps the lush satin and velvet would provide a sufficient barrier between dead flesh and living.

The girl turned to face her. Joanna gripped her shoulder, holding her on her side. "Look away," she ordered.

"No need for shame, *mademoiselle,*" the girl, a child, really—better to think of her as a child—whispered.

"Do it!" she ordered and laughed at the sound of her voice. Her—so stern.

Silent, obedient, the girl rolled back on her side. Joanna pressed close behind, her face buried in the velvet, her hands moving beneath satin and lace over the mounds of her breasts, the hollow of her waist, then lower.

She heard the girl gasp as her fingers parted the hidden folds of flesh, rub the tiny nub that gave the most pleasure, slip inside and out and in again. Deeper. Faster.

As she had done with Colleen, she distracted with pleasure. In the moment when the girl could no longer lie quietly, but began to struggle to get away, she pulled back the top of the cape and bit hard into her back.

The girl's struggle went on and on, moans of pleasure heightened, it seemed, by the pain. Finally, both sated, Joanna loosened her grip and turned to look at Arthur.

He stood pressed against the wall, the candle burning just above him. But even in the shadows tossed on his face, she could see the hard set of his lips, the hands balled into fists, could hear his quick, shallow breaths.

"Come. Take what I cannot," she told him and moved away from the bed.

He held back—modest, perhaps—though she had revealed such intimate things to him.

She stood, walked past him to the door. "Stay awhile. I have a place I must visit."

"Will I see you soon?"

"Outside. Wait for me." She pulled open the door, scanned the hall and was gone. Arthur had to close the door behind her, his body blocking Antoinette's view of her sudden departure.

He turned back to the bed where the whore lay with Joanna's cape beside her. Her eyes were glazed, but her body more than ready to receive him.

She laughed softly as he lay beside her. He could smell violet candy on her breath that barely masked the scent of gin. "First your friend, now you. I am twice blessed tonight," she told him as she undid the tiny hooks on the front of her gown. He watched her slip it off, one hand idly fingering the velvet cape beneath him.

"So much has been done to me, it is your turn, I think," she went on as she kissed him on the side of his neck, his chest, his stomach. "And here?" she asked as her hand curled around his erection.

"The tip only. Hold me back," he asked.

As her tongue circled it, he reached down and fingered her hair, her neck, the wound Joanna had made, still wet with blood.

As the whore straddled him, he raised his wet fingers to his lips and tasted.

Some time later, Joanna reached the cottage in Chelsea. It was late, and the rooms were dark. She entered in misty silence and found the rooms exactly as she recalled them, obviously used but now empty.

Had Colleen found a sweetheart to occupy her time? For all the jealousy she had to fight at that thought, Joanna hoped she had. She allowed herself the luxury of human form and took a seat in the chair she had always used. She wondered if she should leave some sign of her visit, and decided she must, if only to prove that Colleen was not abandoned.

She couldn't write. She had no coin. She looked down at her hands, but the ring Arthur had given her seemed too precious to him for her to give it away. There was nothing else but . . .

Perfect. So perfect. She went into the room she still thought of as hers and found a simple dress. Pulling off the green lace gown, she draped it over a chair. It would look so magnificent with Colleen's coloring. It never occurred to her where an Irish working girl already living well beyond her class would be able to wear it.

She let out a quick, delighted giggle, releasing all the emotions she had felt tonight, and left.

Returning to the club, she found Arthur already outside. He draped the cape over her shoulders and led her down the narrow street to a boulevard where his carriage was waiting, driver in place, to take them both home.

"Did you miss the kill?" he asked as they drove.

"It was not necessary," she replied.

"I thought it was. Everything I've heard—"

"Has been a lie." She knew he wanted an explanation, but she did not want to think of Illona tonight. "Why do humans kill? Why did you?" she asked instead.

"Fear," he replied after some thought. In the dark, his expression was somber.

"Then we are not so different after all."

"And the force you believe gives you life?"

"Took a part of my soul, but not all of it. Not as long as there are memories." For the first time since she'd come to him, she took his hand and held it as they drove.

Once home, he helped her from the carriage. They walked a time in the garden, her hand still in his. Finally she turned to him. He saw that she was smiling, delighted. "I was dead," she whispered to him. "For centuries, dead. Now I remember life."

"I saw the whore's expression as you drank from her. Take from me," he whispered.

She drew in a slow breath. "I would not want to rule you. Trust is better." Her hand brushed the side of his face, and though her hand was cold, his body responded to her touch.

twenty-nine

For the fourth night in as many, Colleen roamed the narrow, dark alleys of London's East End, looking for an ideal victim. They were all around her, leaning dazed against dark lampposts, sleeping in windowless hovels and putrid dormitories.

She carried a carving knife with the blade broken off and the tip ground to razor's sharpness. All she had to do was cut and take, such a little bit to quell the hunger and return her to normal for another few days.

As her need grew, she found the courage, coming across a drunk sleeping off the gin behind a broken wooden gate leading into an empty courtyard. The area was lit only by the faintest sliver of a moon and a single lamp burning in an upstairs window. It seemed safe.

She nudged him with the toe of her shoe; he did not stir. As she crouched above him, she held her skirt well away from his filthy clothing. Licking her thumb, she cleaned a spot on the side of his neck, then keeping her finger there to guide the knife, she cut.

Not deep, just deep enough. She could smell the blood even before it touched her finger. Holding her breath against the reek of sweat and oily hair, she pressed her lips to the wound and began to drink. Mercifully, he did not stir until she had taken nearly enough. Then, with the sudden move from sleep to waking of all desperate creatures, he gripped her arm.

"Robbing me, are you?" he said with a growl, then coughed.

"No, kind sir. I was merely making sure you were all right and to give you this so you could find somewhere safer to sleep." She pulled a few coins from her pocket and held them out, shaking them so he could hear.

As she hoped, he let go of her to take them.

"Well and well," he said as he fingered the coins. "Maybe you'd best come with me . . . and keep me company so's we both—"

But, once freed, she had gone, running down the dark street, tripping once and falling hard, then finding her feet again.

The rush was unnecessary. By the time she'd reached the corner, he'd fallen back into his stupor, with only the coins to remind him that her presence had not been a dream.

As soon as she arrived at the cottage in Chelsea, Colleen stripped off her dress and scrubbed her lips with soap and water so hard that they bled. Only then did she allow herself to feel the euphoria the blood gave her. Smiling at her courage, she turned up the light on the table and saw the lace gown draped across a chair.

Nearly a fortnight, and Joanna had finally returned to find her gone. Colleen sat at the table, and in spite of the glow the drunk's blood gave her, tears came to her eyes. She fought them. Joanna was still thinking about her, still nearby. Colleen had not been abandoned.

Knowing this made the change easier to take. Perhaps her ordeal was even some sort of test to determine if she were worthy to become one of those nocturnal creatures. If so, it seemed she was doing well. She had fed three times and had not fallen for the obvious—and unthinkable!—method of stealing helpless infants from their cradles or children from their mother's side.

She lit another set of lamps, put the gown on, and studied herself in the mirror. The high neckline that Joanna preferred to hide her pallor demanded a cameo. She had one of those and pinned it on. The long sleeves, which tapered over the backs of her hands, were perfect alone. Her hair needed a bit of work, though, perhaps pinned up? She played with it and achieved a disheveled but potentially elegant look.

The effect was pretty, more modest than she liked, but perfect for a night at the theater or dinner with a beaux.

Having neither, she heated some water and fixed a cup of tea. With the blood in her satisfying her most primal needs, her appetite returned. She trimmed the moldy edges of some rye bread and cheese and feasted, wiping her fingers delicately on a kitchen rag, pretending it was a linen napkin.

Just before dawn, she went into Joanna's room and, as had become her habit, lay in the box of earth. It seemed so soft against her, so comforting as she drifted off to happy dreams.

She woke late in the afternoon, with enough time to slip a dark cloak over the green lace and venture out for a copy of the *Times,* a pint and a bit of bread and meat from her favorite pub. Human hungers satisfied, she concentrated on the newer, stronger ones. The blood she had taken still warmed her, enough that she would have a day or two more before she needed to hunt again. She marveled at Joanna's control on their long journey from the East. But perhaps once the human half shut down, the vampiric half would be less demanding as well.

No matter, she would adjust.

The following afternoon, her slumber was interrupted by a loud knocking at the door, a messenger bringing her a sealed ivory vellum envelope. She broke it open, noted the signature on the enclosed letter and read as quickly as the unfamiliar hand would allow, the salutation convincing her that Joanna had dictated it.

Draga Colleen,

I am safe here in Kensington. As I had hoped, my host has been good to me and I am happier than I had ever hoped to be in this strange and crowded land.

Last night I went to the opera, and while I listened to it, I thought of you and had to visit. But I had no way of communicating with you except to leave a gift. Now Lord Arthur is writing this for me, as I think someone will always have to. I have no skill with letters, and am likely long past the age when I could learn.

Sora, I want you to want for nothing. With this note comes a letter from Lord Arthur, a duplicate of one he sent to a local bank where a fund has been set up for you. Arthur assures me that £20 each month is more than sufficient for your needs, since there will be no rent on the house. It is yours for as long as you are alive, and perhaps after.

Next time I come, it will not be on a woman's whim. I will write you first. Cu drag, Joanna

When Colleen finished, she looked down at the paper and laughed. A creature who did not know how to write had thought to send her a letter. Yet it had never occurred to her to contact her mistress in that most ordinary fashion.

She pulled out pen and ink and paper; the last not nearly as grand as Lord Arthur's, but it would do. She paused, thought and began to write:

Dearest Joanna,

When I found the gown, I did not know whether to laugh or cry but decided on happiness because, though you missed me, you did keep your promise and come back.

No, I have found no one nor will I ever, it seems. Sadly, the change you had hoped would not come until after death is now on me. I sleep by day and am wakeful at night. I have fed three times, all without detection, and will have to hunt again tonight.

I do not know how long I will remain between two worlds. I pray it will only be a little while and that you will be here when the final change occurs. Cu drag, Colleen

She posted it immediately, then made another quick trip to the baker's, stopping for flowers on the way back. She might not have a garden for her mistress, but she would give her what she could.

Since Arthur Holmwood had learned of Van Helsing's visit, he had been waiting for the old man to storm the walls of the Kensington estate. Instead, the onslaught was far more subtle, coming as it did in the bright afternoon light in the hands of a postman.

First there was a brief note from Van Helsing saying that he was going abroad and returning Arthur's key. Arthur had no doubt that the man was moving, but doubted it would be even as far as Dover, let alone Paris or Vienna.

The second was a letter postmarked in Exeter. He recognized the writing immediately, tore it open and sat in the music room, taking in every word.

My dear Arthur,

Van Helsing has written me and told me that he believes you have managed to find Joanna Tepes and that she may be living under your protection in Kensington. He, of course, wants me to come to London immediately, to help him with his stakes and mallet. I've refused because I know you too well to believe that you would harbor a murderer in your home.

I remember our conversation of just a few short weeks ago—how you would give your soul for a chance to speak to one of those creatures. You seem to have gotten your wish. I presume your soul is still in your keeping and that you have learned much.

But like Van Helsing, I am concerned. So please, Arthur, spare me a tedious trip to London. Drop me a quick line telling me that you are indeed all right. Better yet, send me an invitation to call on your guest. I should like to meet her under calmer circumstances than those terrible hours in Castle Dracula. Mina

Now, that would be an interesting meeting. He wondered what Joanna would say if he suggested it, and decided to wait a bit longer before asking her.

In the meantime, however, he had to return Mina's letter or risk having her—and probably Jonathan and Van Helsing and, if he were particularly unlucky, Jack Seward—prowling outside his gate. He decided to reply in the same spirit she had, and tell her exactly how he felt.

Dear Mina,

You are correct. I have gotten my wish. I have found my houseguest to be civilized but usually shy to the point of being reclusive. She has shared her thoughts with me, and her life.

Yes, I have seen signs of the strange hysteria you spoke of when you told me about your journey east, but I think much of it came from her own life in the castle. I gather that she and Karina were all but prisoners there and she lived in constant fear.

So far as I know she has not killed since coming to London, but did admit to slaying a sailor on board the ship that brought her here. Understandable, since my own investigation assured me that he was trying to rob and rape her at the time.

She has not answered the questions I've asked about Lucy quite as directly as I had hoped. But I gather that the vampire is under the control of the one who made him. In her case, your killing of Illona and Dracula freed her from his control, as it might have freed my Lucy. Would that we had known that. Do you suppose Van Helsing did and thought it made no difference?

That question troubles me even more than the ones about Lucy. Oddly, knowing all of this has been a comfort rather than a source of renewed guilt. At least my only sorrow is that it is too late to change the past.

When the time seems right, yes, I will invite you here.
Arthur

He read the letter over and decided it was enough to keep her away. The fact that it was the truth made it all the better.

But he hadn't told her everything, for that would have sounded insane. The blend of timidity and power in the woman was more arousing than any mortal woman could ever hope to be. Arthur wanted her—physically, though he guessed that would be disquieting at best. But he could live without that if he could merely give her happiness, make her grace him with one of her broad, fleeting smiles.

He almost threw out the last letter. The scrawled hand led

him to believe it was merely another request for funds from some bold, poverty-struck clerk or cleric. But there was a decisiveness in the strokes that made him think it might be important, so he opened it.

Inside was an envelope, thankfully unsealed, addressed to Joanna. A quick note to him made the contents clear.

Dear Lord Holmwood,

My mistress wrote me and I need write her back. I have news that she must know and soon. Please see that she gets this. Read it to her and tell her I ask nothing but that she come to me soon if only for a little while. There is much I need to know. My thanks, Colleen O'Shaunnasy

He stared at the envelope a long time before opening it and reading the contents. He felt a stab of pity for the girl, mixed with a surprising envy. She would know things he never would, would see a future beyond him. Her request was so humble, so hopeful and so full of hidden need. He knew that once Joanna went to her, it was likely Joanna would never return to him.

He read the letter again, noting that the girl was doing well on her own. Judging from how slowly Mina's condition had progressed, a week would make no difference to her, but for him it might be enough to assure that Joanna would return for a visit only.

No, he would not lose his prize.

And so he said nothing that day, nor the next. By the third, Colleen was rarely on his mind. Yet once, with no warning, he saw Joanna's brow crease, her eyes grow troubled. "Is something wrong?" he asked.

She shook her head. "Nothing," she mouthed, a breathless, silent dismissal.

thirty

Mina studied Arthur's letter carefully, looking for any signs that he might have been controlled but finding none. That evening she shared it with Jonathan, who concurred. "He hardly sounds like Renfield, or even you in the worst of your delirium. And yet . . ."

"What is it?"

"Nothing. I was thinking of the castle, but I can't ever recall seeing the sister alone. She was always with the others. Perhaps they goaded her on or forced her to join them, in which case, Arthur is probably right."

"And you're not dreaming of her?"

He laughed, kissed her cheek. "Dearest, I usually dream of you, and in the most embarrassing of positions, I might add."

Since Van Helsing's frantic letter five days before, there had been positions—far more than she'd ever expected. They'd gone to her cottage and calmly alerted Essie, who took the news in stride. "She likely won't know where to find you anyway, unless your friend tells her," Essie added.

Essie was right. The firm's address was on the papers Dracula had signed, their house in town well known. But she had kept this place something of a secret, just as Gance had. Better to be discreet in a town so small.

"We might be safer here, or at least get some warning should she come," Jonathan admitted with obvious reluctance. And so they stayed.

Perhaps the presence she had sensed the night of the storm

was still roaming these halls, because that night, after she got into her bath, Jonathan brought a bottle of wine from the kitchen and poured them both a glass. When she suggested there was more than enough room for two in the bath, he did not hesitate to join her.

Soap and washcloth became hands and caresses, kisses, embraces and an utterly unsuccessful attempt at something more. They dried off quickly and, laughing, ran for the bed.

He was voracious, more than her match. By the time they were done, something as innocent as the touch of his hand on her arm made her shiver with remembered delight.

She sat on the edge of the bed, lit a lamp and began combing the tangles from her damp hair. He got up, went to the doors and threw them open, letting in the cooler night air. He stood by them awhile, looking out at the dark garden, the river beyond.

"Karina had beautiful hair," he said, almost absentmindedly and without looking at her. "Joanna, those incredible green eyes. As for Illona, it was her body that could not be ignored. But though the others had sparks of life in them still, Illona had none. She terrified me as the others never did. And yes, I am certain she terrified them as well."

Mina didn't answer. It was the first time he had ever spoken of those women without being forced to by either Van Helsing or herself, and the first time he'd ever given details.

"There were nights when I was so weak I could barely move. Those where the times she would come and lie beside me, touching me, forcing me to respond when I thought I hadn't even the strength to draw another breath. Then she would invite the others to come and feast."

Mina got up, moved behind him and wrapped her arms around him as he went on, "And then there was you, so alive, so kind. And all I could think of for too long was her and what she had done to me. Whenever I would respond to you, I could not help but think of her. Everything got jumbled up, too much so. I'm sorry. I never knew how to speak of it before. But I should have. You of all people had the right to know."

She felt him catch his breath, a quick sob. Then he turned to her, held her until she led him back to bed.

In the morning they found Essie dozing in a chair in the solarium, her face to the bare window and the yard. There was a gold cross around her neck, the dinner bell on the table beside her.

So much for Essie's nonchalance.

Mina woke her, only to send her off to bed. "But what about breakfast?" she protested.

"Mr. Harker and I will take care of that ourselves, Essie. You need some sleep."

The nights that followed were long and passionate. Mina dreaded the day that the danger had passed and Jonathan would suggest that they go home.

But when the letter from Arthur came, Jonathan said nothing about leaving, only made the quick suggestion that she allay another's fears and write Van Helsing immediately.

She penned a quick note, intending to address and post the letter immediately. But since she was out of envelopes, she decided to post it after she left her work at the shelter the next day. She was just finishing up when one of the carpenters building a fence around the backyard cut his finger nearly to the bone when his saw slipped.

Dr. Rhys was the closest physician. By the time he had the man's cut stitched and she remembered the letter, it was too late to send it, her last chance until Monday.

"You're fortunate to have found me in," Rhys said. "I'll be leaving for London in two hours. Van Helsing and I are going out for supper tomorrow."

"Are you! Then perhaps you would do me a favor and deliver a letter to him. I'm wondering how he's faring; it's been so long since I've seen him." She found an envelope and handed him the sealed note.

He started to put the letter in his bag, then changed his mind and placed it in the inside pocket of his coat instead. "A physician's bag always looks so inviting to thieves. I would not want to lose it," he explained.

"It's hardly that important. I could always write another."

"I suppose. Are you leaving soon? Perhaps you'd do me the honor of walking with me to the station."

"I'm leaving now and I would be happy to," she replied, grabbing her hat and cloak and taking his arm. Her fingers brushed the back of his hand, and she noticed how cold his skin was, then how stiff he moved, as if he dreaded the journey. More concerned than curious, she asked him about his work.

"The rich come to my private clinic with every petty ailment, most of which they bring on themselves. The poor put off a call until death is sitting on their shoulder. I lost two children this week—one to a beating by his father, the second to venereal disease."

"Dear lord!"

"Lord, indeed. Sometimes I wish I had the solace of a Christian faith and could indeed think of them as innocent and bound for a happier eternity. But in truth, it was the parents who deserved to die. And nothing will be done to any of them. It's more convenient to arrest thieves stealing bread from those thought of as their betters."

She squeezed his hand. "You'd make a marvelous socialist," she commented.

"I'd rather be a judge."

Something in his tone made her pause, turn and look at him. "No, I am quite all right. Just tired and disillusioned," he said, managing a wan smile.

"Then a weekend in London is just what you need. I've never asked, but do you have a sweetheart there?"

"No one. An old teacher. A handful of patients who have become friends. Two distant cousins I see only rarely. And now Van Helsing, who is more interesting than all the others put together."

"Have you ever thought of visiting your home?"

"India? I was raised here. I have thought of going there, though. I'd like to see where my mother was raised."

"You speak of her so often. When did she die?"

His pace slowed, as if the memory took too much effort for anything else. "I was seven. My parents were never married, and my father abandoned us when he became ill and went home to be nursed by his family until he died. While he spent his last months in luxury, tended by his own, we were forced to give up our rooms and move in with friends near St. Bartholomew's. When my mother began showing signs of the same illness that affected my father, the people feared contagion and forced us to leave.

"My mother took a job as a seamstress, then when her eyesight began failing, as a washerwoman. We moved from a flat, to a shared flat, to two rooms, to one.

"And just when we thought our next sleeping spot would be a dark alley in Spitalfields, my father did the decent thing and confessed our existence to his family. Just before he died, he made his sister vow to find us and take care of us. And so she did.

We lived under her care nearly a year before my mother died. After that, my aunt cared for me. She died some twelve years ago. I was just out of medical school and tended her in her last days, and so we came full circle, she and I."

"Were the cousins you mentioned her children?" Mina asked. She knew the answer already but wanted to hide how much Winnie had already told her.

"My uncle's. Rowdy brats who grew up to be rowdier adults. They would have done my father proud. I'm pleased that we have nothing in common."

"I'm sorry. I shouldn't have pried."

"You took my mind off the week. That's a good thing," he replied.

She squeezed his hand again, and they went on in silence. At the station, she waited for his train before finding a cab to take her to Jonathan's office for their ride home.

As she did, Rhys was traveling east, away from the clinic, his practice and the facade of a life he'd built. There was no reason to feel that way but he did, and success only made the sham that much clearer.

Mina's questions had opened old thoughts, ancient wounds and reminded him that wealth hardly changed the person its trappings affected. Having never shaken off those early years of his life, it now seemed that only in the company of strangers of the lowest sort did he find himself feeling completely at home.

As the train pulled into one sleepy village after another, he watched families enter and leave, the quick good-byes of lovers and friends, and the dark, sleeping houses of the towns. He might wish for that life, but like the rakshasas or the vampires of Western lore, he could only observe that happy world, forever apart from it.

The train pulled into Blackfriars Station a little after midnight. Though it was raining, Rhys walked the distance to a single room he kept at a boardinghouse on Queen Street. He carried a razor in his pocket with the tip sharpened to a surgeon's precision but was otherwise blind to the danger the night and neighborhood presented. Along the way he stopped in a pub for a drink and a bottle to take with him.

Alone in his sparsely furnished room, he drank a third of what he'd purchased before changing into clothing more suited to the neighborhood. That done, he put on his coat once more and headed for an all-night club he often frequented near the river.

"Hullo, Chancy!" the barkeep called out as he entered the sooty room, then turned to get the doctor's regular order—a shot of rum and a pint of ale to wash it down.

Anonymous here, he blended with the workingmen and gamblers, all with a few quid to spend and nowhere else to go. He did not believe in demons, but some terrible urge drew him to these places, an urge that could not be denied. He contemplated this as he watched the foam on his beer slide down the inside of his glass, then ordered another and waited for oblivion.

Long past midnight, a woman walked in alone. The barkeep glanced at her, then went back to his conversation at the end of the bar.

Rhys barely noticed her until she came up beside him and pulled on his sleeve. "Doctor?" She looked at him, eyes half focused. When he didn't react, she repeated, less certain now, "Doctor?"

He shrugged, shook his head. "You've got me confused," he said in his best Indian accent, so unlike his usual crisp English.

She continued to stare. "You look just like him . . . the doctor who treated my little girl."

"Wasn't me," he said without looking at her.

She stood beside him a while longer before finding a table, a pair of friends who bought her a drink.

He finished his own, slowly, glanced at his pocket watch, then left. In the shadows outside the door, he paused to breathe in the thick, damp air.

It was nearly two in the morning and he seemed to be the only living soul outside in all of London's East End. Silence surrounded him, broken only by the distant trickle of water, a pretty sound for something as disgusting as a sewer emptying into the Thames. With his coat wrapped tightly around him to protect him from the damp and chilly air, he walked in the direction of the river, stopping occasionally to listen for the hard and even sound of a patrolman's booted steps. In spite of the alcohol he'd consumed, every sense was alert; only his judgment had been skewed.

He should have walked the few blocks back to his room. It would have been the wise thing to do in this part of town. Instead, he turned down a street that pointed toward the river, the silent wooden walkways, the dark and pressing fog.

He'd almost reached it when a woman stepped out from between two buildings, then retreated to let him pass. Though he could no longer see her face, he could sense her watching him, weighing the danger. No wonder, when there had been four murders in London that summer and whispers of another Ripper heard from pub to pub along the docks.

He stopped, leaned against a hitching post and took a deep breath. His hands were shaking and he seemed to have no control over them. He knew how this must look to the woman and waited to see what she would do. Out of the corner of his eye he saw her move toward him, slowly at first, then with more purpose.

"Now, here's a sorry sight," the woman said as she came toward him. "Are you able to speak?"

Head down, he nodded. "Yes," he replied.

"Do you have a place to sleep it off?"

"On Tower, 'cross the bridge. Not far."

"Come on, then. I'll see you home."

He looked at her for the first time. Tall and thin, with long, fair hair tied back beneath her modest bonnet, she hardly seemed the sort he would find on the streets so late at night. And her clothes were too well cut, too clean.

"I'm all right," he said. "I just need to catch my breath. You go home, yourself."

She looked at him doubtfully, let go of his arm, then headed away from the river toward the Gateway and the empty stretches of open land between the warehouses.

He watched her go, then went on his way, quicker now, seeking the sort of woman with no purity to her intentions.

thirty-one

There had been no easy victims that evening. An early storm had sent the drunks scurrying for whatever shelters they could find, and Colleen dared not hunt indoors. She'd almost decided to head for the market at Spitalfields and find a chicken or out-of-season lamb to satisfy the blood lust, when she'd spied the drunk near the river.

Not drunk enough, it seemed, and there was something about his keen interest in her that made her wary. She was glad when they parted company, and walked away from him as quickly as she was able.

She had not gone far when she heard a sigh, soft but distinct, coming from someplace closer to the river. She cut through a narrow walkway between two buildings and found herself back on the wharf. Thinking it might be the man she'd just met, she stepped back into the shadows and waited.

The couple came into view—the drunk and some woman, arm in arm. She leaned against him, her voice low, whispering in his ear. She seemed to be leading him at first, but when she stumbled, he caught her. Remarkably quick for one even slightly inebriated.

The woman did not notice the shift. Instead she laughed and moved closer to him, slipping an arm under his coat and around his waist. "You're the quiet onc, aren't you?" she said and laughed.

He did not look at her but kept his eyes straight ahead.

"Don't worry. The police don't much come down here, and my room's right around the corner."

They turned onto a street so narrow that, by the time Colleen got to the corner of it, the blackness had swallowed the pair. She cocked her head and listened.

There was a sound—a faint moan. It might have been the sound of lovemaking; more likely the man had lived up to Colleen's expectations and robbed the poor woman of the last pennies she owned. In that case, she might be hurt, swooning and helpless.

The last thought gave Colleen a sudden jolt of pleasure, a feeling so beneath her that she felt sickened by it. Nonetheless, those feelings would likely increase as the change continued and, being practical, Colleen could only accept them. Besides, she wouldn't hurt the woman, not really. And she'd follow with the service of seeing her home.

She moved up the street, slowly so as not to trip and give her presence away. A light burned in a window farther up the block, and she saw a shadow move in front of the curtain.

Crouching low, she crept close to the window and peered inside.

The man sat at a table close to the window, his back to her, pouring himself a drink from the bottle on the table. The woman, what Colleen could see of her, lay on the bed. Only her feet were visible. Her boots were still on, and there was mud caked to the soles.

She might have been drunk, or didn't care, since the place was little more than a hovel. The bed had only a straw mattress, obvious since the stuffing was poking out of a ripped corner. The rest of the room held only a single ladderback chair and a table. An oil lamp on it shed a dim light in the space.

Colleen began to retreat, then paused when the man got up and walked toward the bed. The action allowed her to glimpse the woman's face—expressionless, as if she had passed out. The bleeding cut on her head said something more sinister had transpired. Holding her breath, Colleen watched the man raise a hand, saw the knife he held. He lowered it, only to cut through the fabric of her blouse and part the halfs.

The woman stirred, turned her face toward him, managed to grip his wrist. He jerked back, slicing across her palm. Blood flowed. Colleen, hungry, fixed on that, then on the pair.

The woman would surely lose if someone did not help her soon. Convinced that the two of them would be a match for the man, she rushed to the door, threw it open and ran inside.

Her arrival startled the pair, and as the woman lost concentration, the man sliced down. The knife moved through her shoulder, her breast, her belly.

Finished with his victim, the man turned to deal with the witness. Colleen backed up a step, and when he charged, she threw the table down between them. The oil from the lamp flared, catching the dry straw in the mattress. The woman did not stir when the flames brushed her leg. Already dead, or nearly so.

Colleen turned, tried to run, but he was quicker. Grabbing her by her hair, he pulled her close, clamped a hand over her mouth. "I'm sorry," he whispered as he dragged her outside and toward the shadows well away from the blaze.

She responded with a hard kick against the back of his knee. He went down sideways, dropping her. She kicked backward again, less effectively, then scrambled away from him on hands and knees. She'd just found her footing so she could run when he grabbed her and pulled her down again. Her head struck the pavement at his feet, leaving her dizzy but still conscious enough to cry out once as the blade descended. His hand shook but the blade was sharp, cutting upward across her shoulder, her breast and deep into the side of her neck.

Not a killing stroke, likely not intended to be. "It shouldn't have been you," he whispered, and raised his knife again.

She made one final weak and strangled cry, more of protest than of pain.

She had gone searching for blood. Now blood was all around her. The scent of it stayed with her as consciousness faded.

• • •

When Joanna spoke of the feelings the arias had raised in her, it was with an intensity Arthur had never glimpsed in her before. Seeing her passion, he had arranged a box seat for a special August performance of the London Symphony. After assuring her that the seats would be just as private as the ones at the opera house, she agreed to attend.

She had no way of knowing that the program—a blend of Mozart and Tchaikovsky—was odd, only that the music ran an emotional gauntlet that exhausted her. She commented on that as they rode away. Arthur, ever diligent to her needs, suggested another trip to Impostors, speaking casually, as if he were discussing a late supper. She placed her hand on his and nodded. He called a Holburn address to the driver, and the coach lurched forward.

She said nothing as they traveled, but in spite of her weariness—a weariness that should have raised only hunger—an odd and disquieting emotion seemed to have taken hold in her, one that could not be dispelled by thoughts of the music or the meal to come. She glanced sideways at Arthur, but his serene expression told her this wasn't some feeling she'd acquired through proximity to him.

The emotion stayed with her at the club. Even those moments when she lay with the pliant Antoinette—such an innocent in her way!—could not dispel it. Arthur must have sensed her uneasiness because he showed no desire to remain with the girl after Joanna had finished with her. Instead he seemed in a rush to get them on their way.

They'd traveled only a short distance when she thought of Colleen and decided that tomorrow night she would definitely visit her again, and stay if the girl were not at home. Decision made, she tried to relax but found that impossible. She shivered, nerves on edge, waiting for something worse, something terrible. A scream cut through her mind. She winced, squeezed Arthur's hand so tightly he cried out in pain for both of them.

"What is it?" he asked.

"Colleen," she replied.

"In Chelsea?"

She hesitated, shook her head. "The river . . . near the bridge by the prison."

"How can you know?"

"The blood we shared makes a bond. I know. Find me there. Come soon."

He wanted to ask something more, but she was already gone. Leaning forward, he rapped his cane against the driver's box. "Take us to Tower Bridge instead," he called.

"No good part of town this time of night, sir," the driver called back.

"Just go, and quickly."

Arthur sat back in time to brace himself against the hard right of the coach. He thought of Renfield and of Mina's tie with Dracula and understood what possessed Joanna now. And sadly, he understood all too well what possessed him to follow her.

Joanna moved as quickly as she was able through the narrow, silent streets. The cries in her mind grew louder as she approached the river, then stopped altogether. The shadows hid her as she took on human form once again, and with all senses alert, cocked her head and listened,

Her hearing, so much keener than a mortal's, detected a distant sliding of fabric on stone; and in the opposite direction, a woman's cry for help followed by a man's bellowed, "Fire!"

She glanced in the direction of the voices, saw a faint flickering glow between the buildings. People, most half dressed or covered with ragged blankets, were coming out of nearby buildings, forming a crescent around the blaze as they waited for the firemen with their water truck and buckets. She could smell charred flesh, burning hair. Moving as close to the fire as she was able, she saw the body. Badly burned already, but the knife strokes were still visible. It wasn't Colleen.

Had Colleen felt that surge of fear for the woman inside, or was it something more? Not sure, Joanna scanned the street, noticing the line of blood stretching from the front door to the turn at the next corner. So much of it! Too much!

She followed it, arriving just in time to see a man bending over Colleen, the golden reflection of distant flames off the blade of his knife as he raised it for another stroke.

Rage stole any shred of caution or fear. With the quickness of thought, Joanna was behind him, her hands fumbling for his neck.

He jerked forward, whirled and saw her. His recognition strengthened her own. Yes, they had met before. Would that she had killed him then.

He sliced the knife across her body; this time, prepared, she didn't even wince. He took a step backward, slipped on the bloody stones and fell across Colleen's feet. As Joanna reached for him, she detected no pulse in her servant, no heat of life rising from the flowing blood.

Without even being aware of the act, air filled her lungs, released with a loud and terrible keening. The killer slid crablike away from her, soles slipping on the wet and bloody pavement until he found his footing. Reaching for him, she caught the hem of his coat. He shrugged it off his shoulders and ran, leaving it in her hand, not turning to see if she would follow.

She started to, but her cry of grief and pain had attracted the attention of some of the spectators gathered around the fire. Much though she wanted to find the killer and give back more agony than he had caused, she had no choice but to abandon the chase for now. There were more important matters.

She ran a hand over Colleen's bruised face, then covered her body with the killer's coat. Lifting her servant, she retreated farther down the street, vanishing into the shadows by the time anyone turned the corner. Moving down the darkest streets as quietly and quickly as she was able, she traveled in the direction of Tower Bridge, reaching it moments before Arthur arrived in the carriage.

Seeing her, the driver reined in the team and started to get down. "Stay where you are," Arthur called to him and helped Joanna lift Colleen inside, thankful he'd hired a brougham instead of the more common small hansoms. They lay Colleen on the seat facing him, her head in Joanna's arms. "To Chelsea," she whispered, her trembling voice revealing all the hysteria she'd managed to keep in check.

He did not have a vampire's senses, but the reek of blood and death was unmistakable. "How was she killed?" he asked.

Joanna's lips brushed the forehead, the blood-soaked hair, the open, sightless eyes. "She isn't dead," she replied, punctuating the remark with a soft titter of hysteria.

She's gone over the edge, he thought. Or perhaps she hadn't. Perhaps he was going to witness the most wondrous thing of all.

thirty-two

If their driver had noticed Joanna's sudden departure from the carriage, her just as sudden reappearance and the nature of the burden she'd carried, he gave no indication. When they reached the Chelsea cottage, Arthur helped Joanna lower Colleen from the cab, then tipped the man handsomely.

The driver whistled at the amount. "Should I come back for you later, sir?" he asked.

Arthur shook his head. "I'll be staying the night," he said and went inside.

Joanna had laid Colleen on the table and begun to remove her bloody clothes. She undid the buttons on her servant's blouse, parted the sticky folds of cloth from the body gently, then raised the head and shoulders slowly so she could pull the blouse off her. She worked as if Colleen might still feel the caresses, the pain.

With the first real sight of the wounds, her hysteria increased. Silent sobs shook her, interspersed by bursts of quick, sad laughter. If this had been any other woman, Arthur would have rushed to comfort. But now, faced with madness and grief in a creature so deadly, his courage failed, and he dared not speak to her, let alone approach her.

He heard someone on the street outside, forced a comment, "It's late. You ought to be quieter. This is hardly a time to have your neighbors decide to pry."

The keening stopped. She raised her head, eyes glowing

through the long hair that had fallen over her face. Her breath was audible, broken. "Late?" she asked.

He checked his watch. "Nearly four."

She still trembled, but silently kissed the cold forehead and lay Colleen flat on the table again. Her own body became transparent, words seeming to hang in the air, coming from everywhere. "Clean her. Find something for her to wear."

"And what—"

Of course he got no answer. With Joanna those nagging little questions always seemed to be left hanging in the air. The habit was, he thought, the one obvious sign of her noble blood. He took off his coat and shirt and set to work.

Colleen's skirt and undergarments were filthy—the excrement that came with death mixed with blood and dirt. He stripped it all off. Not certain how to proceed, he filled a pail with water and began to clean the wounds first; then, trying to think of her less as a woman or a corpse than a helpless child, he cleaned the rest.

Joanna returned, but only long enough to drop off a pair of flower boxes from the neighbors' windows. She returned some time later with three more. Working with one box at a time, she pulled out the flowers and carried the earth into an inside room. When she returned, she replaced the flowers in the empty boxes and set them outside.

When she'd finished, she left. He heard the clatter of the wooden boxes as she moved down the street. He glanced out the doorway and saw her replacing each of them, soiless, on their windowsills.

By the time she'd finished, Arthur, who had managed to clean the body by himself, was wrapping the wounds with strips of cloth. Joanna found a dress in the closet, a loose empire design in deep crimson. With his help, she put it on the body, then combed out the wet hair.

By then the sky was already light. "Come and help me," she said, the first words either of them had spoken for well over an hour.

He did as she asked, helping her mix the added earth with that already in the box in the windowless room. "Her soil," Joanna explained as they smoothed the folds of soft cloth over it.

"If you put her in there, where will you sleep?" he asked.

She looked at him as if he were a fool. "This was my brother's. He was quite a large man."

As he watched, she lay the girl inside. "Will you stay?" she asked.

He nodded, wondering how much the killer had learned about his victim and if they were in any danger here or elsewhere. After the lid was closed over the pair of them, he went to the outer room and turned the chair to face the locked door. He had his cane, and thanks to Colleen's well-stocked pantry, a sharp knife. Certain he'd sleep with one eye open, he sat down and tried to rest.

In late afternoon, a sudden burst of sound woke him. He all but leaped to his feet before realizing it was thunder rather than someone beating down the door. The air felt thick and charged, the darkness intense. Joanna, and possibly her servent, would likely wake soon, and as he looked at the room in which he slept, he realized he could be making better use of his time than in uneasy slumber.

Cleaning was something he'd last done during his brief time at Eton, but even in Kensington it would be up to him to clandestinely dispose of this much blood. Servants could be discreet, but even Ian had his limits.

He carried the bloody pail of water around the cottage, dumping it onto a small patch of flowers. It puddled on the ground, then sank in slowly. By the time he returned to the house, the rain had started. He found a basin to set on the stoop, then filled the pail from the last of the water jug in the kitchen and began to clean.

The table was spotless when he finished, a glass pitcher in the center of it. The floor was a worse problem. He washed it as best he could, laying the ripped and bloody clothing by the front door. He looked around for something to wrap those in before he carried it to the trash pile and noticed the coat they'd used to cover the body.

It might be wise to get some idea of the murderer's identity, so he went through the pockets. He found a knife, a bit of money, and a sealed and rumpled envelope. Unaddressed, but there was a note inside. Moving close to the dim light of the window, he ripped the envelope open and read quickly:

Dear Doctor,

I have heard from Arthur. He assures me that he is quite all right and I have every reason to believe him. He tells me he will be inviting me to London soon. When he does, I shall see for myself if you have any reason to be concerned.

You might accuse me of being a fool for not taking his situation more seriously, but it is what I must do.
Mina

Arthur read the note again, trying to deduce who might have possessed it. Not Van Helsing, surely. Though he might easily kill Joanna should the chance arise, he would hardly attack an innocent girl.

Then he thought of Colleen's own letter and of Lucy and how her teeth had already grown to a lethal length before she died. Might that have happened here? If so and in the darkness, Van Helsing might have been confused.

It was time to face the professor—and ask him directly if he was a murderer.

Before he could leave, he heard the floorboards creek behind him, turned and saw Joanna standing in the doorway; still, silent.

He knew her moods well. Such intense calm was not a good sign. "Is she . . . all right?" he asked.

She took a moment to answer. "I don't know. I know so little," she said. "They never told me. I thought they kept their power from me. Now I wonder if they really knew themselves."

"Van Helsing says it only takes a drop of vampire blood." He knew he sounded foolish. A drop would take a long time to complete its arcane work. Yet he had the sudden vision of Joanna spending months sharing a coffin with a rotting corpse, waiting for that miracle. He went and took her hand, for his sake as well as hers he added, "And Mina was with your brother only twice, we believe. She would have changed."

She noticed the cleaned table and floor, the pile of bloody clothes beside the door, the coat—the killer's coat—on top of them.

She moved beside it, fingering the collar. "I almost killed him once. Out of fear, I let him go. Now he takes her life, as if he wanted to curse me again. Human life is so precious, Arthur. Being in London has taught me that."

He hardly heard her, focused instead on the fact that the man had crossed paths with Joanna before. He thought of Van Helsing again. "You saw the man. What did he look like?" he asked.

"Older than you. But only a little."

She frowned, as if she could sense his relief. "What is it? she asked. When he did not reply, she repeated the question more insistently.

"Nothing. I just wanted to know, since you've encountered him twice. Go on."

Thankfully, her description was of no one he knew. "And how did he act when he saw you?" Arthur asked.

She detailed their first meeting. Apparently the man was only a killer, another night hunter whose path had crossed hers. The only unanswered question was how he'd come by that note.

"I need to go out for a little while. I'll be back as soon as I am able. Tonight. I promise. Before I go, may I look at her?"

"It will not harm?"

"It didn't with my Lucy."

She let him pass into the little room. He lit a candle and opened the box.

Colleen lay on her side, placed that way to make room for her mistress. Her hair was tousled—Joanna's caresses, no doubt. Yes, she looked like Lucy; as if she were sleeping, not dead. And the wound on her neck seemed much smaller, far less raw. "Do you see?" he said to Joanna, showing her the things she had not observed.

She held him, trembled. This time the emotion, so strong she could not contain it, was relief.

thirty-three

Since moving from Arthur's lodging to Mina's rooms in Mayfair, Van Helsing managed to relax in spite of his shattered calm. Mina's letter unsettled him, but he had to admit that her logic was flawless. So he waited for some word from her or Arthur. He expected to receive a letter from her first, but had never anticipated that Arthur would be the one to deliver it.

When he heard the frantic pounding at his door and Arthur calling to him, he paused to pick up a bottle of holy water. He slipped it into his pocket before letting the young man in.

His concern that Arthur might have been taken over vanished as Arthur stormed into his rooms without an invitation. And there was color in Arthur's face, far more than Van Helsing had seen there in many months.

"Explain this," Arthur ordered, handing the letter over and waiting, watching Van Helsing's face as he read it.

"You are angry because we are concerned about your so-dangerous behavior? What kind of allies would be we if we were not?" the doctor asked.

"Have you seen this letter before?"

"I have not. I was expecting it, though." He turned over the envelope, noted the lack of address. "Why do you have it?"

"I found it in the coat pocket of a murderer."

Van Helsing sat back in his chair, pointed to one nearby. "Sit down, Arthur, and tell everything to me."

Authur did. Every detail Joanna had described, then the nature of the wounds he'd seen on Colleen's body. "All this summer there have been murders, the same sort of cuts as I saw myself. People speak of the Ripper, or someone copying him. And this madman, this killer, had Mina's letter in his pocket."

"He may have stolen the coat."

"Joanna tells me it's the same man she encountered before. He wore a similar coat then. And the letter is dated for yesterday."

Van Helsing's mind moved quickly through possibilities, discarding the least likely, holding on to others until only one was left. If the man hadn't stolen the letter with the coat, he likely intended to deliver it. "Describe the killer again," he said.

Every new detail convinced Van Helsing that his first guess was the right one. "Dr. Rhys," he said.

"That doctor from the Exeter clinic? You can't be serious."

"I am most serious," Van Helsing said. "Mina told me that something about him disturbed her. I noted it too—a hardness in his heart toward those he sees as morally inferior. And there is his Eastern belief in reincarnation. He may not even believe he is committing murder in the sense that we would. He may think he is merely giving some poor unfortunates another turn on the wheel."

"He killed two last night. The woman in the burning shack by the river was likely his usual sort of victim. And Colleen. She may have been only a witness."

"And if he knows that, then he will have committed his first true murder, in his own eyes, no?"

Van Helsing went to a cupboard near the door. Inside, along with the stakes and crosses Arthur had expected to see, he noticed a crossbow and a pair of pistols. Van Helsing handed a pistol to Arthur and stuck the other in his belt. "Dr. Rhys is coming here at four-thirty. We're to go to dinner. He likely meant to deliver the letter then. If you wait with me, we two can take him."

They sat speaking quietly for nearly an hour. Now that he had Arthur alone, Van Helsing questioned him at length about the vampire woman. Arthur answered candidly, evasive only on the details that would put her in danger, far more detailed on what he had learned of her human likes and dislikes—the gardens and the theater.

At six, Van Helsing gave up the wait. "He's punctual. He isn't coming, and he did not send a note to me. All the more reason to conclude that he is guilty."

"He's likely left the city. If he went back to Exeter, then Mina is in danger."

"We'll send a telegram immediately. And we must go to her." Van Helsing tucked a clean shirt and underwear into his medical bag, then found a train schedule among a stack of papers. "There is the westbound train at six tonight."

"I can't go with you. I made a promise elsewhere."

Van Helsing stared at him, weighing possibilities. "Hold out your hand," he ordered.

Arthur did, palm up and cupped, as if he knew Van Helsing would pour holy water into it. When he did, Arthur brought the liquid to his lips and drank.

"If she isn't controlling you, Arthur, what is?"

"Herself, doctor. Not Illona or Dracula or the hunger within her. Herself. And it is herself—that human part of her—that I have come to love. I will not harm her or abandon her. And I will not let you do her harm."

"Nothing can come of that love," Van Helsing said gently.

"So she has shown me. But I can no more change my feelings than you can change yours for the wife you lost decades ago."

"The force that animates her is deadly," Van Helsing warned.

"Should she choose to use it."

"She will, Arthur. It is her nature."

Arthur picked up his hat and cane. "Come, doctor. I'll accompany you to the telegraph office and station just in case the murderer is lying in wait for you."

They said little as they walked together, senses alert for danger. At the telegraph office, Van Helsing labored over how to make the message clear but not to the extent that some operator would violate a trust and alert the authorities. He settled for something cryptic he expected only their little band would understand:

My dear Madame Mina. Something has transpired here that you must know. You may recall some discussion we recently had concerning troubles in London's East End. I believe that your doctor from Exeter is involved. Joanna has informed me of this through Arthur. I am astonished to say that I believe her. I am coming to Exeter on the late train. We can speak more freely then. AVH

When he had finished the one, he sent nearly the same message to Jonathan. "They will get these today?" he asked the operator.

"They should. There's some problem with the western lines, but we should have them repaired soon."

"Soon, he says! We'll see if the messages or I arrive there first. So much for modern inventions."

"And what might the train be?" Arthur asked in an innocent tone.

"An express, I pray," Van Helsing replied as they hurried on.

The train station waiting area was well lit and crowded and therefore safe. "I'll leave you now," Arthur said.

"Be careful," Van Helsing replied and, with unexpected emotion, embraced him.

It was past eight when Arthur returned to the Chelsea cottage and saw a dim light coming from the inside room. He found Joanna in it, standing beside the open box, a hand holding one of Colleen's. Arthur moved close beside the vampire, took her free hand, kissed her cheek. "How is she?" he asked.

She pointed to the girl's neck, the place where the blade had cut an artery now no more than a fading red line. "She'll wake tonight. I'm certain of it. I lit the lamp because I thought the light would be more familiar to her." She hesitated, then added, "I wanted so much more for her."

"Joanna, when she wakes, what will you do?"

"She will need me, and we will need someone to trust for those daytime needs. You, Arthur, if you will agree."

"Of course," he whispered, his throat so dry he felt like

one of them. He went into the front room and rummaged in the cupboard until he found the bottle of brandy he'd spied the night before. Colleen would have no need of it any longer, and after the events of the last day, he certainly did. As he sat, listening to the ticking of the anniversary clock on the mantel of the little fireplace, he wondered how much Colleen would remember about how she died and how the memory would affect her.

An hour later, he heard Joanna call to him. Rushing to her, he looked down and saw that Colleen's hands had curled into tight fists. As he watched for some further movement, they relaxed, as if she were shedding her mortal fears.

Colleen's soul lay in the shadows between life and death, claimed by neither realm. Blind, without feeling, without any concept of form, she thought herself a ghost at first. Frightened, she tensed, with ghostly memories of hands curling into fists. She felt her nails digging into her palms. Felt pain. So the change had come!

Elated now, she forced herself to relax, to wait for the rest to return—for movement, for hearing, for sight, for the possibility of speech.

The numb silence seemed to stretch forever. Then she felt a hand gripping hers, lips brushing against her cheek. "Take your time, *draga,*" she heard.

So she was home, or somewhere safe, and Joanna was with her. She managed the lightest squeeze of her beloved's hand, heard Joanna's cry of delight. Relaxed now, Colleen concentrated only on her eyes, on how to force the heavy lids to open.

When the moment to wake fully came, they opened effortlessly, then squinted shut, assaulted by a painful blast of light from a nearby lamp. Not so intense, she guessed, but her senses had become more acute. She opened them again, slower, focusing on the sight of Joanna standing above her.

She raised her arms, pulled Joanna close so she could kiss her.

Arthur stepped back. He'd seen all he needed to see. This was a moment of such intimacy, such beauty, that his presence would surely sully it. Tears came to his eyes. He brushed them away with the back of his hand and retreated to the outer room, where he poured another, larger, drink.

Not so long ago, he had vowed to stop thinking of Lucy, yet now she was all he could think of. She had awakened alone and confused, had discovered and fought and finally satisfied the unfamiliar cravings, again alone. By the time they reached her, she was likely mad.

She'd deserved much better. Had he known the truths he did now, he would never have abandoned her.

He heard the women murmuring in the other room; Joanna's voice even, the other's broken bursts, as if she were out of breath. She would learn, he thought. Joanna would teach her.

Something happened, a shift in the tone, the voices growing louder, quicker. They came together from the room. Colleen looked down as she shuffled forward, watching her feet; like someone bedridden for months, trying to find some balance in her steps. He got up to help her, but Joanna looked at him with eyes glowing with fury. "Don't come any closer," she warned.

Colleen had remembered too much, he thought. And she'd undoubtedly told it all.

"Colleen said she sent a letter to me through you. Why didn't I know of it?"

Arthur thought he could bluff and say that the letter was never delivered, but he would not lie. Whatever punishment came to him was deserved.

"I would have. A day or two longer was all I wanted. I was foolish, and wrong." He might have apologized, but the words seemed too easy. Even as he thought them, they seemed hollow.

"You took her life . . . the one she might have led." She trembled as she said the words.

He expected her to laugh or scream. Instead she helped Colleen to the wicker chair, then came and grabbed his wrist, leading him to her, pushing him down at her knees. "You wanted me to feed on you. You wanted to know what it feels like. So you shall. You took one life from her, give her another."

He would not have fought, even if he'd had the will to do

so. Colleen's eyes were magnificent, the color of the sea at night. The brush of her fingers on the side of his neck made him tremble. Joanna gripped his shoulders, holding him steady from behind. "Take," she ordered.

It seemed as if Colleen tried to be gentle, but she had little experience. Her bite hurt, and as she dug deeper and began to drink, hc cried out.

"Silence," Joanna hissed in his ear.

He did as she asked, praying that Colleen would listen to the flutter of his heart and stop in time.

But when she pulled away, lips red with his blood, Joanna took her place. Though he would likely die, he raised his arms and held her until they would no longer stay up on their own.

His senses reeling, he heard Colleen hiss, cough, force in gulps of air so she could scream, "Leave him . . . alone! The change . . . was already on . . . me when I wrote you! . . . And it was only . . . what I wanted."

Joanna released him so abruptly that he fell hard on the floor. Too weak to try to stand, he waited, beyond caring, for some decision to be made on whether he would live or die. Before they reached it, he lost what remained of his consciousness.

He woke in darkness in what must have been Colleen's bedroom, laid out on her bed, still in his clothes. He felt his neck, the raw wounds there. When he tried to rise, he realized how weak he was, how drained. But at least he had survived their wrath.

He stumbled into the main room. His breath came hard, his heart fluttered, no doubt low on liquid to pump. He poured himself a glass of water, drank it down, poured another and mixed it with the last of the brandy. Returning to the bed, he sat and sipped the drink slowly. The warmth of it made him feel stronger, more exhausted than weak. He returned to sleep.

Joanna woke him just before dawn, running a finger down the side of his face. He looked at her, and though her expression was frigid, he had never felt such love.

So this was what it meant to be enthralled, he thought. Not so different from what he'd felt before, but then his will hadn't been tested yet.

"I sense there was more you didn't speak of earlier," she said, her voice cold but so beautiful.

She took his hand, helped him to rise and go into the outer room. Colleen already sat at the table. She licked her lips as he sat down. A nervous habit, he hoped. One more feeding like the last and he would be one of them or dead. "There was something else. Most disturbing." He explained about the letter he'd found, his visit with Van Helsing and what he had learned there.

"And this old man, he will be a threat to us?"

"Not if I can help it," Arthur countered, feeling more like himself as the hour went on. "Besides, he's gone to Exeter to protect Mina Harker."

"And the murderer will be there as well—all of them?"

"The murderer lives there. So yes, I would assume all of them."

"Then we go also."

"But you can't." He protested on two counts: the danger to them and his friends, and the distance they would have to travel. It could not all be done at night.

"I crossed many oceans to get to this land, I am sure you can arrange to get us all to Exeter safely," Joanna replied.

Colleen grinned and looked at him. Too intently. Perhaps the newly changed were like infants and had to eat more often. "I'll go later and arrange for a private compartment on the train, and a cart to get you to the station. We'll handle Exeter when we get there."

"Arrange to arrive there this evening . . . it will be easier," Colleen said, still sounding breathless but learning quickly.

"Tonight," Joanna agreed. "I am so looking forward to seeing your Mina Harker again."

Light crept through the cracks in the heavy draperies, reflecting off the polished wood of the floor. When Colleen tried to stand, Joanna had to help her. "We sleep now and wake in Exeter. We'll find the one who did this to you, *draga,* and you will feast."

Arthur watched them go, then made his way to the door. A messenger boy on an early-morning run was pedaling his bicycle down the street. Arthur hailed him, gave him some coins and asked for food and a copy of the *Times*. "I'll double what's here if you bring it back immediately," he said.

"And you would like, sir?"

"Anything. Anything at all. Just plenty of it."

The boy returned with two warm meat pies, a tart and pint of cider. Tipping him lavishly for the service, he carried the food inside, wolfing it down before returning to bed. He'd been awake or unconscious most of the night and needed a few hours of real sleep or he would be no use to the women that evening.

Later, rested and nearly himself again, he sat beside the box containing Joanna and her servant, guarding it as they traveled by cart to the station. As they moved through the streets, he realized that this was the time his own free will should surface, consider, take control. But though he had no inclination to disobey her, it was not the bond she had forced that caused this. Even without it, he would have trusted her still. At her core she was not a killer.

thirty-four

Rhys fled the murder scene with reckless speed; running down unknown streets, tripping over uneven stones, open sewers, a drunk passed out against a hitching post. By the time he was too exhaused to run any farther, his clothes were filthy and torn, his knife dropped in the flight. Streets were no longer marked, and he was lost. He went on cautiously until he reached Lombard Street, then headed west, toward his rooms.

But, of course, he could not stay there. The creature he had encountered twice would have the power to know where to find him, and his only chance lay in getting as far away from her haunts as possible. So he returned to his rooms, discarded his useless clothing and, dressed as a gentleman once again. With another of his surgical blades tucked into his pocket, he headed for the station to catch the morning train to Exeter.

Long after the train left the station, he was still too agitated to rest. Rakshasa! Dakini! Vampire! She would kill his body and claim his soul. He had no idea what to do, how to avoid her, what sort of portent her presence meant for his future life.

But Mina did. He would go to her, confess everything to her, beg her to save him.

Such a good woman. When he explained, she would not refuse to help him.

So he sat in his compartment on the train, huddled against

the inside wall, terrified in spite of the daylight and the reluctant sun peeking through the lowering British sky. Occasionally some passengers from a more crowded section of the train would come by and open his door, ask if they could join him. By the time he replied, something in his eyes—fear or madness or fury, or a mélange of all of them—made them pause, apologize, leave.

It was a long ride, broken every half hour, it seemed, by another stop to take on still more passengers. By the time he reached Exeter it was nearly evening and his clothes reeked of sweat. Instead of going home, he went to his clinic, where he always kept a change of garments.

It was a sunny afternoon and he chose the native cottons. They carried with them some hint of the philosophy of his mother's land, his own blood. When he wore them, he often felt an Eastern serenity. Today, though their comfort was needed, they did not calm him.

He went in search of Mina, starting at the children's hospital. Winnie Beason, who'd been conferring with one of the nurses in the entrance room, looked up when she glimpsed him, smiled a greeting. It froze when she looked more carefully at him. Was the trouble so obvious in his expression? "Are you all right?" she asked, and without waiting for a reply came close to him as if she intended to feel his forehead.

"The nurse is giving the doctor an exam?" he asked, trying to make a joke.

He didn't succeed. "The nurse is worried, that's all. You look exhausted."

"I didn't sleep well last night. I'll be fine tomorrow. Now I'm looking for Mrs. Harker."

"For Mina? She was here earlier this morning. I'll likely see her in the morning. Do you have something you want me to give her?"

"No, not at all. I just wanted to speak to her. I suppose it can wait."

He opened the door before she could ask another question. As he walked away, he was aware of her standing in the doorway, watching him go.

• • •

Rhys had intended to stop at the clinic for a moment before going out again, but someone spotted him going in. Soon one patient came in followed by another, sick with what sounded like pneumonia. He gave brief instructions to each, then went to lock the clinic door. Too late, a patient arrived with a deep cut on his arm that needed immediate attention. Rhys changed from his white shirt into a leather surgeon's apron and began to clean and close the wound. He was so caught up in the routine of his work that when he noticed the blood on his hands, he could only stare at the sight, unpleasantly surprised.

Portents. Judgments. His hands shook as he finished the task. Seeing the man out, he shooed away a pair waiting to see him, then locked the clinic door.

He washed his hands in the sink, far longer than he needed to, trying to clean off every speck of dirt, until even the moons beneath his nails were spotless.

Only then did he dust his torso with talc, put on the white shirt. Departing out the more private rear door, he headed for the river road and Mina Harker. If he had to wait for her there, so be it. Her garden was a much more appropriate place than among the poor of Exeter.

It had been a long week, and as Saturday wound slowly down toward the Sabbath, Essie stopped her work, fixed herself a cup of tea and carried it to the table just outside the back doors. It was a late-afternoon habit she and Mina had fallen into during their first weeks together, one each continued even when alone.

Essie brought a copy of *Ladies' Unity* with her, opened to an article she'd already started and began to read an account of orphans in Manchester. The article was a stretch for her skills, and she had to slow her reading occasionally to sound out an unfamiliar word.

Frantic pounding at the front door made her jump. She ran through the house, peeked through the side window and seeing the doctor, pulled open the door.

"Is Mrs. Harker at home?" he asked.

"No, but please come in. I was just having a cup of tea in the back. The days following storms are always the purest, don't you think?"

"I suppose." He followed her to the garden to sit and wait while she went for another cup and saucer.

"You can continue with your reading," he said when she returned.

She was about to say she had all sorts of news to tell him, and she was happy he'd stopped by when she realized that he wanted the silence. So she did as he asked. Twice she looked up, wanting to tell him something, but he sat with eyes closed, facing away from her and toward the river. He seemed outwardly calm but his hands were gripping the chair arms, his shoulders were taut and though the day was pleasant there were beads of sweat rolling down his neck. Something troubled him, and deeply.

A bumblebee that had been buzzing a nearby rose bush flew close to the doctor. Rhys must have heard it but didn't react, not even when it landed on his hair. "Doctor," Essie warned, walking up behind him. "You've a bee in your hair. Be still." As she went to shoo it away, her hand brushed the back of his head. He whirled, arm outstretched, pushing her away so hard she fell against the nearby table, upsetting her tea and breaking the china cup with her hand.

"A bee," she repeated, surprised that he did not rush to see that she was all right. A piece of the broken china had stuck in her palm. She pulled out the piece and grabbed a napkin to press against the wound. Though he looked at it more intently than even a doctor would, he did not comment, nor move to help her.

But as she picked up the broken pieces of the cup, she noticed him still watching her hand, the blood seeping through the white linen cloth.

Something was wrong with the doctor, terribly so. She pretended not to notice, even a managed a smile when she asked if he would be all right alone for a little bit. "I have some errands to run, but Mrs. Harker will be here soon," she said. "I'm sure she would want you to wait for her."

He nodded—absently, it seemed—and fell back into his taut contemplation. But when she began to leave him, he turned and asked her where she was going, forcing her to repeat herself.

"No! I cannot be alone tonight. Stay until she gets back."

"But doctor, I must—"

"Stay!" he ordered, standing quickly and pointing at a chair.

He seemed almost dangerous, so much so that she dared not disobey him. As she sat facing him in the garden, she could only pray that when her mistress came home, Mr. Harker would be with her.

It began to grow dark. He suggested they move inside. They were just settling into the solarium when someone pounded at the door. Rhys cried out at the sudden sound, and Essie had the urge to lay a hand on him and tell him it would be all right. Instead, she started for the door, with the doctor close behind her, Essie hoping it would be someone who could help her.

Instead it was a messenger boy, too young and thin to be of any help. He handed her a telegram he said was from London and was off again before she could think of how to alert him to her situation.

"Give it here," Rhys ordered.

She gripped the telegram tightly. The doctor might have lost some part of his mind, but she still had hers. "That belongs to my mistress," she countered.

"It's from London and likely concerns us both. Now give it here. Don't make me take it."

The cold way he said the last words, as if he would hurt her more than needed if she disobeyed, left her no choice. She watched him rip open the envelope, read the contents. Shrugging, he handed it over to her as if it would explain everything.

Or nothing. She read it twice, frowned, then set it on the foyer table for Mina. "What does it mean?" she asked.

"It means that I am being hunted, by those same creatures Mr. Harker dreams of. And I need to speak to your mistress to learn what I must do for protection."

Could it be? Perhaps she had misinterpreted his actions, for he did seem most frightened. Even so, she only wished to get away from him. "It's late," she said. "She may stay with her husband tonight."

"We shouldn't try to go there. Not after dark. Is that true?"

Essie would have far preferred the exposed darkness to

the presence of this man she'd thought she knew. On the other hand, with no idea of what he might already know, Essie was afraid to lie. "That's what she told me," she admitted.

Rhys gripped her arm, led her back to the main room, where they sat and stared out at the lawn, the lengthening shadows, the growing dark.

thirty-five

Mina had expected to spend Saturday night at the house in town, but work—hers and Jonathan's— made that impossible. Two more families were moving into the shelter early Sunday morning because it was the only day of the week they had off from work and could move. And Jonathan had a meeting to attend. "Dreary but necessary, and though everything is likely all right, I would prefer you stay with Essie at the cottage rather than alone at night in town," he told her as they said good-bye outside the restaurant where they'd dined.

"Come to me when you're finished, love," she whispered, her lips brushing his cheek.

"I'll try," he said and helped her into the cab.

She hoped he would, for the little place she had inherited from Gance had become more than their refuge. Being in rooms where windows actually opened and uncovered glass looked onto expanses of lawn rather than high garden walls made them both more free. The room they slept in had no one sleeping just the other side of the wall, so they could be more passionate. And while the inside rooms were suited only for small dinner parties, the gardens could accommodate dozens of guests. She'd even begun to consider how to expand the second floor to accommodate another bedroom and sitting room, should they need a nursery.

She'd hinted at the potential expansion to Jonathan and been heartened when his reaction had been thoughtful rather than negative. She hoped that once this new crisis was over and she suggested a permanent move here, he would agree to sell the house in town—a place they had both come to think of a shrine to the deceased Mr. Hawkins.

These were the thoughts in her mind as she traveled home, not the growing dark, nor even Arthur and Joanna.

It was well after eight when she arrived at the cottage, but Essie had not lit the gaslight at the front gate—not so surprising, since Mina had not been expected. She paid the driver and started up the walk, frowning when she noticed that there were no inside lights on either. Could Essie be asleep so early? She doubted it and turned, intending to call to the driver to wait a moment. As she did, the front door opened. She heard Essie call to her, then the unexpected voice of Dr. Rhys.

"What brings you back from London so soon, doctor?" she asked as she walked toward them.

He drew her quickly inside, shut the door and locked it as if she had entered his home, not her own. She noted that the place was not entirely dark. There was a single lamp glowing dimly on the dining room table and that every drapery in the house had been pulled completely shut. "So dark," Mina commented, reaching for the light.

"No! Leave it dim!" Rhys ordered, his voice so loud that Mina jumped and Essie gave a small, startled cry.

"Listen to him, please," Essie said. "He is most upset. Frightening." She spoke the last word in a soft whisper.

"Dear lord," she said, going to him. "Has something happened? Is Dr. Van Helsing all right?"

"All right?" He laughed, mirthlessly. "I suppose he is, but I never saw him. I was too concerned about myself after what I've witnessed."

"I'm so sorry." She sat on the sofa and reached for his hands. He let her take them, almost managing a smile as she pulled him down to sit beside her. She expected him to supply details. When he fell into silence, she prompted, "Was it a patient? An illness?"

"No. I've lost patients often enough. Death happens. But this . . . this . . ." His voice trailed off. He took a deep breath and went on, "I saw a rakshasa."

She frowned, not comprehending.

"A demon. A vampire. I understand you know of them?"

"I do," she said softly, wondering how much Van Helsing had told him.

"Then you can tell me what I must do to defend myself before she comes for me again. I never paid attention to those strange folk tales. They were only words to me, but now . . ." He'd spoken quickly, then stopped altogether in midsentence.

"Did this creature attack you?"

"Twice." In a voice that halted often, he described a woman who could only be Joanna. He told how he had glimpsed her once on a dark street in the East End, how the second time he crossed her path she had come at him so quickly, how the knife he carried for protection had so little effect on her. "I must have injured her, or at least her pride. Now she pursues me. I need to know what to do for protection."

Of course he did, she thought. And she would provide it and in the morning write Van Helsing to apologize and tell him that indeed she would come to London and do what she could to protect Arthur from that creature. "Did Dr. Van Helsing get my letter?" she asked.

He shook his head. "I never went to meet him. And I'd already lost the letter when I ran. Then I could only think to come back to Exeter and you. Essie said it would be all right if I waited," he said.

She saw tears in his eyes, saw the trembling in his hands. What had he been through? "It's all right," she said. "I'll just have to send him another."

"Before you arrived, a messenger came by with a telegram from him in London. It's on the foyer table," Essie said from the doorway.

"Bring it, please," Mina requested.

Essie seemed about to say something, apparently thought better of it, and did as her mistress asked. The telegram had already been opened, but given the state of her servant and the doctor, she could hardly blame either of them. Mina rose and moved close to the lamp, holding the paper up to it so she could make out the words.

Telegrams were not completely private, so Van Helsing had to be discreet, but this was cryptic at best. She frowned, trying to recall what troubles he referred to. When the memory came to her, it brought with it a rush of fear that she struggled to hide as she turned back to her guest.

Apparently she did not hide it well enough, because he asked, "I didn't understand all of the message. Is the doctor all right?"

"He is, but he is most concerned about you," she answered, slipping the telegram into her skirt pocket and struggling to remain calm. Fortunately, she had more than a little experience at it.

"But I never even saw him that night. How would he know?"

She thought quickly, made up a likely lie. "There are others like us in London. They patrol the creature's haunts. Someone likely saw her attack you. If you hadn't escaped, they would have come to your aid."

He seemed to accept this, and fell into an uneasy silence again, staring at the closed drapes. She stood, mind reeling at what Van Helsing had to mean. "Essie could tell me only a little. But I understand that you know much more," he said after a while.

She didn't trust herself to get close to him just yet. "Before we begin, would you like something to drink? Tea? Cider? Some sherry? Brandy?"

"Brandy neat," he replied, though she had never known him to drink alcohol of any kind before.

She started for the cabinet, but Essie was faster. "I'll help you," she said.

"It's not necessary. You need to get some sleep. We'll need you awake and alert well before morning." Since she was faced away from the doctor, she took the opportunity to motion toward the front door.

Esse nodded slowly. "As you wish, then," she said, and started toward her room.

"Wait!" Rhys called to her. "Stay here. It will . . . be safer that way."

"We cannot all stay alert the entire night," Mina countered.

"I can. Please . . . Essie, sit."

Essie did as he asked, taking a seat at the table, her head on her arms as she faced Mina, waiting for some sign.

The ruse would not hold much longer, Mina knew. Rhys

was far too intelligent not to see through their act, particularly if they pushed him much farther. She took the coat she had been wearing that day, laid it over Essie's shoulders and rejoined the doctor.

She'd wanted to keep some distance between them, but as soon as she was close, he held out his hand. She could not avoid taking it, nor fight too strongly his drawing her down into the same place she had been sitting before. But he seemed calmer in proximity to her calm, so she stayed.

"Tell me. Will she follow me here?"

"It will be difficult. She is not what you think," Mina began. Now that she saw the doctor as the threat, she desired to tell him as little as possible on how to defend himself. She went on, weighing her words carefully, telling some truths, some plausible lies. "First, she cannot come into your house unless you invite her in. So you will be safe there and can get the rest I believe you need. The same prohibition will hold for your clinic, since it is also yours. Because she can only travel by night and must return to her haunts for the day, it is unlikely she will ever be able to travel this far to find you."

"To find me? You mean she could but likely won't?"

Mina took a deep breath. "I mean, I doubt she can. First of all, how would she know where to look? You said that she didn't follow you. Did she manage to steal one of your calling cards or just convince you to hand it over to her?"

"No. Not that." He actually managed an uneasy smile.

"Then she cannot know, just as any person would not know. Doctor, you will be safe in Exeter."

He looked at her with gratitude. "Thank you," he said.

Heartened, she slid her chair back a few inches. "My husband went east and actually spent time as a prisoner of these creatures. He managed to escape. He can tell you so much more about them than I can. We could go into town together and find him."

He grabbed her hand, holding it so tight she winced. "No!" he said. "We'll stay here . . . at least until morning."

When she looked down at his hand, she saw a steel handle sticking out of his pants pocket, the outline of a surgical blade against their light cotton fabric. She forced her voice to remain even as she went on, "Doctor, you've had a terrible fright. If this place calms you, by all means we can stay. But if you will excuse me a moment or two, I need to go upstairs."

He released her, no doubt thinking she needed to use the toilet. She went through the house slowly, stopping to move the glasses they had used to the sink, letting him think that everything was well and that her heart was not pounding.

In truth, his attitude alone would have frightened her. Having read Van Helsing's letter and seen the weapon he carried, she was terrified.

As she moved toward the front door, she heard his footsteps as he came up behind her. She met him at the foot of the stairs. "I'm sorry," he said. "But all this talk has me concerned. I want to stay as close to you as possible just in case you need my help."

"Help? Well, unless you're planning on going into the water closet with me, it's best you remain here."

Her comment had the desired effect. He was blushing as he let her go upstairs alone but stayed at the foot of the stairs, blocking her escape out the door. Fortunately, she had another idea.

Upstairs, she moved by memory through the dark bedroom to the bedside drawer where she kept her revolver. Tucking it into the waistband of her skirt, she went to the bathroom, then stood at the sink, splashing water on her face. You've been through worse, she thought. Be logical. Calm. This is nothing compared to the rest.

Given how close Rhys stayed to her, would she be able to shoot him if she had the resolve? Better to shoot from the top of the stairs while he was still at a distance, but she was reluctant even to wound him until she was completely certain of what Van Helsing meant in his telegram. Instead, she decided to force Rhys into a chair so Essie could tie him up. That had its own risks, especially if he were desperate, but she could see no other choice. Hiding her gun in the folds of her skirt, she started for the stairs.

She had debated too long. He'd started up after her and had nearly reached the landing when she came around the corner. "I thought I should come up and—" he began, stopping in midsentence when he saw what she was holding.

"I believe that we need a more conventional defense," she said. "We should go down. I don't want Essie to be alone, either."

He looked uncertain, as if he wanted to believe her. Cautious, he moved sideways to let her go first. As she passed him, she felt a draft of cooler air and heard the French door bang against the back of the house.

Rhys felt it too. As he started to push past her, she thought of Essie, raised the gun and shot at him just grazing his arm. The recoil threw her off balance, and she stepped backward off the top stair. She grabbed the rail for an instant, then dropped the weapon as she tumbled down the stairs. With the breath knocked out of her and her vision blurred, she looked up in time to see Rhys step over her and run down the hall and through the back doorway.

Too dazed to care, she pressed her cheek against the cool floor and fought only to remain conscious. She moved her feet and hands, then her arms and legs. Nothing seemed broken, though everything already felt bruised and the floor beneath her so unsteady that even an attempt to get on hands and knees sent a wave of dizziness through her and a sharp pain to her side. Thinking of Essie, she placed one hand on the stairs and slowly crawled upward, toward the weapon.

Since she'd lowered her head on the table, Essie had been feigning sleep, waiting for some opportunity to come to Mina's aid. Once or twice, in spite of her own fear, she had actually dozed off for a moment or two but always started awake when she heard the doctor's voice. Still, she had waited until he'd gone up the stairs after Mina, then ran for the back door. It took her a moment to unbolt it, and as she left she heard the doctor's voice, dim in the distance but growing louder.

He was coming for her! Terrified, she fled toward the river.

She had hoped to be out of sight by the time he came outside, but her skirts made running difficult. She ducked into the bushes past the formal gardens and, keeping low, headed through them toward the wall that separated their gardens from their neighbors: Nearly five feet high, it offered some privacy without cutting off the sun. Now it was merely another obstacle blocking her escape.

She reached it before he'd even seen her, tried to pull herself up. Her feet slipped on the stones before finding a toehold. She had one foot over the top when he reached her, pulling her back. "Help!" she called, a weak sound not likely to be heard by the family in the distant house, already shut against the night's damp.

"Please, doctor. I meant no harm," she said. "But my loyalty is to my mistress, and you've frightened us both."

She expected him to drag her back to the house, not grip her so tightly by the neck that speech became impossible nor to pull a knife from his pocket. Even then, she thought she knew him and that he intended to use it to control, not to kill. So the first quick slash across her shoulder and neck came as a surprise. She held up her hand, and the second slice cut across her palm. As he raised it again, they heard a shot, another, the sound of breaking glass.

"Damn her!" Rhys muttered. He slashed again, this time slicing her arm, then let her fall as he turned and ran toward the house.

Essie pressed her bleeding neck with her hand, the cut on her arm with the wounded palm. Though she could not see her wounds, the front of her dress felt sticky and wet. She had just decided to try to make it over the wall when her strength failed her and she slid slowly to the ground.

Mina's first shot had lodged in the hallway armoire. The second had been better aimed, going through one of the panes of glass in the rear doors. She considered a third but decided not to waste her bullets. Instead, she remained where she was, back to the front door and side against the foyer wall, the gun balanced on her bent knees. Her eyes were a bit out of focus and her head pounded, but as the doctor came through the doorway, she got off one more shot. She saw him jerk as the bullet hit, saw him fall and lay still.

She'd hoped to sound an alarm and save Essie's life, but the blood so obvious on his white shirt made it clear that she had been too late. Now Rhys was dead himself, or wounded. She should make certain, she knew, but what she had managed to do had taken the last of her strength. No matter. She'd sounded an alarm. Any neighbor who heard would either go for help or come to the door to check on her soon.

In the meantime, she would rest.

Her eyes shut, her muscles went slack, her grip on the gun loosened.

Rhys raised his head slowly, his expression grim as he began to crawl to her. "Why did you do this?" he asked as if she could still answer.

thirty-six

Van Helsing's train pulled into Exeter a little before one on Sunday morning. He should have gotten some sleep while he traveled, but he had been too caught up in how he would explain everything that had transpired in the last day to the Harkers. He tried to look at his story through their eyes and was convinced they would both think him mad.

He decided, finally, that it would make no difference as long as they were warned.

Even at the late hour, there were still some cabs for hire. The doctor hesitated before giving the Harkers' address in town. His rationale was simple: It was the most likely place to find Jonathan. If Mina were with him, they would likely be safe. If Mina were not—well, he was getting too old and stiff for anything but a battle of wits. Young Harker would have to provide the brawn.

As Van Helsing's cab pulled away from the station, Jonathan was arriving home. His meeting had gone on even longer than he'd feared, and they'd still reached no agreement on how to deal with increases in taxes and tariffs and their devastating effects on British businesses. The speaker had actually referred to the colonies a number of times, as if the United States were somehow still as much Britain's as was India.

Afterward, a group of them had stopped at a nearby pub for an informal meeting on the matter that had consisted less of further discussion than of alcohol-softened mutual misery.

None of this discussion put Jonathan in an amorous mood. Since Mina was also likely asleep by now and he didn't want to disturb her or Essie, he decided to spend the night in town.

He'd just gone inside when he heard the sound of hooves and wheels, looked out the window and saw Van Helsing getting out of a cab. Jonathan pulled open the door. Seeing him, Van Helsing called from the street, "Is Madame Mina here?"

"She spent the night at the cottage," Jonathan replied, more annoyed than concerned at the late disturbance.

"Come, come. Put your coat on. We must go to her at once."

"Doctor, if this is about the"—it occurred to him that one or more of his neighbors was likely privy to this loud exchange—"the matter in London, we really—"

"It is not. Come, I tell everything to you on the way."

With no choice but to go, Jonathan grabbed his coat, locked the door and joined the old man at the cab.

They'd traveled only a little way when Jonathan, having heard the main points of the story, leaned out the window and asked the driver to please hurry.

"And I had thought you would be so hard to convince," Van Helsing said.

"No, doctor. The moment you said that you would accept the word of one of those creatures, I knew you were deadly serious. Now tell me the rest of what you know, every detail."

Van Helsing did, including what he knew of the murders. "Rhys and I met in London three times since I met him. There was one killing when he was there. Now this one as well. I think we must be cautious."

"He may still be in London."

"We can pray so, but Jonathan, he speaks of your wife so often and with such reverence that I cannot help but believe that with a so-troubled mind, he would be compelled to go to her."

Jonathan nodded and said little else, for they had turned onto the river road. He called to the driver to stop a few doors down from his house. "No use announcing our arrival," he said.

They got out, paid the driver and walked quietly toward

the cottage. Along the way, Jonathan pulled out his key and gripped the revolver Van Helsing had given him.

Like all the other houses around it, the cottage was dark and silent, though as they approached the house Jonathan saw that the inside was dimly lit. The gate creaked as they opened it, their footsteps audible now on the cobblestone path. Staying well to the side of the door, Jonathan slipped the key in the lock and opened it.

The door swung open. Jonathan entered slowly, Van Helsing close behind. Though the room was nearly dark, they could smell what had transpired—scents of gunpowder and blood.

They moved toward the back of the house, Jonathan ready to fire if need be. But as soon as he saw Rhys, he realized he was too late.

Mina was on the settee, asleep or unconscious, a damp rag across her forehead. Rhys sat on a chair beside her, one hand holding the tip of a surgical knife pressed against her neck the other her revolver, which he pointed in Jonathan's direction. "I was expecting you," he said to Jonathan, then glanced toward the doorway where Van Helsing stood just out of sight. "And the doctor as well. Both of you, come in."

Jonathan shuffled in and moved toward the doors while Van Helsing stopped just in sight near the front hallway. Rhys wisely focused on Jonathan, who having noted the blood on Rhys's shirt, realized that some of it was undoubtedly from a bullet wound, and wondered if he would be able to attack without bringing harm to Mina.

As if reading his mind, Rhys said, "Mr. Harker, put your gun on the floor and slide it over here, please."

Jonathan started to obey, but before he could slide the gun forward, Rhys's attention was diverted by Van Helsing's question. "What are your plans for all of us, Felix?"

Rhys looked at him, expression blank. Jonathan thought he would never have a better time. He stood, kicked the gun hard into the side of Rhys's foot and lunged.

Jonathan had gambled and won. Rhys didn't act on his threat. Instead, he swung the knife up and sideways into the soft spot on Jonathan's side, just below his ribs. He might have twisted, or thrust up with a killing stroke. Instead he shoved Jonathan backward, dropped the knife and with both hands aimed the gun at Jonathan's chest. "Don't force me," he said, his voice still calm and even.

Without taking his attention away from Jonathan, he spoke to them both. "Mr. Harker, take a seat on one of the side chairs. Doctor, there is a rope on the table. Please, use it to make certain Mr. Harker cannot charge me again."

"He is wounded. I should see to him," Van Helsing countered.

"Do what I ask, then see to Mrs. Harker first. After, I will let you examine him."

"What have you done—" Jonathan began, but Van Helsing moved close to him, motioning for him to be silent.

"Come, we do as he tells us," Van Helsing said, helping Jonathan to stand.

He secured Jonathan to the chair, as loosely as he thought Rhys would allow.

When he had finished, he advised Jonathan, in a voice loud enough for Rhys to hear, "Just be silent. Let us old friends work this disagreement out."

Noting that Jonathan's wound was not bleeding overly much, Van Helsing turned his attention to Mina. "What happened to her?" he asked Rhys.

"She fell down the stairs, hitting her side and head hard as she landed. She lost consciousness for a moment, then again later. I moved her as carefully as I could but can find nothing wrong."

"How long has she been like this?"

"About three hours."

"A long time. Let me sit and look at her."

Rhys moved aside for him, getting the lamp when Van Helsing requested it. He lifted her eyelids, examined their reaction to light. He ran his fingers over her forehead and the back of her neck, looking for signs of swelling. He took a stethoscope from his bag and listened to her heartbeat, then removed her shoes and scraped a fingernail down the center of her feet, pleased when reflex made her legs move.

"No sign of internal or back damage. A slight concussion perhaps," he said loud enough for Jonathan to hear, then turned to Rhys. "You say she fell on her side?"

"The right, yes."

He had Rhys help him undo the buttons on the back of her blouse so he could take it off and the corset as well. Lifting her chemise only as much as he needed to, he felt each rib, pausing at one of the lower ones. "None is broken, but I think I feel something here." He took Rhys's hand, had him feel the spot. "A crack, perhaps?"

"You're right. But that doesn't explain her unconsciousness."

"It may be nothing more than pain. We should bandage her. I have none in my bag, however."

"I saw a towel in the kitchen. If we fold it over the fracture and lace the corset tighter than normal, it will brace the rib."

Van Helsing looked at him. "An excellent idea, Felix. But one of us needs to get it," he said.

"Your word that you will stay at her side?"

"If I may treat her husband next, then yes, you have my word."

Satisfied, Rhys went to the kitchen, returning with a soft cloth and a pitcher of cold water. "For her head," he explained, moistening the compress he had been using, placing it over her forehead again.

Van Helsing lifted her torso. Rhys placed the folded towel over the fracture, then put the corset in place and tightened the laces. She cried out once, a response both doctors saw as good sign.

As they lay her back down, she touched Van Helsing's side, hitting it twice. "Mina. Mina, can you hear me?" he asked.

Her eyes twitched but did not open. Her lips moved. He held his ear close to them, trying to catch her soft words. "I'm dreaming," she whispered.

"Dreaming?" he asked.

"As I did on the train. She is coming, doctor. Tell Jonathan to take care and wait."

Rhys, who had been standing on the other side of Van Helsing, could hear only the faintest hint of her whisper. "What did she say? Something about dreams and coming was it?" he asked.

"Yes, she says she is dreaming, which is what she did when

we traveled through Europe and she fell ill. It was a good sign then, Felix. I believe it will be now as well."

"You really think so?"

"I think we've done all we could anywhere," Van Helsing commented. "Now, may I see to my other patient?"

As Jonathan watched the doctors treat Mina, he tried to breathe shallowly and move as little as possible. He had no idea of the extent of his own injury, only that the almost painless cut had given way to an incessant dull throbbing, keeping time to his heartbeat.

He had been considering his dwindling strength and how loosely Van Helsing had tied him and was weighing another attack on the now unarmed doctor when he heard Van Helsing repeat Mina's words.

He understood them perfectly. She was dreaming of Joanna. The vampire had shown no interest in any of them, but given Arthur's story, she would have every reason to come after Rhys. He prayed that it would be soon, because unlike Van Helsing, whose thoughts were completely of Mina, Jonathan had time to observe and consider Rhys's state. Though there was a lot of blood on the man's shirt, he showed no sign of weakness. Either he was incredibly strong, as madmen sometimes were, or else it was not all his.

He wondered what the effect would be on Rhys if he were to ask what had become of Essie. He decided to wait. Van Helsing would turn his attention to the Indian doctor's wounds and learn the truth soon enough.

Van Helsing brought a bottle of brandy and a teacup, a towel and some water. He set it all on the table, peeled back Jonathan's shirt and began cleaning the wound.

"You're lucky Felix didn't want to kill you," Van Helsing commented when he saw the depth and angle. "As it is, he may have nicked a kidney, but I doubt even that." Though he had the items in his medical bag, he asked Jonathan, "Do you happen to know where Madame Mina keeps her sewing box?"

"In one of the drawers in the kitchen. Close to the woodstove, I think."

Again Rhys went to get it, giving doctor and patient a moment alone. "He killed Essie," Jonathan whispered.

"*Ja*, and to remind him of it will likely bring the same fate to one or all of us. You heard Madame Mina. We wait, and while we wait, we work to heal you and keep his mind on his higher purposes."

He poured a cupful of brandy, held it up. Jonathan shook his head, so Van Helsing drank it down, wiped the inside of the cup, and filled it with grain spirits from his medical bag. Moving quickly, he pressed the rim of the teacup over the wound, letting the alcohol flow into it.

This was the way Jonathan had expected the actual cut to feel—searing and horrible. He pressed his lips together to keep from crying out.

Rhys threaded a needle, and at Van Helsing's request dipped it all in the alcohol before handing it to Van Helsing. Jonathan cried out again as Van Helsing began stitching. He must have been weaker than he thought, because the new pain made him dizzy. He slumped sideways. Rhys caught him and held him steady, his hands deceptively soft.

thirty-seven

As he traveled west on the afternoon train, Arthur developed a great respect for Colleen. She had managed to get her mistress across all of Europe, while a simple trip to Exeter had caused him so much grief.

First, the hack he had hired had a door too narrow to accommodate Joanna's box of earth. After much pushing and swearing, the driver had gone in search of a cart. On that, the horse was lame, and one wheel of the cart seemed in danger of falling off, a particular problem since by now Arthur was concerned about catching the train and had to ask the driver to hurry.

When they arrived at the station, two extra men were needed to lift the huge chest onto a boxcar. As they did, one man lost his grip for a moment before they managed to slide it in. Seeing this, Arthur had the sudden disquieting image of it falling, breaking, and the two women inside screaming as the sunlight touched them and their bodies burned.

Should such an event occur, he would disappear and mourn and occasionally spare some small bit of pity for Derrick Smythe, whose cards he was still prudently using.

Of course, no such tragedy occurred, but there were other, more likely ones. Arthur took the precaution of sitting in the passenger car next to the one carrying his precious cargo, and he would leave the train to keep watch over it at every stop in the long ride.

Were the women aware of the journey? he wondered.

Could they be as nervous as he was about the outcome of it?

The sun was low in the sky when they pulled into Exeter. He had just enough time to rent a cart and horses. "And you won't be needing a driver, you say?" the carrier asked him.

"I'm in need of privacy," Arthur replied. "I'll have the team back tomorrow morning."

The man grinned. "I've had a need for privacy myself on occasion. Three pounds for deposit and I'll put a pair of feed bags in the back with your luggage." He looked at the box curiously as he said the last.

"An antique for a friend. One I need to deliver myself," Arthur supplied, nearly grinning at the truthfulness of that statement

"Well, I hope you've some stout help on that end," the man commented.

While Arthur had been arranging for the cart, he sent a messenger boy to the Harkers' house in town, to Rhys's clinic and, since the boy said he knew the doctor, to the doctor's house. The boy came back in record time to report that none of the parties was home. "It's Mina's cottage, then," Arthur commented aloud, wondering if they were awake in back and could hear him.

He drove on through the dwindling light, stopping finally in a secluded spot near the turn to Mina's cottage. Joanna joined him on the driver's seat some time later, sitting silently as she picked bits of dirt out of her hair. He glanced behind him. Colleen was still resting; the young, he thought, usually sleep in.

"How far?" Joanna asked after a while.

"We're close." He explained about the notes he had sent, and his own feeling that Rhys would be at Mina's cottage. "Now that they know about the doctor, they'll likely welcome your arrival."

"Unless they're in league with him."

"They're not."

She looked at him as if she could read his thoughts. "They're not, I assure you of it," he replied more vehemently.

"We will know soon," she said, falling into silence again.

He wanted to take her hand, to touch her thick hair—all the things he had wanted to do before. Again, he wondered. Did he feel any differently toward her now when he was supposed to be her slave through blood? Though the pain of her stare made him think she had more power over him than before, he sensed nothing else. Perhaps he had been her slave already.

"We're almost there," he said when they reached a familiar bend in the road.

"Good," Colleen said from behind him.

Startled, he nearly cried out. She had emerged from her shelter so soundlessly.

Joanna asked him to pull the team over and pointed to Mina's cottage farther down the road. "The husband is there," she said. "The wife too. The doctor as well, I think, for I feel much pain."

"You know this?" he asked incredulously. Van Helsing had never mentioned this power.

"The woman has some power of her own. And the husband's blood is in me. Even after so long, I can feel his emotions and his pain, just as I will always feel yours. And I can cause him pain as well, though I will never be as vicious as Illona was." She rested her hand on his. "Now we shall see about those you call friends, Arthur."

"Should I come?" he asked.

Joanna looked at him, lips curling upward without mirth—a predatory smile. "A half hour, then pull up to the gate," she told him. "We would not want to lose our day home to some curious thief."

He studied the air between his cart and the cottage. A mist curled through the entrance garden, dividing at the front door to circle the house. Colleen was learning about her new life remarkably fast.

By Sunday afternoon Jonathan had fallen into a deep and, Van Helsing hoped, healing sleep. Mina had awakened only twice. He'd given her some water, then held her hand as she drifted off again. She did not act as if she had a concussion, and though he had told Rhys she had done this before, he had lied. He wondered if, knowing Rhys's attachment for her, a part of this was an act. If so, she did a remarkable job.

With both of his patients seemingly in the hands of God, he focused his attention on Rhys. The doctor's body had needed little work, since the bullet that had nicked his arm had done no real damage and the one to the shoulder had passed through. He cleaned both wounds and bandaged them. Like Mina, he was concerned about the amount of blood on the man's clothing and Essie's absence, but said nothing. Instead, he found a clean shirt for Rhys to put on.

During all of this, there had been two occasions when Jonathan's gun was within his reach, but he thought of Mina's advice. She was right, as always. If the vampire woman was really coming, he would have more than one enemy here and would need both wits and strength to survive.

Besides, while Van Helsing had worked on the patients, he had consulted with Rhys often. Doing his work had alleviated Van Helsing's anxiety. And now that he wasn't covered in blood, Van Helsing could almost view him as he once had, as colleague and friend.

The sun rose, burned off the river fog to reveal a beautiful day. Once he was through with the others, Van Helsing thought of Essie and suggested they go outside so he could smoke his pipe. Though he said this most casually, he watched Rhys's reaction and saw nothing unusual but the caution he would expect given the man's fright.

"It is barely noon, Felix, and a bit of sun will do us both good. My old, stiff bones in particular," Van Helsing said and started for the door. Rhys did not call him back, but followed some moments later to take a seat in one of the chairs. The gun was still tucked into his belt, he had the knife somewhere, but he had made no threats for hours.

By then Van Helsing also was sitting in a chair on the far edge of the terrace, facing the river. He commented often on the height of the water and the speed of the current while he scanned the lawn and bushes looking for some sign of the woman.

There was nothing but the buzzing of bees among the blooms, the soft rustle of early-fallen leaves in the soft, shifting breeze. He watched the smoke from his pipe twist and dissipate in the cool air. A puff blew against his face; he coughed. As he did, he deliberately dropped his wooden pipe on the stones. It bounced, stopping on the second wide step leading from the terrace to the garden. He stepped below it to retrieve it, scanning the yard once more as he turned, noting something pale moving in the bushes near the river.

As he peered in that direction, he heard Rhys mumble something. Turning, he saw how ashen the doctor's face had become. "It's just a cat. No need to fear that, Felix," he said, bending over and calling to the animal now moving on the edge of the garden.

The animal, a well-tended marmalade tabby, came forward slowly; then, sensing that Van Helsing meant no harm, more quickly. It curled around the doctor's feet, lifted its head so he could scratch under the chin. As he did, he noticed the blood on its muzzle, on its feet, even a patch on its shoulder.

"Come and look at this, Felix. We may have another patient here," he called as he felt the chin and shoulder, finding no wounds. "Been hunting, have you, you so-spoiled little thing. What did you catch that put up such a—"

Rhys kicked the animal hard, sending it back toward the bushes. It rolled as it landed, then found its feet and fled.

"What did you do that for?" Van Helsing asked, knowing the answer as soon as he saw Rhys's face. The question, unplanned, came from him before he could screen the words for their possible reaction. "Felix, what have you done?"

Rhys shook his head, fell back into the chair. His hand was on the gun but he did not move to pull it out.

Now that things had gone this far, he might as well push the man farther, Van Helsing thought. Saying a quick prayer, he moved away from the terrace, toward the bushes where he had first glimpsed the animal.

He saw a foot first, a bare leg, the rest. Rhys had done this? To read of the deeds had been one thing, but to see his terrible work on someone he knew made him queasy. He shuddered. His knees all but gave way as he knelt beside her.

Dead. She had to be dead, there was so much blood. And

yet as he touched the dry side of her neck searching for a pulse, he saw her hand twitch. "Felix!" he called. "Felix, come quickly. We have another patient here.

"So terrible," Van Helsing mumbled as he turned to her. "So terrible I cannot imagine you surviving the night. We shall help you do the same today."

He tried to lift her but could not, looked toward the house and saw Rhys still standing on the terrace. "Come, Felix, we are doctors, *ja*? This woman needs help so help we must give. Though she is barely more than a child to me, I cannot lift her alone," he called.

Rhys came then, but only to stand above the woman, looking down at her as if he didn't know her. Only the tremors of his body betrayed what he had done.

Van Helsing directed him to the less wounded side of the girl and together they lifted her and carried her to the house, laying her on a stack of soft cushions close the settee where Mina slept. Through it all, Rhys seemed so anxious that Van Helsing found himself praying that the girl would show no outward sign of life, lest the doctor drop her and reach for a weapon.

But she remained lifeless except for that fluttering pulse. Shock, Van Helsing thought. Though the bane of physicians, it must have saved her, shutting down her body's needs and conserving what little strength she had.

As he undressed her, Van Helsing saw that the wounds were deeper than he had imagined. It seemed to him that only God could have directed the way she had fallen, so that her hand was held between her chin and neck, somehow pressing the cut neck closed. He cleaned around the cuts carefully, trying not to loosen the tenuous clots that had formed on her arm and neck until he had stitched the smallest cut shut.

As before, he tried to keep Rhys involved in the work without success. As Van Helsing cleaned and closed the cut on Essie's palm, he could hear Rhys pacing the room, muttering words so soft they sounded like whispered prayers, stopping occasionally to look out the window. "It is daylight, Felix," Van Helsing finally said.

Rhys went to the sideboard, poured himself a brandy. "No

matter, I am doomed anyway. I always have been," he said after a while.

"No, not when there is a God above capable of mercy."

Rhys looked at him, almost smiling. "You would draw me into this discussion after seeing what I've done?"

So much for avoidance of the obvious, Van Helsing thought, looking down at Essie and wondering what she had done to provoke the attack. He wanted to ask, but the words would not come. Other, better ones did. "I am no doctor of the soul, Felix, but I have some years and a bit of understanding if you wish to speak of these matters further."

"I cannot speak ill of the one who gave me life," Rhys blurted. "I never have before. Even my aunt never knew the truth and so revered her."

Knowing some of his history, Van Helsing guessed at his meaning. "She may have thought it was the only way you would both survive."

"It would have been better had my mother sent me to beg in the streets," Rhys said, his wooden tone at odds with his trembling hands.

Van Helsing nodded. As he expected, Rhys began to weep, and it took some time before he could continue. "After we moved from the rooms my father kept for us, we had only one between us. I would sleep with her in her bed unless someone was coming. Then she would make me sleep in the little bed she had prepared in the cupboard. I would lay with the door cracked to let in air, trying not to make a sound, trying not to listen.

"I understood little of it then. Later, long after she died, I understood more. With every man who had paid her, she had passed on that curse, not just to him but also to the man's wife, perhaps even his children."

He took another swallow of the brandy before continuing. "Her last days were filled with horror. Her mind had gone almost completely over to hallucinations. She would scream that there were demons in the walls and they were reaching through the paper, trying to grab at her soul.

"We were alone the day she died. She was coherent enough then to ask for the bottle of morphine we kept to help her sleep. She sent me from the room without even a good-bye."

"If she had, you might have guessed and taken the bottle away," Van Helsing said gently.

"She might have said something to me. Later, I heard her crying out to God and Jesus to save her from her sins and to take away her pain. I knocked on her closed door, asked what she needed. She told me to go away and leave her alone. By the time my aunt returned, she was dead."

"You told me she'd been raving," Van Helsing said gently as he finished bandaging Essie's hand. He began cleaning the wound on the arm, but it began to bleed so heavily that he had to apply pressure and call to Rhys. "Come, Felix. You have to help me now. If she loses any more blood she will certainly die. She needs more in her before I begin to deal with the larger wounds."

"A transfusion? From one of us?"

"From me, I think. I have done but few of them, but it seems I have the greatest success when the blood in closely matched. Being pure Caucasian, I will present a lesser risk. But I cannot do it alone. Now come."

Afraid to leave Rhys in direct care of Essie for even a moment, Van Helsing had him assemble the pump and sterilize the needles. He connected Essie's line, then rolled up his sleeve so Rhys could do the same for him.

As he held out his arm so Rhys could insert the needle, he was conscious of how vulnerable he was at that moment. But Rhys did the work with almost painless precision—amazing, given his mental state. It occurred to Van Helsing that that was likely how the man functioned from day to day.

It took nearly an hour to draw what was needed, leaving Van Helsing flushed and light-headed. While the blood wound slowly down the tube and into the girl, Van Helsing fixed a bit of lunch. Rhys declined any food, pouring another brandy instead. As he watched Rhys sip the alcohol, Van Helsing considered that when the woman came tonight, the murderer would likely be his only ally—a most unsettling thought.

Even before the last of the blood had flowed into her, some of Essie's color returned, and her pulse had steadied. Heartened, Van Helsing began to clean the wound on her arm. With effort, he managed to connect the damaged tissue and bandage it. She lost some blood as he worked, but not as much as he had given her.

But when he examined the wound on her neck, he could only shake his head sadly. Closing this wound was beyond his abilities, beyond anyone's except perhaps for a battle-trained surgeon.

Through it all, Rhys had stood watching the work from a distance, unable to assist or to look away. "I never meant to hurt her," he said as he watched Van Helsing examining the neck wound. "The anger seemed to take control of my hand. It always does."

"Were you the one in London those years back?"

"The Ripper? No. I came before him, though. It is the night I remember best. September thirtieth in '86. I'd lost three women to venereal disease just that week, one leaving three orphaned children. I'd never felt so useless before. I wasn't a drinker, but I went to a pub far away from my clinic and got sickeningly drunk. I was reeling home when the whore noticed me. I'm a doctor. Even in the gaslight, I could see the signs of disease on her face, could even smell it on her breath, but she thought me shy rather than wary and would not leave me alone.

"I carried a knife for protection. I'm not even sure how it got into my hand, only that, when she pressed me against a stone wall and tried to kiss me, I sliced her and fled. My heart pounded with fear for days, but the papers never even reported finding the body.

"Once I knew I would not be caught, a strange peace came over me. It lasted nearly a year, then I found myself in another pub finishing drink after drink to give me the courage to roam the streets looking for another whore just like her."

He went on, explaining how the calm diminished with every kill, how work at his London clinic surrounded by so much misery became impossible.

"Finally, unable to go on and terrified that I would be caught, I admitted myself to a sanitarium for a few months. When I felt calmer, I asked to be released.

"Nervous exhaustion, the doctor there called it. He suggested I give up my practice but I could not. I had made a vow, you see. I vowed to my mother that no person decent save for poverty would suffer the way she did and there were so many with no one else to turn to.

"I went back to that quiet institution three more times, the last for nearly a year. When I was released, I thought a new start in a smaller, kinder city would end my rages. It did, but not for long."

"How many women did you kill?" Van Helsing asked.

"I don't recall. Twenty. Thirty. But they were always of a certain type until the last. All that poor creature had wanted to do was help me. Then I found myself killing her because I had to kill someone that night, had to smell the blood and the fear. So now, my pretense is ended. The demon's arrival merely reinforces what I already know. There is no longer any justification for what I had become."

He began weeping again, muffling his sobs in one of the towels Van Helsing hadn't needed to use.

"We could go to the police together," Van Helsing suggested. "The work you have done here and in London might lead them to show mercy."

"In a prison or a state asylum? Abraham, it would be better to feel the end of a rope."

Van Helsing thought quickly. "I have a friend who runs an asylum. Perhaps—"

"Stop it! There are no options anymore! I've already made up my mind. When the demon comes, Abraham, I will hold out my arms and embrace her. Whatever she takes, I deserve to lose."

Van Helsing looked down at his open medical bag, the mallet, the stakes, the holy water. He fingered the cross he wore through the fabric of his shirt and pulled it out so it could be seen. The sun was close to setting. So much would happen tonight, and he was an old man and exhausted.

The sky grew darker. Mina stirred. Instinctively, she tried to stretch, cried out in pain and opened her eyes. Van Helsing rushed to her side and helped her stand and walk to the straight-back chairs beside her husband. Jonathan remained motionless with his head on the table, still asleep.

"Take care. You've cracked a rib," Van Helsing told her. "But you will be all right, as will he."

"And Essie?" she asked, looking toward her servant.

"I don't know how she still lives. Truly, her fate is in the hands of God."

Mina brushed the back of Jonathan's head, the touch waking him. He sat up and after a moment took her hand, following her gaze as she looked toward the window, not at Rhys but beyond it, the pair of them waiting for their guests to arrive.

thirty-eight

Outside, something moved in the shadows along the side walls. Fog, Rhys thought, until its tendrils met near the river and coalesced into forms more substantial . . . things that looked so deceptively human, so feminine with their flowing summer frocks and unpinned hair.

But they weren't human. He knew they weren't as they glided across the lawn, eyes glowing, thin white arms reaching. As he took his eyes off them for a moment to look for the cord to shut the draperies, they moved with a speed only the supernatural could achieve, standing just outside the doors.

She had said they could not come in unless . . .

Behind him, he heard Mina speak, her voice loud and strong, "Enter freely and be welcome."

"No!" Rhys bellowed and whirled to face her, his word echoed in Van Helsing's voice, his shock reflected in Van Helsing's expression.

Rhys heard the click of the bolt and looked back at the doors. Their handles turned, they swung inward, though to his eyes it seemed that neither woman had ever touched them.

He had vowed to let the creatures take him, but the sight of them, so pale and beautiful and openly erotic, seemed more terrible than any monster would have been. With his resolve in full retreat, he rushed around the table and placed his knife against the side of Mina's head.

He looked from one creature to the other, recognizing the

vampire and his last victim as well. "Stay away," he warned, as if this threat to Mina would somehow protect him.

The green-eyed one drew in a breath, laughed and asked, "Why should we value her life, murderer? She is nothing to us. It is you we have come for."

"But she means something to you, Felix. It would be another death on your conscience," Van Helsing added quickly.

Rhys glanced over his shoulder at the front door, saw the slide bolt still in place. Even if the door were open, he would not make it through, not the way these creatures could move. The women separated, coming slowly around the table from different directions. As they distracted him for a moment, Jonathan used what little strength he had to slam an arm against Rhys's wrist, shoving the blade away from Mina's neck hard enough that Rhys lost his grip on the knife. It slid across the table and over the edge. With a cry of rage, Rhys bolted over the table, heading for the open French doors.

His foot caught the edge of the carpet and he went down hard beside Essie. The gun in his belt went sliding over the tile floor. One of his hands was buried in the bloody rags Van Helsing had used to slow Essie's bleeding; his face hit inches from her seeping neck. Screaming, he scrambled forward, through the doors, only finding his balance when his feet hit the stone path leading to the river.

He could not hear the creature coming up behind him, but he didn't need to. Of course the victim would be the one to come; he would expect no less. And she would claim his soul, hers to do with as she pleased for all eternity.

The river would be a better death, he thought, wondering why he had not considered it earlier, when the sun still touched the murky water and made it seem beautiful. He had almost reached it when he felt her hands on his shoulders, forcing him to turn and face her.

He'd barely noticed her before, when she'd been alive, so he had no way of knowing if she had been so comely then or if death and rebirth had made her so. A deceitful beauty, he reminded himself as, oblivious to his struggles, she pulled him close to her as if he were her child, weak and helpless, in need of comfort.

• • •

The moment Rhys fled, Colleen followed, every newborn power awake and alive. With effort, Mina had pushed herself to her feet and was starting her slow walk to the door when Joanna rushed to it and screamed after her servant, "*Draga,* no! Leave him to me!"

The words came too late. Side by side they watched as Colleen reached Rhys, spun him around, lifted him and pulled him close in a final embrace.

Joanna called out again, but stayed where she was, while Mina viewed what was happening outside with growing horror.

Colleen's back was to then. Shorter than the doctor, thinner, in her human life far weaker, she held him helples now. Only the top of his head pressed tightly against her shoulder was visible in the dim light. She seemed to struggle with him at first, then stood motionless as, all fight gone, he lay silent in her arms.

"You cannot stop this?" Mina asked Joanna.

Joanna shuddered, such a human reaction. "I dare not try, for I want to kill him myself, and in a way that would make my brother pity him," she said. "And I should not take this vengeance from her but . . ."

She did not have to finish. Mina understood. To kill so young, even a creature such as Rhys, would likely doom Colleen to an eternity of killing.

Mina found one of the revolvers and stepped outside. "She has turned completely?" she asked Joanna.

"Yes. Completely, thanks to him."

Raising the gun, Mina fired two quick shots at Colleen's back, crying out as the recoil grated her fractured rib. As she expected, the bullets passed through Colleen and into Rhys. She had aimed for his chest and did not have to see the doctor to know she had killed him. Colleen's reaction told it all.

The human had killed the monster! Killed him and deprived her of her rightful prey. Furious, Colleen dropped the body, turned and moved toward the house, so quickly that she was on the terrace by the time Mina had stepped back to the door. Colleen's face was stained with the doctor's blood, her clothing drenched in it. She wiped her lips on the back of her sleeve as she advanced on Mina. "You took him from me? Did you think you would . . . spare him suffering? Was that why?"

Joanna answered for her. "*Draga,* you know why."

"Did she?" She walked toward Mina, who stood motionless, watching her, unafraid and confident. "Does she think I . . . won't kill a woman? Does she really think I . . . will let her live?"

When only inches separated them, Mina looked her in the eyes and whispered. "I would not let him claim you as his last victim."

Colleen listened, barely hearing, her body taut, ready to strike. She took the last step forward, her hands on Mina's shoulders, when she heard a low, terrible moan, a beating on the floor.

She looked behind her at Essie, lying on the pillows and folded blankets—the wounds, the blood, the bandaged arm shaking as damaged nerves convulsed.

Dropping her hands to her side, Colleen crouched beside the girl, staring not at her face or the blood, but at the cuts. For the first time she remembered those last moments of her life—how the knife had sliced her neck and belly, how she had lain, face scraping on the gritty road as her life flowed from her veins and into her lungs, filling them until she drowned.

"He did this?" Colleen asked.

"Essie was going for help," Mina said. "He hunted her down, then left her to die."

Colleen stared at the girl again, thinking how she would have died had Joanna not given her a different kind of life. She shivered, drew in a breath so she could exhale a dry, silent sob.

Joanna came up behind her, rested a hand on her back. Colleen stood and pressed close, her head against her mistress's shoulder.

Jonathan's attention had alternated between the confrontation he expected his wife to win, and Van Helsing. The old doctor had said nothing since the vampires' arrival, but knowing him, Jonathan was sure he was weighing the consequences of an attack.

It would be carnage, and like Mina, the thought would not sit well on his conscience. So he moved closer to Mina, careful to place himself between the doctor and the women, ready to use what strength he had to stop any attack.

But Van Helsing only watched, silent and pensive while Mina faced the creature and looked as relieved as the others at the outcome.

When Jonathan was sure he would not be compelled to stop the doctor's attack, Jonathan moved stiffly to where Mina stood, started to embrace her and realized his wound would not allow it. So instead he stayed beside her, considering all the words he would say later, when they were alone. How brave she was. How kind.

The moment's silence shattered with a pounding at the front door. Before any of them could reach it, it burst open, part of the frame attached to the bolt, and Arthur rushed in, gripping a pistol. "I heard shots. What's happening in here?" he asked, then noticed Essie and also fell silent.

"Justice," Joanna said, and stepped up to Mina.

To Jonathan she seemed so much smaller than she'd been in the castle, thinner, less vampire than woman. He had feared her then, but only because he'd feared them all. Now, inexplicably, he wanted to touch her, to see if she had shaken off the curse completely and there was warmth to her flesh. In the castle he had not heard her speak a word of English, but tonight she spoke as if she had lived among them for years.

Drawing in a breath, she shuddered a little, an anxiety Jonathan well remembered, forced a calm and began, "For weeks, I prayed for the strength to face you and make you feel the pain I thought you had given me. My brother is dead, his wife, my reluctant friend Karina. My entire world ended because of you."

She drew Mina close, embraced her. "A thousand thanks. Would that Karina had chosen this journey."

Through the exchange, Van Helsing had his hand in his pocket, holding a loosely capped bottle of holy water. At first he dared not use it. The only ally he'd had here was dead, and rightfully so. The Harkers could not be trusted. And Arthur, for all his care in keeping the gun pointed toward the ground, had the long edge of the barrel facing him. No, this was not a battle Van Helsing could win, so instead he wisely listened.

It astonished him that, after decades of viewing these creatures as only beings to be hunted and destroyed, he found himself actually waiting to see what these would do before passing judgment on them.

And truly, Joanna Tepes astonished him.

She was not at all like the creature she had been—that wild-eyed being that had taunted him in the Borgo Pass. Not at all like the others he had seen in Romania, and certainly not at all like her brother. But then Dracula had been a barbarian in life, so why not in death? While she . . . ?

So many questions. Would she answer if he asked them?

Not tonight, he thought. There were still things that needed to be done. "Come, Arthur," he said. "We have a wounded woman and a body in the yard. Best we summon the police and a surgeon soon, or questions will be difficult. You have a coach here, do you not?"

"More like a cart, but it should suffice." He looked to Joanna, who motioned for him to go.

Van Helsing said little on the drive, what energy he still possessed spent in contemplating the fantastic night and day before. But later, as he sat on the cart waiting for Arthur to wake the surgeon, he considered what purpose the box in back must serve. If he lifted the lid, dumped the holy water onto the earth, what effect would it have on them?

No matter. He would never do it. Besides, the box was certainly locked.

He considered what Karina's journal had revealed about the vampire origins—that the creature that created them had been in league with the Devil.

Perhaps even that didn't matter. Men, after all, were children of God, and look at the monsters born among them.

No. For now, he would leave them in peace.

Epilogue

From the journal of Mina Harker dated October 14:

After Arthur left with Van Helsing, Colleen and I sat holding Essie's hands, whispering words of comfort until we heard a commotion outside. The police were coming, and hopefully a surgeon. "You should go," I said to Colleen and Joanna, who sat nearby, beside Jonathan. They waited until someone knocked, then like ghosts, they were gone.

The police behaved as police often do when the victim is known to them. But my own injury, Jonathan's wound and Van Helsing's testimony were enough to convince them that I likely told the truth. My only difficulty was in explaining my reason for shooting him. I said I had not intended to kill him but only to stop him from killing himself, since he was most distraught after his confession. Jonathan corroborated what I said, and his word seemed enough to silence them for a time.

I did not know if they believed me completely, but Essie's wounds made them believe my words held some truth.

And apparently the doctor had spent a great deal of time with his journal, searching his thoughts and seeking mental balance, for when they searched his rooms they found diaries detailing crimes the London police had long since despaired of ever solving. They even compared his handwriting with the Ripper's, but though they were similar—a fact attributed to similarly deranged minds—the writings were not thought to be a match.

So Jonathan and I ended a troubling series of murders and had our moment as heroes. I made a statement to the press explaining that Rhys had told me that the sight of so much London poverty had driven him insane. I suggested there would be more such insanity if something were not done to alleviate the plight of the most desperately poor.

Only the socialist papers printed everything I said, though even the edited comments in the more conservative papers caused some stir and an influx of checks for my own work.

It's been nearly six weeks since that terrible weekend. My broken rib troubles me occasionally, usually before a rain. Jonathan, whose wound was deeper, has healed much more slowly. The doctor who examined him thinks it may shorten his life, but so far he seems better every day.

As for Essie. We had been prepared for the worst, but the doctor Arthur brought—though still in his cups from a night out with friends—had far more skill as a surgeon than Van Helsing. Some four hours after he arrived at the cottage, he had Essie's neck wound cleaned, stitched and bandaged as tightly as he could. He moved her to her bed, propping up her head with pillows so she could breathe with greater comfort until her lungs cleared themselves of the blood.

"Keep her quiet, keep the wound covered and say your prayers that no infection sets in," the doctor told us before he left. "One more thing: The monster cut through her larynx. She'll never speak above a whisper again."

If so, how did she moan and unwittingly draw Colleen's attention from me? A mystery, perhaps a miracle, though not the only one, since Essie did survive.

I never did ask where Arthur and vampire women went after they left my cottage that night. But Colleen alone appeared the following evening so she could learn

Essie's fate. As she held my servant's hand, I could see the human part of her was still strong. Something of her soul had survived her terrible death.

They are staying somewhere close to town. Arthur, still wary, does not tell me where. But sometimes at night I or Jonathan will go to the cottage window and see Colleen in the garden sitting with Essie, or glimpse Joanna walking among the flowers, breathing in the scent of roses she is afraid to touch.

Special thanks:
As always, to Ray McNally for his outstanding research in vampire lore, and J. Gordon Melton for the same. Also, to Tari Urecke, and to Elizabeth Miller, author of *Reflections on Dracula* and *Dracula: The Shade and the Shadow,* for providing me with the Romanian phrases scattered throughout the story. And last to Choral Pepper, whose excellent book *Walks in Oscar Wilde's London* has provided me with both entertainment and illumination on how "those other Victorians" lived.